CRYONIC

A PARANORMAL AFFAIR

MAN

CRYONIC

A PARANORMAL AFFAIR

MAN

JOE DIBUDUO

TooTie-Do pRESS

LoS ANGELES
REDWooD HiGHWaY 101
SAN DiEGo

Cover design by Clarissa Yeo, Yocla Designs
Editorial and interior design by Kate Robinson
Author photo by Mary DiBuduo
Tootie-Do Press logo photo by Carlolijah Robinson

To my writing mentors at Yavapai College
and the Prescott, Arizona critique group
who helped make this novel possible.

⋙Chapter 1

I bit down hard on the cold steel barrel of the Colt .38 to hold it steady in my trembling hands. A big eater, I never dreamed gun oil would end up on the menu. The bitter tang almost made me laugh through clenched teeth.

My finger tightened on the trigger. I shut my eyes, drew the hammer back, and pictured Emily's face for the last time.

Would I hear the gunpowder explode before my lights went out? Terrified, my body went numb as I imagined the bullet tearing through my brain.

Click.

The sound sent me sprawling across the bed.

I checked the cylinders. There were .38 slugs in five of the six chambers. How could I forget that I always left a chamber empty? Maybe my subconscious mind wanted me to play a little Russian roulette, give me an unexpected thrill.

I made sure a slug was under the firing pin, put the barrel back into my mouth, and bit down hard again.

Before I closed my eyes, I saw a reflection of Emily's portrait over the bed in the dresser mirror. Her face seemed to float above me like a disembodied spirit, her eyes accusing me of cowardliness.

I yanked the pistol from my mouth and shouted, "I'm no coward, Emily. I'm doing this to make it easier for you."

I shook with anger, but the reprieve gave me time to consider. It wouldn't be too damn pleasant for Emily to find me in the bedroom with my head blown off. Maybe I should leave a note and take myself out somewhere else. Yeah, that was it; leave a note so she'd understand. Emily would blame herself if I didn't tell her why I did it. I set the gun on the bedside table and tried to imagine what to say.

Dear Emily.

No, I couldn't say Dear Emily, I'm going to kill myself.

To Whom It May Concern, I killed myself because. . .

That didn't sound right, either.

What words might explain why a tough guy like me would commit suicide? How could I describe my lifelong fear, not of dying, but of becoming helpless? People on their way out, lying in bed, unable to wipe their own ass. I always swore that wouldn't be me and figured if I became helpless, I'd find a way to end it all, *quick.*

As I opened the nightstand drawer where Emily kept pen and paper, the perfume of her stationery drifted up along with warm memories of her. They say a dying man's life flashes through his mind and I grasped at my visions like a drowning man.

I crumpled a pillow under my head and tried to enjoy the memories while I worked up the courage to write a note and pull the trigger again.

Chapter 2

I lay slumped on the bed with the .38 in my hand, recalling the night about a month before when Emily insisted I go to the doctor. I'd suffered headaches for a couple of years but they'd been progressively getting worse. I told her after getting whacked in the head so many times since I'd taken up boxing as a kid, I was bound to have a few headaches now and then.

"Well, you go get your whacked head checked," she'd said.

I figured my headaches were no big deal, but to make her happy, I went. Dr. Everett Dean, my family physician, ran a hundred tests on me – blood, echocardiogram, treadmill, you name it and he tested it. A week later I went back to hear the results.

When the nurse told me to go right in because Dr. Dean was waiting for me, I knew something was up. Usually I got stuck sitting in the waiting room, decorated by some pansy who loved flowers. The flowered rugs, wall-coverings, pictures, and furniture with flowered upholstery annoyed the heck out of me.

When the nurse ushered me to Dr. Dean's office, the look on his careworn face said it all. I hoped his "I lost my best friend" look didn't have anything to do with me. But I knew better. For a doctor and patient, we were pretty close. He delivered me twenty-six years before and was my family physician ever since.

"Sit down, Jim."

I sat.

An even more heartbroken expression spread across Dr. Dean's face. He reached over his desk and put his hand on mine. "Situations like this make me regret becoming a doctor."

"Alright Doc, let me have it. I can take it, you know that."

Dr. Dean's eyes began to water. "I wish I could give you some hope, Jim, but I believe telling my patients the truth is always the best policy." He lowered his head and wrote something on the clipboard he always carried. "I don't know what to do except come right out and tell you. You have only a short time left to live."

"You're joking, right?" But I knew by the look on his face that he wasn't. "You know I've never been sick. How can I suddenly be knocking at death's door?"

"I'm so sorry, Jim. Sometimes a person carries a primary benign neoplasm for several years and has no symptoms at all, or suffers only an occasional headache, like you. Dr. Bernard has more experience with tumors than anyone else at the clinic. I confirmed my suspicions with him. Our prognosis is the same."

"The same as what?"

"More than likely, despite any treatment, you'll pass away sooner rather than later."

"What's sooner mean, Doc?"

Dr. Dean's sad eyes softened even more. "Within six months, max."

His words jolted me more than any blow I'd ever received in the ring. "I ain't gonna let no fucking tumor screw up my life. I've got too much going on to die now. Can't you just cut the damn thing out?"

"Unfortunately, at this time, there's nothing we can do. A brain tumor of this type, and its location, makes surgery impossible."

"Come on, Doc. I only have headaches and now you're telling me I'm dying, right before I win the championship?"

Dr. Dean's eyes pleaded with me. "Do you want me to call your wife? Maybe it would be easier for you if I told her."

"No! Don't tell her anything. I'll do it myself. I have a big fight coming up in a few weeks."

"You're done fighting, Jim. Try to enjoy the time you have left with your family."

"I ain't done 'til the day I die. You should know that. . . If this tumor will kill me, how come I never felt it when I took blows to the head?"

Dr. Dean gazed at me thoughtfully. "Do you remember when I treated you for a concussion two years ago?"

"Yeah, what about it?"

"Do you remember how the bump on the outside of your skull hurt but there was no pain inside your head? That's because your brain has no nerve sensors in the meninges to feel and transmit pain signals."

"Well, if I can't feel pain, why can't I fight?"

"It's entirely up to you, but I can't condone your doing so."

"Condone? I don't care, Doc. You know how I feel about stuff like this. We talked about how I'd rather die than live as an invalid."

"But Jim, you won't be an invalid. Your death will come quickly. Fighting might even speed your death up."

"If I can't fight, I may as well be dead."

I didn't want to get into an argument with Dr. Dean, so I got up and left. On my way through the waiting room, I punched a hole through the big flower painted on the door.

I never once thought about dying before. In my prime, I'd recently won my twenty-eighth heavyweight pro boxing match. A victory in my next fight would put me in line for a championship fight. Money I anticipated earning would pay for a dream house to surprise Emily.

Six months! My gut churned in frustration when I thought of little Joe. He'd just turned five months old and I'd be dead before his first birthday. Not only that, Emily dreamed of having a sister for little Joe. It couldn't happen now.

On the way home, I recalled what it was like hearing that a loved one was going to die soon. When my mutt Molly was a pup and I was twelve, I'd take her running every day. Because of running with her, I became inspired to start training to be a boxer. I kept jogging with Molly at my heels for ten years. When she no longer could keep up, I put her out to pasture to relax in her last dog days. That's when I noticed the lump on her head and took her to the vet.

"Could be a tumor or an osteoma," he'd said. "Let's do a biopsy and some X-rays." The bump was benign but he found a little shadow on her brain. "We're catching the brain tumor early, but at her age, she won't beat it," he said. "I'm sorry."

I couldn't breathe when he told me. I wanted to bust out bawling, but remembered what I learned as a boy: *Suffer any pain in silence. Only sissies show emotion. Keep your emotions locked up in your heart.*

But Molly was my best friend and her death was the conduit that allowed my feelings to flow. Dogs ranked high on my list of things that were okay in this messed-up world.

When Molly couldn't hold her bladder or her bowels any more, I carried her to the vet one last time. "You're right, son, it's time to put her down," the vet said. He spread a blanket on an exam table and lay Molly down. Her eyes opened wide as she watched him take a needle from a cabinet.

I let the river of tears flow that I'd held back all my life. "Molly, it's my turn to sit and stay. You're my buddy and I love you."

Her eyes shone at my words, but the delight in them froze into a blank stare.

The vet rubbed her head with compassion. "She's gone."

I cried all the way home like a goddamn sissy, but I didn't care because I missed her so much. "Where are you now, Molly? If there isn't a heaven for dogs there shouldn't be one for people."

I'd never told anyone how I cried over Molly's death, but I knew if I told Emily that my time had come, she'd certainly cry too. A lot. How could I cause her so much pain?

The phone rang, jangling my thoughts. I looked at the bedside clock. An hour had flown past since the pistol's hammer struck an empty chamber.

I picked up the phone. "Yeah?"

"Jim, are you okay?" Dr. Dean sounded excited.

"Yeah, fine, great," I said flatly.

"I'm sorry to intrude, but I've got some better news. By the way, I added the price of a new door and the installation to your bill."

I smiled sheepishly, knowing he said that to lighten the situation and it did make me feel better for an instant. "Sorry, Doc."

"After you left, I consulted Dr. Bernard again to see if there's any experimental treatment that that might help."

"Yeah, and?"

"Well, one thing came up. However, I question the viability of the procedure and maybe I shouldn't even mention it."

"You call me and say there may be hope, but maybe you shouldn't tell me? Don't give me that bullshit!"

Dr. Dean remained silent for a moment. "I was just wondering out loud. There's a new procedure, but it's pretty radical."

"Spit it out, Doc."

"Jim, please keep an open mind and remain calm so we can discuss this realistically."

"Okay, I'm calm and my mind's wide open. Now what in the hell are you talking about?"

"There's a new science called cryonics. Not to be confused with cryogenics. Cryonics is – "

"Could you just get to the point, Doc? I don't understand scientific stuff and I've got important things to take care of here. What does cryo-whatsis have to do with my tumor?"

"Jim, I'm trying to explain that cryonics is a technique that involves cooling legally dead people to liquid nitrogen temperature until physical decay essentially stops. The preservation process is performed in the hope that advanced scientific procedures will allow patients to be revived and restored to good health someday. A person held in such a state is called a cryopreserved patient. The medical community doesn't regard the cryopreserved person as truly dead."

"Oh, goody. Sounds like a sci-fi movie. The zombie fighter rises from the laboratory. . . You're not holding out much hope here, Doc."

Dr. Dean cleared his throat. "It's the only hope you've got to preserve your life."

"How in the hell do you preserve a corpse for that long?"

"Once you're declared dead, the Cryonic Foundation technicians will pack you in ice and water until the preservation process is started. Then they replace your blood with cryoprotectant chemicals, like antifreeze, and slowly lower your body temperature until they can store you in liquid nitrogen. When science learns how to shrink brain tumors like yours and how to rejuvenate cryopreserved individuals, you'll be revived, your tumor cured, and you'll be able to live out your life."

That silenced me for a moment.

"You're right, Doc. That's pretty damn radical."

Doctor Dean sighed. "You asked me to help. Fact is, you'll expire within six months. This procedure may give you a chance to live again, though in the future. "

What did it matter what happened to my body after I died? I wouldn't be around to find out, I hoped. What if I got preserved and still had feelings? I hated the cold worse than anything. What if my mind or spirit remained aware while my body was trapped in a tank full of nitrogen? Even worse, what if I was revived long after Emily and little Joe were gone?

"I don't know. I can see some problems down the road. If I go through with this cryonics stuff, will I have any feeling?"

"You'll be legally dead before your head is cryonically preserved," Dr. Dean explained. "Your mind will be a total blank when we start the process."

I was relieved to know I probably wouldn't know or feel anything. No worse than being six feet under. Then I realized exactly what Dr. Dean had said.

"My fucking head!? I need my entire body, Doc. You know that! I don't want to end up some kinda patchwork Frankenstein. No way."

Dr. Dean was silent for a moment. "Your long-term memory, personality, and identity are stored in the structures of the brain. Neuropreservation is more economical, and the premise is that your body is expendable and regeneration of it may be routine in the future. So far, cryopreservation hasn't worked well with large mammals, but cryopreservation of single organs, such as kidneys and brains, has been successful."

"No fucking way, Doc. It could take a thousand years to figure out how to regenerate an entire body. I'm an athlete. This plan is out of the question."

Dr. Dean sighed. "Cell damage caused from freezing is one of the problems with cryopreservation of larger masses of tissue. The current process can keep your brain in good shape, but it's a dice roll for your body, if they'll even attempt it. . . I know this is a tough decision, Jim. If you decide not to try this procedure, all you have to look forward to is early death. If you decide to do it, one day you may live again. I only mention it because you're young and should have a future ahead of you. And you can afford to try it. Some people can't."

What the hell, I thought. Why not give it a shot?

"Hearing you put it like that, go ahead and make the arrangements," I said. "I'll call my attorney, so he can check into the financial details and set aside some funds for Emily and little Joe. But I insist – and I want this in writing – I insist that they preserve my entire body. What have I got to lose? Nothing, basically. I'm as good as dead now and if they can't revive me, I'm still dead, right?"

"Good thinking, Joe. And putting money away for your family's future is an excellent idea."

Dr. Dean was right. May as well plan for a miracle. We had a little money tucked away already. Maybe I could win the championship before I croaked and leave a good nest egg as well as the insurance. Or maybe I'd be the comeback kid in a decade or two and get back on the championship track, start life over again with Emily and Joe.

After I hung up the phone, I began to wonder just what in the hell I was getting myself into. I swore I'd never be a guinea pig for the guys in the white coats. For all I knew, the CIA or somebody was experimenting with cryonically preserved bodies. I sure as hell didn't want to get mixed up in something like that.

Then I remembered Dr. Dean's reassurance about not feeling anything during the procedure. I may as well relax and spring for the experiment. I'd be dead anyway, so what the hell could anyone do to hurt me?

This cryonics stuff changed everything. I sure as hell would never live again if I blew my brains out.

Chapter 3

I put the .38 Colt back in the closet, tore up my goodbye note, and went downstairs to the kitchen to pour myself a triple shot of bourbon from a bottle someone left behind after a family gathering. I downed the drink in one swallow and poured another. It felt weird to taste alcohol after that fucking gun oil, but I needed to relax.

I downed the second drink and that seemed to slow my racing thoughts. I tried to think logically. How could I nail the championship title before I died? I'd win if I put my mind to it. I needed help to deal with Emily and the cryonic thing, but didn't know where to turn.

I heard the key turning in the front door. Emily and little Joe were coming home from their daily trip to the park. I dashed upstairs toward the bathroom.

"We're home, Jim," Emily sang out. Little Joe made some of his baby noises in the background.

I almost broke down at the sound of their voices. I couldn't tell Emily. Not yet. I didn't have the courage to watch her face dissolve into agony. I undressed, stepped into an ice-cold shower and began to shiver from the chill.

"Think this is cold? Wait 'til you get into one of those nitrogen tanks," I said out loud.

Feeling anything at all was a good thing because I'd soon be gone and probably never feel anything ever again. I let the needles of frigid water pummel me for a long time before I dried off and put on a flannel robe to go face Emily.

When I stepped back into the kitchen, Emily was feeding little Joe from a Gerber's jar. He fussed in his high chair, the mashed peas smeared in green slashes across his lips and chin. I absorbed the domestic scene, the yellow and blue flowers on the wallpaper, the curve of Emily's hip as she bent toward little Joe, and the way the chrome legs of the kitchen table and chairs reflected light against the floor. My heart caught in my throat because I wouldn't be seeing much more of this. I stood behind Emily and kissed the back of her neck so I wouldn't have to look at her when I lied and told her that Dr. Dean said everything was fine.

I spent a sleepless night and got up at 4 a.m., just an hour earlier than usual. I dressed for the gym, kissed Emily on the cheek, and went to little Joe's room and kissed him too. He lay spread-eagled in his crib, his big fists clenched like a fighter, which made me wonder if he'd take after me. I hoped he'd have the good sense to use those hands in a better profession.

After a few hours at the gym, grueling hours of pushing myself to the limit, I couldn't wait any longer to call the Cryonics Foundation. I took another cold shower to clear my head and picked up the phone at the gym's front desk. Help answered unexpectedly in the form of Dr. Remus, the director of CF. He reassured me with his cheerful, uplifting outlook that the Foundation could take care of the cryonic procedure with minimal problems. He almost made dying and getting flash frozen like a bag of peas sound like an everyday occasion, nothing to worry about. He also knew when to be serious and how to get his point across, just like Dr. Dean.

"Jim, you don't have many choices, therefore your worries are limited. The best thing you can do for Emily and Joe is to assure their financial security."

Though his voice sounded somber, I imagined his eyes smiling with kindness. "In the meantime, why don't you take the wife on a holiday and enjoy the time you have left?"

"I'll be going over our finances with my lawyer soon," I told him. "Thanks to my insurance agent's hard-sell tactics, I bought a half-million dollar life insurance policy before I started having headaches. My family's all set. But I need to know more about the financial arrangements for the cryonic procedure. And I need a contract to preserve my entire body, not just my brain."

What I didn't tell him was that I agreed in principle about enjoying my remaining time, but that our views of enjoyment differed.

We went over the financial aspects of the procedure, including the years of storage and maintenance, the difficulties of preserving an entire body, and my chances of revival in the future.

"You may have heard about the rash of recent cryonic suspension failures due either to lack of ongoing funds or caused by equipment breakdowns. If you convert part of your insurance funds into an annuity for the Cryonic Foundation, that will cover the entire cost in perpetuity," Dr. Remus said. "We do not, for example, store bodies at funeral homes, in vaults at cemeteries, or in family cellars as other organizations have done. Our storage facilities and capsules are state of the art, and our maintenance routines are carried out on a regular schedule.

"As for your return to a normal state, it could be a few years, or thirty, or even a hundred, but it's a certainty that scientists will one day perfect the process of resuscitating cryopreserved patients and using nanobots to reverse aging and to repair tissue damage. We can't guarantee top-notch results for the cryogenic preservation of your entire body at this time, but I believe that your age and circumstances merit our best attempt. I'll discuss your case with my colleagues and see if we can add a disclaimer to that effect in your contract. Whenever you're ready to come in with your lawyer, I'll give you a tour of the facilities and you can meet with our legal office."

"I figure no one loses either way, Doctor. I've got one foot in the grave, so if there's some screw-up with my procedure, maybe scientists can sort it out in the future. Otherwise, I'll just stay dead, right? I'll call my lawyer right now and have him get in touch with your people."

"Jim, I think you're absolutely right. The Cryonic Foundation will look forward to serving you on this groundbreaking adventure. Now, please, leave us with your worries. You go enjoy life."

As I drove home, I thought about the biggest joy in my life – in addition to spending time with my family – winning the world heavyweight boxing championship. I could do it in less than six months. The first step was to win the fight scheduled in two weeks. I could just keep training as usual and Emily wouldn't suspect a thing. After winning that fight, I'd be the number one contender for the big one. Then I might be ready to talk to Emily. After all, the tumor hadn't physically disabled me yet – headaches were my only symptom. I'd go on fighting until I lost or died.

After picking up some papers from Zoloti's law office, I sat in the kitchen with a bourbon in hand, waiting for Emily to return from her walk, just like the day before. Although I still felt conflicted about withholding information from her, I wasn't ready to face her devastation, either. Maybe I was a selfish oaf, but I swear my only motive was to make things easier for her.

She'd know something was bothering me and I tried to figure out what to say when she asked. I downed a second bourbon. I needed to make a decision, but when Emily came into the kitchen, I was still uncertain what to say.

She put little Joe in my lap and pecked me on the cheek. "Jim, is something wrong? You're holding something back. You've been awfully quiet."

Little Joe pounded at my forehead and pulled my hair as if to illustrate my dilemma – headaches, brain tumor, hard decisions.

"No, really, I'm fine. Just mentally preparing myself for the next fight."

"Come on, Jim, you can't fool me."

I wanted to take her in my arms and tell her how much she and our boy meant to me, but if I did, the truth would pour out. So I said, "To be honest, there is something."

"Tell me."

"Dr. Dean made a strange request yesterday."

"Request. What kind of request? What did he ask you?"

"He asked me to help with a scientific experiment he's involved with."

Emily's face tightened. "Don't you dare volunteer! Doctors experiment on people and sometimes they end up debilitated in some way."

"It's no big deal. Just something they do after a person dies."

Emily's face relaxed a bit, so I continued. "Yeah, Dr. Dean says he's working on a way to extend the human lifespan."

"That's a pretty lofty goal for a family doctor. How's he planning to do that?"

"By preserving people after they die and reviving them."

"That's impossible, Jim. You know as well as I do that no one ever comes back from the dead."

"Yeah, but he says that scientists are trying."

"Well he's not experimenting on you. Everybody dies, why does he need you?"

Good question. How was I going to answer?

"Guess it's because he knows I'm going to be a champion, and if a boxing champion volunteers, then others will be sure to follow," I said, wincing inside at my lie.

"Why can't you donate some money to his cause and forget about volunteering?"

"You don't understand, Emily. This is something I want to do."

Emily balled her hands into fists and placed them on her hips. "You do? How selfish of you. Did you even stop to think how we bought cemetery plots side by side, so we'd be together forever? If you volunteer for this experiment, I'll be alone after we pass on."

"I promise I'll be buried right beside you. Even if I volunteer, I have to die before I actually become part of the experiment, so if he gets enough people involved now, the experiment will probably be over by then."

Telling Emily so many lies made me sick. I felt like puking, but I couldn't backtrack now that I'd gone this far.

"Look, let's not argue about this." I pulled the envelope with the medical power of attorney and the cryonic procedure form from the dining room table that Zoloti drew up after I called the Foundation. "Here's some papers you need to sign. Just do it and forget all about this conversation."

"Jim! Forget it. Why do you think you can stand there and tell me you're going to donate your body to some crackpot scheme and then order me to sign papers saying it's okay?"

She grabbed the envelope from my hand and threw it on the floor. Her concern overwhelmed me. I wanted to confess, but I could never admit I lied to her. I picked up the envelope and with little Joe tucked in one arm, I led her to the sofa. "We need to talk seriously for a minute."

She looked at me with those blazing eyes and my guts twisted, thinking she must know I was lying to her.

"Once I become champion," I said, "we can take a long vacation, maybe a month-long cruise or even a trip around the world." I knew there might not be a cruise, maybe just a short vacation, but one lie led to another.

"That would be wonderful, Jim. But no more talk about experiments," she said after I ran the vacation line on her. She kissed me hard, her lips opening to allow my tongue to explore their soft, sweet edges. When the kiss ended, we smiled shyly at one another, just like when we first started dating. We'd put romance on the back burner since Joe was born and I started seriously training with an eye on the championship.

I decided to try another direction. "Honey, you know I'm in a dangerous profession, and God forbid."

Emily's smile faded.

"Don't get upset, baby – this is just in case something ever does happen to me. It might be a good thing to have my body preserved at the Cryonic Foundation. That's who Dr. Dean is working with."

She threw the envelope on the floor again and pulled away. I grabbed her by the arm. She looked at me a long time with tears in her eyes. Little Joe looked back and forth at our faces, confused.

"What is it you're not telling me, Jim?"

I thought I wouldn't have to lie to her again, but I looked her straight in the eye and gave her more crap. "Of course, there isn't anything I'm not telling you. You already know I'll be leaving for training camp in the morning. Baby, please sign. You know damn well I'll do anything I can to live a long, beautiful life with you. If I win the world championship, I can retire early, do something else. These papers are just like insurance, in case something bad happens."

If Emily knew how little time I had left, she wouldn't allow us to be apart at all. At any rate, she either couldn't resist my plea or knew I was more stubborn than she was. She finally signed, reluctantly at first, and then with a resolute flourish.

Vincent Zoloti, my attorney, came to the training camp at Cape Cod a few days later. I signed the payment agreements for the cryonic procedure and we reviewed my insurance policies to make sure Emily and Joe were named as the beneficiaries before I died.

Before I died! I couldn't believe I sat there calmly discussing my impending death.

I arranged for the substantial purse from this upcoming fight to be held in a trust fund managed by Zoloti and his associates. If and when I was revived, and we both knew it was a big if, I'd have plenty of money to start my life over.

"Look, Zoloti," I said, handing him a note, "here's what I want on my tombstone if they fail to revive me: 'Jim Jackson, Heavyweight Boxing Champion of the World, born 1950, died 1976.'"

"I'll make sure it's at the top of the list, Jim, but what if you don't win the championship before your time comes?"

"Then have my tombstone say I would have been the champ if it wasn't for this fucking tumor."

≫ Chapter 4

While I sat in my dressing room waiting to enter the ring, some sharp, flashing pains shot through my head. I did my best to ignore them. A fighter has to withstand pain or he's worthless. Soon I wouldn't have to worry about pain ever again, I thought glumly.

Hell, thinking about dying scared me, no, terrified me, but before I went, I wanted to ace my last two fights. There was no quitting as long as there was any breath left in me. I just wished the goddamn tumor had a face so I could punch the shit out of it. It didn't, so I'd punch the shit out of my opponent instead.

"Homicide Hank" earned his unusual name because he'd almost killed several boxers with his unrelenting assaults. Built like a Renaissance statue, the young Italian fighter out of Boston's North End was solid muscle from head to toe. But I knew his muscles were more for show than work and that his stamina wouldn't match mine. He was tough, but not as tough as me. I looked forward to k-o'ing him.

We met center-ring and touched gloves. "Hope you got your life insurance paid up," Hank mumbled through his sneer.

I looked past him as though I didn't hear a word. That rattled him more than some snide remark.

We felt each other out by jabbing and dancing for a round. The judges probably scored us even. Suddenly, a jolt of high voltage electricity seared my brain. My hands instinctively flew to my head. Whoever said the brain doesn't feel pain was dead wrong. Hank took advantage of my hesitation and hit me with a right uppercut. Flashing stars filled my head. I grabbed his arms and hung on tight as I tried to recover, grateful that Emily couldn't see this. She refused to attend any of my fights since her brother brought her to see me get my ass kicked so long ago.

The bell rang. I staggered to my corner, spit out my mouthpiece, and took a deep breath.

"How many fingers?" my trainer asked, sticking his big hand in front of my face. I slapped it away. If my corner-man hadn't already rinsed my mouthpiece and put it back in, I'd have told him to get fucked too.

My head seemed to swell like an overfilled balloon. The pain grew right along with my head size, raging spasms that careened around my skull. Another punch would probably kill me, but better to die like this than in some hospital bed.

My trainer wanted me to throw in the towel. I gave him an evil look that changed his opinion real quick.

The thought of getting beaten got my adrenaline flowing. I wasn't about to let Hank get away with killing me so easy. My anger kicked in and my brain started playing tricks on me. I didn't see my opponent coming at me. I saw a man-sized brain tumor instead, the one causing all my pain. Here was my chance to inflict some hurt on it.

I surprised him by standing flat-footed, waiting for his assault. Just as I expected, he came straight in for the kill. I caught him with a straight right lead to the face.

Confused by my unorthodox move, he hesitated for a second, and that's all it took. I caught him with a left hook and a right cross that sent his mouthpiece and two teeth flying across the canvas. I wasn't about to let this humanoid brain tumor escape. I hit it again and again. Ain't no medical cure for this lump, but maybe I could kill it with a well-placed punch.

The bell rang and the ref pulled me off Homicide Hank. "You got him now," my trainer said. "Go right at him as soon as you hear the bell and finish him off."

The bell rang again. Instantly I was at that tumor with a left-right-left-left. A right uppercut stood it straight up, and laid it flat on the canvas. Once it hit the deck, my vision of the giant tumor disappeared and I saw Homicide Hank lying there.

It seemed the ref took forever to count to ten and raise my hand in victory. "Hope *your* insurance is paid up," I said to the unconscious man.

I took a handful of aspirin as soon as I got to the dressing room, hoping to ease the pressure in my exploding head. The reporters were already there, waiting. Just what I needed, a bunch of morons asking dumb questions.

A little guy in a rumpled suit jammed a microphone at me. "You're first in line to fight for the heavyweight championship – will you fight anyone before the big one?"

I knew I didn't have the time or the energy for any extra fights. "No," I said. "I want to stay focused and take my shot at the championship as soon as possible."

Wasn't I supposed to be happy? When the reporters finally trailed off in search of an interview with the loser, I felt glum. Death was my constant companion and k-o'ed any joyful thoughts about my future.

As I headed for the shower, another surge of pain gave me second thoughts about the cryonics. I didn't believe in the everlasting life preached to me by religion all my life. At least I hoped eternity wasn't for real, because I envisioned an eternity of misery. What if I found myself trapped in that liquid nitrogen forever? I tried to shake off my gloom with a long, hot shower to keep my mind from drifting into a nightmare world of cold and isolation.

The day after the fight, I did my best to put on a happy face. "Let's go to Disneyland. Little Joe will love it," I said after Emily cooked my favorite breakfast – double eggs, bacon, hash browns, and a tall stack of pancakes.

She looked at little Joe, who scraped away happily on his high chair tray with a spoon. "I don't know, honey. Don't you think we should wait until he's a little older? Joey's barely big enough to enjoy the kiddy rides."

That hurt, reminding me I'd never see my son enjoying Disneyland. "Let's get my mom to babysit, then. You and I can go away for a few days."

The following weekend, we drove to the Cape, near the camp where I trained. The High Pointe Inn had a panoramic view of Cape Cod Bay and Sandy Neck beach, the ideal romantic getaway. Emily brought all her honeymoon lingerie – what more could a man ask for?

We were lounging by the fireplace in the great room, gazing out a picture window at the sea sparkling under a full moon when a deep, throbbing pain shot through my head. Maybe this was what it felt like to put a bullet through your brain, I thought, dropping my drink and grabbing my head.

"Jim, what's the matter?" Emily tried to make eye contact with me but I could barely see. "Jim? Jim!"

I couldn't answer and fell to the floor, immobilized. I heard Emily dash for the door. "Call an ambulance," she shouted. A few moments later, I felt hands lifting me, wheeling me away.

Next thing I knew, Emily was sitting beside me, clutching my hand and crying. The eerie wail of the ambulance siren should have been loud, but seemed far away. This was it. As much as I hated leaving her and little Joe to fend for themselves, my biggest regret was that I hadn't held on long enough to fight, the one fight I wanted all my life.

Chapter 5

I floated above my body, watching two ambulance attendants dressed in white jackets give me chest compressions. Down below, my physical eyes were shut tight, as if afraid of seeing Heaven, Hell, or someplace else.

Did my immortal soul exist in this place? And what was this place? I felt nothing, heard nothing, and even though my eyes were closed, I could still see what was going on around my body on Earth. Everything was permeated in a ghostly silver-blue light. Mystified and terrified at the same time, I could only wonder if I'd hover around like this for eternity. If so, then my second worst nightmare had come true.

Then everything went black. I got so scared I could feel my knees knocking, only I didn't have knees any longer. Would I go to hell or someplace worse for considering suicide?

At least I wasn't anywhere bad yet. I found I could still direct my consciousness from this dark space. I didn't live inside my body any more, yet I sensed that my surroundings weren't really so dark. I found myself standing in a waterfall of pure, cool, white light. Understanding and acceptance flowed through me like a river. Suddenly I knew that if a star in the heavens disintegrated in front of my eyes, that it had done so thousands, maybe millions of years ago.

Yet I could still see it happening in the present. I viewed the fusion of my new consciousness, my exit from the physical world, and my receding life in a similar manner.

I watched as the paramedics solemnly carried my dying body into Cape Cod Hospital. Emily walked behind the gurney, then stood beside a strange doctor, sobbing. Apparently she'd called Dr. Dean, because the ER staff packed me in ice and put me aboard a chopper headed to Boston. Emily sat beside me, holding my hand all the way. Cryonics Foundation doctors were waiting for me in the emergency room of St. Elizabeth's, the hospital where I was born. Once CF assumed control of my body, their medical team packed me in more ice and water and put me aboard another ambulance.

Emily stood at St. Elizabeth's ER door with Dr. Dean, her face crumpling with pain as she blew a goodbye kiss. I hovered above her but there was little I could do but brush past her tenderly, hoping she could feel my love. Startled, she looked through me and turned her face upward to the moon as if to look for me there.

The medical techs took turns giving me chest compressions on the way to Cryonics Foundation to keep my blood flowing. Guess they wanted me freshly dead and not stone cold dead when they started to preserve me. At CF, specially trained technicians set up a device similar to those used in funeral homes to exchange blood for formaldehyde, but in this case, they'd use cryoprotectants, like antifreeze. Normally I'd have no idea what went on in a situation like this, but from the world beyond death, I instinctively understood everything I saw.

Attaching my body to this machine took considerable time and effort. The team then inserted cannula into my femoral artery and a vein in my groin. A nurse administered IV drugs that reduced the damage from the decreased oxygen content in my tissues. Once the machine was properly attached to my body, the technicians perfused my circulatory system, exchanging my blood for cryoprotectant fluids to prevent cellular freezing and breakage. The medical team hovered over me until their instruments showed my body temperature had dropped to -59 degrees Fahrenheit.

Then the technicians submerged me in a bath of silicone oil for forty-eight hours, and cooled my body to -109 degrees Fahrenheit. Dr. Remus wrapped my body in a pre-cooled sleeping bag and placed it inside a protective aluminum pod. He then lowered it into an insulated container to which he repeatedly added small amounts of liquid nitrogen.

My body gradually cooled even further over five days to -320 Fahrenheit. My body was basically deader than a doornail, but I still floated over it, observing myself. Finally, Dr. Remus and his technicians transferred it to a cryostat, a large, vacuum-tight aluminum container used for science applications. Filled with liquid nitrogen, the container stood nine feet high, weighed almost two-and-a-half tons, and stored four bodies. Mine was the fourth. Our bodies were buoyant in the liquid nitrogen, so there was no crushing weight or injury. At least I had company for the long sleep.

While my body settled into the dark, induced hibernation, scenes from my life flowed through my mind like a three-dimensional movie. My birth, infancy, childhood, and young adulthood flickered past in minute detail. I could move forward, or turn time back. I wondered what it was like to be born, so I focused on the old maternity ward at St. Elizabeth's Hospital where a young, spry Dr. Dean placed my still wet body on my mother's chest. Soon I watched my parents naming me in the old hospital ward.

"Let's name him after my dad," my father said. "He's a bang-up boxer. Maybe junior here will follow in his footsteps."

Turns out I was number twelve out of thirteen, and received all the stuff kicked down from the top. My baby sister Ellen, the only girl in the family, got all the attention. I got the worn-out hand-me-downs from my eleven older brothers. When Dad got out of sorts with all our shenanigans, he'd whack Mom and she in turn would take it out on one of my older brothers. It didn't matter which one, because the abuse always hit bottom, my place in the family pecking order. No one would dare touch baby Ellen.

An optimist would say our family dynamics were a good thing because that's how I learned to fight. But if that optimist caught my shit, I don't think he'd be positive for long. Yeah, it taught me to fight. It taught me to hate too. I hated everybody and everything. When someone had something I wanted, my guts twisted and turned. My heart raced and my anger flared until I figured a way to get it. Using my fists was the easiest way to get anything I wanted.

By age fifteen, I could kick all my older brothers' asses. The next time I saw the old man hitting my mom, I kicked his ass too. I loved kids and animals, but I sure hated grown people, because most of the ones I knew were rotten to the core. So much shit went on in my neighborhood that I don't even like to think about it.

My sixteenth birthday came and I got drunk to celebrate. I bought myself a case of Old India Beer, the cheapest brew in the store, but it seemed to get me drunker than the more expensive stuff. I did the usual when I got drunk – found someone to fight with. It didn't matter who. A fight was a fight and in my neighborhood, when someone wanted to fight you couldn't say no.

I was drunk and spoiling to fight when Pauly Callahan came strolling down the street with his sister Emily. He was one of the toughest guys in my neighborhood and a few years older than me. That's probably why we hadn't fought yet.

When they passed by me, I walked up and put my arm around Emily. "When are we going out on a date?" I said.

She kicked me in the shin. I laughed.

Pauly got ready to swing. "You want your ass kicked? I'll do you that little favor."

Emily stepped between us. "No! Don't be idiots."

But Pauly Callahan's honor was at stake. If he didn't fight, he'd have to move out of the neighborhood or forever hear the chicken cackle wherever he went. Callahan pushed Emily aside, swung at me and missed. I ducked low to the ground, grabbed his ankles and yanked them out from under him, a street fighting trick I learned long ago. It worked on Callahan – down and out, it was over. But I'd twisted his ankle too hard as I pulled his feet out from under him.

Pauly held his left ankle with both hands, his face twisting with pain. "Damn, you broke my ankle!"

Emily's deep blue eyes blazed at me, blaming me for hurting her brother. I became Jell-O as I looked into those bright, hot eyes. She tried to kick me in the balls and swiped her tiny hands at my head. I grabbed her by the wrists and planted a kiss on those angry lips. She fought all the harder when I did that. I loved her spirit and wanted her. But it was obvious she didn't see it my way.

Right then and there, I decided I wanted her bad enough that I'd do whatever it took to make her mine. Hell, I even helped her brother to his feet and brushed the snow and cinders from his jacket. I lifted his arm across my back and he put his other arm across Emily's shoulders. Good thing the snow on the ground allowed him to slide along on his good leg as we dragged him to a pay phone. Emily called for an ambulance. Tongue-tied, I could only fantasize about asking her for a date. She'd probably never have anything to do with me again after breaking her brother's leg.

"Do you really think they'll show up?"

"Of course. Why wouldn't they?"

Hell, to live in Hano and ask a question like that meant she must live a sheltered life. Somehow, that made her even more attractive to me.

Miraculously, an ambulance arrived. As Emily climbed in to ride with her brother, she gave me a parting half-smile. Right then and there, I decided to reform so I'd have a chance with her.

I stopped stealing for a living and got a job at the box factory to impress her. I made damn sure Emily found out I was a working man. Unloading rolls of cardboard from freight cars was an honest living, but not much to my liking. On my first day, when the foreman told me the rolls weighed eight hundred pounds each, I said, "No way. Nobody can move those rolls all day long."

He showed me how to use a hand dolly and I unloaded a freight car until I thought I'd pass out. After a few weeks, I unloaded two freight cars a day by myself. My muscles swelled, and my newfound strength helped every time I got into a scuffle. I didn't lose a single fight after I started working at the box factory, and my reputation as a fighter grew.

So did my persistence in asking Emily for a date. It wasn't easy to change her mind. She worked for Dr. Kline, the veterinarian, so I started picking up stray cats and dogs to bring in for whatever treatment they needed. After they were healthy again, I found homes or a no-kill shelter for every one of them. Her resolve softened with each visit. I knew that eventually I'd have to make peace with her brother before she'd go out with me.

One Friday as I walked through the door of the Model Café, where I went for lunch every day, a string of bells clattered against the glass door like an accompaniment to the owner's deep bass voice. "Hey, tough guy," he bellowed. Come over here. Sit down, have lunch on me. I want to talk about you coming to work for me."

Gus also ran a stable of three or four fighters. "I've got a job, Gus. I'm not crazy about it, but I'm making money and staying out of trouble."

"I know, I know, I don't mean a full-time job. I hear you've been kicking ass on the streets. I need you to fight tonight and every Friday night from now on. You'll make fifty bucks a fight, win or lose. You're already fighting anyways, may as well get paid for it. Whaddya say, kid?"

Fifty bucks to fight. Hell that was what I brought home for working all week. This was a dream come true.

"Sure, Gus," I said, "but can you make it sixty bucks? I need to buy trunks, shoes, and other stuff if I'm gonna fight in a ring."

"Fifty for now. Let me see how ya do. Tonight's fight is at the Brighton Men's Club." He slapped down two crumpled twenties and a ten on the table in front of me. "Here's an advance. Go get what you need, and don't forget a mouthpiece or you won't have any teeth next time we talk."

The first time for anything is scary. I'd been fighting as long as I could remember and never been scared, not once, but that night my knees shook. I was fifth on the card and the night seemed to drag on forever. The first fight was a heavyweight match between an Italian named Luigi from the North End and an Irishman named Pat from Hano. They obviously weren't professional boxers. They stood toe-to-toe, stationary and slugging each other with all they had. Luigi's nose started to gush blood. The roar that went up from the crowd scared the shit out of me. My buddies used to talk about "blood lust", but I never saw anything quite like this before. Guys loved watching the fighters get the crap beat out of them and the more bloodshed, the louder they roared.

Luigi connected a good one on Pat's right eye, splitting his brow open. The blood flowing into his eyes blinded him, but Pat didn't let that stop him from swinging like crazy. Luigi wasn't bothered by the bloody trickle running over his lips. They both kept throwing punches until the bell rang, the first round of three.

At the next bell, Luigi and Pat rushed to the center of the ring and started slugging it out again. Both were bloody messes, but blood wasn't enough to stop them. I'd been in enough fights to know how much they were hurting. I figured maybe fifty bucks wasn't such a good deal if I got hammered like that. I vowed to use my head. No matter how tough I was, I knew I couldn't take a pounding like that every week.

Luigi hit Pat in his cup. The ref declared Pat the winner because of this low blow. The audience roared and I thought maybe they'd lynch poor Luigi for hitting below the belt.

Three more thumping, blood-gushing matches came and went before I had to get ready for my brawl. Gus came in while his trainer taped my hands.

"How ya feeling, kid? No, don't tell me. I know your stomach is probably flip-flopping, but don't worry about it. I want you to take it easy tonight anyways. Rosario di Angelo, the guy you're fighting, is an old timer and I want him to win for old time's sake. So throw a few punches and then kiss the canvas."

"Fuck you, Gus. I don't take a dive for nobody."

"Listen kid, I'm telling you for your own good, lay down after a couple o' rounds."

I sat there and thought about what he said, *for my own good*. I bet he meant for his own good. He probably bet a bundle against me. The more I thought about it the angrier I got. I jumped up and grabbed

Gus by the throat.

"Nobody's going to beat me unless they beat me. Ask me to do that again, and I quit."

Gus turned white. I don't know if it was from fear or anger, but I didn't give a damn. My face got hot and I shook from fury before I relaxed my grip. Gus stalked off. Rosario di Angelo was going to get his ass kicked tonight or I'd die trying. Gus'd better bet on me winning.

Gus's trainer, Kelly, a wino who slept in Gus's basement, helped me get my gloves on and led me to the ring. I couldn't afford a robe so I walked down the smoke-filled aisle in my trunks with a towel over my shoulders. First in the ring, the crowd cheered because of my Irish name.

Rosario skipped toward the ring amidst loud booing and catcalls. I almost felt sorry for him until he climbed into the ring and I discovered he was a foot and a half taller than me. He took his robe off and I thought, old man, hell. I wondered where Gus got off saying that.

I just might die trying to kick this giant's ass. He must weigh at least two-fifty; I only weighed one-ninety. Sixty pounds would make a big difference. Maybe Gus wanted me to take a dive so I wouldn't get hurt.

The ref called us to the center of the ring and gave us our instructions. He emphasized "no low blows" on account of what happened earlier. Pauly Callahan sat in the front row with Emily beside him. She was probably going to see me get creamed. If I could have left straight away, I would have. Anything so I wouldn't be humiliated in front of her. Why the heck would Pauly bring her to fight night at a men's club? It hit me then, revenge. He probably set the whole thing up to see me get my ass kicked. That would explain Gus telling me to take a dive. He knew about the setup and he was looking out for me in his own way. Rage replaced my fear. I'd show that asshole Callahan.

The bell rang and I charged, my arms swinging like a windmill. My aggressiveness startled Rosario. He backed up and I followed him without letting up. The crowd roared their approval. Pauly Callahan didn't. Emily slipped her hand over her eyes so she wouldn't have to watch. I smiled at the thought.

Rosario sidestepped and caught me on my left ear with a hard right that rattled my brain. He became the aggressor. I couldn't block his swift, powerful punches. I gave up trying to block and traded punch for punch. I felt the noise of the crowd more than heard it as Rosario's fists and the sound both hit me like a hurricane.

I knew I'd lose in the long run because he was bigger and stronger than me. In a street fight, that didn't make much of a difference – there I could use feet, teeth, and other things not allowed in the ring.

Blood started to pour from my nose. Not a mark showed on Rosario's face. I landed a solid punch directly on his solar plexus, knocking the wind out of him. I worked on his face as he gasped for breath. Soon I'd opened a wound on his left temple that bled profusely. Dagos were hardheaded, I'd heard all my life, and as blood poured from his head, I figured that saying wasn't true. We were going down the same street Pat and Luigi went in the first fight. If I wanted to be smarter than them, I had to beat this guy without getting crippled. Of course, I could always get the fight stopped by hitting him in the balls. I saw Luigi do it, and it seemed like a more honorable way to get out of an ass kicking than taking a dive. If things got any worse, that would be my ace in the hole.

I knew I hurt Rosario with the punch to his midsection, but pummeling his head didn't seem to be doing much good, other than making him bleed.

The bell rang. "You did good, kid," Gus said when I went to my corner. "Now lay down before you get hurt. This guy's a professional. He'll kill ya if you stay in there."

I couldn't get more than a mumble out because Kelly put my mouthpiece in after I rinsed my mouth with water.

The bell rang again. I cautiously approached Rosario. Knowing he was a pro made a difference, a big difference. Pros sometimes fought fifteen rounds. I knew he wasn't going to tire in a three rounder. Every swing I took from this point on would have to hurt him as bad as possible. His middle seemed vulnerable, so I aimed every punch there.

I held one hand in front of my face and waded into Rosario, visualizing him as one of my eight hundred-pound rolls of cardboard. Somehow, I managed to force him to the ropes where I landed punch after punch.

Rosario left his head wide open while he protected his stomach. I couldn't resist and swung a right roundhouse into his exposed face. His head swung sharply backwards and his body followed. The force of the punch had knocked him out. You'd think I won the championship the way the crowd cheered. I felt invincible. My first ring fight and I beat a pro hired to kick my ass.

"You're my number one fighter now, Jim," Gus said when I got back to the locker room.

"Why didn't you warn me what was going on?"

"In this business sometimes you gotta do things you don't like. I tried to give you an easy way out."

Deep down I knew Gus was a good guy. I'd stay with him, especially now that I was his number one fighter.

After that fight, my boxing career took a boost. Gus got me licensed as a pro and set me up with some ducks that I wiped out one, two, three. Paydays got bigger with each fight. Soon I quit working at the box factory and trained at the gym all day, every day. Muscles sprouted all over my body, and I outgrew all my clothes. I wouldn't use steroids like a lot of other athletes were starting to. I didn't need them the way my body grew from training and eating up a storm. My weight jumped to two-twenty, a true heavyweight.

People recognized me wherever I went around Boston. Word spread that I'd be the next champ, and I did everything in my power to make that come true. My respect soared in Hano, and I saw my chance to finally call on Emily and make my peace with Pauly.

I stood on the Callahan's front doorstep with a bouquet of roses, hoping I didn't look like a sap. I rang the bell and Pauly answered the door.

"What the hell are you doing here?"

I stuck my hand out. "I wanna apologize for picking a fight and breaking your ankle. Booze made me do it. I've quit drinking, so it'll never happen again."

Pauly looked me in the eye and stuck his hands in his pockets. "Yeah, if you're so sorry why'd it take you so long to say so? Don't think I'll shake the hand that broke my ankle."

"I've got to tell you, Pauly, I intend to marry Emily. . ."

He swung as soon as he heard that. I took his punch to the chin and shrugged it off. "That makes us even. Do it again, and you'll get one right back. Now shake, damn it. After all, we're gonna be brothers."

Emily walked up behind Pauly. "Don't you dare shake on that," she said.

She'd been listening the whole time, but I was glad. Now I didn't have to repeat my intentions. Emily graciously accepted the flowers, but she wouldn't listen to anything I said.

I continued to visit the animal hospital where she worked, and after weeks of bringing in every stray I could find, Emily finally agreed to go to a movie with me. *Bonnie and Clyde* starring Warren Beatty and Faye Dunaway was playing at the Egyptian Theatre where everyone always took their dates. Emily thought the movie glorified violence. I agreed with her and didn't let on that I thought it was probably the coolest flick I'd ever seen.

We got along great. Anything she didn't like, I didn't like either. Whether I really did or not was immaterial. I always agreed with her to sway her opinion of me, and it worked. Before long, we started going steady.

Friday and Saturday nights were our date nights. The sun always shone on those days for me, even if it rained. Every person I knew became a better human being because I began to see the world through Emily's compassionate eyes. She told me once, "I work at the clinic because animals are so helpless and sometimes, I can make their lives a little better."

"It's a job," I callously replied the first time she said this.

"It's not just a job, it's a vocation. I would have been a nurse, but

I couldn't stand to see so many people suffering."

That's the way she was, committed and compassionate, as well as the prettiest girl in Hano. Once my career took off, I proposed marriage.

Emily wanted just a small wedding. I thought it was because her parents were poor and couldn't afford more. I offered to pay all the expenses for a bigger reception, but she declined.

"I don't want to spend so much on a reception where everyone drinks, and there'll be fights and other trouble," she said.

I understood her worry. Almost every wedding reception in Hano turned into a brawl. Once the cops came to stop the fight, all combatants turned on them as a common enemy. There were lots of bandages and black eyes sported after those weddings.

Our tiny wedding and reception didn't have one altercation and after our honeymoon in Florida, we got along great. When our son Joe came along ten months later, life couldn't be better. Due to Emily and boxing, things were going my way. I could actually say that happiness graced my life for the first time.

But I still loved boxing more than anything, maybe even more than Emily and little Joe. Fighting gave me recognition, pride, and an honest way to earn a living.

With that thought, a host of spirits surrounded me. Like little darting clouds of light, they came and went in the blink of an eye. Without words, they told me this wasn't my final destination, just a stopover until I tired of reviewing my life.

I only wished I could review a future with Emily and little Joe. My body continued to float in liquid nitrogen waiting for something to change. I sensed it would, and soon.

⨞Chapter 6

The images of the last five years, the happiest of my life, faded away. Over the next few hours, I jerked back and forth between reviewing other parts of my life and watching over my body. I couldn't seem to control what I wanted to do. Gradually I became used to this quick, new manifestation of reality whenever I had a thought: *I think, therefore it appears.*

Then I tried to imagine myself back to life, but that didn't quite work, so it isn't true that you can make anything happen by thinking about it. There is still a barrier between life and the world after death.

Though I was still keenly aware of my connection with Joe and Emily, I couldn't interact in any way with them. I know some people report visitations from the spirits of loved ones, but I couldn't seem to do anything but view them, though it seemed like I was in the room with them when I did. I couldn't tell if they noticed my presence or not, or if I was even really with them.

After I had my fill of reviewing life with Emily, I began to concentrate on my relationship with little Joe. I knew I'd been lucky not to work a nine-to-five job. From the time Emily first told me she was pregnant to the night I'd raced her to the hospital when she labored faster than normal, I'd been around to share things that a lot of guys missed. I gazed with longing at the images; Joe's little puckered-up newborn face, and his sweet, toothless baby smiles. Emily and I were playing with him in our living room together when he pulled himself up at the coffee table and stood for the first time just a few days before I passed over. It pulled my heartstrings to see him look puzzled by my absence now, and I knew he'd probably forget about me soon. But because of my love for him and my deep connection with Emily, I knew I'd be able to watch him grow from this netherworld.

After two or three days of earth time passed, I'd gained some profound revelations, shit I never would have thought about before. I realized that on this plane of existence, time is an illusion. Time exists only because humans devised a way to calculate it. By simultaneously watching the present and reviewing my personal history, I discovered that time is also fluid, subject to our perception. That's why time seemed elastic to me during fights, speeding up when I was winning or going slow motion when I was getting beaten to a pulp. Our brains don't just track time – they create it.

I also began to understand some quirky things about the nature of reality. I discovered that there are many worlds and that souls take on many forms, all composed of energy. Instinctively, I began to understand that when any form of energy is disrupted, it always reforms as something else and is never destroyed, because energy is indestructible. That's why religious types always say that life is eternal. Maybe this eternity stuff wasn't so bad after all.

Though linear time had little meaning here, things changed quickly on Earth. I was astonished to find that Emily nurtured Joe's memories of me by sharing photographs and memorabilia with him, telling him that his dad was a big hero. She explained to him how I donated my body to science for the good of humanity and that he might grow up to be the doctor or scientist who would revive me. Her conversations with Joe reflected her compassionate nature. It humbled me, knowing damn well I'd signed up for a cryonic procedure to benefit number one, Jim Jackson.

Emily didn't rush to remarry. She used some of my life insurance money to open an animal shelter named after me, and devoted herself to rescuing as many animals as she could. In her spare time, she tutored Joe and taught him everything she learned about cryonics. By the time he was in middle school, his goal in life was to revive me. He took every science class he could and instead of going out for sports, he read medical journals and textbooks after school. I watched as he graduated high school with honors, then went through pre-med university classes and medical school.

He did all this because he wanted to discover how to reanimate corpses. How much more love could a son have for his father? He loved me so much it might have been better for him if I'd been buried or cremated. He could have moved on instead of devoting his life to me.

As fifty years went by in Joe's world, I discovered that I could only see people if they remembered me. As people's memories of me faded, they faded from my perception too. In the case of my son, I remained connected because he cultivated a deep connection with me. When it became harder to see Emily, I thought she'd forgotten me. But I found out through my connection with Joe that she began to struggle with Alzheimer's. Her memories of me, along with countless other memories, were disappearing. Eventually I could see Emily only when Joe spent time with her.

Because of the timeless awareness of this existence, I never gave up hope that I would live again, but I could see Joe losing hope that he would ever meet me. During my fifty-year sojourn in the spirit world, no cryopreserved human had been resuscitated. Though Joe began to gray, gained a few pounds, and began to question his efforts to revive me, he still made weekly visits to the assisted living facility where he placed Emily after her early onset Alzheimer's began to advance. Although only in her early seventies, she needed constant care because of the progressive disease. Her physical appearance changed, of course. She'd aged over the years to the point where I wouldn't have recognized her if I hadn't seen her deteriorate year by year. But I still loved her with all my heart, just the same as if I'd grown old with her. I realized that in her own way, she probably still loved me as much as I loved her.

One frigid afternoon in January, I watched Joe celebrate his fifty-first birthday with Emily. They sat together in Emily's room, a Victorian refuge that Joe had paid a decorator to furnish, reminding me of the bedroom we'd shared so long ago. Emily probably hadn't remembered his birthday, so I suspected that Joe gifted Emily with the festive birthday balloons and the flowers in her favorite colors.

Joe had a tender way with his mother. He always spoke patiently to her, sometimes reaching out to touch her hand or smooth a stray lock of hair from her face. When I watched them, I experienced their conversations as though I were in the room.

"Look, Mom." Joe turned his laptop around so she could see the screen, a scientific paper posted online. "Researchers at Yale University have found a virus that effectively attacks an aggressive form of human brain tumor."

The new discovery aroused my interest. Did this mean Joe harbored renewed hope that he'd revive me in his lifetime?

"What's that mean, Joey?" Emily asked.

Joe's excitement showed in his voice. "'By using time-lapse laser imaging, researchers have watched the virus rapidly home in on brain tumors. It selectively kills cancerous cells while leaving healthy tissue intact.' Basically, Mom, this means it might be possible to cure Dad's brain tumor with this method soon."

Emily squirmed uncomfortably in her chair. "Do you really believe after all these years your father will live again?"

Joe didn't answer right away, surprised by her reply. He sometimes discussed technical details about things he worked on, perhaps to help clarify his thoughts, but she usually didn't understand him.

"The central premises of cryonics show that memory, personality, and identity are stored in the structure and chemistry of the brain," he said softly. "We've found that brain activity is known to stop and later resume under certain conditions."

The boy made me proud. He'd certainly educated himself in many fields in order to rejuvenate me.

Emily smiled politely, unable to follow Joe's explanation. "Are you saying that if you do bring him back to life, he'll remember who I am?"

Joe looked distracted, as if he was already running calculations in his head. "I don't know," he said. "It's not generally accepted that current methods preserve the brain well enough to retain previous memories. We've completed studies showing that high concentrations of cryoprotectant circulated through the brain before cooling can largely prevent freezing injuries. This also preserves the fine cell structures of the brain in which memory and identity reside. Believe me, the Cryonic Foundation has assured me many times that Dad received the highest possible concentration infused before he was cooled. So maybe, just maybe he'll have his memory when he's revived. We won't know until we bring him back."

Emily looked bewildered. She frowned and spoke with difficulty. "What about his soul?"

My wife was a devout Catholic and regularly attended Mass. Her priest visited her at least once a week since her confinement.

"I believe his soul is asleep and in God's care," Joe said.

Her voice broke. "Will God return it after fifty years?"

Joe reached out and patted Emily's hand. "Babies are born after years of being cooled in liquid nitrogen storage while they were embryos. People awaken after years spent in a coma. Their soul is always intact."

"I'm glad we're talking. . . so many questions. . . bottled up all these years. I never understood how Jim could be brought back. . . Only Jesus can do that." She raised her eyes heavenward as though in prayer.

Joe took her hand in his and once again spoke as much for his own benefit as hers. "As we learn more about life and how it works, our ideas about death have changed. Once scientists believed life required breath, then they learned to restart breathing. Scientists knew life required a beating heart, and we learned to restart hearts. Then they discovered life merely required a functioning brain. Now, science knows that brain death is simply a natural process that may be reversible."

Emily struggled to brush her hand across his cheek. "We all die. I never believed your father could be revived, Joey."

"Mom, listen. When a body is cryopreserved, disintegration almost totally stops and important structures are intact – "

"Joey, please, I don't want to talk about death anymore."

"Okay, Mom, I'll write it out so when you're feeling better you can read it."

He took the pad of paper from her bedside table and started writing. That triggered memories of how Emily always kept perfumed stationery in her bedside drawer. My thoughts were so potent in this realm that I could literally smell the old scent.

While a body is preserved in timeless slumber, the march of science is not, Joe wrote. *Given enough time, the ability of medicine to repair damage to a body will exceed the loss that disease, aging, and cryopreservation inflict. Then, what appears to be a corpse will live again.*

"Read that later," Joe said and handed the note to Emily.

"Thanks, Joey. It's easier for me to understand when I read; you know I can hardly understand most of what you say."

"Mom, I'm not a kid any longer. Do you have to call me Joey?"

"Okay, Doctor Jackson! But I'm still skeptical about the chances your father will ever live again."

Joe kissed her hand and looked her in the eye. "If by chance Dad is revived, most neuroscientists agree that long-term memory is stored by durable structural and molecular changes within the brain, not transient electrical activity. My hope is he'll remember who we are, even so."

Emily cast her eyes heavenward again as though petitioning God. "I hope God doesn't think we're trying to cheat Him. . ."

Joe tried to make her understand that what he was trying to do didn't offend God in any way. I knew Joe no longer believed in the Catholic God he was raised to worship. I couldn't read his thoughts, but heard him talk of it with Emily.

Joe continued to rattle on about things he'd learned from books. "Preservation and reanimation simply reenact an older fantasy. The elaborate preparation a body undergoes prior to cryonic suspension isn't much different from the mummification procedures the Egyptian nobility went through prior to being interred in their pyramids," he said.

"Elaborate preparations are exactly what your dad went through to be preserved," Emily said, suddenly beaming.

I could see Joe realize she might be starting to accept his thoughts about attempting to revive me.

"This doesn't mean that if we're successful and revive Dad, that he'll live forever. At some point in time, he'll still die."

"Of course, we all die sometime," Emily murmured. Her eyelids closed and she lapsed into the dreamworld where she spent much of her time. Joe signaled for the nurse to help Emily to bed, and hurried back to the lab for more work on his reanimation theory.

It wouldn't be long, Joe seemed to think, and for the first time in a very long time, I felt the closest thing to excitement that anyone on this side of the veil experiences. A lot of people believed in reincarnation. But I just might literally return from the dead in my old body and walk in Joe and Emily's world once again.

Chapter 7

The past fifty years had been kind to Dr. Joseph Callahan Jackson. Just a few years after graduating from medical school, my son founded NanoTechnology Restorative Systems (NTRS). The company rapidly grew into a multi-million dollar business. In addition to providing research grants to individuals and to programs interested in advancing cryonics and perfecting rejuvenation processes, such as the Cryonic Foundation, the company also designed, provided, and maintained precision cryonic and nanotech health systems in facilities around the world.

Joe did amazing things with nanotechnology that went far over my head, stuff that sci-fi writers only dreamed about in my day. So far, he'd perfected a process to manufacture nanobots. These nanobots coursed through a person's bloodstream, detecting any trauma in need of repair, and then restored healthy cell structure and chemistry at the molecular level. Joe also created and perfected coated nanoparticles that the nanobots could insert into cells without triggering their self-protective mechanisms.

A few months after his birthday celebration with Emily, Joe made a startling presentation at his company's annual stockholders meeting. I observed the gathering from my world as if I too watched from the curved rows of theatre seats in the semi-darkened auditorium.

"The restorative system we have devised is ground-breaking technology," Joe said, standing at a sparkling, crystal-like podium. "This is the most basic component of what we hope to accomplish. We have the ability to replace organs and body parts when these are defective in some manner. But I'm worried about the long periods of dormancy prior to initiating brain restoration. Some of our clients have been in deep suspension now for nearly sixty years." He directed a laser pen at the big screen behind him, a graph of statistics about NTRS clients.

I assumed my case was also averaged into these numbers.

"I agonize over our limited but growing knowledge about restoring brain function. NTRS has developed technologies for general molecular analysis and the repair of internal organs. Now we're racing to develop the same technology to restore brain function. At this time, successful animal experiments – dog, sheep, pig, and several types of simians – use a drug cocktail compatible with the species' brain chemistry to stimulate their cryonically suspended brains. During our first human restoration, a specially tailored pharmaceutical cocktail will also be employed. As the body is warmed and circulation is restored, injections and intravenously administered dopamine enhancers, as well as drugs designed to treat Parkinson's disease, depression, anxiety and other conditions will help to counter any physical and mental side effects of the cryonic procedure and resuscitation. Narcan, for example, normally used to treat heroin overdoses, is one of the drugs we'll administer in small therapeutic doses as an aid to restore consciousness.

"As you know, our earliest efforts with animals clearly showed brain and nervous system trauma. As our human subject moves from a state of vitrification into a medically induced coma, electrodes will be attached to various points on the patient's body. The electrodes will send electrical signals along the median nerves and the spinal cord to the thalamus. This electrical activity will excite the brain and increase oxygen and blood flow to the cerebral cortex. Both animal and human studies have proven this stimulates axon growth and rebuilds any damaged connections. Of course, the danger is that no one is certain what facets of human cerebral function may be damaged by cryonic procedures and if this damage is repairable."

I listened until the meeting concluded with a polite standing ovation. Joe's presentation thrilled me. The things he said meant I might re-enter my body soon and continue the life taken from me. If I could remember anything of the spirit world, would I be considered living proof of the existence of life after death?

Joe's questions about cerebral complexity didn't stop him from trying to revive me. Within weeks, Joe's legal department reviewed all the documents I'd signed before my death. Everything looked good to go. NTRS and Cryonic Foundation technicians withdrew my body from the tank of nitrogen, and began the resuscitation process by inserting electrodes into my brain and warming them to the temperature that allowed the cancer-suppressing virus to thrive. I felt nothing physically during this procedure; in fact, my consciousness remained rooted in the spirit world and I continued to view the process as though I were nearby.

Joe reviewed the resuscitation procedures with the technicians in the temperature-controlled room where my body would be processed over the coming weeks.

"My father's brain tumor is undetectable now and the blood markers have disappeared. Now we face the onerous task of reversing the preservation procedure and restoring bodily processes and full cerebral function."

Joe then supervised the process of warming my body to match the temperature of my thawed-out brain, gently encouraging the technicians in their work. The room felt cool to my awakening senses, but definitely not as cold as the nitrogen tank. Perhaps this step brought me nearer the physical world, because my dread of cold began to surface even though my body had literally floated like an ice cube in liquid nitrogen for five decades.

When my body and brain temperature matched, the technicians began the months-long healing process by infusing Joe's nanobots into my bloodstream. They immediately began their task of rejuvenating dormant organs and tissues on the cellular level.

Joe unhooked the electrodes from my body and attached me to an advanced heart-lung system that continued to help maintain my circulation while the nanobots continued their repair job. The object was eventually to replace the concoctions made from sugar-based molecules that mimicked chemicals to real blood. In cryonic terminology, these were commonly called cryonic protective agents (CPA). Technicians finally flushed these CPAs out and replaced them with type A+ blood. They periodically tested my organs for function levels, and when they showed signs of activity, technicians raised my body temperature cautiously. At a critical point when all organs functioned well, Joe would give the signal to jump-start my heart.

Though I had my doubts about cryonics before I died, after my demise I accepted that I might live again because all things seemed possible from my vantage point "beyond the beyond." Now I was beginning to have human doubts again. Would my body have aged as much as Emily's? Like her, I was over seventy years old. If the old heart started pumping again, could I spend the remainder of my days in a rocking chair beside my wife, at the very least?

Joe continued to monitor the process one day at a time until the momentous morning when the technicians replaced the CPA in my veins and arteries with blood. One by one, they unhooked the machines except the heart-lung machine that supported my circulation. Two doctors, Dr. Remus and young Dr. McGuire, and two nurses, Braun and Rizzo, joined the team of three technicians assisting Joe in the sterile, temperature-controlled resuscitation room. Joe and this core team had successfully started animal hearts with bursts of direct electrical current by alternately accelerating and decelerating the current. Once the hearts quivered to life, the animals' brains always showed electrical activity. If my heart did begin to pump with all the proper electrical impulses, then hopefully my brain would show electrical activity as well.

Joe elaborated on the subject aloud, saying there was no reason a human body would react any differently than the animal test subjects. The tension in the room began to mount. Nurse Rizzo, a petite brunette, mopped Joe's sweaty forehead with a wad of tissues as he attached electrodes to my cranium. Dr. McGuire and a technician moved my still form into an fMRI scanner. Nurse Braun, a tall Germanic type, turned away from the monitors, set her clipboard aside, and readied a video camera to record the historical event.

Joe answered his colleagues' questions in a firm, quiet voice. He checked all his medical gadgets to be certain they were operational. The medical team fell silent for a few minutes, each focused on a task.

Finally, Joe turned toward the camera. "It's March 10, 2026. The first cryonic patient resuscitation at the Cryonic Foundation has been in progress since January 23, 2026, managed by the NanoTechnology Restorative Systems revival team. Our patient is James Robert Jackson, born March 26, 1950, expired and cryonically preserved on April 30, 1976. I'm Dr. Joseph James Jackson, and I'm joined by Dr. Layton Remus and Dr. Michael McGuire."

Joe leaned over and squeezed my hand. "Dad, we're ready to start your heart."

He checked the amperage, and with a dramatic pause, firmly applied the two paddles and jolted my heart with electrical current.

The world's first cryonic revival team gazed at all the monitors, waiting to observe any brain activity. I'd learned by listening to Joe review the process with his team that even if a brain showed electrical activity, it didn't mean that it functioned in a normal manner. But I suppose any doctor knew this first step in any type of resuscitation. Get the heart beating, the brain active, and go from there.

My body jumped inches off the table and stiffened until Joe cut the juice. Then it sagged back to the table. The medical team stood by, gazing at the many screens lining the room's walls again. Nothing. The monitors beeped for a moment and flatlined.

"Ready, again." Joe turned up the current by a factor of two and applied the paddles.

Same result.

He increased the level by a factor of four and applied the paddles.

My body jerked hard and smoke rose from the contact points on my flesh. The team looked at one another. Dr. Remus stepped forward and put his hand on Joe's shoulder as if to say he'd done a magnificent job of restoring my body even if he couldn't insert that spark of life.

Joe stubbornly turned away and his determination felt palpable. "One more time," he muttered, turning the voltage to the maximum setting. The final bolt arched my back in a spasm that left two large burns on my chest. I felt sucked away from the spirit world, as if drawn to my body. I literally responded to the spark that animated me in every cell in my body. For the first time in fifty years, my body and soul were partners again.

A cheer went up as the monitors filled with undulating lines and beeped like crazy. Dr. McGuire pumped his fist in the air and whooped like I'd just nailed a boxing knockout.

The objective had been to get that spark going. Now I'd be nursed to full consciousness over a matter of days or weeks. As far as anyone could tell, my systems were working fine. The question was if I could function again.

My eyes fluttered open for an instant, but all I could see were lights, shadows, and vague blurs.

"Dr. Jackson, look at this." Rizzo, the younger nurse, pointed to the glowing fMRI screen. "I've never seen brain activity this pronounced before."

Because I was still officially unconscious, the team couldn't determine yet if my brain was damaged from the high current.

"Oh, Jesus," Joe exclaimed, "I must have screwed up." Flustered, he began to scribble numbers on a clipboard.

Suddenly I could no longer see the room. I was aware of hearing the conversation, no more, as if it took place far, far away.

Braun, a dignified woman who wore her blonde hair pinned up under her surgical cap, inserted a Foley catheter into my urethra and she and Rizzo wheeled me on a gurney to a private room. Both stayed near my side that night, and the ICU revival crew stayed on standby as I struggled for survival.

Over the next three weeks, the nursing staff administered intravenous fluids and medications as needed. Dr. Remus, Dr. McGuire, and the various technicians checked in on me from time to time. Joe made long visits and sat nearby as I drifted in and out of my body and into cosmic overview as if uncertain whether I wanted to stay or not. Perhaps this was normal for an unconscious person, because I also stayed in my body for longer and longer periods, as if practicing to be physical again. Finally, I drifted into my body one morning and I felt tethered to it, as if it were a perfect fit. I didn't feel the pull to drift away, earthbound at last.

Would my new chance at life be an improvement over my first twenty-six years, or should I have stayed in my pain-free world?

⋟Chapter 8

Though I still lay unconscious in the Cryonic Foundation intensive care recovery suite, my mind began to focus upon everyday concerns. Normal human doubts that I'd not experienced on the other side began to surface: *2026! How can I rebuild my life when so many things have changed? How would I cope?*

One part of me whirled in excitement at the thought of eating, making love, and enjoying my family again, but another dreaded the pain of physical life.

Joe came into the sterile room where I lay and spoke to me as though I was fully awake, as he always did. He told me that Dr. Dovinsky, a neurologist who specialized in comatose patients, would examine me.

Another doctor, I thought, remembering the old light bulb jokes. How many doctors did it take to raise the dead?

Joe always seemed to have some type of electronic device in his hand. He'd simply point it at me and it would talk back in a mechanical voice, reciting my vital signs – temperature, pulse, and blood pressure. If he wanted anything changed or a ordered a medication, he'd press another button on the device, talk out loud, and within seconds his orders were confirmed on the computer screens in the nursing station.

Today, Joe's monologue seemed to respond to all my unasked questions. "No doctors at the Cryonic Foundation have experience in treating long-term cryonic patients," he said, tapping a ballpoint pen against his electronic pad. "The CF doctors are all experts in other fields. Even Dr. Dovinsky has only worked with comatose patients. But we're combining cutting-edge research from many fields to bring you around, Dad."

Soon Dr. Dovinsky stood at my bedside to examine me. He didn't seem to consider that I might be able to hear what he said. "After fifty years of inactivity, it's unlikely that Mr. Jackson's condition will improve if and when he regains consciousness," he told Joe. "I don't think a mature human brain has the same capability as an embryo to withstand long-term cryonic storage. Essentially, there's a one in a million chance he'll ever be aware of anything. I'm sorry, Joe. I wish this could work out."

Disappointment shadowed Joe's face. He tenderly told me good-bye, left the Foundation, and drove to the nursing home to tell his mother. Because I wasn't yet entirely bound to my body, I could still summon up the will to view him because of his deep connection to me.

"I should have left him in a cryopreserved state until science advanced sufficiently to revive him," Joe told Emily. "There's so much we don't know yet. But I'm getting older, Mom, and I want to communicate with my father before I die. I never had the chance to know him. . ."

Joe's middle-aged face crumpled as though he might cry.

Emily simply patted him on the hand, as if consoling him about a minor mishap. She was quiet while Joe struggled with his feelings and then she suddenly spoke. "You did the right thing, son. I wanted to say goodbye to him too. He left us so quickly. But don't blame yourself for anything. If your plan wasn't successful, at least you've done your best."

Emily certainly seemed lucid for a person having advanced Alzheimer's, I thought. Their sentiments pierced my heart. Maybe I would choose life, would have to choose life, just for them. I recalled how devastating it was to leave my beautiful young wife and son. Would it still be possible to connect with the spirit world if Joe could bring me around? I'd miss my greater awareness. Like all human beings, I figured on either being alive or being in the spirit world, one or the other. Given a real choice, what would I want?

But witnessing Joe's deep disappointment motivated me to do all I could to make his efforts successful. Over the next few days, my heart beat regularly and my brain continued to show electrical activity, but I wasn't truly alive. I still couldn't communicate with Joe even though somewhat aware of my surroundings. This felt similar to my isolation in the spirit world. But I couldn't do anything now to change my circumstances.

The next day, I heard Dr. Dohmed, the neuropsychiatrist, as he called himself, talking to my son. I couldn't see him, but I could view Joe's reactions to other people whenever he was in the room.

"I changed the combination of drugs for your father. Ambien is an old medication that can trigger a cascade of events in the brain known as the GABA pathway. The latest version of Ambien will sometimes awaken a coma patient. I thought we may as well give it a try."

Joe barely listened to Dr. Dohmed. "My nanobots have repaired any damaged cells throughout his body, so I don't know why he hasn't regained consciousness by now," he said. "Maybe he doesn't want to come back."

"What you've done so far is amazing, Dr. Jackson. Your nanobots are changing the way we treat many injuries."

"That may be so, but right now I'm only interested in reviving my father," Joe said, gazing down at me with undisguised despair.

Dr. Dohmed squeezed Joe's shoulder. I could hear him leave the room, shutting the door quietly behind him.

Apparently the Ambien worked as advertised, because I began to feel something, a yearning, a mental tug that seem to fire my desire for physical existence. I felt like I crossed some line, as though beginning to wake from a night's sleep. I tried to open my eyes after three days, but it felt as though they'd been glued shut for fifty years, no surprise.

My mind drifted from thought to thought in the meantime. I could travel with my thoughts in the spirit world, but I couldn't from my body, so when I tried to imagine waking up, it didn't help much. My thoughts didn't project me anywhere or manifest anything as they did on the other side.

Easily distracted, I forgot about my effort and began to let my memories filter in again, but I couldn't view them in the same way. When I thought of my ride in the ambulance after Emily summoned it, the details were less vivid but more emotional. So were my memories of seeing little Joe for the first time from the spirit world.

My mind took off like it had during the rare times when I slept in on a Saturday morning and let my dreams take over before the tumor took me away. I started to enjoy the pleasant sensation of dreaming, the closest thing on Earth to being on the other side. I found myself winning the world championship in a fight where boxers hovered over the ring like superheroes. I played with little Joe on a rocket ship, and traveled with Emily on an old sailing ship at Cape Cod, all sorts of real and unreal things.

Suddenly, I sensed an intruder, the same feeling you get when someone's staring at you, or when you're alone and realize someone has crept into the room. It wasn't scary, exactly, but something didn't feel right.

I snapped back into the present and waited for something to happen. When it didn't, I told myself it was probably the drugs or my imagination. After all, here I was in my old body, back on Earth after fifty long years. Who wouldn't be a little nervous and jerky?

I struggled to open my eyes again, to move a finger or a toe. Anything to prove I lived.

My eyes suddenly shot open without my willing them. Light and form burst around me like images in a kaleidoscope. I felt nauseated by the all the color and movement, but when I tried to close my eyes, they wouldn't budge.

My right index finger moved, something I'd tried and tried to do, but this time I hadn't willed it to happen. It bent and when I tried to straighten it, I couldn't.

This wasn't a dream. Did I imagine a woman's voice saying in a thick accent, 'I'm in control. If you want to live, relax and let me manage everything?'

Confusion and disbelief flooded my mind. *What the hell?*

It wasn't exactly a voice I heard. It felt more like a feminine presence that planted thoughts in my mind.

"I am Erzsébet Báthory."

This revelation ripped through my mind like a fire alarm.

"I choose to inhabit your body. I will return it to you when I finish what I must do."

What the fuck. . .?

Then my eyes closed involuntarily. The old familiar feeling of anger, a hard, bitter punching bag, filled my solar plexus and squeezed my heart.

How could a goddamn female get inside my head? If that's what rejuvenation was all about, I didn't want it.

Only crazy people hear voices. Maybe the tumor damaged my brain despite Joe's nanobots.

Then the bitch told me I wasn't dreaming or crazy.

My surge of anger turned to fear. That's it – I'm psycho. The past fifty years in the spirit world were just a long dream. Maybe I never died at all. Maybe I'd been restrained in a mental hospital all these years.

But what if I wasn't dreaming or psycho? Then this woman probably caused all the electrical activity the medical team witnessed. When she entered my consciousness, *that* was the first physical awareness I'd experienced in fifty years.

The nurse standing beside the bed, who looked to me like nothing more than a patchwork of white and flesh-colored shapes, gasped when my eyes opened and closed. She pulled a cord, which made a light over the door flash and sounded an alarm that summoned the doctors. Dr. Dohmed and Joe rushed into the room. Both stood with their mouths agape, staring at me and then at my brain's electrical signals on the monitors. Dr. Dohmed signed an order to have my ventilator removed. As soon as the nurse did so, I breathed easily on my own.

I felt as if I was tied up and forced to watch a horror movie. I couldn't see well, I couldn't talk, and I couldn't move. Might as well be a goddamn quadriplegic. I should've put that bullet through my brain while I still had the chance.

I wondered if I could breathe without this woman, who lurked silently in the background like a fox concealing herself from hounds. When I started to panic, she somehow generated a soothing feeling, as though ocean waves washed through my mind. But it only comforted me for a moment. I soon struggled for control and resisted her to the best of my ability. Jim Jackson would never give in. I forced my will to flex like a muscle, pushing her with away with all my mental might. But she pushed back like a force of nature, and I couldn't hold her back for long.

I needed a new strategy. Maybe if I didn't resist and ignored her, she might vanish.

Her raspy laugh echoed inside my brain. "You amuse me, Jim Jackson."

I imagined the woman to be a boxing opponent, in the same way I imagined Homicide Hank to be my tumor. I visualized pummeling her until she hit the canvas.

She laughed harder.

How could two different minds share one body? This was unnatural. I tried again to fight back, but she did something to paralyze my brain.

Just as I reached the point of overwhelming anger and despair, she absorbed my pain again.

Joe reached over to shine a light into my pupils and then flicked it away to see if they dilated properly. "Dad?" He paused and tried again. "Dad?"

I tried to move my mouth but my face felt like a jumble of unrelated parts.

"Dad? Joe said once more, "are you there?"

Dr. Dohmed reached out and clapped Joe on the shoulder the same way he had a couple of weeks before, as if to say, *it's too bad your father's not going to respond.*

Joe stepped quickly out of Dr. Dohmed's reach and turned to the charge nurse, Sherrod. The no-nonsense look on her plain face belonged to a Marine drill sergeant.

"Keep tabs on his brain activity. Document all data accurately." As Joe stormed out of the room, I could see that he punched the door from the corner of my eye, reminding me of myself so many years before.

I wondered why this damned Elizabeth –

"Erzsébet," she said. "Countess Báthory, Hungarian by birth."

I did my best to glower mentally.

Joe stepped back into the room suddenly. "I apologize for my attitude. Unfortunately, this case is close to my heart. If my dad is alive but remains comatose, then all my work is a failure. . ."

Even with my distraction, I could feel Joe's pain. While Dr. Dohmed and the nurse reassured Joe that his work would help many, I tried to lift my finger again.

Erzsébet responded with a smirky thought. "Hmm," she said. "See how far you get without me."

"You bitch," I railed. "I wouldn't be surprised if you're blocking me. My son has done everything possible to bring me back. There should be no reason I can't respond."

But Erzsébet Báthory, not Jim Jackson, controlled my wiring. It became crystal clear that she knew everything I thought about. But I had no access to her mind and could only comprehend what she told me.

I couldn't do anything except what she allowed.

Joe and Dr. Dohmed tried every trick in the medical book to bring me around – stimulants, some more IV vitamins, even some old alternatives like Chinese acupuncture and Swedish massage. Erzsébet enjoyed these treatments, but she remained silent while I fumed. Two days went by without much physical improvement, and I learned little about her.

I couldn't believe my predicament. All this time and trouble and now

I was screwed, nailed by a conniving female. My mind whirled hour after hour in a tangle of questions. How could she occupy my mind? Was I hallucinating? Had my brain deteriorated? Had Erzsébet come from one of my previous existences? I'd never believed in such a thing, but my experiences on the other side showed me what Jesus meant when he said that His Father's house has many mansions. And there were definitely evil spirits cruising around the afterworld. Could Erzsébet be an evil spirit or a demon?

Whoever or whatever she was, I, Jim Jackson, world-class fighter, couldn't comprehend going through life commandeered by a woman. My poor, dear Emily was the only woman I'd ever allowed inside my head. Some way, somehow, I had to get rid of this she-devil.

When Joe returned to my bedside a few hours later, I opened my eyes on my own, a first for me. I did a mental feint, like a fake right, and then went in with a left hook, mocking Erzsébet – "see, you can't stop me."

I struggled to move my lips to tell Joe what was happening inside me, but I still couldn't will any other responses. Was Erzsébet still blocking me?

Thrilled, Joe asked me how I felt.

I couldn't say anything, but I focused my vision enough to see him. I knew he'd matured, of course, because I'd been viewing him all along, but in broad daylight he looked just like a tired, aging version of me. How old and decrepit I must be now. Maybe Joe would move me into the long-term care facility with Emily soon.

I lay immobile for three more days. Erzsébet seemed to get restless. She knew I desperately wanted to speak so I could ask Joe to get her out of my head.

Maybe Erzsébet changed her mind, because she suddenly started to try like hell to get me to talk, maybe to break the boredom, I suspected.

On the morning of the fourth day, Joe arrived with the entire rejuvenation team. Dr. Remus and Dr. McGuire examined me, marveling that I was more or less alive, but what they didn't say filled the room with a palpable gloom. Joe directed Nurse Braun to turn on the video camera, just in case, he said. He filmed himself with an introduction as he had when he'd started my heart.

"Vegetable," Erzsébet taunted. "Fool."

She'd figured out that anger motivated me. If you told me I couldn't do something, I would damn well do it.

As I fought to show her I could talk on my own, I could feel her concentrate her thoughts upon my lips, tongue, and voice box. My lips parted again, but I couldn't make a sound. My brain responded by becoming more alert. When Joe passed his light in front of my face, I followed it with my eyes. Nurse Sherrod duly charted the change, but I may as well have remained a spirit. I couldn't even utter a grunt.

I began to understand that morning how Erzsébet's and my mind worked together. When she allowed our minds to merge, I "heard" her thoughts telepathically, somehow reading them with my mind. Apparently this process worked both ways, except I didn't have as much access to her mind as she had to mine.

Without warning, Erzsébet caused me to speak. *"Engedj ki innen. Kik mindnyájan?"*

After not talking for so many years, my voice had grown raspy and hoarse. I wondered if Erzsébet had something to do with it, or if it was a natural consequence of the cryonic procedure. Then, on the other hand, it wasn't me doing the talking. Hell, I didn't even know what I was saying.

Joe and the medical team stared at me in amazement.

I knew Joe and the other doctors had probably seen and heard a few odd things when people came out of anesthesia, but this was way beyond the usual.

"What? What did he say?" Joe slipped his palm recorder out of his pocket and turned it on.

No one said a word. My accented voice grew louder and louder, demanding who knew what. *"Én Erzsébet Báthory,"* I croaked.

Joe shared a shocked look with the other doctors. "There goes your million to one shot, Dovinsky. You said the odds of him speaking were nil, but now he's speaking more than one language," he said.

Young Nurse Rizzo stepped forward. "My grandmother on my mother's side spoke Magyar – Hungarian, that is. If I'm not mistaken, Mr. Jackson first said, "Let me out of here, and then he asked who we all were. The last thing he said – I may have misinterpreted it – but I believe he said, "My name is Erzsébet Báthory."

"Are you sure?" Joe said. "I don't have any idea where he would've learned any central European languages."

"Can you speak English?" she asked in Magyar.

"Yes," I answered in English. I felt as perplexed as Joe looked. I had no memory of hearing Hungarian before. Erzsébet had just demonstrated how she could combine her knowledge and mine.

Between us, we know many languages, I joked. *I know one, and you know the rest.*

But I was disturbed, too. If Erzsébet controlled my speech, how would I ever be able to communicate my true thoughts? If she was always dominant, I could only express her desires. I found myself butting up against my fear of helplessness, trapped inside an incompetent body, the worst punishment I could imagine. How could I get away from this ruthless woman?

Joe locked his eyes on mine. "Can you tell me who you are and where we are?"

"I have told you that I am Erzsébet Báthory."

She ignored our whereabouts, but she spoke in English this time, with such conviction that everyone in attendance would have believed her had they not known it was impossible for me to be Erzsébet Báthory.

"Good," Joe said. "Erzsébet, can you tell me what year it is?"

"1626," she quickly answered.

I wanted to say 2026. I died in 1976 and I knew fifty years had passed since then, but Erzsébet was doing all the talking.

Joe seemed too shocked to welcome me back. He pressed buttons to scroll through data on his electronic devices and compared figures there to figures on my chart. "I can't understand this. Could brain damage from an electrical overload cause this phenomenon?"

The possibility that I might have some kind of split personality from brain damage left me relieved for a moment. On the other hand, would I ever be myself again?

Dr. McGuire, the youngest of the doctors, spoke up. "Could it be that there's no damage? Maybe there's some effect caused by bathing the brain in cryoprotectants for five decades. Or maybe he's just temporarily confused, giving answers like 1626."

Joe turned to me and took my hand. "Maybe I'm expecting too much, Dad, wanting you to speak like you just woke up from a nap. How am I going to explain this to Mom? I need to figure this out."

I felt a surge of love for my son when he worried about what to tell Emily. Obviously, he wasn't going to quit on me, either.

He tried another question. "Dad, where and when were you born?"

"The Kingdom of Hungary, 1560," I said, in accented English.

The answer was totally unexpected by those in attendance, including me.

Joe quizzed the rejuvenation team. "Does anyone have any idea why he might claim to be a Hungarian woman from the seventeenth century and speak Magyar? Has anyone read any psychological studies about anything similar?" Joe asked. "What could possibly make him think he's someone else?"

Dr. Dohmed pulled at his goatee. "There are certified cases of people with multiple personality disorders in which one of the personalities believes it lives in the past. There's a possibility –"

Dr. Dovinsky interrupted. "A disorder seems likely, because if his brain is damaged, how could he answer questions logically?" He reached for my other hand and held it palm up in his. "Can you move your fingers?"

I shut my eyes and focused on my fingers. I moved my forefinger slightly, and then all four. But I knew that Erzsébet had provided most of the energy.

"He's beginning to respond beyond my expectations, physically, at least, considering the long cryonic preservation," Dr. Dovinsky said.

"I am concerned by the answers to your questions, though. Perhaps Dohmed is on to something."

"I know this sounds unscientific, but could your father be possessed?" young Nurse Rizzo asked. "The Slovakian side of my mother's family, well, you know about the Transylvania area. . ."

"Dracula. And you must have watched that old '70s movie, *The Exorcist,*" Joe said.

"Well, no," Nurse Rizzo said. "Dracula is an English invention, but Transylvanian folktales do contain all manner of beasts, shapeshifters, and spirits who enter people."

I tried to say, yes, yes, to encourage Joe to consider the possibility, but Erzsébet stopped me.

"There have been academic studies of people who recall living in another era in a past life," one of the technicians suggested.

Joe listened to the medical team's opinions without comment.

"At any rate, the nanobots are continuing to repair damaged cells and now that his synapses are firing, they should detect any anomalies," he said, speaking in a low voice with his back turned to me. "I want my father under rigorous observation throughout the night, and if there are any complications whatsoever, notify me immediately. Keep him under light sedation to make certain he rests, and we'll see if his mental state improves. I'll pray that his memory is restored."

He turned to me, picked up my hand and gave me a long look. "Welcome back, Dad. You look exhausted. We're going to leave you now to get some more rest. If you need anything, try to ask the nurses for it. As soon as you can speak, we'll put you on a light liquid diet, and if you tolerate that well, you should be able to eat solid food soon."

I tried to nod. I did feel exhausted even though I'd been resting for fifty years. *Come on, do something. Give me a shock or a shot to get this craziness out of my head.*

Unfortunately, no one could hear my thoughts and Erzsébet either wouldn't allow me to speak again or couldn't be bothered.

As the medical team left the room, chattering about the rejuvenation, I felt her crawling through my memories like a spider. I tried to penetrate her mind as she focused on me, but Erzsébet blocked every attempt, somehow rocking my consciousness into a dreamy lull until I drifted away into sleep.

Chapter 9

I still couldn't communicate easily the next morning, or for many mornings after waking up – Erzsébet was cautious about letting me talk. Delighted with my progress, Joe decided that getting my body moving was a bigger priority than speaking. Maybe an active body would strengthen mind and memory, he said.

Though I convalesced in bed for two more weeks, sleeping much of the time, Joe assigned a physical therapist to spend an hour twice a day with me. She helped me stretch and retrain my muscles with some pansy exercises designed for bedridden people. At least I thought they were pansy exercises until it caused me severe discomfort to stretch muscles that were inert for so long. I began to admire Erzsébet her because she took my suffering with fortitude.

When I finally gained some muscle tone, the therapist helped me out of bed to sit in a chair for the first time. I'd kept my hair short before I went into the tank, but once my blood began to circulate, it started to grow again. I discovered that the nurses had pulled it back into a little ponytail.

Before the nurses returned me to bed on my first day up, Joe called a barber. He wrapped a sheet around my neck, fastened it, and began snipping. I watched the tufts of hair hit the floor.

Something wasn't right.

Tufts of black hair lay on the floor, the same color I had when I was twenty-six. It should have been gray, or maybe snow white.

A mirror was the last thing I wanted to gaze into when the barber finished and handed one to me. I turned the hand mirror upside down in my lap, imagining how old and wrinkled I'd look. But Erzsébet didn't seem to care what I looked like, and I assumed she saw me before entering my body.

"Look in the mirror, Jim. It'll make you feel better," she said.

She always flapped her yapper about almost anything. I didn't want to look, but my hair color and her statement piqued my curiosity.

I picked up the mirror and held it in front of my face.

Impossible.

My face appeared younger than the last time I saw it, fewer lines, smoother skin, barely a flaw. Fifty years had passed and I hadn't aged at all.

If Erzsébet wasn't in control and I wasn't so goddamn weak, I would have jumped out of the chair.

"See," Erzsébet said.

"Guess it's good that I look younger than I thought."

Emily had aged, and even my son was almost an old man. I hadn't considered yet how this would affect my relationship with Emily. It felt strange knowing I looked younger than my son.

A nurse and technician helped me into onto a shower chair to wash the stray hairs from my body. I felt Erzsébet luxuriating in the hot running water. I wanted to get out once I saw the loose hairs swirling down the drain, but she said, "There was never a luxury like this where I came from. I'm staying in here as long as I want."

And so the bitch made me motion to the nurses to let me stay in the shower until the hot water ran out, over twenty minutes. When the nurses helped me out of the shower, my reflection in the bathroom mirror revealed how my musculature had deteriorated, but I still looked younger than I ever thought possible. I could hardly wait until I could manage some real workouts.

The next few weeks passed with a flurry of activity, many hours of rehabilitation and mental testing. Joe brought in a speech therapist to see if I had any injury or chemical-related speech problems, and three different neuropsychologists and neuropsychiatrists grilled me to determine if I had any behavioral problems or a mental illness that might have caused the formation of my second personality.

Erzsébet allowed me to handle my bodily functions and any other minor actions, but when it came to important activities, she took complete control. When the shrinks tested my IQ, she answered the questions and scored in the top percentile. The result was clearly her IQ, because I'd never been book smart and barely passed high school. After the IQ test, she gradually let me say more, but kept my conversations simple and basic.

She learned fast and soon absorbed everything I remembered about twentieth-century life. She made me request access to the Cryonic Foundation reference library and she read the medical journals there voraciously, acquiring vast amounts of technical knowledge.

One time I stopped to watch Joan, the librarian – according to her nametag – sitting in front of a pad where all sorts of pictures and text flowed.

"What's the device you're using?" Erzsébet had me ask.

"It's hard to believe there's anyone alive who doesn't know what a computer is, or how to use one," Joan said.

"I've seen the staff use them in the nursing station. Can you show me how?"

Joan took a wide band made of some stretchy type material off her head and handed it to me. "Put this on your head and just think what you want the computer to do, and it'll do it."

"Anything?" Erzsébet said.

"Well, anything a computer can do."

"What exactly can a computer do?"

Joan showed her a list of the software programs, the Internet, and the films, music, and multimedia presentations we could access just by thinking about them. It struck me then that I might be able to use a computer to tell my son how Erzsébet controlled me, but of course, there was no way for me to hide my thought from her.

"Don't even consider it," she said as I fit the band snugly around my head.

With us both thinking at the same time, the computer flashed and gave an error message about an improper mental input.

"Quit trying to operate this thing," Erzsébet said.

"Like hell I will."

She made me rip the headband from my head. I guessed she couldn't stop me from thinking entirely. That was good news.

"Is there some other way to operate this without thought projection?" Erzsébet asked.

Joan nodded. "Sure, you can just touch the screen and do almost anything you want the old-fashioned way."

Erzsébet touched the screen and dragged pictures around that amazed me. The colors and images were vivid and clear, nothing like the old color TVs from my day. She whizzed around the screen for an hour or so and seemed to understand all she encountered. I tried to memorize everything she did.

She looked through news stories about Hungary and Slovakia and found a recent photograph of a seventeenth-century painting of her castle. She looked at it with longing for several minutes. I could only read the caption: *Castle Cséjthe, also called Čachtice, situated deep in the Carpathian Mountains of what is now Slovakia.*

The picturesque setting embraced a bucolic tapestry of fields, meandering stone walls, and quaint cottages. Some scattered chickens roamed among cows, goats, and sheep grazing in meadows. The castle looked typical for its time and place: cold, damp, and gloomy.

When she scrolled the page down, some personal history appeared. I read along. . . *Báthory gathered around her persons of peculiar and sinister arts. These she welcomed into her presence. Among them were those who claimed to be witches, sorcerers, seers, wizards, and alchemists, who practiced the most depraved deeds in league with the Devil. They taught her their crafts in intimate detail. But learning such unspeakable things was not enough. . .*

Erzsébet caused me to throw my head back with a throaty laugh, sparking a deep resentment in me. "What's so funny? Keep your snickering to yourself, bitch. I can see how horrible you were."

She pointed to the text on the monitor. "That's what I'm laughing at."

Under her relatively attractive portrait was a description: *The most evil woman in history by many accounts,* it said.

Jesus, Erzsébet must have been a real psycho. I hoped no one would see me browsing this stuff. I read some more of her history as she scrolled further. She continued to giggle while she read about herself.

She is reputed to have murdered over six hundred girls, and how she killed them accounts for her reputation as the most vile mass murderer ever. The girls Báthory –

"You're a goddamn monster," I yelled mentally. "You're really sick to laugh at such a grisly story."

"Come on, Jim. If what this says were true, do you think I'd be laughing?"

I didn't know what to think or how to answer her question, so I went on the offensive. "What are you doing here, anyway? Why don't you just get the fuck out of my life?"

"Things aren't so simple, Jim. I told you I will leave when I achieve my objective."

Erzsébet seemed pensive but she wouldn't let me penetrate the barrier between our minds. She could shut me out completely whenever she wanted. I got so frustrated I'd have punched myself if she'd let me.

I mentally shouted at her again. "Tell me what you need and I'll get it for you."

"If only you could, I would leave today, you stupid peasant."

"What? You have powers. Go on and take whatever it is you need and leave me alone!"

She answered me with silence. I feared insanity would claim me if this frustration continued much longer.

My physical rehabilitation proceeded remarkably well because the nanobots' repair job restored me to a level beyond my original condition. Weight training and walking on a treadmill built my muscles, and I became stronger and faster than I'd ever been before the tumor. Erzsébet loved having the strength of a man and egged me on to get as brawny as possible, the one thing we didn't argue about. I figured she must have a reason for doing so.

In her era, a man's physical strength accounted for most everything. Erzsébet knew I'd fought for a living and she decided she wanted to try punching a heavy bag, so we had a meeting of the minds. Ready to start training again, I couldn't wait to punch the shit out of something or somebody because of my frustration with her. I asked Joe to get a bag for us. My body instinctively remembered the footwork and combination punches. Erzsébet contributed a viciousness that amazed me. Instinct, the nanobots' rejuvenation, and her unrelenting ambition enabled me to throw punches faster and harder than ever before.

The staff at CF was confounded when I'd introduced myself as Erzsébet and still seemed bemused by her presence. Although awed by my growing physical strength, some snickered whenever Erzsébet insisted they call me by her name. I knew they thought me nuts, and I wondered if maybe I really was. The neuroshrinks continued to dicker around with me because of this. If I could have wrapped my hands around the bitch's neck. . . She never tried to hide the fact that she'd hijacked my body, and seemed to think it was her royal privilege to do and say anything.

"How's it going, 'Lizabeth?" One of the orderlies greeted me when I left the library and entered the common room where I socialized with the staff taking their breaks and watching TV.

"Erzsébet," she made me say. "Just great," I added, trying to sound cynical. Pissed, I decided to head to the restroom.

When the medical team had first removed my catheter, we always used the bedpan, portable urinal, or my private bathroom. But now we had the full run of the Foundation, and when we had to pee, Erzsébet was confused about whether I should use the men's or women's room. In her day, she went to the turret where an enclosed outhouse emptied onto the grounds outside. She never had a gender choice to make then, but she made me stand like a fool in front of the

CRYONIC MAN

two restroom doors. Erzsébet said she was more inclined to use the ladies' room.

"I'm using the men's," I said. "It's bad enough you've got everyone calling me Erzsébet. There's no goddamn way I'm using the ladies' room."

She pushed through the men's room door, then stood staring, immediately taken aback by the urinal. She'd never seen one before, and she continued to stare at it as she headed for the bowl. She was amazed at that the first time we used it too.

"C'mon, I've got to use the urinal to piss." She irritated me, trying to make me sit down whenever I wanted to take a leak.

Once she made her mind up, I didn't have to tell her what to do. She walked to the urinal and unzipped my pants, pulled my penis out, and started peeing. But she forgot to hold on and aim. We pissed all over the side of the urinal and the floor.

I laughed at her surprised discomfort. "That's what you get for having people call me by your name," I said.

I looked at the clock when we left the bathroom. Time for my appointment with a neuroshrink. I walked to the meeting room where my so-called therapy took place. Sitting at a table in one of two chairs was Dr. Dohmed's partner, a short, plump, almost bald man. He looked up when I entered the room, his owlish eyes magnified by his glasses. In fact, he did resemble an owl because of the tufts of hair around his ears, his short round body, and wing-like arms encased in a tweed jacket and held close to his sides. His hooty voice enhanced my impression as I pictured his big hooked nose and his small, tight mouth as an owl's beak.

"Hi, Jim. Or would you rather I call you Erzsébet? I'm Doctor Abrams."

"Jim Jackson," Erzsébet said, and I extended my hand. My spirits lifted a bit because she'd decided to use my name instead of hers.

Maybe that little ploy in the bathroom paid off.

"Welcome, welcome," Dr. Abrams said, patting the table beside him. He was beginning to gain Erzsébet's trust with his warm, caring manner.

"Today we're going to try hypnotizing you to see if we can determine where Erzsébet originated. I'm going to give you a little something to make things easier for you."

Erzsébet responded like a kid eager for candy.

Abrams prepped my arm with an alcohol pad and injected me with what he described as mild relaxant. He hadn't told me he was going to use any drugs, and I'm sure Erzsébet didn't know anything about modern pharmaceuticals or she would have pitched a fit.

"All hypnosis is self-hypnosis; patients can't be hypnotized if they don't want to be," Dr. Abrams said. "Clinical hypnosis involves the induction of a trance. That's the reason for the injection; it will help induce a trance-like state."

I reacted to the drug almost immediately.

He began speaking in a low, monotonous voice, leading me through a guided meditation to relax. "Watch the pendulum," Abrams said as he swung the crystal on a chain, telling me I'd awake when he said the words "wake up."

I hoped the hypnotism would work on Erzsébet, though I figured it was sorta hokey, like the time I watched a stage magician hypnotize members of an audience and convince them to squawk like chickens. I wanted to laugh at the situation, but soon found myself relaxed and willing to play the game. Maybe Dr. Abrams would discover I was truly possessed and get rid of her somehow.

"Erzsébet, I need to speak to Jim Jackson," Dr. Abrams said in his monotone voice. He quit swinging his pendulum and set it on the table.

"You're speaking to Jim Jackson," Erzsébet made me say in a haughty tone that seemed more feminine than masculine.

Right then I knew Erzsébet wasn't in any trance. I'd read that the usual procedure when a person has multiple personalities is for the examiner to ask to speak with the most distinctive or primary personality first.

"But I genuinely thought you were Erzsébet Báthory," Dr. Abrams said.

"I am, but I'm also Jim Jackson."

"How can you be two people at the same time?"

That was the question I wanted answered.

"You're the doctor, you figure it out."

"Why do you inhabit Jackson's body?"

"I need it for my purposes," she said.

"And what are those?"

"To save the world from an unspeakable evil."

"What is this evil you speak of?"

"Zsombor."

"Who in the hell is Zom-bor?" I asked Erzsébet. She ignored me.

Dr. Abrams leaned forward. "Is that a name? A place?"

Silence met him.

Dr. Abrams sighed and took another line of reasoning. "Tell me about where you lived in Transylvania."

I'd looked at a recreated photo of Erzsébet's castle on the internet, but I knew little about it.

"I lived, among other places I owned, in Castle Cséjthe, a mountain fortress overlooking the village Cséjthe in the Carpathian Mountains in Transylvania, ruled by Hungary in my day. Today both castle and town are located in Slovakia and called Čachtice. Do you want detailed descriptions?"

"Yes, please tell me whatever details you remember."

"Other towns I frequented during the sixteenth and seventeenth centuries were Brasov, Sibiu, and Sighisoara. Sighisoara is the home of a distant relative, Vlad Tepes, a great warrior. One of the most beautiful towns in the heart of Transylvania, it served as a military stronghold. A beautiful clock tower stood in the main gate of the defensive wall, a modern marvel built in the fourteenth century."

As she spoke about these places, she allowed me to view the pictures in her mind's eye.

"You have a good memory, Erzsébet."

"My name is Jim Jackson," she rebuked him sternly.

A small victory – no more being called Erzsébet.

"Yes, I know, but clearly I'm talking to Erzsébet. May I please have a few words with Jim?"

"I'm speaking for Jim," she answered. She apparently didn't want to cooperate, so Dr. Abrams spoke into his handheld device. "Computer, find maps of sixteenth century Transylvania. Almost instantly, he began to read from a list of all the towns and villages Erzsébet named.

He dragged his finger across the miniature screen. "Project," he said.

The computer projected maps on the wall and recited, in English, a brief history of each location.

"Mute," Dr. Abrams said, and the handheld stopped speaking.

While she chatted with Dr. Abrams about her life in Hungary, I tried to figure out some way I could fool her into letting me talk to him. A clever diversion, I thought, when he glided from his conversation with Erzsébet and tried to speak to me again.

"Jim, how do you feel about Erzsébet? Is it difficult emotionally for you to make room for another personality in your life?"

Erzsébet made me shrug. When Dr. Abrams tried to press me again for an answer, she forced me into silence.

Damn bitch. This isn't helping at all, I thought. But Erzsébet was using my name, at least. She must realize that the doctors would never release me until they thought I was sane. When I was released, I wondered what she'd do.

Dr. Abrams returned for a follow-up visit a week later. We met in the same room, but this time there were three chairs lined up along the table. I could feel Erzsébet staring at the extra chair.

Dr. Abrams noticed me looking at the vacant chair. "I thought I'd have a chair brought in for Jim."

"I told you, I'm speaking for Jim," Erzsébet said.

Abrams patted the empty chair. "Well, I thought if Jim wanted to say something, it might be more comfortable if he had his own chair."

"I don't know what kind of witchery you're using with this chair trick, Doctor, but whatever spell it is, it will be useless against me. I already told you, I speak for Jim."

Erzsébet's anger leaked into my consciousness like a sour poison.

Abram's chubby cheeks reddened. "I'm never sure if I should call you Jim or Erzsébet. I thought if I gave you each a chair to sit in, I'd know what name to address you with by your location."

I was able to cut in for the first time ever. "Do I look like or sound like an Erzsébet? If I'm going to get by in this world, I want to be called by the name that suits my appearance, and that certainly isn't Erzsébet."

"Okay, Jim. Now that we have that settled, can you tell me how you know so much about Transylvania?" Dr. Abrams held his pen over a notebook, waiting to write down my answer.

Erzsébet let me know she thought the doctor was an idiot. "Are you dense? I told you I lived there."

"Yes, I know Erzsébet lived there. I'm asking Jim how he knows so much about it."

"I'm speaking for him," Erzsébet snapped, "and he knows so much, because I told him all about Transylvania."

Dr. Abrams' expression let me know he thought I was nuts. He walked away from our session that day, shaking his head in confusion. Based on Dr. Abrams' diagnosis and my perfect physical health, I was transferred to Evergreen, a psychiatric facility frequented by wealthy celebrities.

I became an overnight sensation when the video of my rejuvenation was leaked to the internet and network news. *First human resurrection since Jesus!* the tabloids screamed. Requests for interviews poured in. But Joe wouldn't allow any reporters near me and hired extra security to guard my room. By putting me in an asylum, I figured they were not only protecting me, but hoped to avoid any bad publicity about the first CF patient revived in a state of confusion.

Erzsébet could be more than a pain in the ass. She'd learned to imitate me, so she mimicked the things I would do and say if I had control. She was keenly aware of the powerful people in this world who would lock me up and throw away the key if they wanted to. She allowed me to view some memories of the years she lived walled up in her living quarters at Castle Čachtice as punishment for her alleged crimes – an excuse to strip her of her property and her title, she said.

The experience put a serious fear of incarceration into her. A damn good thing, because some of the thoughts she shared were totally unacceptable in today's society. Like the time an orderly raised his voice to tell me to hurry up. She wanted to whip him for his disrespect. Another time, she didn't like a question Dr. Abrams asked me and stabbed at his face with a pencil. Fortunately, I was able to stop her before Abrams noticed.

Erzsébet had a fiery, unpredictable temper. Maybe my sequestration was for the best until someone figured out how to separate her from me.

☞Chapter 10

Several psychiatrists studied my case history and talked with me over the next few weeks, but Erzsébet never changed one word of her story. She revealed more and more details about Hungary in the sixteenth and seventeenth centuries that proved to be factual, and even shared previously unknown facts that jibed with historical documents. But she still tiptoed around our identity issues and the mystery of her presence.

Joe finally confessed that the Cryonic Foundation Board of Directors insisted I continue to be confined. They didn't want the world to see me insisting to be Erzsébet.

"You don't have to worry about that any longer; she now insists everyone call me Jim."

"But Dad, do you really need this other personality? I'm beginning to think she's some kind of security blanket."

That set Erzsébet off into peals of laughter and exasperated the hell out of me. If only he could hear her private thoughts, he'd understand what I was going through.

The staff of the psychiatric facility conferred and scheduled a confidential symposium in an attempt to determine my problem. The Foundation couldn't explain how I'd emerged a different person than the one they'd cryonically preserved. Not only was I a different person, I was possibly insane. The neuroshrinks were sure there was a rational explanation for my condition and would do their best to diagnose it by sharing their conclusions.

Joe informed me that I wouldn't be allowed to attend the symposium as an observer, but he'd arranged for me to watch it from my room on closed circuit TV. He also explained that he and my psychiatric team had also invited other eminent psychologists and experts in spirituality and other topics relevant to human rejuvenation to speak at the event, including Father O'Malley, the leading exorcist of the Roman Catholic Church in North America.

Joe spoke first at the opening of the symposium in the same auditorium where he'd spoken prior to starting my rejuvenation. When he stood at the translucent, crystal-like podium, a polite round of applause acknowledged his accomplishments in restorative nanobot technology and his achievement in rejuvenating me after my lengthy cryonic preservation.

Joe glanced solemnly around the room. "You all know why we're here this morning. Without further ado, allow me to present a quick overview of all the events leading up to this meeting. After I elaborate on our findings regarding the patient's mental and emotional state and summarize the proceedings, I'll open the floor to discussion. I'd appreciate hearing your theories on why my father not only genuinely thinks he is, or rather, why he has assumed the persona of an infamous noblewoman born in the sixteenth century. So far, he is able to substantiate his claim with verifiable historical facts, no matter how unorthodox and far-fetched this may seem."

Joe's overview was brief because all attendees were provided with an abstract and my case data. He soon finished clarifying the case highlights and opened the floor to comments and questions. The attendees gave Joe another polite round of applause. Afterward, murmured rumors drifted around the room about a possible nomination for a Nobel Prize.

Proud of my son, I was truly relieved that the simple possibility of a nomination for such an award meant Joe hadn't wasted his life because of me. Hell, I thought, he might even win because of me.

"And me," Erzsébet said, sniffing out my thoughts.

Irritated, I bit my tongue and turned my attention back to the closed-circuit screen.

Joe introduced Dr. Everett Johnson, the world's leading expert on reincarnation.

Dr. Johnson acknowledged the luminaries attending the gathering. "I've been researching the controversial phenomenon of reincarnation for over twenty-five years. In this field of inquiry, we record and analyze subjects' claims of past life memories. We have found that young children sometimes recall a previous life and talk about events and people from that life at length. Typically, the child begins talking about these reminiscences around three years of age, and loses these recollections around age seven. In some cases, the locations and people mentioned in the child's recollections correspond closely to actual locations and events.

"If scientists can interview these children before contact is made with the supposed previous family, then an objective comparison can be made between the statements made by the child and the features of the previous environment.

"In this particular case, we have verified numerous names and events related by Jim Jackson as Erzsébet Báthory. I believe what we have here is a reincarnation, but not in the usual sense of a rebirth. In a normal reincarnation, a child has years to assimilate body and spirit before communicating with anyone. In this instance, I suspect we have a spirit reincarnated into a fully grown human with little assimilation time."

I squirmed in my chair. Dr. Johnson forgot to mention that I'm still here with that goddamned spirit he thinks got reincarnated.

When Dr. Dohmed, acting as the meeting coordinator, opened the floor to questions, Joe stood up. "Dr. Johnson, are you saying the person I revived is not actually the same person he was before his cryonic treatment?"

"Legally, he's the same man even though his body holds a different spirit," Johnson replied.

How about two spirits? Mine and the bitch's, I groused.

Erzsébet gave me a mental kick.

"Doesn't that make him a different person, then?"

"That depends on what you mean by a person. When reincarnation occurs, children mature naturally with a new personality and carry memories of a previous life. In this case, a mature reincarnated spirit appears to be the second awareness in the revived adult body. But there is continuity over time, and what appears to be a linear progression of separate personalities, even in separate bodies, may be an illusion. I believe that Eastern spiritual disciplines such as Buddhism address the illusory nature of personal identity. At any rate, our next speaker will provide additional insight into another possibility."

Dr. Johnson sat down at the speakers' panel table and the next speaker rose and took his spot at the podium.

Dr. Jared Kowalski, an imposing figure with a bald head and piercing blue eyes, needed no introduction, known worldwide for his work on dissociative identity disorder, popularly referred to as multiple personality disorder.

"The usual way that dissociative identity disorder presents itself is when an individual breaches the barrier of reality and fantasy due to overwhelming physical and mental stresses," Kowalski said in rapid-fire speech. "Once the patient displays an alter personality, a search for more alters surrounding the host personality begins. Sometimes the original two or three personalities proliferate to as many as ninety or a hundred. At least one alter must be of the opposite sex. Sometimes an alter is an animal – a dog, cat, or even a cow must be found and made to speak! In Jim Jackson's case, there is just one persistent personality. This is highly unusual, and I think we can rule out DID / MPD."

At least he got that right; I sure as hell don't have any animal personalities. It's bad enough being stuck with a bitchy woman.

Dr. Kowalski then sat down without fanfare. Joe introduced my favorite neuroshrink as the next speaker. Dr. Abrams spoke softly and with great kindness, as always. "All our testing finds this subject normal in every aspect, except his delusion of having lived in the late sixteenth and early seventeenth centuries. While the patient's claims of being possessed are unique, I think they're harmless, and I don't see any reason for his continued confinement."

What's Abrams saying? Doesn't he believe she controls my actions? At least he wants to spring me from this loony bin.

Father O'Malley, the exorcist representing the Catholic Church, spoke next.

I didn't have much patience with his religious blather. The Church tried to become involved in my case from the first day of cryonic treatment. They had an open policy on cryonics. Their philosophy stated that by bringing someone back from death, one might carry memories of where they'd been – Heaven, Hell, or Purgatory – thus presenting proof of an afterlife. Now the Church believed I might have, at the very least, proof of the existence of evil spirits and spirit possession because of my brush with the infamous Erzsébet Báthory.

". . . I realize science is purely logic driven," Father O'Malley said as I tuned back into his spiel, "and what I have to say may be met with disdain, but I must say, Dr. Abrams, I wholeheartedly disagree with you. This man is suffering a clear case of possession. According to the narrative presented by Dr. Jackson, a disembodied spirit possesses his father, Jim Jackson. Erzsébet Báthory has committed capital crimes in the past and professes to have an agenda in our time. Possession by evil spirits is reaching epidemic proportions worldwide."

My son jumped to his feet. "Just a minute," he said. "Granting you the point there is such a spirit, you're saying that it's evil? How accurate are the legends about Erzsébet Báthory?"

"It's a matter of historic record," the priest replied.

"So is the Inquisition. Historically, the Church doesn't have an exemplary record in regard to power struggles with its perceived enemies and tends to rewrite history at its own convenience."

Father O'Malley took the high road. "Don't you understand? This spirit could very well be the one to open the gates to Hell for others to follow."

"As you so aptly stated, Father, we scientists trust logic and your statements are illogical, based on hearsay and scriptural dogma."

Joe, raised by Emily as a devout Catholic, was raking Father O'Malley over the coals for his beliefs. And little did any of the physicians and scientists know that the priest's opinion matched my experience better than their theories about my mental health.

Father O'Malley moved one hand over his chest in the sign of the cross. "We cannot allow a profane spirit to possess a body belonging to a Christian soul. I implore this audience of respected scientists to allow the Church to perform an exorcism before it's too late."

Erzsébet's mind squirmed at the mention of exorcism. Though I wasn't in the room, I wanted to shout out loud that I agreed with the priest, but she wouldn't let me.

Dr. Dohmed requested that Father O'Malley leave the room while his proposal was discussed. Dr. Remus, the Director of the Cryonic Foundation, took the floor.

"We all know that inexplicable things happen in this world. If indeed, as Father O'Malley claims, Jim Jackson is the victim of spirit possession by Erzsébet Báthory, then the claim must be studied in context. She is popularly labeled as 'the most evil woman in history'," Dr. Remus explained. "The reasons for the deeds recorded in Báthory's lifetime and in historical records after her lifetime are unknown to us. History has shown that a woman of wealth in her era might be accused of witchcraft, or otherwise discredited to seize her property. Is the entity truly evil or – "

Joe jumped up from his seat. "Hold on," he interjected. "What is your point, Dr. Remus? You speak as if it's entirely possible for an entity to transport itself in time and enter an already occupied body, to "possess" someone, as Father O'Malley calls it, a phenomenon clearly demonstrated by science to be a manifestation of mental illness. While religion postulates belief in the concept of the soul or spirit, science has been unable to prove conclusively the existence of said soul or spirit. We must reject outright the medieval concept of exorcism, a practice known to cause considerable mental and sometimes even physical harm to vulnerable patients. Until we fully grasp what is happening with my father's psyche, I don't want to risk his mental and physical health because of an ill-defined, misunderstood concept."

Erzsébet breathed a sigh of relief at Joe's words.

Dr. Dohmed signaled for a chance to speak. "We're getting inquiries from the families of current and potential cryonic patients," he said. "They're worried that when their family members are revived, they'll also be possessed, as some say Jim Jackson is."

They should be worried, I thought. What if every cryonically preserved person *is* possessed like I am?

Dr. Remus, the CF Director, stood at his chair. "I concur with both Dr. Jackson and Dr. Dohmed. We shouldn't take any unnecessary risks with this patient. We must proceed with caution, both in the matter of his treatment and in how we deal with the public perception of his rejuvenation. We are being approached with many requests for cryonic procedures by terminally ill patients. Next week, a bill goes before Congress. If passed, it will allow candidates for cryonic preservation to submit to the procedure prior to their legal deaths. Animal rejuvenation data suggest that pre-death preservations have greater viability than post-death preservations. Passage of the bill will likely create more demand for the procedure, and the subsequent scientific and financial gains from these ventures will open up avenues for further achievement. While Dr. Jackson and I respect the expert opinions offered during Mr. Jackson's convalescence and during the course of this symposium, these have yielded no conclusive findings. Clearly, more study of Jackson's condition is needed. We feel that the most logical and therapeutic treatment is to reintegrate him with society. I propose that Mr. Jackson be released to the care of his son."

Dr. Dohmed called for a referendum on Dr. Remus's proposal and all voting members of the symposium approved unanimously.

Erzsébet's happiness that Father O'Malley's opinion hadn't swayed the vote entered my mind, as I'm sure my dismay entered hers. I think we were both eager to get out into the world but were also fearful of leaving the watchful eye of these scientists. Me, because I wondered if I would ever make anyone understand what was happening, and Erzsébet because she had a captive audience at Evergreen and the Cryonic Foundation.

Joe's desire to take me home made sense, but releasing Erzsébet into an unsuspecting world worried me. What did she hope to accomplish?

⚳Chapter 11

On the morning after the symposium, Dr. Remus came to my room to tell me goodbye. He brought my release papers and said Joe would pick me up the following day.

With this news, it was time to convince Erzsébet to put me back in control of my body.

"You'd best let me take charge once we're out the door," I said. "You don't even know what a traffic light is and you'll probably get us killed crossing the street."

"Do you take me for a fool? Don't forget, Jim, I'm using your mind along with mine. Everything you know, I know. We will be just fine."

Resigned to another of her quick comebacks, I signed my way through the stack of releases without bothering to read them. As usual, Erzsébet took note of all the details that could only be fascinating to someone not used to such things. I put on a happy face and handed the papers back to Dr. Remus.

Overjoyed about our release from medical detention, Erzsébet could hardly wait to experience the modern world. I had to admit I was also curious to see how things had changed in fifty years. But deep down I worried about what she'd do once we were free. If

Erzsébet was even half as evil as popular history claimed, what in the hell would she force me to participate in?

She backed off and let me have these thoughts without her usual interference.

I clung to some hope when Erzsébet casually mentioned it might be harder to dominate my mind as I engaged more in the outside world. As soon as the thought reached me, she realized she'd made a mistake to tell me that. I felt the old ocean wave rocking my mind sensation as she did her best to do some damage control. I fought her projected serenity, but I couldn't stop it from enveloping me.

All my old doubts surfaced. Why had Erzsébet chosen me, of all people? Just because she had a high IQ didn't mean she knew what she was doing. I'd been out of circulation for five decades – what did I know that could possibly help her? I didn't want anything to do with this Zsombor business, whoever or whatever this was.

She responded instantly. "I chose your body for two reasons. First, you're a fighter and have the heart to do whatever is necessary. You are young and ambitious. Secondly, when I entered your body, your spirit was nearly gone. I took possession during your rejuvenation, an event unprecedented in the history of mankind. I could easily have sent your spirit back to the other side since you had all but abandoned your body, but I sensed we could learn much from each other, so I allowed you to remain with me."

"You allowed me? Who or what gave you the power to choose?"

She clammed up at this question and I faced the stark fact again that I could control little except my emotions.

I didn't have anything to pack other than the few sets of pants and shirts Joe had purchased for me, so I spent my time wandering around Evergreen saying good-bye to the staff. Erzsébet behaved herself and seemed as sad as I was to part with our friends. Soon, Joe and I left Evergreen, side by side under the last rays of the setting sun.

"Brand new worlds to conquer!" Erzsébet said aloud, excited by the prospect of freedom. She looked back at the white Georgian pillars and red brick walls of the facility and pronounced it worthy of her status.

Joe patted me on the back and led the way to his car.

I hardly noticed Erzsébet's running commentary, so great was my excitement. Before we arrived at the parking lot, I was turning my head this way and that. The world seemed a lot more crowded. The way women dressed with so much leg, midriff, and chest showing all at once amazed me, as did the sleek, aerodynamic auto styles.

The parking lot fascinated Erzsébet as much as it did me. She scanned my mind for answers to her questions: how many people rode in each vehicle and the differences between cars with internal combustion engines, hybrids, and electric vehicles.

I figured one good point about Erzsébet having access to my mind was that I didn't have to voice a lot of answers. When I didn't have an answer, I asked Joe for one.

As Joe waved his hand to open his electronic car door for me, Erzsébet wanted me to hop into a luxury sports car and go for a joyride.

"If you break our laws and get me locked up, you'll be sitting there with me," I reminded her.

She made a quick comeback. "If you get locked up, I'll leave your body and go elsewhere, Jim Jackson."

I was tempted to get myself locked up to get rid of her, but as soon as I thought that, Erzsébet had other reflections on the matter. "The experience of dying and possessing another is not painless, something I'd rather not endure again unless absolutely necessary," she confessed.

Maybe this was something I could use to gain some ground, but she refuted that too. I would have to keep trying.

When Joe started driving, his talking dashboard communicator transmitted and received GPS directions, something right out of a science fiction movie. He enjoyed watching my head spinning in amazement at the skyscrapers and the hustle and bustle of Boston streets. Once he pulled onto the freeway, he set his convertible on cruise control by voice command and turned to me to chat.

"Dad, as you probably noticed, I've avoided talking much about Mom.

You know she's in managed care, but she's worse off than I've let on . . . it's Alzheimer's. I'm not sure she'll know who you are when we visit her." He sucked in air after he said this, trying not to tear up.

Of course, I already knew this, but with Erzsébet's manipulation, I couldn't tell him so. I felt pained for us both.

I'd dreamed of the moment when I'd hold Emily again since my rejuvenation began months before. I loved her, but Erzsébet controlled my physical reactions and didn't seem to care much for my memories of Emily.

At that thought, she let me speak, the better to let me blow off some steam, I figured.

"Son, I don't care if Emily remembers me or not. She's my one and only, no matter what. I want to tell her I still love her."

That is, if Erzsébet would let me.

Joe seemed relieved at my response and changed the subject, pointing out things that had changed in the past fifty years.

"Notice there's no engine noise?" he asked.

"I noticed how much quieter this car is."

"Most vehicles run on water. The process produces hydrogen, but air power is the up and coming thing," he said.

"Wow. I would have guessed electric car. When we didn't have much money for gas in my day, we used to wish we could put water or air in the tank," I said. "Some egghead figured out how to really do it, huh?"

Joe flashed a thumbs up. I wondered how many more technological surprises were in store.

If I was shocked at how busy the world had become, Erzsébet was even more so. I could only imagine how this world affected someone with a seventeenth-century perspective.

Erzsébet could hardly sit still as she absorbed the sights. The high-rise buildings reminded her of castles, and as the solar lights of the city came to life at dusk, they dazzled us both, but she quickly noticed the lack of stars overhead. She scanned my mind with questions about everything around us. When she couldn't lift the answers from my consciousness, she deluged me with more questions. Most everything we saw had some counterpart in my era, but I was glad when she became speechless, or I should say thoughtless, because this kept her at bay.

Evergreen was over fifty miles from where my wife and son lived in a suburb of Boston. During the one-hour drive, Erzsébet said she saw more dwellings than she had seen in her entire previous life. With her mind more prominent than my own, I felt like a voyeur from another world. I avoided my usual irritation at her by thinking of the alternative. I decided this was better, at least physically, than floating in liquid nitrogen.

It was after dark when we approached West Newton, an upper-class suburb on the outskirts of Boston. I was eager to see Emily, but Joe wanted to wait until morning to visit her. "She's probably asleep by now," he reminded me. "Anyway, Dad, I want you to meet my wife and get a good night's rest. All this newness might be over-stimulating."

When Joe called me Dad, it felt weird. I studied him closely. He really did look like my father, and I'm sure people who saw us thought this was the case. Little did I know this was one of many paradoxes I'd live with during the months to come.

I wondered for the millionth time if could communicate with Joe without going through Erzsébet. And again, I asked myself if she was the serial killer that history claimed. I wanted to tell Joe that he might be in danger by associating with me, but Erzsébet immediately made her presence known. She scuttled any plan I could come up with. If only there was a way to think without thinking! On the other hand, Joe was well aware of Erzsébet's history and her alleged crimes. Maybe I didn't have to warn him.

As a member of the ruling class in her time, Erzsébet could do almost anything she wanted without worrying about consequences. She saw nothing wrong with wanting my son to smash into a car that pulled in front of us on the freeway. "Teach the peasant to cross in front of a countess. Smash him to pieces," were her exact words.

I warned her again about imprisonment for speaking and behaving impulsively. She remained calm until Joe stopped at a tollbooth.

"Don't pay this highwayman any tribute…" she forced me to say.

"Shut up," I told her mentally. "This is a toll road. I'm pretty certain Europe had toll roads, even in your day."

"I never paid tribute in my life and I'm not starting now," she said.

"Erzsébet, the toll is for the vehicle. This is how citizens contribute to maintain the roads."

"The nobility exacts tribute."

"You're Jim Jackson, remember?"

Erzsébet sulked as Joe cast me an odd look, then swiped his plastic card across a small screen under a box emitting a red laser beam as the toll taker watched.

Joe looked worried whenever I had one of these outbursts caused by Erzsébet. I did my best to suppress her inappropriate statements. Even when I stopped her, I must get a funny look on my face when I argued with her, judging by other people's reactions.

I hoped Joe didn't think it a mistake to take me from the clinic. On the other hand, maybe I should let Erzsébet put her foot in my mouth as much as she wanted. Maybe Joe would send me back to Evergreen where one of those smart doctors might eventually figure out how to separate Erzsébet's spirit from my body.

Erzsébet read my thoughts and laughed. "Not a chance. From now on I'm going through your mind before I open your mouth."

This proved she wouldn't be easy to fool in any way, shape, or form. I had no choice but to play a waiting game.

Joe pulled into the circular driveway of his large, Tudor-style home, an emblem of his financial accomplishments. I felt proud of Joe's education and his social status. What a long way from Hano we'd come.

Erzsébet stared at the fountain installed at the center of the driveway. A bronze nude emptied a vase of water into a large pool populated by shimmering carp and white and pink water lilies. She compared it favorably with our previous residences.

Joe parked near the front door. I stepped onto the driveway, inhaling the smells of suburbia: new-mown grass, jumbles of flowers, shrubs, and trees, and the faint odor of industrial pollution that triggered memories of the times Emily and I strolled through the public gardens in downtown Boston.

Erzsébet compared the smells to her Transylvanian home. The air where she lived, she said, smelt of pig shit, unwashed people, and human waste. She far preferred the modern scents to the old ones.

We walked to the entrance and Joe opened the heavy oak door. "We're here, Audrey," he called into a foyer decked out with mirrors and flowers. I heard the click of heels on the marble floor. A petite, well-dressed, and regal-looking woman emerged from a spacious living room.

"Welcome, Mr. Jackson, I'm thrilled to finally meet you," she said, her voice mellow with class and culture.

"Dad, this is Audrey, my wife," Joe said, clearly proud of her.

"I'm sorry we haven't met before this," Audrey said. "Joe mentioned you've had so much to deal with that meeting me might increase your burden. But I followed your progress with great interest."

She opened her arms and hugged me. I inhaled the sweet wildflower scent of her perfume and thought of Emily again. Her scent also aroused Erzsébet sexually, and this scared me.

"Stop that right now," I warned her mentally. What kind of creature was this? Normal for me to be aroused by a female, but. . . I couldn't help wondering if what I'd read on the internet about Erzsébet was true despite all the speculation by serious historians. My stomach turned as I imagined Joe and Audrey hung from a wall and sliced with blades like the servant girls Erzsébet employed. If only I could explain to Joe that Erzsébet and I were *not* one and the same person.

"I've made a light dinner. I hope you're both hungry," Audrey said.

"I'm always famished," I said, smiling.

Joe showed me the luxurious but small bathroom where guests freshened up before dining.

I shut the door and put my hands under the faucet in the enameled lavatory.

It automatically dispensed hot water. It still amazed Erzsébet to turn a handle or to activate an electronic faucet and have hot and cold water emerge. If she had the luxury of hot water and herbal soaps and lotions in her previous life, her problem with aging skin would have been less severe, she let me know. I washed my hands and dried them with a thick, Turkish hand towel embroidered at the top with Greek designs. Erzsébet thought the cotton towel fit for royalty, meaning it was good enough for her. She adored the little basket of guest soaps and lotions, and insisted I choose one and put it in my pocket.

When I glanced at myself in the mirror, Erzsébet studied my body and the scar on my face.

"Hard to believe the youthful face staring back at you belongs to a seventy-six-year-old man, isn't it?" she reflected.

What would Emily think when she found I hadn't aged? At least my scar hadn't changed. The long gash running from the edge of my right eyebrow halfway down my face contributed to a tough look. At that angle, my face appeared meaner than I really was. I glanced down at my forearms. Superb, shapely muscles bulged underneath taut, unblemished skin, thanks to my son's nanobots.

"Tough, masculine, scarred," she said. "A handsome warrior."

Erzsébet scanned my mind to learn how I got the scar. I never told anyone how I'd fallen and gashed my face when I was a kid. I'd tried to outrun a queer – a pedophile – who tried to abduct me on my way home from school. Back when I was in second grade, people were a lot more trusting. This guy had called me over to his Cadillac. I thought he was asking for directions, but when I stood at his window, he asked me if I wanted a candy bar. He laid a Hershey bar on his lap and told me to take it. I reached through the window but my hand grasped his dick, hidden under the candy bar. I tried to jerk my hand away, but he wouldn't let me. He held me by the wrist and tried to make me masturbate him. I spit in his face. Surprised, he loosened his grip and I pulled free. I ran like hell. He followed me down the street.

I looked over my left shoulder as I veered off a curb to get away from the car, but tripped and smashed my face in the gutter. I don't know what happened to the guy, but I bet somebody beat the shit out of him if they caught him with his dick hanging out. I woke up in the hospital with eleven stitches. I told my dad I'd gotten in a fight, and I carried a hatred of people like him ever since.

Erzsébet was enthralled by my memory and told me I should have cut his dick off. Though I agreed in principle – after all, I was an innocent kid, victimized by a pervert – I sighed at her violent nature, wondering what other outlandish ideas she had in store for me.

As I walked into the formal dining room of Joe's opulent home, I saw that the light dinner Audrey mentioned was truly a sumptuous-looking New England boiled dinner.

"How refined," Erzsébet said to me.

"What pretty bone china," she made me say out loud.

I wouldn't know bone china from stoneware, I thought.

"The Vera Lace Iris dinnerware belonged to Mom," Joe said.

"Evidently Emily has good taste," Erzsébet made me say.

Joe and Audrey laughed politely, but I could see that they were puzzled by my comment.

In a light-hearted mood despite the aggravation, I said to Erzsébet, "Damn right she does. Married me, didn't she?"

My good fortune to be alive and with my family made me happy until I became acutely aware how my son and daughter-in-law appeared so much older than me. I wanted to ask Joe how he felt about this, but Erzsébet blocked my question.

Joe wanted to go down memory lane. "I owe everything to Mom," he said, between bites of food. "My first memories are of her telling me stories about you, Dad. Once I was old enough to understand that you'd died and were taken to the Cryonics Foundation, I became determined to get you back. She sometimes talked about how you became ill, and when you were revived, how you'd fight for the championship and win it."

This showed me how much Emily cared about me and how deeply she wished Joe could know me. I teared up, at a loss for words.

"When I wanted to go to medical school so I could be the one to revive you, Mom backed me all the way. I always said if we waited for others to solve the problems of cryonic preservation, we'd probably never see you again. Now that you're back, unfortunately, she's gone. Well, not gone, but her mind is in another place. . . I'll never forget how much she sacrificed for both of us. Now that my nanobot research is perfected, I'm working on an Alzheimer's cure. Wouldn't that be a miracle if I cured both my parents?"

My heart overflowed with pride at having such a caring son.

Erzsébet seemed to enjoy my dinner while I could only imagine how good it must have tasted, so emotional did this tough guy feel.

After dinner, Erzsébet recalled her sexual arousal from our contact with Audrey. Repulsed that she thought of my daughter-in-law that way, I chided her, realizing that she probably also enjoyed pushing my buttons. My theory was soon proven when she deliberately allowed me access to her thoughts as she wondered how men felt when they had sex.

Lord, what next, I wondered.

Erzsébet complained to Joe how tired I was and asked him to escort me to my bedroom. I wanted to yell at her, but of course, she wouldn't let me.

Once we were alone, she unzipped my pants and slowly stroked my penis. "What the fuck," I said. I wished I could knock my own hand away. I felt nothing, but Erzsébet evidently did as my body became aroused. I breathed heavily as she stroked harder and faster, and faster and harder. My body became rigid as I ejaculated into the tissue she held around my dick.

How easily a man ejaculates, Erzsébet thought.

Me, I wished I'd enjoyed it more. At least I knew all my body parts worked after fifty years on ice.

I showered, and as usual, Erzsébet luxuriated in the hot running water and abundant shampoos and soaps. My shower used to be five minutes tops, but since Erzsébet took control, I found myself spending immense amounts of time bathing. When she finally finished, I lay naked on the bed, or I should say, we did.

Hopefully tomorrow would bring a chance to rid myself of this pest.

I shut my eyes and began to drift off.

Unfortunately, the act of masturbating filled Erzsébet's mind with memories of her sexual escapades. She allowed me to view intimate moments with her husband and several blazing encounters with lesbians.

I didn't want to watch her pornographic thoughts, but she didn't give me any choice. The bitch turned me into a goddamn voyeur. I'd been sensuously deprived for so long that in the end, I didn't reprimand myself for enjoying her encounters. The sensible part of my mind warned me that this was totally creepy and insisted I should concentrate on finding a way out of my predicament.

I closed my eyes again. Restless, I stayed awake while Erzsébet dreamed. To my surprise, the part of her mind that normally shut me out weakened its grasp. I found that if I concentrated upon her presence in my mind that I could slip into hers. I saw images of girls hanging by their arms on a wall, tormented with burning torches. Once I became attuned to the visions, I realized these were dreams, not memories.

I didn't want to see any more. I would have immediately left her mind the way I'd entered, but knew I'd best take advantage of this opportunity to learn more about her. Maybe I could discover a weakness. I might never get another chance like this one.

Chapter 12

Watching Erzsébet's detail-studded dreams caused me to wonder if I tend to forget my dreams because most were so ordinary. While I searched for memories that might help me rid myself of her, Erzsébet's dream drifted into scenes from her childhood.

A convivial dinner party crackled to life at Castle Ecsed, where her family lived in Hungary. Maidservants carrying platters of delectables – meats, freshly baked breads, pickled and steamed vegetables, and sweets of all descriptions – bustled in an out of an enormous dining room while the cream of Hungary's nobility gathered with the wealthy Báthory family. Erzsébet and her younger sisters Zsofía and Klara, lined up at the nearly endless table among their elders, squirming in their lavish gowns.

Shouts and the sound of a scuffle broke out in the courtyard outside. Erzsébet's father and the other nobleman glanced at one another and excused themselves from the feast. The women took Erzsébet and the smallest children into the kitchen, while all peered from the open windows at the scene below.

One of the castle guard accompanied a scruffy mob from the village of Ecsed who held a gypsy man with his arms tied behind his back. "He sold his daughter into slavery," one of the self-appointed jailers shouted.

Another peasant bowed before Erzsébet's father as he approached the gypsy.

"Sir, what kind of man would sell his own child?"

Lord György Báthory gazed at the trembling prisoner with contempt and then at the newly dead horse lying at the edge of a path that led toward the stables.

"Is this tale true?"

The gypsy rolled his eyes heavenward and begged for mercy. "I swear I didn't mean to. I thought I was bargaining for her marriage."

Báthory looked again at the carcass, beginning to swell and buzz with hundreds of flies. He motioned to his soldier to slit its belly.

"I beg you, Lord, please have mercy." The gypsy fell blubbering to his knees.

"Sew him in up to his neck. Leave him." Báthory dusted his hands together as though he'd done the work and turned back to the castle. He and the other noblemen laughed as they returned to their meal.

Lady Anna Báthory stood holding her younger sisters' hands. Erzsébet stole away from her mother to make her way from the kitchen to a servants' entrance that led into the courtyard. As the noblemen shut the enormous door to the castle's living quarters, she crept behind the small mob of servants and peasants who gathered to watch the gypsy scream and beg for mercy. Three soldiers bound his legs together and jammed him into the horse's belly, forcing his head through the throat and out its mouth.

"Oh, God, please. Please have mercy on my soul."

The stench wafted its way to Erzsébet's nostrils but she was not repelled.

My father has chosen a fitting punishment for the crime, she thought. Pity the lout's suffering and death will not last as long as his daughter's.

Erzsébet's mind wandered from her dream into a state of semi-consciousness. Even though her horror at unnecessary bloodshed was acute, as a member of the ruling class, she felt satisfied when criminals were duly punished for their crimes.

Erzsébet's mind moved forward. During her childhood, she enjoyed wandering at the edges of the woods surrounding Castle Ecsed, gathering wildflowers and cavorting in the streams. If anyone supervised her activity, guards would accompany her and she'd have to wear her undertunic when swimming. Chafing against her father's strict rules, she found she could leave the castle unnoticed by donning boy's clothing and sneaking away. His harsh response to the gypsy's crime two years before had made her fear of assault or rape almost nonexistent. She could see how men stared at her and thought her attractive, but none would dare utter a word to her because of her father. Betrothed to Ferenc Nádasdy, the son of Baron Tamás Nádasdy and his wife, Orsolya Kanizsai, she would soon go to live with them until a marriageable age, as was the custom.

Erzsébet's life changed little after her father and his entourage deposited her with a rich dowry of jewelry, household goods, and livestock at the Nádasdy estate, with the exception that she missed her sisters and the tender attention of her mother. She still endured long sessions with her tutor, who schooled her in the literary classics and mathematics, and taught her to read and write Magyar, Latin, Greek, German, and Slovak, the tongue of many in the servant class.

Erzsébet still evaded maidservants to stroll into the woods whenever she could. One bright summer morning after her fourteenth birthday, she quickly undressed in a stand of reeds and cattails by a small lake near the Nádasdy estate. She loved to bathe in the clear, cool water and dry herself in the warm sunlight afterward. She'd just climbed from the pool when she heard the sound of a branch snapping.

"Who's there?" she called out.

No answer.

Erzsébet assumed the sound was one of the woodland creatures, a deer, a hare, a squirrel, or even a bird. She scrambled atop a boulder to air her wet body. As she stretched luxuriously, she childishly imagined how the men from the castle would love to see her reclining nude along the stream.

Snap! The sound seemed nearer now. She stood up and turned around, looking in every direction.

Nothing.

Then suddenly, she heard the sound of breathing and a quick movement right behind her.

A young man stood staring from the brush, the stable boy, Gregor. She grabbed her clothes and started to run. But he ran faster, tackling her and holding her tight against him while he attempted to loosen his trousers. He smelled like the animals he cared for.

Erzsébet remembered what her mother and father said might happen if she wandered about alone. *You must always fight for your honor,* they always told her. She fought, but couldn't get loose. He forced her to the ground. She screamed and spit and tried to bite him, but in the end, he raped her. When he finished, he rolled off her and lay still, catching his breath. She saw the knife he carried lying with his pants on the ground. She snatched it and attempted to plunge it into his throat. He resisted and they wrestled on the ground again until he pinned her and took the knife away, throwing it into the water. But he bled from a cut on his neck that she'd managed to inflict. He raised his fist to hit her, but before he could, he fell back, faint from his loss of blood. He still lay upon her when her father-in-law and a dozen of his men came upon the scene. Their natural conclusion was that Erzsébet and the boy were mating, and in her excitement, she'd bitten the boy's throat.

Erzsébet cowered from them, trying to cover herself with her dirty tunic. When she tried to explain what happened, her father-in-law wouldn't listen. Any mention of·the incident caused Baron Nádasdy to curse the day he found his son's betrothed lying with the peasant boy.

Erzsébet never learned what had happened to Gregor, outside the fact he was wounded and not dead, but a new boy soon replaced him in the stable, one who turned away whenever she came near.

Her mother was summoned. A week later, Erzsébet overheard Baron Nádasdy tell her, "Whenever I think of that peasant atop your daughter with his throat bleeding and her lips covered with his blood, shivers run down my spine. If she bears some low-born peasant child, I want her far away so that no one ever knows. I am only glad that

Ferenc is not here."

Whether this was but a fantasy or a real event, I didn't know. But for the first time since I became aware of her, I felt a tinge of compassion for Erzsébet.

❧Chapter 13

The instant Erzsébet surfaced from her dreams, I felt her stirring in my mind. Her outrage surged through me like an electrical probe. "You! How could you invade my privacy like this?"

I felt a strange, kinetic energy building up in my heart. If thoughts could kill, I'd be dead.

"You know everything I think – why can't I know what you're thinking? Before you do something we'll both regret, remember, we both live in here."

My reminder that if she hurt me, she'd only hurt herself, seemed to work. Erzsébet paused for a moment and calmed herself, a response she was clearly just learning to cultivate.

"You're right. We need each other whether we like it or not," she admitted.

"I saw some of your, um, uncomfortable circumstances. I hope things improved later."

Maybe she'd volunteer some information – something, anything that might help me get rid of her. I didn't have much hope of prying anything from her.

I felt Erzsébet's thoughts enter my mind. Sometimes she'd plant information in the same way that she'd scan my mind and instantly know something about me, but this time she slowly fed me information word-for-word in a conversational narrative.

"My life did improve after the incident in the woods when I was fourteen. My mother intervened and saved my honor, with few regrets on my part. My betrothal to Count Ferenc Nádasdy at age ten was a blessing in disguise, for only he would still accept me due to whispered rumors about the incident.

"Publicly, Ferenc boasted of the large dowries I brought him and praised the alliance between our families. Privately, he believed, like my father-in-law, that I'd bitten the stable boy in passion. He admired my viciousness and sensuality, how it exceeded even his own. Ferenc had also heard the baseless rumors about my family's sordid history – my aunt Klara was called a lesbian and a witch, my uncle, an alchemist and devil-worshiper, and my brother, a reprobate around whom no child was safe. Ferenc felt aroused by any mention of violence or deviant traits and saw me as he fantasized rather than as who I was. 'No one but you has these unmatched family attributes,' he told me."

Erzsébet spoke about her family with no sense of shame or regret, as if she accepted their oddities or perhaps knew that the tales weren't true.

"So Count Ferenc admired your family," I said, trying to draw her out.

"Yes, he did. The rumors about my pregnancy became more prevalent. It didn't matter to him. No one really cared about it except to give the bastard away to pursue the advantages of our union afterward."

Erzsébet paused as if to enjoy the discomfort I felt about her dilemma. "But it got worse. After our marriage, rumors spread and turned the simple rape by a stable boy into a tale that I'd conjured up a demon for my pleasure and bitten it to death. Later, tongues wagged about how I'd fornicated with and killed the Devil himself.

"I blamed my father-in-law and his men for starting these unfair and inappropriate rumors. This defamation of my character evolved because I defended my honor, as I was always instructed.

CRYONIC MAN

"I lived an exemplary life after my marriage. To deflect the unwanted attention, I immersed myself in books and small pleasures to avoid listening to all senseless talk. I tried to help peasant girls by employing them and educating them. I supported midwifery, and gave my time and money to the church. I spent much time traveling and managing my husband's estates. The few people who knew me personally thought me saintly, but the rumors persisted.

"Ferenc continued to be pleased with the outlandish stories. Anyone who conjured up demons for their own amusement had to have supernatural powers. My supposed powers boosted his standing in the secret societies he belonged to, and his colleagues believed he could somehow acquire this knowledge from me.

"Ferenc moved me to Castle Cséjthe, his ancestral home, which stood atop a mountain in the Carpathian Mountains. He left soon afterward to battle with the Turks. Meanwhile, he made a name for himself in the long war, distinguishing himself as a feared and legendary leader. When he traveled in the East, he sought out practitioners of magick. He learned many secrets and many new methods of torture that he enjoyed testing upon his enemies. When he was at home, which wasn't often, he liked to hear of my struggles with the servants and taught me disciplinary measures that increased their respect for me."

I started to ask about her so-called disciplinary measures, but thought better of it. Maybe Erzsébet wasn't as twisted as history portrayed her. But that didn't make me forgive her for dominating me.

I continued to listen carefully, not wanting to interrupt the flow of her narrative. She confided her willingness to learn the magick that Ferenc shared, but noted emphatically her revulsion of her husband's cruelty.

Ferenc had described how Báró Zsombor, one of his officers, watched him as he tried to extract information from a captive without success.

"I can show you a method that will get anyone to tell you all they know," Zsombor bragged.

"Get this prisoner to tell me where he hid the gold icons he stole from the Church," Ferenc ordered.

To comply, Zsombor had a brazen bull brought into the chamber. Made of brass, the hollow, life-sized bull was hollow, fashioned with a door on one side. He put the prisoner inside, built a roaring fire under it, and heated the metal until it became red hot. When the man bellowed in pain, Zsombor asked his questions and the captive quickly answered them because no man could bear the pain of being roasted alive. Once he confirmed the truth, Zsombor added fuel to the fire anyway and the prisoner roasted to death, screaming horrifically.

When Zsombor opened the bull, the victim's scorched bones shone like jewels. He found a jeweler to make these into bracelets. He presented bone bracelets to Ferenc and other noblemen, an act that endeared him to many. Before long, Ferenc, Zsombor, and other high-ranking Hungarian warriors wore these jewel-like bracelets made of human bones.

"What you're describing doesn't endear these gentlemen to me at all," I told Erzsébet. "They were sadists and psychopaths of the worst kind."

I thought I'd lived a rough life, but mine was a piece of cake compared to anyone who'd endured the demented acts of those perverts.

Erzsébet ignored me and continued her story.

After a minor battle, Zsombor and Ferenc tortured captives to extract information on the numbers of men they traveled with. Afterward, Zsombor said, "I know of a great historical secret that will intrigue you, my Lord."

"What secret would that be?"

"Before time began, the god Marduk, a very young god, killed all his enemies and wrested from them the Tablets of Destiny. Under his reign, he created humans to bear life's burdens so that gods like himself could live at leisure. But humans frequently died of deadly diseases and the injuries of warfare. Marduk created incorporeal bracelets of fire that granted eternal life to any who possessed two, one on each wrist. While wearing a pair of these bracelets, a mortal human would not die from any natural cause. If he wore only one, he could reincarnate by choice when death came. Because of the bracelets, the gods had no need to make a new man each time one died.

"Men were lonely, and Marduk created women for them. Out of love, men gave one of their bracelets to their female companions. With this, men lost their immortality but retained the power of reincarnation. The reincarnated man or woman wore an invisible bracelet of fire on the right wrist of the new person they had become. These bracelets became visible if one knew the incantation prescribed by Marduk. If one didn't know the chant, that person might forget if he or she wore a bracelet or not. Many wearers didn't learn how to use the summons to see their bracelets. These became lost spirits, reborn repeatedly over eons of time, never knowing how or why.

"If a man desired, he could retrieve a second bracelet from a woman or another man and regain immortality. Because of this, murder became common. Every man wanted a woman for himself, but had to give her one bracelet to keep her. But all men wanted both their own woman and two bracelets, so each had a reason to kill on either account. Many owners of the bracelets grew to understand the burden of owning them, and acquired spells to transform the bracelets into physical form. Then they could destroy them in the heart of an active volcano, thus preventing their acquisition by men with negative intentions. The owners of any remaining bracelets hid them, and almost all were lost over time. Only two of these bracelets are known to remain in existence," Zsombor said.

"So you believe that you and I can locate and acquire the last two for ourselves," Ferenc said.

Erzsébet admitted that her husband was skeptical, but if there was truth to this outlandish story, he also must consider the long-term consequences of finding the bracelets. That Ferenc and Zsombor would gain great power was certain, but what would happen if either man preferred to own both bracelets?

Ferenc asked only how and when they would begin to search. Zsombor explained that once they knew the bracelets' location, it would be possible to gain possession of them. He described how a sorcerer-scribe named Heka-senu had learned Marduk's incantations from Thoth, the god of writing and knowledge. One incantation made the bracelets visible and another incantation transferred the bracelets from the wearer's wrists to the wrists of the summoner. Heka-senu had chanted the first incantation while standing near Pharaoh Thutmose and proved his suspicions when he saw both bracelets glowing on Thutmose's wrists. He knew then that Thutmose wasn't sharing a bracelet with his wife, Queen Ahmose. Heka-senu schemed to use this information to his advantage.

"In the old Egyptian tradition," Zsombor said, "royal brother and sister marry, but barring that, then a Pharaoh must marry a royal woman as his first wife to legitimize his reign. Women in Egypt carried the royal bloodline, not the males. Thutmose I was not a noble himself and his status depended upon his wife Ahmose."

Heka-senu worked to gain the queen's confidence over many months. When he became one of her most trusted advisors, he revealed that Thutmose had possession of these rare bracelets. Heka-senu swore to Queen Ahmose that only he could take the bracelets from Thutmose, and that if the Pharaoh died, and she married him, she could declare him the new Pharaoh. Then he would grant her the gift of reincarnation by giving her one bracelet, and she would forever be reborn upon her death. But first, they would have to take the bracelets from Thutmose.

Hungry for this new power, Queen Ahmose agreed. They planned for Heka-senu to recite the incantations near Thutmose in order to steal the bracelets of fire.

Heka-senu told her his plan to make Thutmose ill with a specially crafted poison, but she had to take care not to give him so much he would die. An accidental death would cause the bracelets to travel with his spirit to his next life. So Queen Ahmose added a few drops of this poison to her husband's wine, enough to sicken him, but not enough to kill.

When Thutmose became ill from the bit of poison and his physician was unable to provide a remedy, Queen Ahmose recommended he send for her healer. When her cohort Heka-senu arrived, she ordered everyone out of his chambers. Heka-senu took hold of Pharaoh's hands. Then he leaned toward Thutmose and started to chant the invocation to transfer the bracelets from the Pharaoh's wrist onto his own.

The bracelets slowly started sliding from wrist to wrist. The Pharaoh struggled to break free himself of Heka-senu's grip, but weakened by the poison, he was unable to resist. Once the bracelets of fire slid onto Heka-senu's wrist, the Pharaoh fell to the floor and shriveled into a wrinkled corpse.

Queen Ahmose faced Heka-senu and said, 'If you intend to keep both bracelets for yourself, you should know that I consulted my priest, who informed me that Marduk will allow me to take your life in any way I want. Give me one now, or die."

Heka-senu took Queen Ahmose's right hand in his. "I never thought of doing such a thing. You promised to make me Pharoah, and I promised you life everlasting." He then grasped her right hand in his and whispered the magick incantation into her ear. The bracelet of fire slid from his right wrist to hers.

Erzsébet and Ferenc felt Zsombor's story might be little more than legend, but if not, then what was there to lose?

"The rest is simple," Zsombor told Ferenc. "All we have to do is track the bracelets from the era of Thutmose I, Heka-senu, and Queen Ahmose. We can determine where the wearers have reincarnated. If the bracelets are present in our era, we can easily take them for ourselves."

"And so," Erzsébet said, "Zsombor and Ferenc began their search for immortality."

Stunned by where this story was leading, I remained silent, but I couldn't staunch my thoughts. Many believed in witchcraft and magick in the sixteenth and seventeenth centuries, but these guys were attempting a global search for something I would say did not exist if it wasn't for the impossible situation of Erzsébet possessing my body.

The immortality bracelets were the reason for Erzsébet's appearance in the twenty-first century. I couldn't help but assume that Báró Zsombor and Gróf Ferenc Nádasdy had finally found them.

Despite my thoughts, or maybe because of them, Erzsébet continued her tale. She revealed that Zsombor needed Ferenc's financial support and that he suspected Zsombor would use anyone for his gain, so he played up his skepticism in order to determine how much Zsombor knew about the bracelets.

"There are a million stories told about the gods, and these are mostly meaningless legends," Ferenc told Zsombor.

"Look, my Lord," Zsombor replied. He reached into his robe and pulled out an ancient scroll fashioned from animal skin, covered with hieroglyphics drawn in faded colors. "I tortured a great many men to gain possession of this. Couriers carried news of the discovery to Rome. None of them knew the exact location of the scroll, but I extracted bits of information from each until I knew exactly where to find it."

"Where was it?"

"It too was on its way to Rome from Constantinople, following the messages. I discovered it just in time. If it had arrived at the Vatican, it would have disappeared into the archives and no one would ever see it, as the Church now considers the doctrine of reincarnation heresy."

Ferenc narrowed his eyes. "And it may well be."

"And if not, Lord, we can share an eternity together. Just imagine, you and I born many times over, what wars we might glory in!"

Ferenc grilled Zsombor further. "Why would you want to share these bracelets of fire if wearing two gives you unlimited power?"

"When we find the bracelets, we each can take one and go our separate ways, if you desire. I swear it," Zsombor said.

Erzsébet stopped to gather her thoughts and then continued her narrative.

Ferenc examined the scroll again and decided he could not refuse an opportunity such as this. The search began in Egypt, the last known location of the bracelets. Ferenc learned from an alchemist to read hieroglyphics, so Zsombor could not deceive him.

They speculated whether Heka-senu and Queen Ahmose tricked one another to steal the other's bracelet. If one had the pair, he or she would be alive, though with a new identity. How could Ferenc and Zsombor determine when they had reincarnated, who they had become, or where on Earth they had returned?

Their first destination was the tomb where grave robbers discovered the scroll. Not one inhabitant would answer their inquiries until Zsombor captured the leader of the robbers. Zsombor laid him on his back, bared his feet, and fastened chains around his ankles. Then he smeared the soles of the robber's feet with lard. Zsombor built a roaring fire and placed the robber's feet above it, near enough to roast over the red-hot coals. When Zsombor's questions were not answered to his satisfaction, he pumped a bellows to control the intensity of the flames. It didn't take long to extract everything the man knew about the tomb.

Unfortunately for the poor man, Zsombor wanted to demonstrate his technique to Ferenc. So he continued roasting the robber's feet until they were charred to the bone, and odd pieces of phalanges and metatarsal fell to the floor. This was only one of the many forms of torture Zsombor taught Ferenc during their quest for the bracelets of fire.

Satisfied he had shown Ferenc the efficacy of his method, and to assure his victim would never seek revenge, Zsombor dumped the hot coals onto the chest of the immobilized man. He and Ferenc put their hands over their ears to block out the robber's cries of agony and watched as the red-hot embers seared his chest. When his screaming finally stopped, both turned away from the smoldering corpse to breathe the cool night air.

Now they knew the location of the tomb where the scroll had come from. They needed to enlist help to unearth any other buried secrets that might have been left behind. Ferenc sent his soldiers to capture another ringleader of the thieves who regularly robbed royal burial places. This thief heard what had happened to his predecessor and cooperated, freely supplying his knowledge. He also sent a dozen experienced diggers to help search the tomb.

When Zsombor's party arrived at the tomb, it appeared empty, except for the nearly perfect hieroglyphics that covered the walls from floor to ceiling. Some appeared to indicate locations in the desert, another, a map of the heavens – it would take months of study to determine a starting point for their search for the bracelets of fire.

As Zsombor and Ferenc studied these figures, trying to determine their next move, they noticed a rat skittering through the stone wall. "Impossible," they both said, but there it was, in front of them. When they looked closer, they saw the rat hadn't come through a solid wall at all, but through an almost invisible crack running across it. They soon located a hidden chamber behind the wall.

Not wanting to let the tomb robbers or their soldiers know what they had found, they began to dig themselves. Before long, they pounded a hole large enough to crawl through with a torch in each hand. Rats scurried away. Hundreds of beetles, scorpions, and ugly winged things dropped from the ceiling onto their backs. The insect bites didn't deter them in the least, so entranced were they by their find.

Zsombor and Ferenc found brackets on the walls and set their torches into them. Rows and rows of scrolls, some intact and some half-eaten by vermin, lined one wall. On a platform against the far wall hung two golden amulets the size of Zsombor's large hands, with hieroglyphics carved into them.

Erzsébet invited me to view her visualization of the scene. Count Ferenc Nádasdy appeared to be a giant of a man with a muscular build. He wore a sleek tunic of chain mail and an Egyptian-style taqiyah, a skullcap, rather than his usual armor and helmet in the desert heat, which allowed me to see his uncommonly handsome face.

Báró Zsombor was bigger than Ferenc Nádasdy and his physique would rival any of today's bodybuilders. His appearance struck me as ferocious and evil because of the scowl lines on his face and the glowing intensity of his green eyes. His scruffy red beard made him all the more fearsome. He wore thick leather body armor and a helmet with a sharp spike on top, which dangled from a strap of leather around his waist. Both men carried broadswords that appeared to be quite heavy.

"Thankfully rats don't eat gold," Ferenc said as he wrapped the golden amulets into a bit of rag and placed them in his taqiyah. They gathered what scrolls appeared to be readable, and returned to their tent to study what they'd found, calling off the search in order to leave their find undisturbed.

Erzsébet pushed me from her mind and all the images vanished.

"The surviving scrolls were all related to alchemy and Ferenc thought they might prove to be invaluable. Alchemists had searched for centuries for the secret of transmuting lead to gold and those instructions could possibly be in these ancient documents," she explained. "Normally this secret would be an exciting find, but searching for clues to the whereabouts of the bracelets took precedence over gold, for the time being."

Ferenc organized a caravan loaded with other plunder they had confiscated, and sent it off to Hungary and Castle Cséjthe. As Ferenc and Zsombor voraciously studied the amulets, the clue they sought emerged in the star charts. After an intense investigation over several days, Zsombor concluded that the bracelets could be followed by using astronomical charts. He drew a large chart, copied information from the amulets, and traced the bracelets for the previous two millennia, right back to the time of Heka-senu and Queen Ahmose, where the history ended, or rather, began.

"We need to prepare a new star chart like this one," Zsombor said, "but adjust it to display only the last five hundred years. Then we will find the bracelets by following the alignment of the planets."

"How do you know this?" Ferenc said, assuming a cool tone.

Zsombor placed his forefinger in several places on a parchment. "Look at the chart, and you can see that every time the rings changed hands, Mars moved to this unusual position."

"That may tell you when. How do you know where?"

"By using triangulation."

"What are you talking about?"

"See here. All we have to do is draw a triangle through Mars, Earth, and the Sun. See where the point of the triangle touches Earth? I marked each point, and the year when the bracelets were at each location. I tested this by using every location I knew the bracelets were at a specific time, and it matched up perfectly with the calculations."

"Commence, triangulate so we can see where the bracelets are now," Ferenc ordered.

Zsombor did so, and they were both pleased to see the point of the triangle rest upon Turkey, a country Transylvania had been at war with for many years. They needed no excuse to invade to search for the bracelets. Ferenc immediately ordered his troops to Turkey, though several months passed before they and their equipment arrived at the border.

"The bracelets must be in the city the triangle pointed to, just thirty miles from the border," Zsombor said as they neared their destination.

"How can you be sure both bracelets will be there?" Ferenc asked.

"Because the planets' alignments differ when there is only one."

Zsombor showed Ferenc a duplicate of the chart. He pointed out the periods when they knew the bracelets were shared, and matched up those planetary alignments. The pattern also differed when both bracelets were transferred at once.

"How will we know *who* has the bracelets?" Ferenc asked.

"Remember the first scroll and the story about Heka-senu and Queen Ahmose? We must get near the proper suspect and recite the incantation in order to see the bracelets," Zsombor said.

Ferenc and Zsombor searched for the wearer of the bracelets, and when they found that person, they had no qualms about doing whatever it took to gain possession of them. Ferenc was feared in these lands; his reputation as a fierce warrior had preceded him and there was token opposition to his advance.

Zsombor revealed his latest discovery after a series of victorious military forays. "I've pinpointed the exact location of the bracelets' wearer in the city of Şanlıurfa," he said.

"Where exactly is Şanlıurfa?" I asked.

At this point, Erzsébet visualized an old map for me, focusing upon a spot in southeastern Turkey, about eighty kilometers east of the Euphrates River. She then continued to describe what her husband had told her.

Zsombor spread a large map on the table, and pointed at Urfa.

"I thought you said Şanlıurfa?"

Zsombor touched a place name on the map. "That's the old name; it's now called Urfa."

When Ferenc's army neared the city, a delegation from Urfa arrived to greet him. They wanted to buy peace at any price, so Ferenc invited the city's leaders to the camp to negotiate peace terms. Zsombor greeted the leaders individually. He held each one by the hands and whispered an incantation into their ears. It seemed logical that the wearer of the bracelets might be among the city's leaders.

Twenty-one men comprised the delegation, and when Zsombor whispered to the twentieth official, he saw two bracelets glowing on his wrists. He immediately chanted the incantation to transfer the bracelets, but he couldn't draw them onto his wrists.

Zsombor held on for dear life to the man's wrists and shouted for Ferenc. "Gróf, come quickly, I have the wearer of the bracelets. Hurry, before he gets away."

Ferenc came running with soldiers right behind. "Send the remainder of the delegation back to the city," he told them.

Zsombor held the man tightly so he couldn't get away with the others.

"I know why you're here," the official said.

It dawned upon Zsombor why he couldn't transfer the bracelets. "Somehow this man knew we were coming and must have used a magick spell to prevent theft of the bracelets," he told Ferenc. "Give me the bracelets," he demanded of the official, "otherwise we will burn the city."

"Whether he acquired the bracelets or not, Zsombor planned upon burning the city, as he never spared his enemies any pain," Erzsébet said. "It also dawned upon Ferenc that if Zsombor had been able to transfer the bracelets, he would have possession of both and wouldn't need him any longer. Ferenc vowed to never give Zsombor an opportunity like that again."

"The bracelets belong here," the official insisted.

Zsombor sneered in the man's face. "No. They belong to me now that I've found them. The gods sent us for the bracelets."

The official laughed. "And which gods sent you?"

"The gods of Egypt," Zsombor said, pulling an old scroll from his robe and waving it in the man's face.

"My God is more powerful than all the Egyptian gods combined."

"I find that hard to believe since you're our prisoner," Ferenc said.

Just then, the Earth shook, and the official laughed. "Perhaps my God does not care for the way you treat me. If you don't release me, He'll destroy you and your army."

Zsombor held on to him tighter than before. "I want those bracelets and I'm willing to fight your God or anyone else for them."

"What happens if we cut his hands off? Will we be able to take the bracelets then?" Ferenc asked.

"Shall we find out?" Zsombor drew his sword and forced one of the official's hands to the table. Then he raised his sword high and forcefully brought it down just above the bracelet. The severed hand fell to the ground with the bracelet glowing brightly. Ferenc grabbed the hand and tried to take the bracelet off.

The official's face twisted in shock and pain as he watched his blood pour from his severed wrist.

"You only have one bracelet now. You're no longer immortal." Zsombor grabbed his other hand and cut that one off as well. The man died, shriveling into a pile of dust.

Ferenc gazed with disbelief at Zsombor. "How can these bracelets make anyone immortal when we so easily cut the wearer's hands off and killed him?

"The immortality conferred by the bracelets only assures one doesn't experience a mortal death. When the god Marduk created these bracelets, there was no such thing as murder, because there were few men. Then Marduk created women for men and women begat many murderers."

"Hellfire, then these bracelets won't do us much good, will they?"

"I'm not concerned with the legend of immortality," Zsombor said. "It's knowledge I want. With both bracelets, one sees into the mind of Marduk and acquires his infinite wisdom."

Ferenc scoffed at this. "What good is Marduk's knowledge without his powers?"

"Knowledge *is* power," Zsombor replied.

Erzsébet recounted how Ferenc and Zsombor transferred the bracelets of fire to their right wrists. If killed in battle, both would be born again in a time of their choice, still in possession of their bracelets.

Erzsébet laughed. "And both, of course, began plotting to gain possession of the other's bracelet."

Chapter 15

"Just weeks before Ferenc acquired the bracelet of fire, a feeling of dread overcame me. I knew my husband needed me," Erzsébet said. "I immediately traveled to Turkey, preparing myself to assist him in any way I could. As fate would have it, I arrived at his camp the very day he and Zsombor acquired both bracelets.

"Almost as soon as I arrived, a spy I planted in the camp said Zsombor told his lieutenant at arms 'to put his plans on hold' because he had heard of my powers. The rumor went around that Zsombor was willing to fight a god for the bracelet, but not a powerful witch like me. So you see, my reputation worked to my benefit at times."

"If a guy like Zsombor fears you that much, I'd best be careful too," I said, disguising my fear as a jest.

Erzsébet laughed and continued to speak. "Zsombor tried to impress me with his profound knowledge of the occult by putting on a display of his magickal prowess. He ordered his men to construct an arena. They placed large stones into a circle with a sixty-foot diameter and provided a canopy to protect me from the sun in a reviewing area. To add a bit of drama, extra sand was strewn on the ground to soak up any gore from his demonstrations.

"When the preparations were complete and Ferenc joined me in the reviewing area, a chariot drawn by a team of horses ran straight toward Zsombor. As he was about to be trampled, the chariot, horses, and driver suddenly disappeared. While awe-inspiring to others, I had learned that trick long ago and I was not impressed," Erzsébet said.

"Zsombor approached me. 'My magick is by far inferior to your majesties' powers, but perhaps you haven't seen my next trick.'

"A slave girl stood in front of me, and Zsombor chanted and waltzed around her, shaking a rattle made of lion's teeth until the slave started to disappear bit by bit. First one arm, then the other arm, and then her right leg went next. The girl wobbled and hopped about on her left leg, trying to remain upright. Zsombor shook his rattle and chanted loudly until that leg disappeared too. Her torso fell to the ground, and lay before me with only her head attached. Zsombor chanted his magickal incantation, shook his rattle again, and the head disappeared, leaving nothing but a torso lying on the ground. He stood over it, and with sword in hand, he struck the regions where there should have been arms, legs, and head. After plunging his sword into the chest of the living torso, he reached in and pulled out the still beating heart."

Jesus. Erzsébet chatted about this horror story as if it was a common event.

"Zsombor impressed me with his skills," Erzsébet said, "and I worried that he might outmaneuver Ferenc. That night, my husband confided in me about the bracelets."

"I'm not sure how to take Zsombor's bracelet," Ferenc said, "because I know him well. He's shrewd and vicious, and wants my bracelet as much as I want his. You've seen his magickal powers, so I can't just steal it from him. I fear his magick may overcome me."

"What will stop his taking your bracelet?"

"Only my army."

"With the powers he has, I doubt that is good enough."

Ferenc seemed ashamed. "My magickal powers are not insignificant, but. . ."

"What I saw tonight suggests Zsombor's powers are far beyond yours."

"Then I shall simply kill him first thing in the morning and take the bracelet."

"Give me your bracelet," I urged him. "If something goes wrong, he'll not be able to take it from you. I'll leave immediately, so it will be out of his reach."

"You will return it to me as soon as I secure the other?"

I kissed my husband good-bye. "We have always shared our occult discoveries. Why should this time be any different?"

"Did you intend to return the bracelet to him?" I asked Erzsébet.

"Of course I did. I respected Ferenc, and appreciated his trust."

Erzsébet's spy told her what happened next. After she left, Zsombor ordered a servant who resembled him to sleep in his tent. When a cadre of the Count's loyal soldiers rushed in, they found the servant sleeping there.

"There it is," a soldier said.

On the servant's wrist was a physical bracelet Zsombor had crafted to resemble his bracelet of fire. Although it looked the same, he had filled it with snake venom. Once removed from the servant's wrist, small barbs would protrude, and when slid onto another wrist, the barbs would release the venom into the wearer's skin. Death was assured in a few minutes.

The servant awoke to a sword crashing down on the arm that held the bracelet.

Zsombor followed some loyal soldiers who carried the severed hand. They took the hand with the bracelet still attached to Ferenc's tent. Zsombor cut a peephole in the tent to observe what would happen next. The soldiers asked for leave to enter the tent, then dropped the severed hand onto the table in front of Ferenc. He dismissed the soldiers and when they had exited the tent, he picked up the bloody hand, tore off the bracelet, and jammed it onto his left arm.

Once he did this, Zsombor told his soldiers, "Stand guard while I retrieve my bracelet." He entered the tent.

"My spy was among Zsombor's trusted soldiers, and he peered through the peep hole Zsombor had made, watching Ferenc's face distort in surprise when Zsombor burst in, still alive," Erzsébet explained, making a face in my mind.

"Did you not wonder why my hand did not disintegrate as the hands we took the bracelets from did?" Zsombor asked Ferenc.

"You tricked me, you swine. I'll make sure you never do it again." Ferenc attempted to draw his sword, but the toxin was already weakening him. "You may have gotten the best of me, but you'll never get the other bracelet."

"My spy said that Ferenc attempted to laugh, but choked instead, fell to the ground, and died. Zsombor bent over his body and chanted the incantation to make the real bracelet of fire appear, but Ferenc had transferred the bracelet to me. Furious when he discovered the deception, he ranted and cursed. "It had to be that witch wife of his. No one else but Erzsébet could have talked Ferenc into giving up the bracelet. Somehow, I will retrieve it from her, and I'm prepared to do anything, anything at all!"

"My spy said Zsombor returned to his own tent and raved for hours," she said. "He babbled on about my connections to the royal family, my uncle, the King of Poland, and all the obstacles he would encounter. Finally, his Lieutenant-at-Arms entered the tent and Zsombor explained his plan to destroy the favor of my royal relatives and make me vulnerable to public condemnation by starting more rumors to discredit me."

"After all," Zsombor told the soldier, "she is related to Vlad the Impaler. Make transcripts of Vlad's history and post them everywhere. I'll use this information to create the illusion she's also draining peasants' blood for her enjoyment. Write about how she bathes in blood, tortures young girls, and bites her servants to death. Kill a few girls, drain them of blood, and dump the bodies around Erzsébet's castle. That will lay suspicion at her doorstep."

Man, Zsombor wasn't fooling around, I thought.

"I've told you about the rumors that had circulated about me. I tried desperately to counteract Zsombor's plan as soon as his dirty deeds were accomplished and the new rumors began, because I desperately needed the protection of my sons-in-laws and cousins now that Ferenc was gone. When word returned to me that Matthias II, King of Hungary, and later the Holy Roman Emperor, and my cousin, the Palatine Thurzö, did indeed believe these evil stories, I knew these powerful men simply wanted my inheritance for themselves. I began locking myself in my rooms so no one could murder me in my sleep. I begged my friend Anna Darvulia for help with her spells and visions. She revealed that Thurzö encouraged Zsombor and thwarted assassination attempts against him."

"Why do you not send an army after Zsombor?" Anna asked.

"My castle guard has been disbanded by orders of the King himself," I told her.

"Some royals poison those they want deposed, so be cautious. Once the king proposes an act, success usually follows. There is no doubt your superiors will persuade you to surrender your wealth," Anna said. "Or they will simply plot to take it. You have to be alert at all times."

"After that conversation, I constantly looked over my shoulder. I rarely allowed anyone to handle my food and always studied my teacup, searching for dregs of poison."

A rush of euphoria passed through me in response to Erzsébet's familiarity. Obviously, she'd finally shared with me her reason for possessing me. But did she also allow me this addictive emotion in order to keep me involved?

"That's quite a story," I said. I wondered exactly how much of it was true and what exactly she'd left out.

❧Chapter 16

After witnessing Erzsébet's dreams and listening to her life stories, I conceded she probably wasn't as cruel as history portrayed. On the other hand, even though hers had been a difficult life, it didn't justify her hijacking my body. She'd messed my new life up. When I thought of Zsombor harassing her, I felt animosity creeping through my brain – anger toward him and a mixture of empathy and irritation for Erzsébet.

Erzsébet didn't care for getting up at the crack of dawn, but she loved the strength and energy of my body and tolerated the one hundred sit-ups and one hundred push-ups of my wake-up routine. I learned to develop some minor control over my bodily functions, so if she complained about the physical exercises, I concentrated upon shutting down my plumbing. She hated constipation because even though I attacked my own body, she also felt the pain. I hoped I could discover a way to harass her right out of my body.

Erzsébet continued to marvel over modern conveniences. The first time she used a telephone, she thrilled to the voice transmitted through the instrument, even though she already knew all about them due to her ability to scan my memory. Televisions and computers were like old-fashioned magick to her, and I avoided them whenever possible because it became difficult to peel her away once she began channel and internet surfing. She continued to adore hot running water and spent so much time in showers, baths, and Jacuzzis that I felt in danger of getting waterlogged.

The morning after I arrived at my son's home, I was lolling in the living room when the phone rang. Audrey answered the call in the kitchen and brought a mobile phone to me. "It's for you."

"My first phone call in fifty years," I said. After a vacation of five decades, I figured just about everyone I knew was dead.

"Jim Jackson here," I answered.

"Hello, Mr. Jackson, this is your attorney, Vince Zoloti."

My God. He had to be over ninety years old, I thought.

"Zoloti! How's it going? Aren't you a little old to still be working?"

"I'm sorry. I'm Vince, Jr., Mr. Jackson. My father, Vincent, your original attorney, died twenty years ago. I inherited your file along with his business. I'm calling about your trust fund. Do you recall setting it up with my father?"

"Of course I do. I had a half million in life insurance for my wife and son, so I put my last purse in trust for me."

"Your initial investment has multiplied many times over despite the recessions of the '80s and '90s and the crashes of 2008, '11, and '16. You're a wealthy man, Mr. Jackson. If you'd like to come in, we can review your assets. You may take control of them, or if you'd prefer, I can continue handling them for you."

"How much are we talking about?"

"I don't have an exact figure at this time because of market fluctuations, but you're worth multiple millions of dollars."

"You mean like a billion?"

"Not quite, but if you play your cards right, you should be there in a few years."

I pretended to be nonplussed at this disclosure, but Erzsébet had my body trembling all over. Almost a billion dollars, she knew, was a vast amount of money.

Maybe I could bribe Erzsébet to leave, somehow.

"In that case, put ten million dollars in an account that I can easily access, and I will see you when I have an opportunity," she made me tell Zoloti.

"I'll have the money transferred right away, Mr. Jackson. Where do you want me to send the paperwork?"

"Here, I suppose."

"I'll send an electronic device to your son's house so I can reach you whenever I need a signature or confirmation on any issues that may arise."

"All right, send one over. Goodbye for now, Mr. Zoloti."

Erzsébet's excitement surged through my body. My wealth meant I could live like royalty, in the manner to which she was accustomed. To top it off, she was itching to get her hands on Zoloti's electronic device.

If only she'd had one back in Transylvania! She sent a shudder of dismay through my body whenever she thought about connecting then and now.

She turned her concentration back to the present. Her libido, or maybe it was mine, got her thinking about sex. She wanted to use my body to satisfy her urges. Our masturbation the night before had whetted her desire to experience more sex from a man's perspective. Her thoughts were interrupted when Joe stuck his head in and called me to breakfast.

Audrey and Joe had teamed up to cook another sumptuous-looking meal, a breakfast buffet filling an entire countertop of their gleaming, ultra-modern kitchen. Joe sat at the round granite-topped table looking at pictures of Emily taken before he was born. My heart skipped a beat. *So beautiful*, I thought. Erzsébet agreed. Did I detect a twinge of jealousy?

Again, I envied Erzsébet's enjoyment while she ate my breakfast. Being stuck inside my body with little connection to my five senses was like making love through an interpreter. I could barely taste a thing. Apparently, Erzsébet was still keeping me on a short leash despite her midnight confession. I tried to complain to Joe, but Erzsébet quickly stopped me.

"Are you nervous about seeing Mom?" Joe asked between bites of his fruit salad.

Mom?

"Oh, Emily," I said. Joe couldn't yet talk when I went into the nitrogen tank and hearing him call Emily "Mom" made me feel nostalgic for the years I'd missed.

I answered in the affirmative, and Erzsébet told him I was ready. After we finished breakfast and I helped clean up the kitchen, it took only twenty minutes to drive to the managed care facility where Emily lived. As we pulled up and I gazed across the green lawns and lush gardens, Erzsébet proclaimed it fit for nobility. I made a mental note to reward my son for taking such good care of his mother.

"She's on the third floor, Dad," Joe said as we walked through the facility's double doors and headed for the elevators.

If I had control of my body, I'd have trembled from nervousness. Mostly I could only wreak havoc on my mind, worrying about how Erzsébet would behave when she met Emily. Would she let me hold her or show her any affection? I had no way of knowing what this bitch would do. Erzsébet resented my thoughts and we engaged in a power struggle as we walked along a hallway with custom-designed doors and entryways to create the appearance of unique residences. As usual, our mind war was a hopeless struggle that Erzsébet won.

At a door with ornate Victorian hardware and a leaded glass panel, Joe stopped, gave a light knock, and went inside. I held back and stared at Emily as my son walked toward her. I'd seen her many times from the spirit world, but to face my young and beautiful wife in this condition shocked me. To see her hair thinned and gray, her smooth, flawless skin as wrinkled as the prunes I ate for breakfast, and her twinkling eyes dimmed; the mother of my son, the only woman I ever loved. . . how she looked didn't matter, I still loved her!

I walked to her, put my arm around her shoulders and attempted to plant a kiss on her lips.

"Get away from me! Who are you? Joe, Joe, get this man out of my room."

She screamed so loud, I jumped back.

"But Mom, this is Dad."

"No, you're trying to trick me, Joey. Get him out of here."

She pulled the throw on her lap over her face and started to cry.

Joe turned to me with hands upturned and a pained expression on his face. "I'm sorry, Dad, I never expected this reaction."

I stepped outside the door and pushed it almost shut so Emily wouldn't have to look at me any longer. I knew better, but I let my thoughts have the best of me: *My own wife doesn't want any part of me.* All my dreams came crashing down.

I took a deep breath. Could I blame her? What if I was in my mid-seventies and Emily waltzed into my room, still a young woman. How would I react? Erzsébet nudged me then, reminding me that being a man, my reaction would likely be different. And the Alzheimer's probably muddled things more for Emily.

I bristled when a thought clearly belonging to Erzsébet filtered into my mind. *Maybe it is for the best.*

I peered through the leaded glass in the door and I flinched when I saw my son check the diaper that Emily wore. I wanted to cry. Erzsébet stared at Emily, and decided that the toll time took on a woman's body was an affront to her senses.

I should have realized this might happen.

"I think it's best if we leave now," Joe said as he came out of Emily's room. "I'm sorry. I had no idea she'd react this way, Dad. Mom's memory of you comes and goes. Maybe once she recuperates from this visit, we can try again. It's likely she won't even remember this tomorrow."

The way things were going, I was happy to leave.

Chapter 17

As Joe drove me back to his house, I obsessed about Emily. She was right about the cryonic procedure. It did make our separation more extreme. She'd weathered fifty years without me, and soon I'd weather fifty years or more without her. If I'd gone to the grave as I should have, we'd be together soon.

I knew there was nothing I could do now except to have patience, but I still felt like crap.

Joe glanced over at me and patted me on the thigh. "Don't worry, Dad, Mom still has lots of good days. She'll remember you soon and be thrilled to see you."

"But when does she have good days?"

"I hate to admit it," he said sheepishly, "but they're getting farther apart."

I figured that might be the case. I didn't know what to think. My wife didn't recognize me and I had some fiendish woman controlling my every move. . .

"Don't worry about anything, Jim Jackson," Erzsébet said. "Things will get better."

She sent me that wave of euphoria she was so good at producing. I reclined the seat and began to watch the scenery go by. Soon I relaxed and my thoughts of Emily faded.

As we approached Joe's house, he stopped when we saw a large object hovering two feet above the ground in his driveway. The long, sleek vehicle seemed to change colors as the sun reflected from the iridescent black finish.

"What in the hell is that?"

"Wow, that's the first VTK2500 I've ever seen," Joe said.

Limousine was the only term I could relate to it, especially when a clean-cut young driver wearing a traditional chauffeur's uniform emerged through a gull-winged door and dropped gracefully to the ground. He approached my window as I hit the switch to roll it down.

"A gift from Mr. Zoloti." The chauffeur handed me a thin square of plastic with rounded edges, about three inches by three inches.

"Um, what's this?"

"A PVA, sir," he said with a look that indicated I must have been living in a cave to not know what it was.

"PVA?"

"Personal video appliance. Like a smartphone on steroids. Latest model, state of the art, sir."

"What do I do with this?"

"Oh, I'm so sorry, Mr. Jackson. Forgot you've been away awhile."

He took the device from my hand and tapped it once. It unfolded to about three times its original size.

"Watch me," he said, and showed me a screen with multiple pictures on it.

"First thing we need to do is authenticate who you are. Place your thumb here."

"Wait a minute. What do you want with my thumb?"

"Sorry, I meant to say, please press your thumb against the screen so it can scan the print to verify you're the registered owner."

"How would it know that I am?"

"Zoloti took your prints from your database and registered this in your name."

I pressed my thumb on the screen. "Okay, I still don't know what to do with it."

"You can just say who you want to call, or touch a picture on the screen and it will dial that person."

"Are you saying this complex thing is just a telephone?"

"It's much more than a phone. You can do hundreds of things with it. You can sign documents for Mr. Zoloti with it, but the most important feature is that you can purchase anything you want with it, like a debit card. It's linked to your brokerage account and is much more secure than a bank card."

"I don't understand how that works."

"Just scroll through shop sites, touch a photo of anything you want and follow the on-screen cues."

"But what if I want to buy something in a store, or rent a hotel room?"

"Simple. Just physically point it at the sales scanner and verify your thumb print, and the cash will be instantly transferred."

What a complex world I came back to.

I glanced at Joe and he smiled and nodded. Apparently, he was used to this high-tech money stuff.

Enthralled by the device, Erzsébet could hardly wait to get her hands on this too.

"Mr. Zoloti is concerned that your driving skills might be rusty, and that it may take you awhile to adjust to today's automated vehicles. So he sent me along with the VTK," the young man said. "I'm Mike, by the way. I'll be your driver, and the car will be at your disposal for as long as you need it."

PVA, VTK, alphabet soup, I thought. Nice touch. The Zoloti family probably made a small fortune from handling my money over the years. Still, a nice gesture. But I felt intimidated by the technological advances, and though Erzsébet would never admit it, I could sense her confusion as well.

"May I look at your vehicle for a moment, Mike?"

"Certainly, sir." Mike reached out and opened the door for me.

"I find it difficult to believe machines like this actually exist," Erzsébet said, running my hand over the highly polished surface of the VTK. "Can you drive such a machine?"

"I used to," I told her mentally, "but I have no idea how to drive a car that rides on air. I don't even know how it would stop without wheels on the ground."

I smiled at Mike. "Good thing Zoloti sent a driver. I'd never figure out how to operate this monstrosity."

Joe got out of his car and wandered over to look at the VTK. I turned to Joe to say something, but Erzsébet abruptly said, "Thank you for everything, but I need to be alone for a while, so I'll be staying at Nine Zero."

"Hold on, Dad, you're supposed to stay with me so I can keep an eye on you," Joe said, perplexed by my sudden streak of independence.

Annoyed, I stepped back. On second thought, I mused, Joe and Audrey might be safer with me staying somewhere else.

"Look, Joe," Erzsébet said through me, "I will keep in touch with you. I just want some time to think about things."

"Uh, this is a little abrupt," Joe said. "But you're a big boy and I'm not your daddy, after all. Promise you'll call me if you have any problems, any at all."

"Okay, I promise," Erzsébet said. She let me hug Joe and then told Mike to take us to the Nine Zero.

"Where the hell are we going?" I growled.

"To one of Boston's better hotels, or so the internet claims," she said, sniffing like I was some kind of rube. "It's a high-rise hotel I saw on the drive over here. It is located downtown, near the Freedom Trail, and only a block away from the Boston Commons."

At the hotel desk, I aimed the unfolded PVA at a scanner affixed to the counter and put my thumb on it. Within seconds, a paid receipt appeared on the small screen. A robotic bellhop showed us to the penthouse, an opulent, ultramodern suite of rooms on a scale I'd never experienced in my previous life. I wondered what to tip the bellhop with, computer bits?

Erzsébet lived an uppercrust life in the sixteenth and seventeenth centuries, but compared to this, that luxury was literally primitive. Like a child, she ran about to play with all the gadgets through my hands, opening and closing the motorized drapes and turning on the three-dimensional TV and digitized hypersonic music system with the prescribed hand positions and finger snaps – even the fairly mundane jade thermatic massage bed thrilled her. She especially loved the Jacuzzi tub surrounded by mirrored glass that allowed lolling in the bubbles and gazing out over the city. She even spent a good twenty minutes playing with the hot shaving cream dispenser.

Opening the sliding glass door, she moved my body onto the patio and gazed across the city, dazzled by the sea of lighted buildings and streets surrounding the hotel. When I looked down, she froze and I stepped back. Her fear of falling amused me, because I never had a fear of heights.

"I've never been higher than the castle turret before. This may seem like nothing to you, but I need to accustom myself to these great heights."

When I walked back into the room, she snapped my fingers to turn the television on. She scrolled through the channels until she found an adult channel where a hot S&M movie played with a heavy breathing soundtrack. The 3-D presentation on a wall-sized screen practically put the actors in the room with us. I waved my hand and the volume increased. As before, Erzsébet became aroused, but I had to settle for mental stimulation. Not having a clear connection to my own physical sensations was a tough way to live, but it beat the alternative, as they say.

After a few minutes, Erzsébet's attention wandered. She picked up a hotel brochure from a writing desk. A photo of a Latino couple dancing in a lounge specializing in Latin music attracted her, and she decided to go downstairs. She dressed me in a dark blue designer suit she had purchased for me by using the PVA device to send the tailor my measurements. A courier had delivered a half-dozen suits within hours of the call. The delivery included all necessary accessories, because as Erzsébet told all vendors, "Just send the best that money can buy."

She let me get by with a quick shower this time. After I dressed, I stood before a wall of mirrors and my handsome face looked back at me. The suit hugged my body like a second skin. The blue shirt set off my fair face, framed in thick, wavy, jet-black hair combed straight back. The scar running from my right eyebrow down to my lip made me look dangerous, hardening what would have been a pretty-boy look.

As we left the room, I took one last look at the movie. The closing scene aroused Erzsébet. She snapped my fingers and the TV shut off. I walked down the fire stairs to the ground floor because Erzsébet refused to take the glass-enclosed elevator. I passed unnoticed through the crowded lounge until I found an empty stool at the bar.

I looked around me. There were quite a few couples, but also enough single women, mostly in pairs and trios, to keep me happy. Most looked soft and delicious, and Erzsébet described them as a "perfumed garden of roses."

If I had control of my senses, my mouth would have watered at the sight of so much delectable flesh. Instead, my eyes wandered and settled on the man who sat next to me. He was around the age I looked, mid-to-late twenties, tall and well dressed. I found him strangely appealing when he introduced himself and warmly shook my hand. "Alex," he said.

"Jim Jackson," I told him, trying to gaze around again at the honeys. But Erzsébet glued my eyes on Alex.

What the fuck was she doing? Then I remembered. I started to panic. "No!"

Entranced with Alex, she ignored my mental agony. Erzsébet chit-chatted and flirted. Alex became chummy.

"Did you hear the one about …?" he said, telling me the latest joke about some politician, leaning in on the punch line as an excuse to throw his arm around my shoulder.

"Erzsébet, get his goddamned arm off of me," I mentally yelled. She ignored me and continued chatting with Alex.

I tried to tolerate it by rationalizing that Alex was just being friendly. Then I felt his hand on my leg, slowly moving towards my crotch. Sweating and on the verge of a panic attack, I felt his hand on my stuff, and my stuff was getting hard. While I'd heard this was all quite acceptable in twenty-first century society, I couldn't forget my experience with the pedophile years ago in Hano. How could this be happening again?

Transfixed, Erzsébet enjoyed every sensuous moment. She responded in kind and put my hand in his lap. Repulsed, I begged her to stop, but she continued to ignore me.

She and Alex decided to go up to my room for a drink. Would this insane encounter end up with me having sex with another man? If Erzsébet went through with this, I'd never be able to look in a mirror without calling myself a faggot.

Erzsébet was so excited about her conquest that she'd forgotten her fear of the glass-enclosed elevator. She had me running my hand through the guy's tousled blond hair on the way to the fifteenth floor. I had to close my eyes and withdraw my consciousness to tolerate it. When we went inside my room, Alex took his jacket off. Erzsébet took my jacket off, and we sat side by side on the couch. Alex leaned toward me with his eyes closed and his lips pursed, posed for a kiss. Goddamn Erzsébet made me lean forward to kiss him. When I saw my reflection in the mirrored doors, my scar was vivid, and I remembered how I got it.

Rage! The thought of me about to swap spit with another man was just too much. I erupted and somehow I took control away from Erzsébet. I punched Alex in the face as hard as I could. Taking my anger at Erzsébet out on him, I punched him again, breaking his nose. Seconds later, he lay on the floor, bleeding and perplexed.

"Why, what?" he mumbled as I kicked him in the ribs.

"Get the fuck out before I kill you!"

The door slammed as Alex found his way out. Without a word, Erzsébet fought me mentally for dominance. I ran to the balcony, threw one leg over the railing, and took a good, long look down.

"We're going over if you don't back off."

I wondered if this was how it worked for those poor bastards with multiple personalities, always a fight for control. I tried to reach further into Erzsébet's mind and saw her fear of plunging through space and hitting the pavement.

She relented.

Now I felt *my* wants and desires. The damn bitch had gotten my libido worked up, and I needed relief. I picked up the phone and called an escort service. It was me talking, not Erzsébet. "Send two of your best girls to the Nine Zero penthouse immediately," I demanded.

Two hours later I was sated and enjoying that loving feeling.

"Did you enjoy it as much as I did, Erzsébet?"

She surprised me when she answered, "yes." Not one word about poor, handsome Alex.

I thought of Emily. How could I have done this? Come on, I told myself, she'd understand. After what I'd been through, I really believed Emily would forgive me. Erzsébet found it strange that a man of my means would worry about something so trivial.

I soon fell asleep. Big mistake, because when I woke up, Erzsébet had firmly taken control.

I tried to tune her out but I didn't have any choice but to listen.

"Your anger is dangerous for both of us. I'm willing to compromise. If you're so repulsed by men, I'll only encourage women from now on."

I knew she compromised only because she feared I might overcome her permanently one day. I demanded she leave my body in no uncertain terms even though I had no leverage. She sent that ocean wave feeling coursing through me again. I had no idea how to combat the sorcery she used on me.

A light bulb came on then. As much as I disliked admitting it to myself, maybe I could use her brute determination to my benefit.

"I want to claim my right to a championship fight."

Her response surprised me. "Nothing could please me more. I always wanted to be a warrior. To fight a man as an equal is tantalizing, a dream come true."

It was time to lay down some conditions. "The first thing you need to know, Erzsébet, is that sex is an absolute no-no while I'm training. Second, we'll need to train every day."

"Fine, where will we train?"

CRYONIC MAN

"I can join a gym and. . ."

"Why join one? With all the money we have, we will buy one."

I began to bristle at the word "we", but thought better of it. We'd have to work as a team to be successful. I would never have thought of buying a gym, but why not? I called Joe and informed him of my plans.

"But, Dad, you can't, your brain, your age, your – "

"Look, son, I appreciate all you've done for me. You gave me life again. Surely you don't want me living it out in a nursing home."

Silence. Those were Erzsébet's words coming out of my mouth. I couldn't imagine being so blunt, what with Emily having Alzheimer's and all his years of struggle to revive me.

"No, no, of course not," he said, "it's just there are so many unknowns. Theoretically, you're a fit, twenty-six-year-old man because of the nanobot cellular treatments, but your chronological age is seventy-six. That's a large span and no one knows how your body will respond to strenuous exercise or if it will withstand the pummeling you'd take from boxing."

"I exercised hard at Evergreen with no ill effects, so I don't see any problem. Do I have your support or not?"

Damn, Erzsébet is rude, crude, and insistent, I thought.

"You are my father, and even though I'm your doctor, I don't have the right to tell you how to live your life. So I'll wish you luck and pray you don't disintegrate from a hard punch to the head."

"How would you like to be my medical advisor as long as I fight?"

Erzsébet might be blunt, but she also knew the art of diplomacy. This is exactly what I'd been thinking.

"I'd like that very much. We'll spend some more time together and get to know one another," Joe said. "I always wanted to know you as a fighter, Dad."

We began to search for appropriate facilities the next day.

❧Chapter 18

The next morning, we had an early room-service breakfast and went out shopping for a training gym. After seeing every viable commercial property available, my son recommended that I offer to purchase the gym I'd always trained in. Although located in a rundown section of Boston's South End, it was just a short commute from Joe's office. Besides, I felt a kinship with the down and outers who frequented this part of the city. Maybe I could do something for the kids there while I trained.

Erzsébet wanted the gym remodeled, nothing but first class for her. Fit for royalty was the term she used when telling the contractors what improvements to make. The construction crew worked 24/7 to complete the work as quickly as possible.

While I waited for the gym's grand opening, I started my conditioning program by running ten miles a day, doing calisthenics, and shadow boxing. My physique had already improved from the cell-by-cell nanobot revitalization. My program improved my endurance astronomically. My reflexes were sharper, probably better than ever. Before the gym was even open to the public, I felt ready for the big fight.

Joe examined me every day. He monitored me for at least a few minutes during each activity. I wore a halter monitor to record my heart rate. He drew blood several times a week.

"Your physical condition is astounding. It's way beyond my expectations for a person rehabilitated from a cryonically preserved state, especially in light of your initial problems."

Erzsébet went on high alert. She didn't let me communicate much when my son was around. Obviously, she didn't want me telling him anything about her. If only I could tell him that she still controlled me, he just might allow Father O'Malley to perform an exorcism to get rid of her. All I could do was play a waiting game and look for an opportunity to get around her.

In a matter of weeks, the refurbished gym opened for business. Unfortunately, the gym seemed to be too classy for the type of guys that normally hung out at a training gym. Erzsébet's decorating style leaned toward the gothic, to say the least. Tapestries and sconces hung from the walls, suits of armor lined the hallways, and sixteenth- and seventeenth-century weapons adorned the dressing rooms. When my training began, Erzsébet also intervened at first, and then agreed to let me run all aspects of my career.

I dreamed up a practical solution to attract some sparring partners. We offered free membership to anyone in my weight class who could spar with me and last one round, figuring this would attract some quality fighters while keeping the deadbeats away. Evidently, free membership wasn't incentive enough to get my fellow pugilists interested in our spa-like amenities. We didn't acquire one member with this offer.

Erzsébet suggested a monetary motivator, a bonus of a thousand dollars and a free membership to anyone who could last one round in the ring with me. The only protection allowed would be eight-ounce gloves, a mouthpiece, and a cup. We didn't want to fight a bunch of pansies with headgear and pillow gloves trying to hang on to complete the round.

Erzsébet wanted warriors who thought they could beat me. And we wanted to be able to end the fight quick, if we thought my opponent didn't deserve the gym membership.

Fighters queued around the building the day following the new advertisement, and to my surprise, the first in line was a pretty woman named Cwia. At first glance, she looked too feminine for boxing with her rose-petal skin, wide-set golden-green eyes, and long mane of curly red hair. When Erzsébet found out women could compete in this gladiatorial sport, she loved the idea.

Me, I was dumbfounded that women were allowed to get near the ring. I realized a lot had changed since the '70s, but it took me some time to adjust. I reminded Erzsébet that we hired models as ring hostesses to carry 'round numbers during fights. I found the models enticing, but Erzsébet reminded me of our no sex agreement. And that was okay with me because my conscience continued to bother me that I'd strayed. Emily still wouldn't allow me to visit, and her refusal to talk to me on the phone gnawed at me. I knew she was sick, and she likely worried about our age difference, but I desperately wanted her companionship again. I fantasized that maybe she could somehow help me regain control of my body and mind.

Anyway, Erzsébet liked the idea of going face-to-face with a woman and wanted me to spar with Cwia. I had to convince her that fighting a mid-weight woman with my enhanced heavyweight body would be unfair and unequal.

She insisted I hire Cwia as a trainer. I agreed to interview her for the position because by being prepared to fight me, I knew she nurtured a warrior's spirit. Along with her pumped-up, muscular body, the rumors calling her the best cutman in town swayed me. For a woman, she had an impressive dedication to the sport.

I questioned Cwia about her cornerman's knowledge. She talked fast, a true Bostonian.

"A minute between rounds isn't long, but enough time to make a difference. I know what drugs to use and not to use; for example, Avitene can only be used if a cut is actively bleeding, and thrombin can only be used if blood is removed first and the surface is dry! For nosebleeds, use Q-tips soaked in adrenaline hydrochloride and for –"

I interrupted her spiel. "You're my cutman, all right. But I want you to consult with my son. I believe he's developed a drug to instantly stop bleeding on any surface injuries."

A good cutman is invaluable to a fighter and can truly make the difference between winning and losing. I'd seen countless fights stopped because no one in the corner knew how to prevent a simple cut from getting worse. Cwia's feminine nurturing instincts along with her knowledge of medicine and boxing would probably make her emerge as one of the best cutmen in the sport.

Over six hundred fighters signed up on the first day. They all had to pass a physical, a stress test, undergo X-rays to see if they nursed any broken bones, and take a psych exam before fighting me. The five grand was a great motivator, and not one applicant refused the exams. We supplied a free lunch or dinner to all who tested, and this motivated a handful who looked like they hadn't eaten a good meal for a while. These men were in no shape to fight and so I fed them well and gave them a hundred-dollar bill for showing up.

One-third of the applicants passed the exams with acceptable results. Now I had two hundred potential gym members. We would accept applications until we had as many sparring partners as I wanted or needed. If they lasted three minutes in the ring with a man who hadn't fought for over fifty years, they'd be amply rewarded. I'd get tuned up by going through the amateurs first and save the professional fighters for last.

Monday, opening day, I'd finally get to punch some galoot again, and I could hardly wait. I'd start fighting ten men a day, which meant ten rounds a day. I'd schedule thirty days straight, and I'd fight three hundred sparring partners. This would have been way too many rounds in the old days, but my rebuild gave me the physical strength and endurance for this agenda. I could run and fight all day without getting tired since the rejuvenation. My son's nanobots were truly amazing.

Monday's ten fighters showed up early and were standing around the brand-new boxing ring before I arrived. Word had spread about my offer, and a few reporters milled around interviewing fighters. The reporters expected to see me humiliated, but hoped I'd win anyway so they'd have a story. If I won any of the bouts, a seventy-six-year-old guy fighting guys in their twenties, the story would sell e-news. Even newspapers were delivered electronically on PVAs these days.

As I walked toward the ring, some asshole played the "Rocky" theme song over the loudspeakers. If Erzsébet weren't in my body, I figured she'd do something like that. The ten boxers started warming up, skipping rope, punching speed, and heavy bags. My first opponent was already in the ring, flexing and stretching. I knew he weighed in at two hundred and sixty pounds, forty more than my two-twenty. Mostly solid, the Puerto Rican had just a smidgen of fat covering his extensively muscled body, the best physique for a heavyweight.

I climbed into the ring, removed my robe, and braced myself for my first round in nearly fifty-one years. The ref had us touch gloves and the fight began. My opponent charged me, trying to force me against the ropes. I easily sidestepped him, giving him a good right to the kidney as he passed me.

Erzsébet thrilled to the challenge as her dream of participating in combat was fulfilled. She had my adrenaline flowing and I went on the attack too soon.

"Lay him out," she urged.

I took a hard punch to my head because of her eagerness.

"Let me lead the fight. Remember our agreement? I'm the boxing expert."

Erzsébet mentally flipped me off, but she was smart enough to realize that I spoke the truth, and returned control. I wouldn't make a mistake like that again, getting punched by some amateur.

My opponent tried to seize the initiative after landing that one punch. He charged again, and I easily sidestepped to his right this time. I caught him on the side of his head with a good straight right. It dazed him and his eyes glazed over as I followed through with a kidney punch, and then a left uppercut that caught a corner of his jaw, snapping his head back.

He tried to counter, but he didn't have the speed and was rather clumsy, not the type I wanted hanging around my gym. I finally put him away after a minute and a half, a bit longer than I thought it would take. The other nine went easier, and there wasn't a one I deemed

CRYONIC MAN

deserving of a gym membership.

"Hey, champ," one of the reporters yelled, "good job, you showed those youngsters how an old-timer can fight."

I might be old in chronological years, but physically, I was probably younger than anyone I fought that night. But the media started calling me the "old man boxer."

"How about a statement?" another reporter asked.

Before I could stop her, Erzsébet had a Muhammed Ali moment. "Yeah, I have a statement. You are looking at the next heavyweight champion of the world. There is no one out there who can beat me."

I tried to get her to shut up, but she ignored me like she always does when she doesn't want to listen.

"Do you think tomorrow night's fights are going to be as easy as tonight's?"

"Of course," Erzsébet said.

When I returned to my dressing room, it was half-filled with electronic devices and Joe was there with a team of doctors. I submitted to a thorough exam.

"Looks like you've got a super body, Dad, not one thing out of place. Even your bruises heal at an accelerated rate. He held a mirror in front of my face so I could see where the punch had landed in my first round. It was visibly bruised when I passed a mirror right after the fight. Now, just a few minutes later, I had only a vague yellow spot.

The story made it to the second page of a few e-newspapers. "Is it witchcraft? Seventy-six-year -old man knocks out ten young boxers." The story carried a short description of my gym membership drive and a few details about the rumors of my possession by Erzsébet that went around after my rejuvenation at the Cryonic Foundation. The reporters had a way of digging up dirt that the CF wanted kept quiet. I figured some public knowledge might help me personally, even if it put a crimp in CF's style.

When I left my dressing room on Tuesday, the "Rocky" theme played over the loudspeaker system again as soon as I walked through the door. Erzsébet made me parade wave like a movie star as I walked down the aisle among a capacity crowd who cheered me as I passed. This reminded Erzsébet of the crowds cheering the Gróf and Grófnő – Count and Countess Báthory-Nádasdy at their formal appearances after one of the Count's military campaigns. She gloried in such moments.

I saw fear in my opponents where the day before I'd seen nothing but cockiness. I could almost read their thoughts: "He must be tired after yesterday, drag it out, make him come after me."

They were living on dreams. I felt great and intended to come after each one of them. The second day went like the first. The matches bored me. Erzsébet and I put our heads together and offered compensation of one thousand dollars to any amateur who would withdraw from the tournament. That way maybe I'd find some competition sooner and fight the pros. All but eight of the amateurs accepted the grand. Those who took the offer knew the deal was better than fighting me in the hope of winning 5k. Whatever qualities the remaining eight had must have been on the inside because I couldn't see anything special when I looked them over.

I looked forward to getting the remaining amateurs out of the way. The papers now called me the seventy-six-year-old bully who used his vast experience against a bunch of unsuspecting novices. They all predicted a different outcome when I started fighting the pros in line.

My first contender the next day was another big but sloppy-looking man. When I immediately went after him, he surprised me, dancing easily out of my reach, light on his feet. I left jabbed, he blocked. I right crossed, he blocked. I left hooked and followed with a right cross. He blocked the hook, dodged the cross, and came back with a right uppercut that glanced off my chin. I danced backwards, amazed at his speed and agility. I wanted him to be a gym member, so I let him last the full round. Nevertheless, I felt the need to let him know who was in control, and proceeded to beat him bloody without finishing him. He was the first one to last an entire round. Now I had at least one sparring partner.

I fought the next six contenders and guessed the only thing special

CRYONIC MAN

about those guys was their need for money. I made certain each one received a check for fifteen hundred for their effort. The last opponent surprised me, a Mexican I outweighed by a few pounds. When the fight started, he circled me, smiling and jabbering in Spanish. He feinted at every other step I took. I held back to see what he'd do. He came directly at me, hands by his sides. I threw a jab he avoided and then he threw his arms around me. I bucked. He hung on. The ref tapped his back and told him to break. He pretended not to understand, trying to get the clock to run because he only needed another two-and-a-half minutes. Finally, I broke away, backed him up to the ropes, and threw a body punch with my right. He wrapped his arm around mine. I tried to kidney punch him with my left. He wrapped his other arm around that one. He hung on my arms with all his weight, trying to tire me out, but I never got tired. I admired his perseverance and courage. A boxer needs to know how to combat this type of fighter, one who wears you down and beats the heck out of you when you're too tired to defend yourself. He'd make a fine addition to my gym, and I let him hang on until the round was over.

"Old man boxer finally meets his match with underweight Mexican fighter" ran as the next morning's headline. The story said I'd fight professionals the next day, meaning my joyride was over.

The stories got to me and made me determined to show the reporters that they didn't know shit. The first ten professionals only took me thirty minutes total to obliterate. The media suddenly changed its tune and started calling me championship material. I went through the remaining boxers and found thirty-three to my liking. Now we had a total of thirty-five sparring partners and one woman trainer.

Erzsébet was awed by Cwia's courage after what she'd experienced with me in the ring. In her day, women could never meet men in hand-to-hand combat, yet she'd just faced some of the toughest men in Boston. Erzsébet asked me again to spar with Cwia. I refused again. Cwia had trained for years in martial arts and boxing, but as I reminded Erzsébet, even the toughest mid-weight woman was no match for a heavyweight man. Erzsébet didn't want to risk upsetting me emotionally during training by making me do something that felt unnatural and unfair, so she relented.

My next step was to renew my boxing license. The state boxing commission statutes didn't allow anyone over fifty-five to be licensed. I argued that since I'd been cryopreserved for fifty years after dying at age twenty-six, I was physically a young man, just a few weeks shy of my twenty-seventh birthday.

"I'm sorry," the clerk at the commission office apologized, "rules are rules."

I reached across the counter and grabbed the skinny clerk's collar.

"Yeah, rules are made to be broken, so why don't you just break one and give me my damn license."

"Break his neck," Erzsébet shouted inside my head.

She wanted me teach him a lesson, but her anger subsided when she realized how much trouble that would cause.

But I couldn't fight for the championship without a license.

⋙ Chapter 19

Stumped, I called Zoloti.

"Because your circumstances are unusual, I'm certain your license can be reinstated, but it'll take some time to wade through the red tape."

"Time! I've already waited fifty years for my shot. I don't want to wait any longer."

"If you can't wait to fight, there's no law against holding boxing matches in your gym. It's a private club isn't it?"

Pure genius. Zoloti Jr. was a chip off the old block.

Erzsébet suggested I offer a large purse and take on all qualified comers. I'd attract the top boxers if I offered enough, but I only wanted to fight the best. I settled on Monday, Wednesday, and Friday night elimination fights. Eventually, through an elimination system, the best fighters would face me. Then I wouldn't have to wait for the boxing commission to tell me it was okay.

I set up thirty-four elimination bouts for the next week, ten bouts each on Monday and Wednesday. Friday would have nine bouts and Saturday, five. The emergent winners would fight each other on the following week. There would be an odd fighter kept in reserve in case of accident or illness. I set the minimum weight at two hundred and five pounds with no maximum. We didn't need any accusations about pounding smaller fighters.

Thirty-four of my gym members would compete against me in the first round. I knew if I could beat these, then qualified fighters would clamor to fight me. These elimination bouts would go on weekly and keep me supplied with competent opponents.

Erzsébet convinced me to offer a million dollars to anyone who could last ten rounds with me, and five million to anyone who beat me. I had to call Zoloti about setting up an account, just in case someone actually won.

Cwia told me about pay-per-view video streaming. I called a network and asked if they'd carry the fights. Even with some national attention, I couldn't get the network interested, so Joe found a local public access channel to broadcast the opening fights.

Even though the first Monday night fight had a half-million dollar purse, mostly local fans and gym members attended it. The same two or three reporters who'd followed my story before showed up, plus the director and cameraman from the local access station.

The dossier on my challenger for the night was impressive: thirty fights, twenty-eight won, and twenty-six of those by knockouts. Just two losses and both of those came when the fight really mattered. Henrik Bekker, aka Big Bek, had aced the elimination bouts two weeks in a row, easily knocking out both opponents. Our fight was no big deal for him – Bek hung out for the money and hoped to last the full ten rounds. Hailing from South Africa, he had the blondest hair and bluest eyes I'd ever seen. Big wasn't the word to describe him. Humongous sounded more like he looked – a Biblical Goliath – tall, well-muscled, about two hundred and fifty pounds. The two guys who beat him must have been behemoths.

When the fight started, Bek tried to overpower me. Surprised when he couldn't move me backwards, we stood toe-to-toe, trading punches. I blocked most, but a few grazing blows got through. If it wasn't for my amazing nanobot rebuild, I couldn't have absorbed the blows as well.

Big Bek must have felt overconfident because I easily caught him square on the jaw with a right uppercut in the third round and sent him sprawling to the canvas. Not as tough as he looked, but he was still the type I wanted for gym membership. He didn't win the purse, but I awarded him a $10,000 check and a membership card for his effort.

The viewing statistics for the public access channel were dismal that first Monday night. By the Friday night fight, the number of viewers had tripled and the channel began to feature fight reruns three times a day. By the end of the month, an entire network of local access channels picked up the broadcasts and the viewing statistics online went viral. As I became a national sports phenomenon, boxing fans, especially old timers who remembered me, loved watching the old guy beat the heck out of young fighters night after night. Of course, there was some speculation about my youthful energy, how the nanobots might make me stronger than normal.

One night during a particularly heated fight, someone in the crowd yelled out, "Hey champ, those bots better than 'roids?"

I never took steroids in my life, but the nanobots obviously enhanced my performance. There was no law against them, so I ignored the comment.

"Steroids hell, he's using witchcraft," someone else shouted. Another guy stood up and started yelling "witch, witch, witch." The hypnotic chant caught on for a minute. Network news picked up the clip and aired it 24/7 to create a bigger stir than it was in the first place.

Father O'Malley inserted himself into the picture again and started appearing on talk shows to discuss his obsession with Jim Jackson and Erzsébet Báthory. He attracted a worldwide following. Jim Jackson gained household name recognition and it seemed I had a place among the thousands of people inspired to seek exorcism for their alleged possession by evil spirits. I sympathized with them – oh boy, did I ever – but now that I was set to win the championship I'd dreamed about for so many years and Erzsébet's energy aided my plan, I wouldn't touch an exorcism with a ten-foot pole. I'd get my belt first and then I'd deal with the bitch.

My schedule of four fights a week amazed boxing fans. Pay-per-view networks had a change of heart and begged for the rights to my fights.

The public clamored for me to fight the 2025 Heavyweight Champion of the World, Aziz Alhason Abbas. The first and only Arab champion to date, his name translated to English as Determined Handsome Lion. American men envied his traveling with a harem of beauties. But no one could beat him. He'd won sixty fights in five years and up until now, had refused to fight me because the Boxing Commission wouldn't license me. This brought him nothing but ridicule. Under public pressure, he petitioned the Commission to reinstate my license for one fight. The huge purse offered by pay-per-view, not his good nature, prompted this request.

Abbas was a prolific boxer who fought twelve matches a year. If I beat this worthy opponent, I'd reach my lifetime goal – heavyweight champion of the world! I recalled how hard I'd worked toward that day with Emily's loving support. Guilt and regret washed over me. I shoved any thoughts of her aside because they always brought me pain. She still wouldn't consent to see me and even if she had, I'd been tied up with training and fights.

The Boxing Commission finally relented and reinstated my license. How could they refuse a man in his prime? Zoloti managed to secure the venue at TD Banknorth Garden so I could face Abbas in the richest fight in history, right here at home. The tremendous demand for tickets gave scalpers three and four times the original price weeks before the fight.

Finally, fight night.

I took a deep breath and entered the ring to thundering applause mixed with hoots of derision, as ready as I'd ever be. I didn't want Joe to watch me fight, but he insisted and as I scanned the front rows around the ring, I saw his and Audrey's eager faces. Not only did he want to be on hand if I suffered an injury, he also wanted to recover what we'd both missed in his childhood. No way could I let him down.

When Erzsébet gazed at the hulking champion with his goofy-looking red and white keffiyah and pointy boxing shoes, she saw through the facade. Behind his masquerade lay a vicious fighter. A member of his entourage, dressed like a belly dancer, unwrapped the keffiyah from his head to let his long, black hair flow to his shoulders. Abbas stared me down with icy, calculating eyes as she tied his mane into a ponytail knotted at the back of his head. The corners of his mouth twitched upward. I fired a good-natured Irish grin right back at him, wondering how someone could put so much malice into a smile.

The ref directed us to touch gloves and the bell rang. Instantly, the energy of a real fight confronted me. My first punches bounced harmlessly off the Lion. His strong, swift counterpunches took me by surprise. No damn wonder Abbas was champ for so long.

His solid right hit me in the exact spot where my brain tumor lived. I hesitated for an instant. He took the advantage and followed through with a left that split my right eyebrow above my scar. I bled profusely as the referee had me count fingers.

When the ref let the fight go on, I wondered if I could hang. Abbas came at me again. I covered up, trying to shake the numbness in my head. He unanimously took the first round.

I thanked my lucky stars that Cwia was in my corner as she staunched the blood flow from the open gash above my eyebrow. "Your face looks like a swollen balloon," she shouted above the loudspeakers.

Second round. I boxed Abbas to a draw, staying away from his vicious punches. Cwia used the ice-cold Ensell between rounds and tried to reduce the swelling around my eye.

Third round, I landed a few that stunned The Lion.

"Thumb him, blind the bastard, make him bleed," Erzsébet shouted.

"Calm down, I'm in control. Don't worry about a thing."

At the end, Abbas leveled his malicious smile at me again. I didn't return it this time. Fourth round, I wiped the crooked smile off his face with a hard right uppercut that would have knocked out a normal man.

The bell rang, and I went to my corner.

"What the fuck?" Cwia said, staring at me.

I didn't know what she was talking about and stared back at her.

"The cuts are almost healed and all the contusions on your face are fading already."

Good news. The nanobots were still at work, repairing my body. If what Cwia said was any indication, the bots were working at an accelerated pace. They'd quickly repair any damage Abbas inflicted.

"Don't you dare take any chances, make this guy bleed, make him show fear," Erzsébet said, practically panting with desire.

"Like I said, chill out. We'll get him." I wondered if she'd take charge if she got too excited. I couldn't let that happen.

Fifth round, I attacked, and we slugged it out toe to toe. Erzsébet had a creative idea – she made me step on the toe of the Lion's pointy shoe. I drove into his solar plexus. He tried to back up, lost his balance, and fell to the canvas.

The ref ruled a knockdown.

Pissed, Abbas pointed to me. "He tripped me."

I figured the American ref might rule in my favor any opportunity he got, and in this instance, he did.

Abbas took the nine count, and then ferociously attacked me, trying to end it. I bobbed and weaved, then danced away from him. Still pissed, he charged me. Big mistake – I caught him with a right hook that put him down. Only the bell saved him from a knockout.

In my corner, Cwia wiped sweat from my brow. I had him now, but I didn't want to win by cheating. I scolded Erzsébet for tripping him.

"Worked, did it not?" she said.

Sixth round. Abbas didn't smile, but I did. When I went after him, I saw fear. Just a flicker, a momentary hollow look creasing his face. Erzsébet saw it too. Once it infected him, he might as well have quit. I feinted with a left jab and threw a wicked uppercut, just missing his chin. He threw a left to my head. I ducked, countered with a left of my own to his solar plexus. He sucked in air. I followed through with a right and a left to the same area and he staggered back.

"We've got him now," Erzsébet screamed, her voice careening inside my head. "Beat him bad. Make this bastard bleed buckets!"

Insane bitch. No time to think. I would inflict more fear. I backed Abbas into the ropes and worked him over.

Seventh round. The fight announcers jabbered about my miraculous comeback. They noticed my cut closing and my bruises disappearing faster than more bruises could be inflicted. Abbas ran the whole round. His awe at my healing obviously confused him. The punches meant to destroy me were all for naught as he could plainly see.

"Quit playing and finish him now," Erzsébet demanded.

Eighth round. I needed a knockout to win the title clearly, so I went all out. The Lion backed away. All he had to do was last two more rounds, and he'd still be champ. Decisions usually go with the reigning champ. I chased Abbas for the entire round. He managed to stay out of reach and lasted through the eighth.

Ninth round. Cwia warned me about some substance she observed the Lion's corner-man wiping on his gloves. Meaning I couldn't let him put his gloves in my face; if I did, the stuff might temporarily blind me. I circled and danced. He dropped his gloves, a signal that meant "Come on, I dare you." I blasted him with a triple combination that stunned him before he had a chance to raise them back up. I followed through with some hard body shots until Abbas dropped his guard to defend his body. When he did this, I got in his face again. He raised his gloves. I went for body shots. He dropped his gloves again. I went for his face again. Blood leaked from his nose, mouth, and eyes; he staggered with every punch.

Inflamed at the sight of The Lion's blood, Erzsébet screamed like a banshee. I prayed she wouldn't get so excited that she'd cause me to make a mistake. Maybe her spirit would infect me with her psychosis.

I had to hand it to Abbas; no matter how much pain I inflicted, he wasn't about to give up. The bell rang, round over.

Tenth round. This was it, now or never, and we both knew it. I had to knock him out.

"Get him, crush his thorax!" Erzsébet said.

No wonder they called her the Lady Vampire. I continued to worry she'd take control away from me in her lust for blood.

I got Abbas in a corner. He dropped his guard for a second, tried to push me out of the way. I hit him on his chin with a full roundhouse right. His eyes glazed and rolled before he dropped to the canvas, out cold.

"Get up, Aziz," his harem screamed. His right leg twitched and bounced up and down on the canvas, but he was beyond getting up. Other than the twitching leg, he didn't move until long after the count was over.

The ref raised my hand in victory. Cwia jumped up and down. Through an exhausted haze, I could see Joe and Audrey waving their arms in the air and hugging one another.

But the crowd was strangely silent for what seemed a very long time. When the cheers came, there were a few at first, then a few more, and slowly the voices built up into the sound of a normal championship victory. Someone suddenly shouted out "cryonic man!" and this caught on until the arena filled with the chant "cryonic man, cryonic man, cryonic man!"

Why did I suddenly feel numb to the celebration all around me? Now that I wore the heavyweight championship belt around my waist, something I'd wanted all my life, it didn't mean much. I thought again of Emily and my heart sank. My interest in this victory dried up and blew away.

I left the ring in a funk and headed for the locker room. Ecstatic, Erzsébet wanted to celebrate our bloody victory. I warned her to leave me in control or I'd resist her in every way possible. She relented and hovered quietly in the back of my mind. Maybe she wanted to relive the fight and not bother with questions from the reporters and photographers who swarmed around me. Especially the snarky bald one that shoved a mic in my face asked, "Did Erzsébet Báthory help you win the world heavyweight boxing championship?"

Chapter 20

"If you're talking witchcraft, this is 2026, man. Dedication and hard work made me a champion, not hocus-pocus. It's no secret that I'm the first human revived from cryonic preservation. If you're interested, we'll talk about that," I said, skirting the issue.

I glared at the reporter and turned to another, trying to put on a happy face. I refused to answer anything except normal questions about the match and kept my answers short and sweet, heading for the shower as soon as possible.

Someone either leaked or innocently reported my first words after the rejuvenation – or rather, Erzsébet's – but did this new question mean that someone had hacked into my records at Evergreen? All this newfangled digital storage made unauthorized snooping easier than ever before. I had a hell of a time trying to sort out Erzsébet's presence after my rejuvenation and suddenly the media seemed to think they knew more about her than I did. Of course, now Father O'Malley would repeat this story and beat his exorcism drum even harder. . . but maybe it would help me get rid of Erzsébet.

Joe and Audrey insisted on hiring a limo to take us over to the Nine Zero. We shared a bottle of champagne and appetizers delivered from one of the hotel restaurants to my penthouse suite, a private party of three – well, four, if you counted Erzsébet. Though I felt guilty to rush Joe and Audrey off, I pled exhaustion so I could pout alone.

I guess Erzsébet thought it best to back off and give me some space, because she said little, keeping an unusually low profile. Her only jab was to remark how long I stayed in the Jacuzzi as I nursed my aching muscles and stared wistfully over the lights of downtown Boston.

"At least you could order more champagne if we're going to sit here so damn long," she complained, oblivious to the irony.

But Erzsébet was in fine form the next morning. She took control, making me crawl from my nest under the snowy white Egyptian cotton sheets and duvet on the sprawling king-sized bed to turn on the 3D television.

"Uh-uh," I told her. But she just *had* to see news reports of the match on Sports24, the international, 'round-the-clock sports network. The best of the reports called me a "real-life superhero" and the "Comeback Kid."

Erzsébet whooped and hollered. "Jim Jackson, you are a true blue celebrity now!" She loved the way the holographic clips of me pummeling Abbas looked like we were fighting in the room. The slow-motion shots with beads of sweat and drops of blood spraying from our faces mesmerized her.

Then came the reports I dreaded. Rather than cheering my victory, the next one called me a "freak of nature." Erzsébet bounced me up and down on the bed, booing and throwing pillows at the monitor. The most sensational story, titled "Witchcraft fuels Jackson championship," raised my hackles. If I hadn't channeled so much energy into punching the shit out of Abbas the night before, I probably would have punched a few holes in the wall while I watched it.

This report accused Cwia of using black magick to heal my cuts and bruises during the fight despite common knowledge of my cryonic preservation and rejuvenation with nanobots. Might be a smidgen of truth to the black magick charge if you considered the nanobots magick. I was no scientist myself, but anyone with half a brain

150

should be able to understand the reason for my rapid healing.

But there was no way to get around the Erzsébet issue. She helped me all right, and she was still controlling my body, but not in the way the media slanted it.

"My encouragement isn't really any different than Emily's support," she said, proud of her contribution to the championship.

Steamed that she'd compare herself to my Emily, I felt like decking myself or going over the balcony railing to shut her up. But she was right in a way, I had to concede. She'd propelled me with a ferocious determination that matched mine. And there was no way anyone besides me would ever understand that.

Erzsébet sensed my distress and let me turn the television off, much to my surprise. My victory turned bittersweet the moment I'd knocked Abbas out and now I regretted my comeback. But what else did I know how to do but fight?

I sat for a long time, replaying the fight in my mind. I wanted to think that my focused training and my drive to win the championship was so great that I emerged as the natural champion. What could I have done, drain my blood to get rid of the nanobots before each fight? On the other hand, maybe I did have an unfair advantage. Maybe anyone undergoing nanobot repair in the future would be banned from competing in professional sports. Or maybe the opposite would happen – all athletes might be allowed to undergo nanobot treatments to maintain peak health and performance levels. Who knew what might happen?

Nevertheless, neither of these issues had anything to do with Cwia. She'd gotten a lot of heat for nothing.

"I can't believe your media drags Cwia into this. She knows nothing of the ways of sorcerers," Erzsébet scoffed. "Why, I –"

"STOP!" I yelled mentally.

Erzsébet made me pick up the PVA and call Cwia. I knew she'd be raring to kick somebody's ass, so it was good she answered when her line rang. She'd need my support and protection to make it through this.

"Can you believe the bullshit they're saying about me?" Cwia groused.

"I know. Sorry, it's my fault. I feel like shit. I hate the way the media sensationalizes the nanobot issue to sell news. Hopefully, people will forget about it when something more interesting pops up."

"I hope so. God, can you believe people buy this witchcraft bullshit? It's the twenty-first century, for crying out loud!"

I wanted to tell Cwia more about Erzsébet, but I could feel her block me as soon as I thought that.

"Just stay out of sight for a few days. In fact, maybe we'll get someone to manage the gym for a few weeks while we take a nice vacation somewhere they've never heard of boxing."

"Sounds good," Cwia said. "Keep me posted, boss."

But I didn't believe fiery, redheaded Cwia would meekly stay out of sight. Like Erzsébet, she didn't take any guff.

To add insult to injury, Erzsébet started surfing the internet on the PVA after Cwia and I disconnected. "These witchcraft accusations are a little too close to home," she said, watching some newsfeed headlines about the match scroll past. "That exorcism priest is riling people up with his talk about the gates of hell. He claims the only reason you're world champion is because you are 'possessed.' Maybe I should get out of Dodge and go to Transylvania where I'll be safe."

Erzsébet loved that "get out of Dodge" line ever since she discovered American Western movies. And I loved the bit about Transylvania being safe, what with all the Dracula lore I watched in horror movies growing up.

"Oh, that gives me lots of confidence about my own safety, seeing how you're in my body," I teased her. "What's the matter, I'm not good enough for you?"

I didn't pay any attention to Erzsébet's answer, figuring she was just venting. I persuaded her to lay low and stay in the suite for the next two days. On day three, I decided to venture downstairs for breakfast and then outside for a good run in the Commons, as I'd done many days during my pre-championship training. The way people stopped to stare as I jogged by made me think Erzsébet's plan was spot on. It just might be a good idea to head for Europe until things blew over. Cwia could come along. It might distract Erzsébet from focusing on me. Maybe I could make Cwia aware of my predicament somehow and figure out a way to end my captivity.

The media stuff kept snowballing because Father O'Malley wouldn't shut his trap. In addition to jawing about my possession by Erzsébet, he gained a following by claiming that the Great Goddesses of Virtue, the world's largest organization of neo-pagan witches, was the power behind both Erzsébet's possession and the misconception that Cwia healed my injuries. Despite the triumph of medical science that reworked my body, some people started to consider me "raised from the dead" and rather than associate this with something positive like Jesus raising Lazurus, they compared me to Frankenstein. Yeah, my original fear.

O'Malley was sounding more and more like a fire and brimstone fundamentalist preacher than a Catholic priest. I don't see why in the world the Church would continue to endorse him and his controversial claims, but I guess the Church approved of his casting paganism in an evil light. The anti-witchcraft position was catching on in the Irish, Italian, and Latino populations of Boston and propelling O'Malley to worldwide fame. Reporters never seemed to grow tired of interviewing him claiming he would send the demon that possessed Jim Jackson back to hell if given the chance. Did he really care about helping me or did he have a hidden agenda?

I was beginning to think I was better off to send Erzsébet back to wherever she came from my damn self. Sometimes, I had to admit, I almost liked having her around now. Of course, she probably planted that thought!

To add insult to injury, Aziz Alhason Abbas filed a protest with the boxing commission, claiming that I knew the nanobots would continue to heal any injuries I sustained, citing the unfair advantage. He also got on the occult bandwagon and claimed I used witchcraft to win the fight. After a short deliberation, the Commission announced they would consider his request.

Anybody with a message could easily gather a crowd at Boston Commons. Erzsébet insisted that I listen to Father O'Malley on a talk radio show the morning after the Commission's announcement. He said he'd speak at the Commons that night.

There was no way in hell I'd go down there. I didn't even want to watch the old blowhard now that he was ranting about witches, but Erzsébet wanted to keep an eye on O'Malley. Joe was also keeping tabs on the situation and said he'd call me. Erzsébet made me pick up the PVA and found some link for a video in the Boston Commons. When I opened it, the film showed a crowd waiting for O'Malley to speak. Some were in a party mood, passing around bottles – part of the appeal of gathering over there was the drinking and carousing.

The handheld camera seemed to bounce around and then focused on O'Malley. He appeared as usual, dressed in his black clothes and clerical collar. He looked different, the way he walked with a confident swagger, his eyes blazing with an interior fire. Maybe fame went to his head. The crowd quieted down respectfully and loud applause greeted him when he stood on a bench and started speaking.

"It's an outrage, it's a sin, it should be illegal to allow a man to freely walk the streets of any city when he's possessed by a witch," he shouted. "Great Goddesses of Virtue is what witchcraft is called today, ladies and gentlemen. Wicca is what witchcraft is called today. Just look at who Jackson chose for his cutman. A woman named Cwia. Move the letters around and you get W-I-C-A. Don't try to tell me this is a coincidence. Don't try to tell me Jackson didn't use her magick. Witchcraft is the most popular expression of devil worship and is disguised as neo-paganism. It's the fastest-growing religion in the United States. Practitioners are reviving ancient pagan practices and beliefs. They're adapting them to contemporary life before our very eyes. The result is that not one of you is safe from their evil."

I sighed and tried to put the PVA down, but Erzsébet made me turn up the volume. The camera zoomed in from a long shot to O'Malley's face.

". . . That's right; the devil is a lot smarter than we give him credit for. He doesn't want anyone to know his minion controls you. We must stop those gates of hell from opening. In order to do that, I must cast out that demon Erzsébet Báthory before it's too late—"

"Send her back to hell," someone shouted.

"Witch, witch, witch," the crowd chanted as they had during one of the preliminary fights at the gym.

This broadcast segued to someone carrying a big sign with a picture of Cwia and the slogan "WHICH CORNER HAD THE WITCH IN IT?"

The gathering was sounding more and more like a diatribe against women. Now I understood better about what happened to Erzsébet after her husband died. In this case, the media couldn't crucify Jim Jackson, but Cwia and Erzsébet were easy prey.

I wanted to stop looking at this stuff, but Erzsébet wanted to see more. The film went blurry with static for a moment and when the picture cleared, the scene seethed with anger. The camera focused on a group at one side of the crowd. Dressed in white and carrying more signs about witchcraft, this mob began to chant, "Down with witchcraft, stop all witches."

To my surprise, the camera moved away and zeroed in on Cwia. Her distinctive mane of wavy red hair stood out like a flag. She appeared to have entered the Boston Common on her way somewhere else. As she passed the back of the crowd, someone yelled out, "There she is, there she is."

The crowd turned to watch her hurrying toward the subway.

The mob in white began chanting louder. "Witch, witch, witch!"

"I lost a month's pay because of you, witch bitch," yelled a man dressed in white robes like Jesus.

Cwia stopped walking and turned to face the crowd. "Who are you calling a witch bitch? Step over here and say that," she taunted.

The group kept yelling. Some people in the main crowd joined in. Father O'Malley stopped speaking to watch. Two policemen patrolling the front of the crowd nearest O'Malley began to stride toward the disturbance.

Cwia let her temper get the best of her and waded into the crowd. She surged toward the man in robes who seemed to have started it all. She laid the guy down with a kickboxing maneuver. When others, both men and women went after her, she left them in various states of pain, conscious and unconscious.

Maybe if the mob were smaller, Cwia might have dispersed them. Close to a hundred people surrounded her when some from the larger crowd joined in. She bent both knees and raised her arms in a defensive martial arts pose.

Someone yelled, "String her up!"

A skinhead with tattoos wrapped around his skull grabbed the rope belt from around the Jesus guy's waist and fashioned a noose. He motioned to a man and a woman in front of Cwia to rush her as a distraction, and as they did, he approached from behind, threw the belt over Cwia's head and pulled it tight around her neck. She didn't have a chance against this three-hundred-pound hulk. A woman screamed in the background. "They're killing her!" a man yelled.

The policemen dashed through the crowd toward Cwia, brandishing nightsticks. I jumped out of my chair, put on my shoes, and headed for the door. Erzsébet stopped me. "The incident's over, remember? The speech started nearly an hour ago. This is news, no? The police are there."

"I don't care, I'm going for Cwia." I tried to put the PVA down and reach for the door, but she wouldn't let me move.

"It's not over–" Erzsébet made me stare again at the PVA.

"Oh, my God," I said, looking at the URL. "BVine.com – this is some kind of livestream. This isn't a news recording. It's happening right now."

I tried to leave again but Erzsébet seemed mesmerized by the incident and wouldn't let me move.

The camera bounced around and the sound of the cameraperson's heavy breathing became audible for a moment. Cwia's eyes bulged as she tried to resist. The rope prevented her from screaming, but she fought her heart out, twisting and turning, kicking and thrashing. The big skinhead and two other pale, skinny men in denim jeans and jackets flung the rope over a tree branch and hauled Cwia up, lifting her on her toes. Her face reddened and she held her hands to her throat as she struggled to free herself.

In the background, the chanting started anew. "Burn the witch, burn the witch, burn the witch."

The mob surged forward again and broke branches from surrounding trees. They attempted to start a fire, but the wood was too green and they had nothing to kindle it. The camera turned toward the officers, frantically swinging their batons and shoving their way toward Cwia. In the distance, the sound of sirens could be heard over the crowd's screams and curses. Opposite the cops, a group from the main crowd fought their way toward Cwia from the opposite direction, also trying to push the thugs back.

When the camera turned back, the sight sickened me. The skinhead who put the noose around Cwia's neck drenched her with a can of lighter fluid and bent down with a lighter. The ankle-length boots Cwia wore emitted a puff of smoke, smoldered, and then burst into flames that licked at her jeans and rose upward. Her jacket and then her mane of hair burst into a ball of fire. Still conscious, her face blistered and she twisted and turned in agony, her toes still digging at the ground. The thug pulled the rope tighter and drew her flaming body up until it went limp and the flames surged up the rope toward the tree limb.

It was all over in a moment. I would never forgive Erzsébet nor myself. I should have gone for Cwia. I could have been there in less than two minutes. Erzsébet, not Cwia, should be burned as a witch.

Tears of shame slipped down my cheeks as I tried to toss the PVA across the room.

"Jim, I know you hate me, but look. Look! Look what haters do to women!"

I grit my teeth and looked again.

"Cops! Run!" someone yelled off-screen.

A contingent of Boston's finest mounted officers spurred their horses toward the mob, and in one case, nearly trampled a man who chose to challenge the officer rather than retreat. With batons flying, the policemen decked a few more idiots who tried to resist.

But they were too late. Cwia looked like little more than a dark, limp effigy.

"Call an ambulance!" A police sergeant dismounted, cut Cwia down, lay her gently on the grass, and loosened the noose. He searched her neck for a pulse and then gingerly opened her blackened lips to try to give her CPR. He gazed around and looked for someone to help him, waving a over fire department EMT, who rushed from one of the emergency vehicles just arrived in a flash of red, white, and blue light and a clash of screeching sirens.

The camera panned away toward the backs of fleeing bystanders – O'Malley was nowhere in sight and the platform he had stood on was empty. Officers lined the skinhead and three of his cronies up along a low retaining wall with their hands cuffed in white plastic zip ties behind their backs.

The EMT looked Cwia over and shook his head. "Too late," he said. "Too late. Do they really think she's a witch?"

"Mob mentality. Someone yells witch and the rest of the morons pick it up."

The EMT and his partner, a short African-American woman with cornrowed hair, hefted a gurney from the back of their vehicle. She pulled a folded sheet from atop the gurney and unfolded it over Cwia.

"Step back, now. Clear the scene for Homicide," the Sergeant ordered.

Erzsébet shuddered. My heart broke in two.

"Stuff like this happens in third world countries – witch hunts, religious government crackdowns. Never thought I'd see it here," the EMT said.

"Unbelievable," the cop said. "I watched that Abbas-Jackson fight and I couldn't believe it when his cuts and bruises healed before my eyes. It was spooky, sure, but Jackson and his people looked just as surprised as everyone else. He's a cryonic man, all right."

Just then, the Sergeant noticed the livestreamer with a PVA camera. He ran toward it with his hand out until his face filled the screen like a big moon, and then everything went black.

≈Chapter 21

Cwia's tragic demise made dramatic news. Television channels broadcast continuous reports about the spirit of the Salem witch trials returning to Boston. Often the newscasts included footage of Cwia tending to me between rounds in the championship fight. I couldn't bear to watch any of it.

"Cwia was my best friend. If you make me watch this shit again, I'll go to O'Malley."

Erzsébet didn't laugh at my threat when she made me turn on the television, but even so, she gave me no choice but to watch. I managed to force my eyes shut when a time-lapse clip of my injuries healing during the fight streamed across the screen, but she wouldn't let me plug my ears to avoid hearing the voiceover.

"The Salem witchcraft hysteria leading to the trials of 1692 is well-known to the public, but few people recall the episodes of suspected witchcraft and what was termed "diabolical possession" in colonial Boston. Witchcraft and possession hysteria have come to light again in the twenty-first century with the murder of Cwia Alexander by an unruly mob in the Boston Commons. Employed by world heavyweight champion and native son Jim Jackson, also known internationally as the "Cryonic Man," Alexander's position as Jackson's "cutman," and Jackson's high-tech cellular healing treatments after a cryonic preservation, exposed both to accusations of witchcraft and demonic possession. Fueled by the growing number of converts to pagan nature religions and a misunderstanding of advanced science, Boston has again grown wary of the occult.

"Alexander's death may be linked to a series of fourteen murders – twelve women and two men – committed between 2011 and 2025. Shortly after rumors and accusations surfaced in local communities about alleged practitioners of black magick, parish priests or local ministers approached some individuals who were later found murdered, some in a ritual fashion. City prosecutors still lack sufficient evidence to charge anyone in connection with these deaths. However, four members of a conservative Moral Right group were apprehended at the scene and arrested as the prime suspects in the Alexander 'witchcraft murder.'"

As I opened my eyes, the voiceover stopped and a clip of a young Asian reporter began to roll. The reporter stopped Chief City Prosecutor Rowan Willson on the Boston Municipal Courthouse Steps as he exited the building.

"Mr. Willson, sir, will the City of Boston and the State of Massachusetts charge local parish priest Father O'Malley for verbally inciting the mob responsible for Alexander's murder?"

"The public can be certain that we're exploring that possibility," he said briskly, "but I'm not at liberty to discuss an ongoing investigation."

The reporter attempted to ask another question but the camera showed Willson turn his back and trot down the stairs.

Below the news clip, the breaking news scroll read: *Bostonians claim Cwia Alexander levitates in midair before hanging.*

"Looks like Salem all over again," Erzsébet said.

"Plenty of people are too dumb or too emotional to distinguish between science and witchcraft, I guess. I've heard about all the climate denialists earlier in the century and these witchcraft alarmists are probably the same types."

"The ignorant are always with us. And I'm so sorry my presence stirred this up. Still, I don't understand how such a gruesome murder could happen here. In my country, this wouldn't be allowed."

Erzsébet's claim of lynching not happening in central Europe was laughable, considering the region's long history of violence. I understood why Cwia's death frightened Erzsébet, but the loss for me was greater. If O'Malley hadn't spouted off so much and this bitch hadn't taken over my body, then Cwia would still be here. I'd love to beat him bloody, I thought, picturing myself pounding O'Malley to death in a boxing ring.

"Don't be stupid," Erzsébet countered. "That's just what he wants you to do, so he can prove what he says is true. Instead, you should offer a large reward for the apprehension and conviction of any thugs who escaped the police. Maybe if the public takes this act seriously, the government will indict O'Malley. At the very least, they'll be more aggressive about rounding up the others responsible for Cwia's death."

I'd offer a reward *and* I'd get even some day, I swore. The fight truly challenged me, despite the nanobots. Joe and Dr. Remus appeared on "XXVI," a massively popular national talk show, to explain how the cellular treatments had healed my cuts and bruises, not witchcraft. They made it clear that even the rejuvenation team was astonished the nanobots remained active in my body. Remus also explained that though this might confer some small advantage in an athletic competition, the fast healing was in no way a guarantee that I could defeat Abbas. "Jim Jackson had years of training and took a lot of hard knocks before winning this championship, just like any ordinary fighter," Dr. Remus said. This clip aired repeatedly on national television venues as a counterpoint to Father O'Malley's propaganda.

"Suck it up, you can handle it. It's only a damn athletic award," Erzsébet sneered. "You're getting a taste of the medicine I got so long ago."

But I continued to whine. On top of possibly losing my championship belt, I now had to worry about Joe and Audrey's safety and even poor Emily's as well.

Erzsébet let me call Zoloti for legal advice.

"You earned the championship," Zoloti said. "Why should you care what anybody says now? If the Commission wants to strip your title, it will take months to resolve. You can try holding your ground. But there's a possibility that if you resign now, they'll let you keep the belt and title as the retired champion. You'll have to take a risk either way, Jim."

I called Joe and popped into his office at NanoTechnology Restorative Systems to meet him over lunch. Erzsébet was curious enough about my concerns to butt out and let me do the talking.

"So you and the team had no idea the nanobots would keep working this long? Am I imagining that I didn't have an unfair advantage over Abbas?"

"We hadn't even thought that far ahead about the nanobots, Dad. Our only concern was to repair any damage caused by the tumor and the cryonic preservation so we could revive you. We saw no evidence after our animal experiments to indicate that the nanobots could continue to work. In fact, they appeared to cease activity as soon as healing and revival were complete. Hell, if they continue to operate indefinitely, it may mean you're practically immortal."

Joe seemed real pleased with this immortality idea. For me, it sounded equivalent to my nightmare of becoming helpless.

"That doesn't answer my second question, though. I hate to think what would happen if someone overheard this conversation."

Joe went silent for a moment. "Sheesh, I guess you're right. I'm going to have to think more about this."

Erzsébet quivered with delight over the "I" word, but she knew as well as I did that my gig was up. If word got out about this so-called immortality, my goose was cooked. I'd either end up like Cwia or become the NTRS and CF guinea pig again.

I sent an electronic letter of resignation to the Boxing Commission that afternoon. The Commission accepted my resignation and allowed me to stay on the books as the oldest heavyweight champion ever. The decision only took a two-day deliberation.

Except for not being able to get Cwia's death out of my mind, I relaxed a bit for the first time since the fight. What next?

"Jim Jackson," Erzsébet said, "Your dream is over. It is time for mine to begin. I only agreed to let you make decisions about boxing. I want to return to Slovakia, and if possible, purchase my castle."

"What about your purpose here? When will you accomplish that goal and set me free?"

"My purpose may find me better at home than here," she said.

I had to agree it looked like a good time to leave the United States. I could keep a lower profile in Europe and that seemed like a good thing for my family. Out of sight, out of mind.

Even so, Father O'Malley continued to encourage people to revile me. According to him, I was still in league with the Devil. I couldn't help but wonder if I really was, by proxy, because of Erzsébet.

I reserved a seat on a red-eye flight to Budapest and called Joe. "I think it's best if I go to Europe for a while. Just until all this witchcraft stuff quiets down. I won't come over to say goodbye because those nuts out there might follow me and make trouble for you and Audrey. I'm going to miss you. I hope we'll spend more time together soon."

Joe was silent for a moment. "I've been thinking about doing more research. The Cryonics Foundation is willing to fund a study about your body's continued healing. We need you here."

"Sure, for experimentation," Erzsébet made me say.

Joe sighed. "I can understand your feelings, Dad. It's probably time you took a vacation. When are you leaving?"

"Tonight. It's better if we, I mean, it's better *I* slip away unnoticed. Zoloti has a buyer for the gym and will transfer the deed tomorrow."

Somehow, the media got wind of my plans. Probably tracked me buying airfare with my PVA or online from my application for an electronically expedited passport. What was supposed to be a quiet trip to the airport became a circus, with the avenue leading from my hotel to the freeway lined with middle-of-the-night spectators waiting to see the Devil.

I'd called Zoloti to send Mark and the VTK2500 to avoid recognition. The ruse didn't work as the paparazzi caught me entering the VTK a little more than two hours before the flight. They tweeted, twitched, and sputtered the news ahead electronically, and passersby gathered to pelt the aircar with garbage and bottles from freeway overpasses all the way to Logan International Airport. Erzsébet worried a mob might block the road somewhere and overturn the car. I half hoped they would so I could get my hands on a few of them. But we made it to the international terminal at Logan without stopping.

Things sure had changed in fifty years, particularly the security. Despite the hour, hordes of sleepy-looking business people and families queued up to pass through the security checkpoint. Of all the modern marvels, the most interesting to Erzsébet was the amount of luggage passengers carried for flights.

"An army of ten thousand men in my day didn't carry as much while campaigning with my husband," she said, staring through a window at a pile of luggage stacked near a departing jet.

"Just wait until you see the luggage carousels for arriving flights when we get to Europe."

I felt her quiver with anticipation. When we finally went through the series of X-ray and Iris-ID scanners and boarded the plane, Erzsébet demanded the best seat on the airplane.

The attendant peered at my boarding pass. "Why don't you just rent a private jet," he said sarcastically.

"Why didn't I think of that?" she said.

So of course, she insisted I turn around, forfeit my airfare, and lease a private jet. At least I'd have some privacy. Who knows what might have happened on a flight with over three hundred people aboard?

At the specialty flight desk, an attractive young man who pleased Erzsébet no end helped me with the transaction. "Your aircraft is one of the newest generation of hydrogen-fueled planes that is faster and safer than the older fossil-fueled aircraft," he said.

An electric cart picked us up at the ticket desk and drove us to a hangar where a Lear jet clone awaited us. As we boarded the craft, I couldn't take my eyes off the svelte blonde welcoming me with a big smile and a pair of equally big hooters that put a grin on my kisser.

"Hello, Mr. Jackson. I'm Gloria Stefanowski, your flight hostess. If there's anything you want, anything at all, I'm here to serve," she said, looking me up and down.

"Tramp," Erzsébet complained to me privately.

We chose a reclining seat near a window. As the engines accelerated with a quiet hum, Erzsébet nearly gave me a heart attack. Terrified of the quiet but alien noise, her panic caused adrenaline to surge in my body. The plane immediately taxied down the runway, pausing only for a few moments before being cleared for take-off. The speed increased her fear. When we left the ground, my heart rate must have soared to two hundred beats a minute.

Gloria emerged from a galley with a tray of drinks and snacks. "I've watched all your televised fights, Mr. Jackson. May I have your autograph, please?" She handed me a cloth napkin and a pen and when our fingers accidentally touched, a spark passed between us that even Erzsébet could feel.

"Calm down, Jim Jackson," Erzsébet said.

As I scribbled my name and best wishes, Gloria put her hand on my shoulder asked if everything was okay.

"Ask the pilot how long the flight will take," Erzsébet said, interrupting our connection.

Gloria laughed. "There's no pilot."

"What!" Erzsébet exclaimed.

What the heck? I wondered.

"That's why we suggest that a host or hostess fly with passengers on their first private flights. The company feels you may need a little human guidance if you've never flown on an UAV autoflight before."

Gloria handed me a goblet filled with a blue liquid. "I think you'll like this."

The drink looked so refreshing with the crushed ice and sugary rim that I figured it must be okay, or she wouldn't have given it to me. I nearly emptied it with one swallow, surprised by the warm feeling that surged through my body.

"Wow, what kind of margarita was that?" Erzsébet had grown fond of the margaritas served in the Latino lounge at the Nine Zero.

Gloria laughed. "It's not a margarita, but it looks like one. This is the charter's specialty drink."

"Oh," Erzsébet let me say. "Well, then."

"I'm so lucky that you decided to take a private flight. It gave me a chance to meet you," Gloria said, batting her eyelashes at me.

Erzsébet didn't respond because she seemed to be having another panic attack. My pulse raced so fast I thought my heart might explode.

Gloria noticed my discomfort. "We're now gaining altitude and we'll automatically level out around 30,000 feet for the big journey across the pond."

I peered out the window, but could see nothing but a few stars and the vast blackness of the Atlantic below.

Erzsébet suddenly disappeared and I wondered if a soul or spirit could faint.

My emotions soared. Was I free at last? I searched my pocket for my PVA to call Joe and explain exactly how Erzsébet had invaded my mind and controlled me.

But Gloria suddenly sat on my lap.

Startled, I gazed into her elfin blue eyes.

She gave me another of her seductive smiles. "I can feel that the mood enhancer has already taken effect. . ."

"Mood what?

"Oh you know, the drink you like so much. It's the rage now, Moody's Elixir. Pink for girls and blue for boys. It makes air time so much more pleasant. Everyone who hires a UAV gets a bottle gratis."

I forgot about finding the PVA as Gloria leaned forward to kiss me.

Chapter 22

Once Gloria's lips touched mine, I lost control. I couldn't stop myself and Erzsébet didn't stop me either. I pressed my lips against Gloria's soft, giving mouth, the most passionate kiss I'd laid on anyone since Emily. Erzsébet faded into the background as I lost myself in Gloria's soft curves. Within minutes, we shed our clothes and shared our most intimate secrets. Perhaps the drink intensified the experience – at any rate, I became unusually tired and fell asleep soon after our lovemaking.

I awoke as the jet's tires touched ground. Erzsébet was back and I kicked myself for not calling Joe when the opportunity arose. I rationalized my disappointment away by thinking if those high-priced doctors couldn't understand how Erzsébet controlled me, then how would Joe be able to understand? He, like the others, scoffed at possession and believed I suffered some sort of harmless psychosis caused by the cryonic preservation.

I gathered from her thoughts that Erzsébet had temporarily relinquished control from a combination of her fear of heights and the sensation of flying through the air at great speed without human control, exaggerated by the effect of the Moody's Elixir. I hoped there was a way to terrify her again – next time I vowed not to become distracted and to get free of her. Maybe I'd even buy a case of Moody's Elixir if she'd let me.

Erzsébet made no response to these thoughts and suddenly had me squirming in the seat as we approached the international terminal. Gloria slipped me her PVA number and I promised to call her. I expected Erzsébet either to take a verbal jab at Gloria or to want to talk about our sex, but she was distracted by arriving home.

"I cannot wait to walk on my home soil again," Erzsébet purred to Gloria in my voice. "I can feel it calling me. My favorite memories of home revolve around nature. I used to travel into mountainous heights with the Earth's most incredible scenery. Pine forests, meadows, running deer, and natural thermal springs that can cure almost any ailment are just a few of the mountain delights in the Carpathians."

"It sounds like you'll enjoy getting away from city life," Gloria said.

"I hope Slovakia has not become anything like America," Erzsébet said as we prepared to deboard the UAV. "Have you ever visited my castle at Čachtice?"

Gloria stared at me, startled by the odd question. "Oh, you're quite a joker, Jim," she said, laughing. "There are many beautiful castle ruins near Budapest in both Hungary and Slovakia," Gloria said. "I'm sure you'll enjoy them."

As we passed through the terminal, I noticed a crowd waiting at one end. For me?

A roar erupted from the crowd when I became close enough for them to recognize me. I expected garbage to fly at me at any moment, as in America. But the tone wasn't jeering, it was a cheer. Some young girls in national dress tossed flower petals from baskets at my feet. The crowd treated me like a homecoming hero. I didn't know that Hungarians followed American boxing enough to recognize me.

"The cheers aren't for your boxing skills," Erzsébet informed me. "They're for me. It's a celebrated fact throughout Hungary, Slovakia, Romania, and the Czech Republic that I've been reincarnated in America."

"It doesn't mean anything to them that your previous life was filled

CRYONIC MAN

with murder and torture?"

"Get serious, Jim. To modern Transylvanians, Vlad Tepes III is a national hero, a great warrior who defended his homeland from the Turks."

"You think that madman is okay?"

"Many of the stories about him are exaggerated or false, like the stories about my evil deeds."

As far as I knew, Vlad's cruelty wasn't confined to impaling people: he decapitated, blinded, strangled, hanged, burned, boiled, skinned, and otherwise sliced and diced people. He rammed stakes into the breasts of mothers and thrust their babies on top. When his armies invaded the Germans of Transylvania, Vlad's army hacked people to bits like cabbage.

One legend was particularly appalling. One year Vlad asked the old, the ill, the lame, the poor, the blind, and the vagabonds of his country to a feast in a large dining hall in the capital city. At the conclusion of the meal, he ended their misery by burning down the hall. Vlad Dracula's problem solving skills had probably inspired Adolf Hitler.

Once I squeezed through the crowd of Erzsébet's adoring fans, she hailed a cab and ordered the cab driver, in Hungarian, to take me to the best hotel in Budapest. I still found the ability to speak and understand foreign languages because of Erzsébet amazing. She glowed with happiness on the ride to the hotel, soaking in the city's wide, tree-lined boulevards and ornate buildings.

"Budapest is one of Europe's most beautiful cities," she said. "With so many buildings from my era gone, I want to curse those responsible for destroying the old churches and other beautiful architecture."

At the hotel, I requested the penthouse, but Erzsébet remembered me putting my leg over the railing and interrupted me to request a room on a lower floor. The hotel had equally luxurious rooms on each floor. Used to opulence by now, the ritzy hotel and our lifestyle didn't affect me anymore. Erzsébet encouraged me to take full advantage of everything: massages, manicures and pedicures, hair styling, and custom fittings by a tailor for European suits.

Erzsébet insisted that we immediately hire a limousine and driver to take us to the Slovakian village where the ruins of the Castle Čachtice, known as Cséjthe in old Hungarian, sat atop a steep hill. We traveled on the motorway until Nové Mesto, where we had lunch.

"Just follow the signs to Čachtice," Erzsébet told the driver afterward.

We soon came to the village situated between the Danubian Lowland and the Little Carpathians. Erzsébet's first venture was a visit to the old Nádasdy family burials at the village church. She guarded her mind and emotions as she viewed these. I did not know at the time that the final resting place of her remains is a mystery, because the townspeople had demanded that her bones be removed from this sacred ground. But I imagined she must have a sense of triumph over death as she pondered her previous mortality.

Erzsébet pointed to the impressive remains of the castle. "This is what is left of Castle Čachtice. On the other side of the hill is a village called Vrbové. Čachtice and the surrounding lands and villages were a wedding gift from the Nádasdy family upon my marriage to Ferenc. Can you believe the government declared this a national reserve? They say the hill is covered with rare plants. I think they declared it a reserve because they didn't want the world to know how much I am revered in this country because of my embarrassing international reputation as 'The Blood Countess.'"

I gazed around at the rolling agricultural lands interspersed with the jagged outcroppings of the Carpathians and then at the Castle Čachtice. The beautiful land remained but the passing years had taken their toll and left the once grand castle in ruins. After the driver took us as close as he could to the top of the hill, Erzsébet steered me toward the dungeon-like rooms of the decaying tower where she was held on house arrest, walled in to spend the final four years of her life.

Her mixed emotions of gratitude, fear, happiness, and anger flowed through my body in a confusing snarl. She ran my shaking hands over the walls to search for something. Bewildered, I had no idea what I was searching for until I felt a small, round hole with the

CRYONIC MAN

tip of one finger. About the diameter of a ten-penny nail, it appeared to be deep, as though someone had driven a nail into the solid stone and then removed it. I kept searching and found three more holes in the same wall, making a total of four, one hole in each of the four corners, evenly spaced.

Erzsébet exuded relief to find the four holes, but I didn't know why. "Let's take a break," she said.

So we toured the rest of the massive, crumbling castle. Five-star accommodation of the seventeenth century convinced me that twenty-first-century life is much better.

When Erzsébet tired of the ruin, I asked the driver to take us back to the village. At the foot of the hill in the center of the village stood a small building dedicated to the memory of Erzsébet Báthory. It appeared to be a museum of some sort. I could feel the pleasure emanating from Erzsébet's mind as she looked it over.

Word of my visit spread. Many residents of the village gathered to cheer Erzsébet, a great swell of voices that seemed louder than a championship fight crowd. Some of the goodwill, I hoped, was gratitude for the publicity I'd brought to these tourist attractions.

The mayor, Ioan Ilionescu, strolled over to greet me – well, Erzsébet. He insisted that I move from our hotel in the city and stay in the recently restored manor house owned by the village. Ilionescu proudly recited a short version of the castle's history. Then he guided me to a quiet spot away from the other tourists.

"I hope you're not offended if I ask if it's true that the spirit of Erzsébet Báthory resides in this body standing before me?" he asked softly, visibly nervous.

"I'm not offended by the question, and yes, it's true. But whatever you do, don't call me Erzsébet or Báthory. My name is Jim Jackson."

I gave the mayor a stern look so he wouldn't forget.

Ioan Ilionescu took a small step forward. "I'm so happy I could kiss you!"

He looked like he'd make an attempt, so I stepped back from his reach.

"The esteemed Báthory family is revered in our village." He explained that even though accused of great cruelty in oral folklore and written history, and despite the fact that some of the distant descendants bearing her or her husband's name do not acknowledge her, "the Countess Báthory is from a family of great warriors."

"Yes, so I've been told by Erzsébet. Like Dracula, she says. In the States, we think of him as a vampire," I said. "And we call her Lady Dracula and worse." I suspected the mayor simply liked the tourism value of the Báthory story and my visit.

Ilionescu found this hilarious and tossed his head back in a rumbling belly laugh. "Cruelty was far more common in those days. Do you know that Vlad Tepes III, the Dracula of your legend, adopted the method of impaling criminals and raising them aloft in his town square for all to see? Almost any crime, from lying and stealing to killing was punished by impalement. Why, he was so confident in the effectiveness of his law that he placed a golden cup on display in the central square of Tirgoviste. Thirsty travelers could use the cup but it had to remain on the square. It was never stolen and remained entirely unmolested. Crime and corruption ceased. Commerce and culture thrived throughout Vlad's reign."

I didn't know the story about the cup. Maybe Erzsébet was also cruel for a reason, as she'd hinted. Maybe she just enjoyed lying to me.

She suddenly interrupted my thoughts. "See, I told you people here view Vlad Tepes as a hero to this very day," she said.

We had dinner with Mayor Ilionescu that evening. He questioned Erzsébet about village families in the early 1600s.

"My servants were peasants from this village," Erzsébet said. "They spoke a Slavic tongue, full of gutturals and hard consonants unknown to me. I struggled for the longest time to communicate with them. Katalin Beneczky, my trusted servant, helped with many things, including the language barrier."

I absorbed this history for the first time along with the mayor.

"What do they say about her cats?" I asked.

Ilionescu looked at me timidly, shifting in his chair.

"I heard that the Countess used these animals as her wicked emissaries, sending them out to attack her enemies."

"What if I told you the story was true?" Erzsébet said, through me. The mayor seemed to accept the oddities of two minds speaking through one body and one voice.

Ilionescu didn't comment.

I wanted to say *cat's got your tongue*, but Erzsébet wouldn't let me.

Erzsébet seemed to enjoy the mayor's discomfort but deftly changed the subject. "Mayor, I knew a family named Ilionescu in Cséjthe at the turn of the sixteenth century. Two brothers and a sister who often came to the castle to assist me. Likely they were your ancestors, no?"

I thought this was an innocent aside but the mayor seemed shaken by this revelation. I realized she was hinting that his ancestors possibly participated in torturing the inhabitants of this very village. His wary behavior seemed proof enough that fear as well as acceptance of Erzsébet Báthory still existed in Čachtice.

Erzsébet grew more talkative, perhaps because of the red wine served during dinner.

"You know, Mayor Ilionescu, when I first arrived here, I was barely literate in the ancient arts until my husband initiated me into the occult. He taught me that Occultism has its roots in ancient Babylonian and Egyptian lore, augmented by Jewish mysticism."

She took a long drink from the goblet I held throughout the conversation.

"Yes, yes, I've heard many stories of your husband," the mayor said, refilling his goblet. "I trust you viewed many of his artifacts in our little museum at the bottom of the hill. By the way, the museum is dedicated to you, Countess Báthory. I hope you enjoyed your visit."

Erzsébet nodded at him graciously. She already knew the information the mayor supplied, but she let him ramble on anyway. I learned quite a bit about Erzsébet during the conversation, but this created more questions for me than the new information answered. I'd begun to relax with Erzsébet, but now she seemed nothing more than a master manipulator.

When I returned to the manor house, dozens of women of all ages stood around it, waiting for Erzsébet. Not only had she somehow become revered as a national heroine, she was quickly embraced as the most powerful witch who had ever lived by these modern pagans.

The leader of this mass of women prostrated herself before me.

"We've come to pay homage to the mistress of Čachtice. Please accept our offerings." She rose and pointed to the thousands of flowers spread around the perimeter of the manor house.

"Offerings for what?" Erzsébet asked.

"For your guidance and intercession with the spirits," she replied. "My sisters and I stand firm and proud as daughters of the Mother Goddess. Long ago, we chose to practice the traditions of the craft. You are spoken of with great reverence in covens throughout the region, and now that we've found you, you will be revered in covens around the world. We know you have enemies and we offer our combined powers to help you defeat any who may wish you harm."

Overcome with emotion, Erzsébet caused my body to walk shakily to the top step of the manor house front entrance, allowing me to experience her thoughts and emotions. Clearly, she was deeply moved by these women's reverence. From the top step, I turned to face the throng of supporters. In a voice I never knew I possessed, Erzsébet spoke. She must have used some sort of magick to produce that much volume from my lungs. She reminded them how cruelly pagan practitioners had been treated, and then continued to give a lengthy speech.

"Because we chose to walk another path on life's spiritual journey, society perceives us as evil. I am personally accused of being vile, yet I've treated my associates with respect and kindness."

I wondered how this could be true, considering all the testimony her contemporaries had offered about her alleged crimes.

"Since the conception of the Christian Church until this day, one is to believe only in God or go straight to hell. I respect the tenets of Christianity and their supreme deity, but I know there are many other deities and that I'm not going to hell."

I had to agree with her statement. I couldn't deny it after my experiences on the "other side." The Christian God seemed to exist in a universe of many other deities.

"It's difficult to understand why so many people have no idea what so-called witches do or don't do in this age of information," Erzsébet said. "There is abundant material about the goddess religions on the internet, and many attempts have been made to share the Gospel of Wicca and other Pagan traditions, but we're still perceived as servants of the Devil.

"I choose to do what's right because it is the right thing to do. As with others who practice the craft, I believe in the law of karma. I know what I give to this world I will reap as well. My creed is, 'If it harms none, do what you will.'

"My goddesses never threatened harm to drive me to do what is right and good. I am motivated by the natural love that lives within my heart. Love cleanses me, heals me, gives me strength, gives me hope, and builds my faith in myself."

I now questioned the wariness I'd felt at dinner. This speech was a revelation to me. I had no idea Erzsébet carried such ideals. My anger at her for hijacking me subsided whenever I noticed these spurts of compassion transcending her crude and bossy ways. Maybe she was different than the legends described her, or somehow became different on her journey to this century, as I had. After hearing her reveal her innermost thoughts to these women, I realized my best interests might be found with this strange being who invaded and conquered my body. Had we each caused the other to grow?

When Erzsébet finished her speech, the women applauded and began to disperse. No one seemed to mind that she was sheathed in the muscular body of a man with little knowledge of feminists and goddess religions.

The Pagan leader, a striking gray-haired woman with large amber eyes handed me an electronic business card with her PVA number on it.

"If you need help or anything at all, just touch this icon." She pointed to a symbol on the miniature, wafer-thin touch screen and shyly glanced at me before she turned and walked away.

Chapter 23

Still jet-lagged and exhausted, I removed my jacket, loosened my tie, and stretched out on the enormous carved bedstead dominating the bedroom suite at the Čachtice manor house. Erzsébet invited me to reminisce with her, recalling the day she arrived at the castle with Count Ferenc Nádasdy. I closed my eyes and listened, drifting near sleep.

"It was beneficial for Ferenc to carry the illustrious name of Báthory, so he kindly added my surname to his," Erzsébet explained.

"Though he was often away at war, Ferenc was an occult practitioner, and whenever he was home, he introduced me to the arts of astrology, alchemy, and ceremonial magick. He studied rites for evoking spiritual beings with other noble members of a well-informed group who believed that the science of ancient Egypt was the most sacred science. As it incorporated esoteric disciplines like magick and astrology with sciences such as mathematics and chemistry, they felt this unified philosophy rivaled, if not exceeded, the discipline of ordinary sixteenth- and seventeenth-century religion or science. But some Egyptian secrets are hidden by code and metaphor, and Ferenc believed he could unlock those secrets. The capabilities of the ancient Egyptians amazed both Ferenc and me."

Erzsébet's thoughts stopped abruptly as she spotted a large yellow toolbox left in a corner of the room by one of the workmen who'd spent the day readying the house. She directed me to get up and go to it. It looked heavy. I grabbed the handle and it rose into the air. Startled, I almost dropped it.

Erzsébet laughed. "It has an anti-gravity device built into the bottom," she said.

I'd never heard of such a thing. Sometimes she scared me with her knowledge of modern stuff she shouldn't understand. She insisted I look through the tools.

"How handy," she said. "We would have had to purchase some of these tools tomorrow."

I unlatched the toolbox and took out a hammer, a pry bar, four long, thin finish nails, and a long dowel shaped like an ice pick. I placed these items in a small gym bag, not knowing what use Erzsébet intended for them.

Erzsébet couldn't sleep and wouldn't let me sleep either. She rattled on and on about astrology and astronomy, flooring me with her vast knowledge. She laughed at my meager understanding of the subjects.

At least she was sharing, and I ended up knowing whatever she shared, I told her.

She anticipated returning to the castle tower in the morning and began to plan a way to make sure we weren't disturbed there. She finally quieted down and allowed me to sleep a couple of hours before dawn.

We went to the mayor's home early that morning. "Mayor Ilionescu, I have a request concerning the castle," I said. "I'm wondering if I could restrict anyone from entering it for a few hours today."

He gave me a puzzled look. "Why would you want to do that?"

"I want to photograph some areas in time exposures. If anyone walks near my setup and causes even the tiniest vibration, my pictures will be spoiled."

"Why don't you use one of the new floating recording devices that vibration doesn't affect?"

I didn't know what he was talking about, and this time, neither did Erzsébet.

"No sense in admitting our ignorance," she said.

I thoroughly agreed. I hated being perceived as stupid, probably because I often thought I was.

"I want to use twentieth-century equipment. That way my photos will have a more authentic look."

"Okay then," the mayor conceded. "The tour buses don't arrive until noon. You can have it all to yourself from eight until twelve."

I'm sure he also readily agreed because he probably hoped the photos would be published in some international magazine, thus increasing tourism to Čachtice. The mayor called the one limousine that serviced the town even though we could have walked.

Erzsébet felt disappointed when an antique 1999 Lincoln appeared with a uniformed driver who stank of mothballs.

"Load all the photo equipment in the car. Then drive us to the castle," she said with a sniff in her voice.

When we arrived at the castle and parked near the sign reading *Čachticky Hrad – Csejte Vára – Čachtice Castle* in Slovak, Hungarian, and English, she tipped the driver. "Stand by the car and if anyone approaches, honk the horn in long, loud bursts."

"Wouldn't it be easier if I just call your mobile device?" the driver asked.

"Just do as you are told," Erzsébet said curtly.

He was right, of course, but any idea she didn't think of, she wouldn't do. Erzsébet was a hardheaded bitch.

I hefted the photo equipment and gym bag up the hill and up a narrow staircase to the largest room in the tower, which was now missing a wall, but in her day bore only a tiny window and a slot where Erzsébet received her meals. If she wasn't insane when they walled her in, she must have been by the time she died there.

"Shut up and take the hammer and four finish nails from the bag, and hammer one nail into each of the four holes we found yesterday," Erzsébet said.

When I finished, she said, "Take the dowel and drive each nail as deep as it'll go."

When I'd driven the fourth nail, I heard a clicking sound like a lock turning when a section in the middle of the wall made a barely noticeable movement. Erzsébet instructed me to insert the edge of the pry bar into the small crack and try to pry the protruding rock out. I feverishly hammered and pried around this three-foot square rock for nearly an hour. Finally, it began to protrude far enough to get a proper grip on it. I wiggled it back and forth while pulling as hard as I could. When the heavy stone finally came loose, I dropped it to the floor, sweating from the effort. The dark, hollow space behind the wall crawled with an infestation of insects.

"Light a torch."

She read my thought, wondering why the hell we hadn't thought to bring a flashlight. She'd missed this fact in her excitement.

"You know when I lived here there was no such thing as a flashlight."

I trudged back to the limo, hoping the driver would have one.

"Do you have a flashlight, I mean a torch?" I said through the open driver's window.

Startled, the drowsy man opened his eyes and sat at attention. "Yes sir, I carry three torches at all times."

He opened the trunk. Lying inside was something like no flashlight I'd ever seen. One round-looking lens was attached to a head strap; another was no bigger than my little finger. The third was a six-inch square yellow cube. Not one of the things was big enough to hold a good old-fashioned D-battery. Even Erzsébet wasn't sure what to make of them. She scanned my mind for more information, but I didn't know anything about these modern flashlights.

The driver must have seen the confusion on my face.

"The flashlights you're looking at all use a Luxeon 10-watt LED. A single Luxeon can deliver more light than a 4 D-cell Maglite, and it will never burn out."

He reached into the trunk and grabbed two of the lights. I took them and hurried back to the tower. When I placed one of the lights in the opening, and turned it on, the brightness astounded Erzsébet. I moved it around until I saw a chest placed directly under the opening. I'd have to lean into the hole up to my waist in order to grip it. I didn't want to because of the disgusting vermin that covered it. We hadn't thought to bring work gloves, either.

"Quit fooling around and get it over with."

Erzsébet's command hit a sore spot. It wasn't like I had a choice. Anything she wanted me to do, I did.

"See, the chest isn't so heavy," she said when I finally swallowed my anger, braced myself, and reached into the wall.

She would know better than me, I groused. I gagged a little as I brought the chest up, thinking I probably squashed hundreds of bugs with my body.

"Hurry up. Get it out of there before someone comes and discovers what we're doing."

Erzsébet panted with excitement as I lifted the chest through the opening that fit around it in a perfect match. I let it thump to the ground, vigorously brushing bugs and dust from my hair and torso.

What did the mysterious-looking, sixteenth-century wood and leather box contain?

"I know what is in there, so don't worry about it," Erzsébet snapped.

She directed me to replace the heavy stone in the wall. It still fit perfectly, and when I pushed it all the way in, a loud click resounded as it snapped shut. I rubbed a handful of dirt from the floor on the stones to obliterate the marks where I'd pried and hammered. We stashed the tools and torches and managed to carry the dusty, bug-infested chest and the rest of the lot to the car.

"Put it in the boot," Erzsébet told the driver.

"You can't take anything from here," the driver said. "It's a national monument."

"You impertinent peasant! Do you not know who I am?" she shouted.

I expected a puzzled reaction from the driver because I was clearly an American and speaking rudely to him, but without uttering another word, he dragged the chest to the back of the limo and placed it in the trunk. Evidently he did know about Erzsébet.

When we arrived at the manor house, Erzsébet continued to issue orders. "Set the chest on the dining room table."

I swore I'd never eat at that table again. "What's inside?"

Erzsébet was in no hurry to open it – she already knew the chest's contents and wasn't interested in sharing. She seemed to be absorbed in some sort of calculations about the contents.

I showered, washing the odds and ends of bug carcasses and dust from my hair. When I'd dried and dressed, I came back downstairs and sat by the trunk.

"Come on, Erzsébet. Hurry up and open this damned thing so I can see why I crawled into that bug-infested hole."

She sighed and let me in on her thoughts. She recalled the day when Ferenc had carefully packed the unlocked chest. Then she opened it with dramatic flair, pulling the lid open slowly at first and then flinging it up. The first item she shared was an ancient-looking scroll made of animal skin and imprinted with hieroglyphics. Next, Erzsébet lifted out a pair of gold amulets with similar hieroglyphics carved into them. She said these glyphs indicated how the bracelets' location could be tracked by charting planetary alignments with astronomical calculations.

"What bracelets are you talking about?"

"We are wearing one."

"What the hell?" I shivered with excitement. At long last, Erzsébet had revealed her agenda, or part of it. I looked at my wrists and ankles and saw nothing.

"They're invisible. Once the incantation is chanted, the bracelet becomes visible, and once the bracelet is visible, the wearer becomes vulnerable to the theft of the bracelet."

Then Erzsébet mused about how to make a new star chart to find the wearer of the bracelet that matched hers. She assured me that this person was diligently seeking me, and it would be better if we found the seeker before he or she found us.

My anger and anxiety rose. "This has something to do with your possession of me."

"Yes, it definitely does," she admitted.

"And?"

Erzsébet didn't reply, but began to muse again about the charts and calculations instead, stuff I didn't understand.

Now I knew why she studied new technology so meticulously. Using the hieroglyphics carved on the golden amulets, anyone could triangulate a position using the Sun, Mars, Earth, and the other planets in the solar system to pinpoint the exact location of the other bracelet. But with all the advances in science and astronomy, along with the proliferation of hundreds of satellites beaming information back and forth from space to Earth, she knew we might learn something to gain an advantage over our pursuer. I must admit that I was more than a little intrigued. Anyway, what choice did I have but to cooperate with her?

As she worked, Erzsébet recalled the years she'd spent confined in the tower. She revealed that the person who wore the other bracelet, Zsombor, was the man partially responsible for her captivity. He'd spread negative rumors about her before she'd married Ferenc. Then he'd plotted to get Ferenc's bracelet during the war between Hungary and Turkey. The Turks had finally gained the upper hand in one last ferocious battle with the Hungarians. Zsombor took advantage of this and wounded Ferenc after poisoning him to make him appear to be a war casualty after stealing his bracelet. The Count's dispirited troops fled the battlefield.

As Erzsébet demonstrated before, Ferenc had given his bracelet to her and Zsombor was left with nothing but his magick and one bracelet despite harming Ferenc. He desperately wanted both bracelets but knew that taking the other from Erzsébet would be difficult. As a member of the royal family, the king might have his head if he harmed her.

Zsombor resigned himself at first to the fact that he might never have a chance to enjoy the power the bracelets would give him. But his deviousness prevailed. He, along with her family confidante György Thurzó, spread rumors about Erzsébet's cruelty toward her servants and the village people, greatly exaggerating her crimes, or so she said, and paid people to testify against her. These ghastly tales of torture and murder eventually revolted her closest relatives. Even the king turned against her. Erzsébet recently read for herself the documents at the memorial museum in which Zsombor and Thurzó convinced the king of her guilt.

"'I wish only to avenge her innocent victims,' Zsombor wrote in a letter to the king, who gave him and Thurzó written permission to go to my castle and isolate me. The bastard tried from the beginning to undo me," she said.

Erzsébet was the only one with keys to the rooms in the tower. She had the secret compartment built with the help of her most trusted servant, Dorothea Szentes, a burly peasant woman also known as Dorka. Erzsébet stored the chest containing her most important possessions in this compartment after willing her lands and other holdings to her surviving son and daughters.

Erzsébet continued to reminisce. "Zsombor tried in vain with all his magick to make the bracelet on my wrist visible before he ordered me walled up in the tower. He surmised that after a year or two I would want to be released so badly that he could return and demand the bracelet. But I would not be moved. I lived in that damned tower four long years, always worried someone would poison the meals shoved at me through a slot in the wall. After all, the king wanted to be released from his great debt to Ferenc and many other nobles who wanted to divide my lands.

"When I heard Zsombor would come a third time to the castle with the king's blessings in order to try to wrest the bracelet from me, I ironically swallowed the vial of poison I'd stored away in the chest for such an occasion.

"While I waited to die, I meditated upon bringing about a conscious rebirth, hoping that my magick incantation along with the bracelet's power would manifest my intent. I vowed to be reborn as a warrior, knowing Zsombor would pursue me until he got what he wanted, or would die trying.

"That's why I chose you, Jim Jackson," she said. "You have a warrior's heart. Your mind wasn't active and your body almost frozen, but your destiny was to live again."

"Yeah, but my mind is active now. So why don't you find another body?"

"We've gone over this many times. I'll leave you in command of your body once I find what I need. Right now, I need you in order to survive in this era. As a reward for your cooperation, I will leave your body while you still have many years ahead of you. Once I acquire what I need – or some unforeseen event causes me to leave before I accomplish that – you will live the remainder of your life in peace."

The soothing narcotic of Erzsébet's artificial euphoria washed through my mind. I hated to be disarmed like that, yet I was beginning to love the blissful feeling.

Her thoughts revealed that the wearers of the remaining two bracelets – her nemesis Zsombor and herself, and by extension, me – could find a body nearly dead or recently vacated and move in, or even enter the body of a fetus or newborn, though that path required much patience. The bracelet's owner could reanimate the body of someone thought to be dying, which explained some miraculous recoveries, Erzsébet said.

What had happened with my consciousness returning at the same moment she occupied my body was a historical first. No one in human history, except for the owners of the magickal bracelets, had ever returned from the dead, except maybe Jesus or Lazarus. And none was ever possessed in quite the same way, she assured me.

With Erzsébet present, I accomplished the one and only thing I'd ever desired. Even though forced to retire to retain my world heavyweight title, I'd still won it. I knew life would turn dull after this achievement. But because of Erzsébet, I felt more alive than ever.

I chided myself for beginning to accept Erzsébet's possession of me, but there were many advantages. My senses became sharpened by sharing our minds. My knowledge and vocabulary were increasing. I could zero in on any abnormality, perceive things I'd never noticed before. Aware of my surroundings with an animal's innate sensitivity, the slightest noise aroused my immediate attention. These developments began to excite me more than my championship victory.

I didn't like the idea that an unseen and unknown enemy stalked me. I preferred to face my enemies in a boxing ring. Erzsébet brought me into this conflict, and if it weren't for her, I'd be. . . Well, exactly where would I be? Presumably, leading an ordinary life, a has-been reliving past glories. Plus, the championship fight had been cloaked in rules and regulations and I could identify my opponent. With this unknown enemy stalking us, there were no rules. Whom would I confront, what would I do when it was time to face this enemy? Could this Zsombor take any form he wanted?

Erzsébet hadn't revealed exactly what to expect – perhaps she didn't know herself. At least she was on my side in the approaching battle, especially lucky since brainpower and magick might be deciding factors.

Erzsébet revealed how I could do more than wait. First, she arranged fencing lessons. I wondered why in this age of automatic weapons anyone would train for battle using swords. Maybe it was just a custom in outback Slovakia. Erzsébet let me know in no uncertain terms that it was a necessary technical skill. She insisted that I continue training until fencing was as natural for me as boxing.

I trained four hours a day, seven days a week, and as she did with boxing, Erzsébet allowed me to use my own skills, steadfastly offering helpful hints. I always considered fencing a sport for sissies, but soon learned swordsmanship required a great deal of skill and endurance. Fortunately, my boxing training melded with fencing.

One day when my fencing instructor and I used rapiers to practice with, he suggested we change to broadswords. The heavier sword suited me fine. I could slice through the practice dummies with one stroke, a feat not matched by either the instructor or any of his other students.

After training sessions, Erzsébet insisted I sit at the dining room table and examine items from the old chest we recovered from her dungeon. She studied the Egyptian scrolls for hours, not only to learn how to locate the second bracelet, but to learn all she could from the ancient documents. Though she spent much time on the internet reading about modern technical marvels, I could see she still embraced her ancient beliefs.

When I expressed my confidence in science over the gods, she laughed. "How do you think I was able to reincarnate into your body and exert control over you if it wasn't for my gods?"

Chapter 24

"Then curse your gods," I said, "if they're responsible for my subservient position in my own body."

"You say that, Jim Jackson, but I've known you to pray at times to the same gods you're now cursing, asking to be released from your bondage."

"I'll pray to anybody or anything that can grant that prayer," I declared, knowing my Catholic mother would roll in her grave to hear me say this.

Erzsébet remained silent for a moment, searching for some memory.

"Did you know that my husband believed in a universe with three heavens? Two heavens were above the sky – the heaven of the stars and the Earth. The underground of Apsu and the underworld of the dead was the third heaven."

I couldn't resist. "Does that mean if I miss getting into one heaven, I have two more chances?"

Erzsébet laughed. "Don't ever say I don't have a sense of humor. Anyway, Ferenc wanted me to learn everything I could about Marduk, the god who created the bracelets. He made me memorize this passage: 'Marduk created the Earth as a raft floating on Apsu. Ea caused Apsu to fall asleep, and then killed the god, and from the clay of Apsu, Marduk fashioned man.'"

I conceded that her stories fascinated me, especially the ones about the gods.

Erzsébet said that the gods managed more than one planet, so this idea didn't shock her as it shocked other seventeenth-century Christians. While I lived at Evergreen, she learned that modern scientists had discovered that the ancient Nubians and Egyptians built pyramids in an alignment so accurate with the stars in Orion's Belt that it could not be accident or coincidence. This information reinforced her belief in the ancient philosophies.

"Where are these gods? Why haven't I ever seen one on Earth?"

"They have many worlds to manage and can't always be here when we need them. That's one of the reasons why the bracelets were created."

"You'd think I would've seen at least one god here if there are as many as you say."

"This planet was a playground for the gods until they created mankind and the world became infested with humans. Now they only come here occasionally to reward their faithful adherents."

"What happens when you pray to your gods? Do they hear you?"

"Of course. My gods hear my every prayer, no matter what worlds they're visiting."

"What are some of the things you pray about?"

She thought for a moment. "Marduk made the numbers three, four, and seven sacred, so I always use these numbers in my prayers."

"I don't understand how you use numbers in prayer," I said.

"Before long you will. Marduk told men he created the four elements – fire, water, air, earth – as manifestations of his divine power. He informed his creation that the human soul is also composed of the four elements, which when united, took the ordinary form of fire or flame. The scrolls we have describe how Marduk made the elements eternal and how nothing can be annihilated, but only changed – souls by transmigration and matter by transmutation."

"So, are you saying that the bracelets are a simple combination of the four elements?"

"Ah, now you're thinking, Jim Jackson. Yes. That's the reason they appear to be made of fire," she said. "The ancient scrolls reveal to those who seek the secret of life, that the tree was the most perfect symbol for the miracle of reproduction. Trees shed their leaves in autumn, rest in the winter, and bloom forth again in spring, and this conveys the divine assurance of renewal; in other words, 'dying to live.' This belief is the framework of the old religions and enabled mankind to welcome death rather than fear it."

"I can see that Zsombor has no fear of death. And now that I've transcended death – almost accidentally – maybe I really am his worthy opponent."

If a spirit could smile, I'd say that Erzsébet responded to me with a great big grin. "Eureka. Now you see another reason why I chose you, Jim Jackson."

After several hundred attempts to create an accurate chart, Erzsébet finally concluded that Zsombor seemed poised to find us at any moment, but she couldn't find a way to recognize him or distinguish him from anyone else. A problem, because Zsombor could easily locate me because of the publicity surrounding my rejuvenation and my championship fight.

"We need to get his bracelet or he will follow me for eternity," Erzsébet fretted.

"Worse," I said. "Now that he's likely entered Slovakia, I hope to hell we can identify what form he's taken, because whatever it is, he intends to kill me. Just tell me how to proceed. You're safe in my form, but I need *your* protection."

Physically, I was a match for any man. But would physical strength be enough to confront supernatural powers? I had faith that Erzsébet's mental agility would surpass Zsombor's, but could we manage an adversary with superior magickal ability?

Erzsébet encouraged patience as she sought ways to alert us to Zsombor's approach. She discovered that one scroll revealed a story about an ancient king whose priests created a spell to make his bracelet emit a magnetic pulse. He felt the pulse as a vibration when another bracelet was nearby.

She gripped my wrist with the fingers of both hands and followed the document's directions to chant this incantation, hoping it a sufficient warning to defend myself against Zsombor.

The next morning we sat with my coffee, poring over the newest astrological chart she'd cast. "Look here," she said. "The planets reveal that Zsombor is not only in the region, but on his way here at this very moment."

Would I figure out who Zsombor was before he either killed me or succeeded in taking the bracelet from my wrist?

Suddenly, the front doorbell buzzed. I opened the door, ready to lash out at whoever appeared. Erzsébet stood ready with her magick.

A scrawny UPS deliveryman speaking Slovakian stood meekly on the doorstep with an express package. I didn't see why Zsombor would manifest himself as a ninety-nine pound weakling and breathed a sigh of relief as he checked my passport and confirmed the signatures. Satisfied that my face and picture matched, he handed me the small package.

I placed the package on the dining room table and stared at it, afraid it might explode.

"Open it," Erzsébet urged.

"Not so fast. What if it's a bomb?" I went to the living room, brought back a poker from the fireplace and gingerly prodded the cardboard box. Nothing. I picked up a table knife, held my breath, and pressed a hole in the packing tape. Still nothing.

I sliced the packing tape along the length of the box, surprised to find a letter wrapped around a disk inside the package.

Erzsébet allowed me to read the letter to her rather than the other way around.

"'Don't ask how I acquired this holo, but I think you need to watch it,' I read. An avid boxing fan had sent me this holo V-SIM chip recording that he'd made of Father O'Malley, the letter continued.

"'Since Cwia Alexander was murdered, there have been weekly exorcisms in Boston. Those accused of being possessed are afraid to refuse exorcism, because they may end up as she did. O'Malley started it all. I think he's the one who is possessed. Signed, A fan and a friend of Pagans.'"

I put the holo in my PVA holo reader slot and hit play. The hologram appeared in the middle of the room. Like the 3-D television broadcasts, we could walk around the images as though the images were people in the room.

I remembered vividly the heavy face and voice of O'Malley from when he tried to convince the symposium at Cryonics Foundation to allow him to perform an exorcism on me, and later, when he spoke in the Boston Commons the night a mob murdered Cwia. Seeing him again made my adrenaline flow and I clenched my fists, thinking of what I'd like to do to him.

Erzsébet crept into my mind to calm my emotions. She didn't want me doing anything rash, and what she wanted, she got. I looked again at the images. O'Malley sat with an older man in a bishop's garb.

"I now believe more than ever that Jim Jackson is possessed, Bishop Cheney, and I'm determined to send the demon back to hell," Father O'Malley said.

The bishop moved a forefinger to encourage O'Malley to continue.

"Look at the evidence," O'Malley said. "Our Mother Church believes one true sign of possession is the display of superhuman strength. Look at how often Jackson fought – more than any man in history. Are not changes in personality and the ability to understand and converse in languages not previously spoken also sure signs of possession?"

Bishop Cheney held his hands out and placed his fingertips together. "We can't break any law to perform an exorcism that hasn't been requested. What you're asking me is unusual. I don't see the urgency in this situation."

"Bishop Cheney, when revived, Jackson spoke fluent Slovakian and Hungarian, languages he'd never spoken before. A possessed person may suffer a complete personality change. The demon dominates the victim whenever it chooses."

"Again, Father O'Malley, the alleged victim does not seem to be suffering in the throes of a demonic possession. I admit that Jackson's circumstances are quite unusual, but he doesn't seem to be a threat to himself or others. Even if what you say is true, how can I justify an act of kidnapping?"

"Diabolical possession is a threat to humanity. Satan has sent one of the most evil humans that ever lived to do his bidding. We cannot wait for Jackson to request an exorcism."

"The question is, can we believe anything written about Erzsébet Báthory?" Bishop Cheney asked. "Her history is not well-recorded and has attained the status of legend."

"I believe to not do what I'm proposing is a dereliction of our sworn duty. I know Jim Jackson is praying for me to rescue him. I sincerely believe if we don't expel this demon, the gates of hell will be opened and our world will soon be overrun with demons."

"I'll consider your request. If I agree, I can authorize you to act as you see fit and will send a dispatch to the Vatican verifying my permission," Bishop Cheney said. "I'll inform you of my decision tomorrow."

O'Malley took leave of the bishop and walked to a chapel nearby.

"Look at him," Erzsébet said. "He will probably pretend to pray about how to find you."

Inside the dim chapel entry, another priest came and stood beside O'Malley. I wondered how the cameraman could pick up clear audio and video without being detected. Perhaps with one of those floating cameras the mayor mentioned, or some other new technology.

"Father Flynn," O'Malley said, "I believe I may have convinced the Bishop and we can proceed with our plans to kidnap Jackson."

"Are you positive about this?" Flynn asked.

"I'm positive Jackson is possessed," O'Malley said. "King Matthias II of Hungary issued a warrant for Erzsébet Báthory's arrest in 1610 for practicing witchcraft and torture. People downhill in the village claimed to have heard screams emanating from within the castle and spoke of disappearing girls, but no one dared approach the Countess.

"Word filtered through the ranks of the nobility that she'd kidnapped and killed nine girls from good families. Missing peasant girls were one thing, but the king could hardly allow her to molest the children of nobles. He used this as an excuse to send the Palatine Thurzó, who bore the warrant, and Báró Zsombor, a noble nearly equal in status to Erzsébet, to search her castle. When they arrived at Cséjthe, they hoped to catch her in a deviant act."

"I know you speak the truth about some things, but you also make rash statements than don't contain an iota of truth," Flynn said. "A journal kept by Zsombor has been held in Rome since his death in 1616. In it, he admits how he arrived at Castle Cséjthe and discovered a body. His men had planted it there earlier that night. Thurzó was set to be rewarded by the king with Erzsébet's fortune. Yet scores of witnesses detailed abuse and the grisly deaths of dozens of young girls at the hands of Erzsébet and her most faithful servants. The question is, was she guilty of the alleged crimes or was she framed?"

O'Malley looked at Flynn with surprise. "If Erzsébet was innocent, then why did she commit suicide when she heard the king would send Zsombor to question her a third time during her house arrest, asking her only to repent? Only a demon would show such a lack of remorse.

"Regardless of her crimes or lack thereof, the historical record clearly condemns the Count and Countess for their involvement in witchcraft. I attended the special symposium at which Jackson's physicians and neuropsychiatrists discussed his case. They dallied around, thinking that perhaps Jackson simply has some brain damage due to the cryonic procedure and that engagement in normal life will set him straight. But I and I alone could smell Satan's hand in this. Clearly, Erzsébet Báthory has somehow managed to free herself from hell. She's in possession of Jackson's body and soul and it's our job to free him."

The hologram faded from view and the PVA menu affirmed its completion. Erzsébet and I were both quiet with our own thoughts for a moment.

"The person who sent this says he wants to help me," I said. "Maybe the true adversary sent us this holo disk to throw us off track.

On the other hand, maybe this will give me a chance to get my hands around O'Malley's throat."

"Stop," Erzsébet said. "Think about what you are saying. If you attack him, it will just prove his point that you're possessed. O'Malley has become famous for performing Saturday night exorcisms. That means he will have plenty of help getting you tied to a table for an exorcism. If he succeeds, it may coincidentally assist Zsombor to attain the bracelet."

"Hopefully O'Malley knows better than to interfere with us in my territory. Plus, he is distracting you from your confrontation with Zsombor."

"Whatever he was trying to plan with Father Flynn didn't seem to work," I said.

Erzsébet ignored me as she often did. "Only one other person on Earth can consciously choose a new life because he wears an immortality bracelet – Zsombor. We must stay focused on him. He is creeping inexorably toward us because he wants the immense knowledge provided by having both bracelets. My spies used to tell me he bragged that once he had both, the very universe itself would be his. He wants to subject the entire world to his wishes and many new miseries."

Erzsébet seemed awfully humanitarian for a woman who reputedly tortured and killed many young girls.

She scoffed at this thought and made me turn on the evening news. We recognized O'Malley right away in a delegation of North American clerics arriving in Bratislava from the Vatican. A chill ran through me.

"The priest is stubborn," Erzsébet said. "He followed us here to perform an exorcism."

"If he succeeds, will you be leaving me?"

"I'm not going anywhere until my mission is complete."

We watched as O'Malley was welcomed with open arms.

Witchhunting and exorcism had become big business in Boston after Cwia Alexander's murder. The Church seemed to forget that she, like the Salem witches, was a victim of hysteria. O'Malley started a reality show in which he led a group of priests that exorcised people every Saturday night, embraced by Catholics and Protestants alike. Other reality shows aired in which people nosed around communities looking for witches.

When questioned by the media about his visit, O'Malley bluntly revealed his plan to visit Čachtice to convince Jim Jackson that exorcism was his only hope.

"That will never happen," Erzsébet said.

"If he gets anywhere near me, I'm going to avenge Cwia," I vowed.

"I'm not going to allow you to play into his hands. Hate him in your mind all you want, but before we can do anything to make him pay, we have to stop Zsombor."

I went out for a jog early the next morning and when I passed the village council house along one side of the town square, a small group of people stood together as if celebrating something. Mayor Ilionescu saw me and waved me over.

"Mr. Jackson, may I introduce you to our visiting dignitaries and the American priest?"

My heart sank. Erzsébet began to chant one of her incantations. I asked her what to do, but she ignored me. I stood near the group of smartly dressed men and women and as Father O'Malley approached us from a small electric car parked near the council house, I felt a small tingle on my wrist.

My mouth dropped open. Was Erzsébet's nemesis also mine? Could Zsombor have come to the twenty-first century as Father O'Malley? Why hadn't we expected this?

I took a fighter's stance with my legs wide and my arms at my side and readied myself for an attack. Maybe I should go on the attack first, I thought.

Mayor Ilionescu stepped forward with a cheery smile and held out his hand. "Welcome, Father. The faithful are lined up to receive your blessing."

I understood the welcome. After all, many people were good Christians here. They might enjoy the novelty of Erzsébet returning as Jim Jackson, but they would not offend an emissary of the Catholic

Church, and especially not if publicity and tourism might be involved. And who could resist seeing Father O'Malley finally coming face-to-face with Jim Jackson in Erzsébet Báthory's old stomping ground? I was surprised O'Malley hadn't enlisted major network media to be here.

O'Malley made the sign of the cross and muttered a prayer, blessing each dignitary and villager as they lined up to shake his hand. A throng continued to gather in the square and a small group of longhaired teenagers gathered nearby along the sidewalk in front of a café, gawking at us.

Could Zsombor be among them instead? I glanced at the priest and gazed around at the onlookers' faces, but it was impossible to know if O'Malley or one of the villagers wore the other bracelet.

When it was my turn to approach Father O'Malley, another vibration tingled at my wrist.

Erzsébet finished her chant and her presence became stronger. "I don't know who it is. But Zsombor is going to try something. Be ready."

"Make way, make way," the mayor said, and the ever-growing crowd parted to let me through to where he stood with Father O'Malley and another priest who could only be Father Flynn.

I extended my right hand and Father O'Malley gripped it tightly in both of his large, meaty hands. If we were in the ring, we'd have been evenly matched.

As I tried to pull back from his grasp, he exerted a mighty force as if he were a human magnet. Leaning forward with a smile as if giving me a blessing, he whispered an ancient language into my ear. At the sound of the first word, Erzsébet repeated her protective incantation.

Father O'Malley smiled with his mouth, but his eyes narrowed. People stepped forward expectantly. What would the famous exorcist say to Jim Jackson?

O'Malley dropped my hand and made the sign of the cross in front of me, and then crossed himself. Without another glance, he moved on to the next person, not missing a beat. More villagers crowded around to see the spectacle.

CRYONIC MAN

Even Zsombor wouldn't risk cutting off my hand in front of the rapidly growing crowd.

Erzsébet berated herself for letting me walk into a trap. "Now that Zsombor knows I can resist the incantation to transfer the bracelets, next time he will have a sharp blade ready, witnesses or no witnesses."

≈Chapter 25

As I jogged back to the manor house, Erzsébet obsessed about why she hadn't spotted Zsombor's identity as Father O'Malley from the beginning. "Zsombor could not have recently possessed him," she said. "The priest has a long, illustrious career in the Church, according to articles online. He hasn't had any severe illnesses, at least none that were publicized. Zsombor must have acquired O'Malley's identity through a natural rebirth by consciously choosing to enter an embryo or infant, a practice that takes great skill, timing, and patience. O'Malley is a perfect incarnation and the priesthood a perfect cover for a rogue like Zsombor."

"Sounds like O'Malley aims to corner us with the blessing of the Church," I said, breathing hard as I scaled a hill lined with enormous oak trees. "The bastard managed to get the Vatican to overlook his inciting the mob who killed Cwia. He'll have vast resources to help him steal the bracelet from us."

After I showered, Erzsébet insisted upon reviewing the documents in the chest even though she'd scoured the contents many times. There might be something essential she'd missed that could determine who would win both bracelets in the future battle with Zsombor.

I opened the chest and spread the documents and artifacts across the dining room table. This time she directed me to place a bowl of water and a candle at each corner of the table and to burn incense that sent sweet, intoxicating smoke swirling about the room for protection and purification, she said.

This time Erzsébet allowed me to enter her mind and fully examine her thoughts about the scrolls and the astrological charts. First, she pointed out the difference between following one bracelet or two. Then she demonstrated how to trace the history of the bracelets, to be certain that I understood the procedure.

Erzsébet pointed out instances on the chart where her diagrammed lines overlapped. "This is where the possessor of a single bracelet incarnated again in the same year he or she left one body for another. I can tell by the angular differences in the pathways," she said.

I didn't grasp exactly what she was talking about, but I could see how the lines changed at the places she pointed to. I could only accept that what she said was true. My brain wasn't made for these mathematical calculations and I didn't quite understand how one could pick a time to reincarnate.

As she often did, Erzsébet launched into obscure explanations about the complexities of the spiritual world. "Linear time is an illusion," she said. "Past, present, and future are woven into a single fabric. Anything that happens or will ever happen occurs simultaneously."

I'd encountered this principle in the spirit world. But when she explained how a spirit could choose a world and a particular time to reincarnate in, I couldn't comprehend this, hard as I tried.

Erzsébet studied and recalculated her charts throughout the night, searching for a new advantage over Zsombor. She memorized incantations in languages I didn't understand, and magickal symbols only she could interpret. I began to understand what Erzsébet meant when she said that spiritual science was "the study of lifetimes."

"If Zsombor knows everything that's in the trunk, what's the sense of going over and over this stuff?"

She ignored me as she usually did when she didn't want to be bothered. I intuitively felt that she'd finally made a breakthrough but didn't want to share it. Instead, she insisted I learn the chant to assure that the bracelet remained on my wrist, something she usually did for me in risky situations. She chanted it word-for-word in the same ancient language that Zsombor used that morning, then translated it into English for me.

"I'll never remember that chant in whatever language you're speaking."

"Sumerian. You must remember it. Just repeat after me. 'I invoke you Marduk, Creator of Man, Son of Ea. Let the flame of eternity burn bright to ensure the life of your humble servant. We faithfully serve you as you created us to do. I beseech you, Marduk, who created also the Tablets of Destiny. Show us the eternal flame which burns in the bracelets of fire. Show us your power. We pay homage to our Creator and Benefactor.'"

After stumbling through the prayer a few times, I finally chanted alone. I must have gotten the words right, because a flaming bracelet finally glowed on my right wrist as I completed the prayer. I ripped the tablecloth from the dining room table and wrapped it around my arm to put out the fire.

Erzsébet howled with laughter. "Stop! The flames won't hurt you."

To my amazement, she was right. My skin didn't blister and neither my shirt cuff nor the tablecloth was scorched. Hell, this was more amazing than floating cars or any other futuristic thing I'd seen so far. But I still couldn't imagine why Erzsébet and Zsombor had taken their own lives for this flaming bracelet. I could never do that, even for immortality –

"Excuse me? Is this the man who sat with a pistol thrust into his mouth because he was afraid of a tumor?"

"Busted. I guess we all have our reasons, don't we? But it seems inconceivable to die in order to travel into the future on an uncertain quest."

Erzsébet coughed and I could feel the question marks in her mind.

"Oh. Even though I finally died naturally, I signed up for an adventure, didn't I?"

"Just one more reason I chose you, Jim Jackson. We are far more alike than different, my friend."

Erzsébet turned her attention back to her investigation. Exhausted from the events of the day, I fell asleep, my head lolling over the table. Somehow, I slept soundly in this uncomfortable position until vibrations coming from the bracelet awoke me around half-past four in the morning.

Zsombor lurked here somewhere. Instantly alert, I grabbed my broadsword from the mantel in the living room and drew it from its sheath.

"Be careful. I've discovered Zsombor may have mastered the principle of invisibility," Erzsébet cautioned.

If I couldn't see him, then maybe if I turned the lights off, he wouldn't be able to see me. I scuttled to the newly installed breaker box in the kitchen and switched the breakers off. I hoped that with his extensive knowledge he couldn't also see in the dark.

Erzsébet began to summon her goddesses. "Athena, help me and ye also, O all-powerful Diana. Protect me, your faithful Erzsébet. I am in peril! Send me nine and ninety cats, for thou art goddess of all cats. Bid them assemble and to come to my aid."

Suddenly a cat screeched. I felt a breeze and a thump as though it flew through the room past me and landed at my feet. Erzsébet directed me to pick up the flashlight sitting near the kitchen door. I shone the light across the room and stepped back in astonishment. Cats galore, dozens of them, big, small, tiger, tortoise, calico, black, white, gray, and brown materialized in mid-air and dropped gracefully to the floor.

Suddenly, one screeched as unseen force flung it against a wall. The others didn't let this deter them and converged on a spot at the far side of the room.

I stared in disbelief. So many cats clung by their claws to the unseen intruder that a human outline formed underneath them.

I flung open the kitchen door and the heap of cats dashed toward it.

"Strike him now!" Erzsébet commanded.

I raised my sword but couldn't bring myself to slice through that pile of cats. Angry, Erzsébet hissed at me like a large feline and willed me to strike with every ounce of her might when the form passed through the door.

"Track this man. Hurry," she ordered.

The bracelet's vibrations weakened as the pile of cats stumbled into the dark. I reset the switch in the breaker box and turned on the security floodlights that lit up the manor house grounds like a football field. This set off the security cameras that would record the intruder's movements. I ran outside and followed the screeching, man-shaped pile of cats as it staggered along around the back of the house and across a wide lawn toward a stand of trees toward a gaping hole cut in a chain-link fence. Here and there, a cat dropped from the pile, wounded or dying from the efforts Zsombor made to protect himself. As he passed through the trees and struggled through the gap in the fence, he managed to fling one unfortunate cat into a tree and impale another on the sharp points atop the fence. Still invisible, he freed himself from the last cat hanging on his back and vanished.

I went back inside the kitchen and opened the big double cabinet where the security monitors corresponding to the security cameras installed around the manor house and gardens were stored. With Erzsébet's help, I found the right monitors and replayed the incident. Luckily, the cameras caught almost every detail of Zsombor's encounters with the cats.

"Zsombor surprised me with his carelessness. He should have known I would have familiars waiting for him," Erzsébet said. "Summoning cats is one of the most elemental hexes, but quite effective, no?"

"I wish I'd cut through those cats. Zsombor would have been finished. Now I'll have to face him again."

"Yes, you will. He'll just consider us the lucky winners of this battle. But don't worry about the cats – look." She pointed across the room at where the first stunned or dead cat fell on top of a buffet after hitting the wall.

I watched with disbelief as the body of the "dead" cat faded into thin air. The sobering sight inspired my healthy new respect for Erzsébet's magick and the terrifying challenge that lay ahead.

Though we only left the manor house for a short walk that day and were the only witnesses to the cat incident (along with Zsombor), a portion of the security video was leaked to the media. Perhaps Mayor Ilionescu or his assistants wanted to stir up more interest in Čachtice, as they were the only ones with a spare key. Perhaps O'Malley had tricked them. The metaphysical cat "slaughter" started a worldwide stir in cyberspace.

Pressured by animal rights groups, the Slovakian government promised a full investigation. Rumors spread like wildfire among the Saturday Night Exorcists about Erzsébet Báthory being up to her old tricks, but in Slovakia and Hungary, this only strengthened the love affair with her.

Goddess worshippers began to converge upon Čachtice, some with real cats. Esmé Deschamps, a young, nubile Pagan leader from New Orleans who sported golden skin and a mane of curly rainbow-tinted hair, was one of the first to arrive. Her mission, she said, was to organize a Pagan resistance to protect Erzsébet from harm.

Soon the media reported that Father O'Malley and his entourage would move on from Čachtice to stay in Trnava, the oldest town in western Slovakia. Dating from 1211, Trnava was settled by Franciscans, Dominicans, and other religious orders of the day. News analysts speculated about our brief meeting in Čachtice and wondered why Father O'Malley hadn't spoken with me about an exorcism. I refused to talk to any of the reporters who called me or showed up at our doorstep, and suggested to all that they might want to ask Father O'Malley why he seemed to have a rather nasty-looking scratch on his face.

Chapter 26

Two mornings later, another holographic V-SIM chip arrived by overnight mail, this time from an address in Trnava. "Don't be too complacent," Erzsébet said as I signed the electronic card for the package. "Someone may want you to become used to signing for packages, then take you by surprise."

The identical package contained a brief note in the same hand as the first. I activated the holo program on my PVA, aligned the signals, and played it.

Father O'Malley seemed to be attempting to placate Father Flynn, who sat before him at a small desk. "I tried to reason with Mr. Jackson, but was confronted by the demon Báthory and a horde of cats. She's far more powerful than I suspected. Now I've got to treat all these scratches so I won't get some nasty cat disease. Before we leave Čachtice, I must teach the witch a lesson."

O'Malley picked up a pad from a desk and wrote his instructions on it as he described them to Flynn, tapping his pencil beside the names of the herbs and minerals.

"Get five hundred pounds of fish, enough to fill five barrels, and put them in water. Go to the local pharmacy – the chemist – and ask for this list of herbs and crushed minerals. Add four ounces of this powder into each barrel."

Father Flynn looked puzzled. "What will you do with so many fish?"

"The herbs and crushed minerals will cause an agonizing death for any cat. Hire some local boys to distribute the fish around the manor house where Jim Jackson is staying. There are dozens of cats there, all controlled by the Báthory witch."

"Are you certain you want to do this? What if the villagers' cats are affected? There's already quite a stir about some cat deaths on the manor house property. I've heard there are some strange security videos of an incident online. We can't be perceived as responsible for any sort of misery, even to animals."

O'Malley looked at his watch, exposing another deep scratch on the back of his hand. "Just more hocus-pocus designed to implicate me and avoid exorcism. We're leaving this afternoon – you have only four hours to accomplish the task. Wear civilian clothes."

The holo ended with O'Malley displaying a smug look of satisfaction. I knew he didn't foresee the problems he'd created for himself. Flynn must have followed his orders because later that day, a few sick and dying cats began to sprawl along the roads and fields. By the next morning, dozens of cats littered the countryside. Their contorted bodies made it obvious they died painfully. TV crews cruised around the countryside filming the horrific event. Local authorities installed an emergency incinerator to dispose of the bodies and the cremations became front-page news. Cat lovers were infuriated for the second time that week.

The Slovak national police analyzed the fish remains and identified the poison. The fish peddler stepped forward to describe the person who'd purchased the fish. The chemist confirmed that the same individual purchased the herbs and minerals. It took a few days to tie the loose ends of the case together and locate Father Flynn in Trnava, just as the Ministry of Interior and Administrative Reform took control of the investigation and assigned local police to a subordinate role. The Ministry scrambled to smooth the situation over with ambassadorial damage control while the Vatican made it clear that the Church had many ways to put pressure on the Ministry if Slovakia tried to prosecute Father Flynn. Suddenly, all mention of poison disappeared from news reports because the Ministry of Health and Human Services determined that a mysterious, new feline virus had killed the cats.

As the Slovakian government sought to accommodate the Vatican, fear spread among the Pagans that Christian persecution might rear its ugly head again. Pagans worldwide recalled the thousands harassed and burned at the stake for the suspicion of practicing witchcraft. The evidence that the American priests were possibly involved in both magick and poisoning animals made the situation even more troubling.

The Pagans already in Slovakia encouraged their sisters to join them. Many legally transported cats as their personal pets to replace the ones slashed and poisoned by Zsombor. Overwhelmed immigration authorities tossed their hands up at the amount of electronic paperwork generated by thousands of quarantine procedures.

Once a respectably large number acquired their visas and legally entered Slovakia, Pagan protesters accused the government of being in league with those who slaughtered the cats and posted pictures online of current and historic cat burnings to highlight the similarities. Slovakian authorities balked and then relented, finally allowing the Pagans to bring their cats into the country with a veterinarian's certificate of disease-free status.

Finally, the Hungarian and Slovakian governments tried to stop the influx of more Pagans into the region, but many entered both countries through unofficial entry points from other European Union nations. Eventually both governments deemed it advantageous to welcome foreigners bearing large amounts of sorely needed foreign currency. Slovakia and Hungary didn't want to admit that their immigration services had lost control of their borders.

All the hotels, hostels, rooms for rent, and caravan parks in and around Čachtice and nearby villages filled within two weeks. The grounds surrounding the castle and the manor house became a hive of activity as Erzsébet took charge and supervised the organization of

CRYONIC MAN

a tent city in the same manner as her former husband had organized military maneuvers centuries before. She transformed the haphazardly placed tents into neat orderly rows. Her crews of Pagans dug latrine pits and constructed a large central kitchen funded by me and staffed by locals who gathered food and cooked for all.

Overrun by Pagans, the manor house teemed day and night with chanters and conjurers of spirits, the practitioners of magick who came to assist their mistress when they heard of the Catholic priest who poisoned cats. I never knew there were so many students of occultism, magick, mysticism, mythology, psychic powers, witchcraft, metaphysics, and spiritualism. I wondered where I'd learned so many definitions and concluded it must be from Erzsébet's thoughts leaking from her consciousness into mine. In my heart, I knew all of these groups attempted to work miracles using hidden but natural forces, forces that are God-given but forbidden by religious suppression.

One night, just before the summer solstice full moon, hundreds of women surrounded the manor house, chanting and praying to their various goddesses when Esmé approached me. "Come into the chapel," she urged.

She led me into a large, carnival-style tent floored with dozens of jewel-colored oriental rugs of many sizes. There were no furnishings other than an altar with hundreds of fragrant candles burning on it. In the center of the floor was an enormous piece of Welsh slate with a square of blue chalk drawn inside a circle of yellow chalk. A large white five-pointed star with a different colored candle on each point surrounded this circle. Esmé directed me to stand in the middle of the square. A small group of women gathered around me. Esmé proceeded to light all the candles and then together they began to chant in a language unknown to me.

Erzsébet chanted with the women. As they performed this incantation, they walked around the circle counterclockwise first, then clockwise, and repeated this several times. Then Esmé stepped up to the altar and raised her arms above her head. In a loud, clear voice, she said, "I call on the gods and goddesses of the old days and those of the new. With your power, break this spell binding Erzsébet. Gods of light, move about Erzsébet's body. Goddesses, come hither to wake her body and suppress all who move against her. Allow the power that you have given her to fulfill any desire she may have."

A hush descended over the group and I felt a powerful and blissful energy surge through me that Erzsébet mentally bathed in as though a life-giving elixir.

After we sat in meditation for a few minutes, the group paid their respects to Erzsébet one by one, as though honoring a great teacher. When the women trailed away, I went back to the manor house and walked through it, amazed by how many women it held. It seemed that not only every room but every nook and cranny overflowed with lovely ladies wearing multicolored robes and gowns of silk of marvelous hues and patterns that accentuated lithe and overweight figures alike. I was thoroughly enjoying the scenery when a tall, elegant woman with copper-toned skin introduced herself.

"We haven't met yet, Erzsébet. I'm Madame LeFleur. Although our magick differs, many of our goddesses are the same. We've come to honor our mistress," she said. "Please come with me to the lawn and see the new ceremony we have prepared for you."

Madame LeFleur's tone was so enthusiastic that Erzsébet left me no choice but to accompany her outside. As I gazed around the great lawn behind the manor house, the frenzied rhythm of Haitian dancers took over my body, making my heart beat in cadence with the ceremonial drumbeats. Erzsébet voiced her surprise and approval. More and more women joined in and danced around a row of columns. Many others wearing red and green robes appeared from the mist that covered the low-lying woods beyond the lawn where Father O'Malley escaped from his encounter with Erzsébet's cats. Women dressed all in white moved like apparitions toward the *poto mitan,* a center pole representing the center of the spirit world, where all the participants want to go tonight, Madame LeFleur explained.

The drums, fire, mist, and moonlight cast a hypnotic spell, drawing me, the only male body, into the ceremony. I couldn't resist joining the dancers and Erzsébet said she felt the same. My feet moved with the drumbeats – when they sped up, my dancing sped up, and when they slowed, my dancing feet slowed with the beat. We danced for what seemed a long time, but when I stopped to catch my breath, I found only fifteen minutes had passed.

As I rested, I watched a priestess dance. She picked up two small branches and held them in the fire until they crackled with a bright flame, and then danced 'round and 'round the fire. Suddenly, the flaming branches turned into twisting, writhing snakes. She held her arms up to the heavens. The snakes turned back into flaming branches, and then she threw them into the fire.

I asked Madame LeFleur if what we watched was a Pagan ceremony.

"Their magick is voodoo," she said. "We're all sisters worshipping many of the same gods and goddesses. These priestesses have powerful spells like ours, though they have different ways of expressing them. . . come, let's go back inside and mingle with the others from covens around the world."

Inside our sitting room, Erzsébet struck up a conversation with another witch, a young woman from Ireland with many questions about our mission. "Zsombor is a master of magick, a wizard," she explained. "He has more magickal powers than any of us. We must find a way to immobilize him."

"We can summon demonic help if need be," the young witch said. "If your adversary uses demons, we don't have much choice but to enlist their help ourselves."

"Only if absolutely necessary," Erzsébet said. "You know those damn demons always extract a high price for their services."

Confused, I asked, "Demons? You actually deal with demons?"

"Demons were originally in fellowship with the gods," Erzsébet replied. "Angels and demons are spirits without bodies. We occasionally harness the power of a demon or two, but only when absolutely necessary. Our struggle is with the powers of darkness that Zsombor uses against us, and we will tame demons to repel him if we must."

"Where do these demons come from?"

"I told you of the Count's belief in three heavens," Erzsébet said. "The demons live in the third heaven or subterranean world. They can live anywhere they want, but most prefer the atmosphere of this inner world. The young demons take at least one tour through all heavens and earths. These are the ones who appear when we summon them."

"Where does the Devil live? I'd like to know."

"The Devil," she laughed, "the leader of all demons, is something invented by the priests to put the fear of hell into pathetic humans. Demons are simply nature spirits who can possess or control animals as well as humans."

I thought of the cats.

"The gods sometimes take advantage of the demons' actions to accomplish their purposes, so I must keep the gods on our side," she said. "Hear all the chanting? That's ego-building stuff for the gods. One of their reasons for creating humans was to have someone worship them. In an earthly sense, we all know anyone who wants to be worshipped is egotistical. We're giving the gods what they want and hopefully they'll grant us what we want."

"What's Zsombor giving them?"

Erzsébet's eyes glittered with mischief. "He is probably sacrificing virgins as we speak."

Was she joking? Queasy, I recalled all the stories I'd read about human sacrifices. "Do the gods prefer virgins?"

"The gods are similar to humans in their likes and dislikes; each has their own preferences. In the past, some required that humans be sacrificed for their benefit, but that became tiring after thousands of repetitions. Some gods were content to have an animal sacrificed to them. Some loved a virgin sacrifice, but most were happy with adulation. That's a Pagan specialty. We chant and pray harder than anyone, including those sexually repressed monks who devote their entire lives praying to a Christian God who doesn't exist in the sense they believe in."

Did she say this about the Christian God because Christians similar to the modern Exorcists had persecuted pagan practitioners for centuries? Too tired to think any longer, I excused myself with Erzsébet's permission and made my way to bed.

Erzsébet planted a spy the day after the ceremony who intercepted a letter intended for Father O'Malley. Someone with a little too much zeal, or more likely, an Exorcist provocateur had tried to burn a village priest at the stake in a remote Slovakian village as we witnessed the voodoo dancers the night before. Slovakian officers converged on a small Pagan camp to arrest the alleged perpetrator of the crime. As the news filtered worldwide, Pagans everywhere braced themselves for the unavoidable confrontation.

"Unfortunately this poor priest was somewhat sympathetic to our views, and I suspect one of O'Malley's followers may have infiltrated the Pagan camp in order to lay the blame on us," Erzsébet told a sober gathering of Pagan leaders the next morning. "Although Eastern Europe has a large Christian population, we can hope that many citizens are on our side because they find our philosophy more tolerant and more self-affirming than Christian theology. I believe that the murder of Cwia Alexander in the United States causes them to suspect that Father O'Malley is building a cult-like following capable of violence."

Erzsébet held up a creased paper in one hand. "I have here a letter from Father O'Malley that was intercepted on its way to Bishop Cheney, his superior. It says, 'Covens of witches have gathered in Slovakia from all over the world. They're attempting to show the strength of their Pagan gods and to change the status quo of men's superiority. They don't consider hexing or "binding" those who try to repel them to be wrong. Don't worry, Your Excellency, I know how to handle all who gather around Erzsébet Báthory. They are Dianic witches, widely known as vicious lesbians who want to displace respectable men as leaders worldwide.'"

Chapter 27

Erzsébet stopped speaking for emphasis and gazed around the room through my eyes at the women gathered around us. Then she began to read the letter again. "'Once the dreadful truth about Dianic Wiccans and other Pagans becomes known, men, particularly Christian Exorcists, will come to our assistance, because we believe our God dominates Creation with a masculine authority; therefore, men are more like God than women. It then goes without saying that men have a God-like authority over women. Therefore, Christian women should not be encouraged to participate in the situation unfolding here in Slovakia, except as spies or decoys to prevent the Dianics from infiltrating our forces.'"

Although Father O'Malley had written these words, I knew the letter was a product of his thoughts as Zsombor and not the genuine philosophy of a Catholic priest.

The attempted murder of the village priest instigated a second influx of foreigners into the Carpathian region – Exorcist men – Catholic, Protestant, and Fundamentalist, who believed in exorcism as pushed by O'Malley and his cohorts in the Saturday Night Exorcism spectacles around the world. O'Malley's cronies and other religious leaders sent hordes of their brethren to protect the clergy of the Carpathian region from the heathens, always portrayed by the

Saturday Night Exorcist movement as vicious, God-hating lesbians. That the village priest's murder was supposedly committed by a coven of Pagan lesbians outraged Exorcist men worldwide and swelled the ranks of volunteers.

In addition to O'Malley's leadership, the Saturday Night Exorcists were spearheaded by "A Boatload from Boston," a militia from Massachusetts. Dubbed by the media as "twenty-first-century Crusaders," this group organized a gun-smuggling ring to keep O'Malley's followers well armed. Bribery and the need for tourist revenues encouraged customs officials to look the other way when trucks loaded with weapons rolled into Slovakia.

Erzsébet mourned this build-up to certain violence. "Apparently, nothing feels better to those so-called Christian zealots than a loaded weapon and someone to shoot at."

I agreed. "Seems to be a man thing."

The male-dominated antics of the Saturday Night Exorcists and Slovakian government officials alarmed Pagans everywhere. Soon more women from around the globe poured into the Carpathian region. I watched a news report showing Christian militants unloading a truckload of automatic weapons in a camp near Trnava. I had no less fear than Erzsébet that this saber-rattling confrontation would turn into a bloodbath. We both fretted about the women, who as far as we knew, were without weapons of any sort except their wits and their prayers.

"As the Exorcists are all men," Erzsébet pointed out, "this is shaping up to be a battle of the sexes. This is unfortunate, as male and female energies are meant to complement one another. Despite their claim that all Wiccans are Dianic, the great majority of Pagan women here are happily married, with families at home, and they practice many traditions. They should not have to deal with the level of violence that these men are capable of creating. Neither should any Dianic Wiccans have to bear their stupidity."

I felt stuck between the proverbial rock and a hard place. Though I despised O'Malley and his religious and political manipulation, I was still none too happy being the only male allied with the feminine side.

But how could it be otherwise? Though I could never support armed men willing to abuse unarmed women, I consoled myself with the fact that I couldn't make a choice anyway. Erzsébet was still in charge.

Erzsébet prodded me to see things her way. "They are a worthless collection of buffoons dependent on firearms. See how weak men arm themselves with any weapon they can get their hands on?"

"What about the priest they tried to kill? A man nearly died for the Pagan cause," I said.

"A real man, a true hero," Erzsébet said. "And we're going to do something about that. We Pagans are dependent upon the gods and spirits to protect us. Practitioners of magick are uniting against a common enemy for the first time in the history of the world. I believe our combined energies will defeat these fools, no matter how well armed they are."

Erzsébet's proclamation was put to the test that afternoon when Esmé and Madame LeFleur led several thousand women through the village where the priest was nearly burned at the stake. The women's colorful dress, as always, made them a sight to behold. Several thousand armed Exorcists gathered to observe.

An onlooker dressed in a military jacket and jeans aimed his rifle at the marching women. "Hey! What do you call a witch with a bullet hole in her head?"

"A holy witch," another shouted amid hoots of derisive laughter from the Exorcist militia, draped with rifles and bullet bandoliers.

"Look at that pussy Jim Jackson, possessed by the holiest witch of all," another man yelled, his red laser tracing my chest as he aimed his sight.

The women gathered in small circles around me and began to chant, reciting prayers or beseeching their goddesses for protection. While I watched, Erzsébet began to chant a familiar protective mantra. The spine-chilling incantations in a variety of native languages rose on the air, at once eerie and beautiful.

A man wearing a military uniform embroidered with Christian crosses and other symbols in place of military patches attempted to approach me. "Are we going to let them march through town without avenging the priest they tried to murder?" he shouted.

The men around him checked that their weapons were loaded and the click of bullets pumping into firing chambers punctuated the women's chants.

Esmé directed a question to no one in particular. "Do you see those armed men? Watch this," she said, and began to dance to her prayer, swirling her multi-layered skirts and long multi-hued hair in a blur of color.

"Look!" An armed man dressed like a biker pointed to the sky. Thousands of birds gathered in dark clots above the Exorcists.

"Watch this," Esmé said again.

"What's that stupid …" A deluge of birdshit fell from the sky on the men's upturned faces, forcing the speaker to drop his weapon.

"I'm not taking this," yelled the man in uniform. He started shooting at the birds with his automatic weapon. The sound of the Pagans' chanting increased with the staccato sounds of gunfire.

"Oh! Oh! What's coming this way?" A man with a cross tattooed on his forehead pointed across a field at what looked like a cloud of dust. Soon hordes of hornets, bees, and wasps converged upon the men and began to sting. Yelps of surprise, pain, and anger arose from those trying to fight this pestilence.

Then a raging shout rang out. "To hell with these goddamn bees!" The tattooed man wildly fired his automatic weapon. He wounded at least two of his brothers, whose screams fueled more chaos. The mob of men panicked, gathered their wounded, and evacuated their position.

The Pagans' prayers were soon answered. In no time, reports began to surface in online news venues, which many of us watched from our PVAs. "Those damn Pagans shot and wounded two innocent men," one angry American Exorcist complained in a mainstream media video clip.

But it was widely known locally that the Pagans carried neither guns nor any other weapons but their prayers, which seemed to garner an appropriate and Biblical response. Despite the ravages of nature, every wounded man was hurt, in reality, by "friendly fire."

When we returned to Čachtice that evening in a motorcade of vans and buses, another UPS delivery package awaited us in the front entryway of the manor house. The holographic V-SIM chip opened with O'Malley telling Flynn that watching the conflict between his followers and Erzsébet's followers unfold was the most fun he'd experienced in years.

"I'll have to lead these redneck evangelist Exorcist militiamen or they'll end up killing each other," he said. "The demon Báthory is appearing in many men's dreams. Some of the men bitten by the demon's insect familiars are breaking out in rashes or having mysterious fevers. Others seem to be on the verge of nervous breakdowns, drooling and babbling to themselves." He handed Flynn a sheet of paper. "Forward this press release to all militia leaders. We will assemble and join all our forces in Čachtice. We must assure our troops that God is on their side and that I and I alone will lead them against Báthory and the evil Dianics."

Father Flynn cast O'Malley a skeptical look, but took the press release and nodded his assent.

Erzsébet released her own bulletin, calling for all Pagans camped in the Slovakian countryside and villages as well as any interested local women to converge in Čachtice for a "Harmonic Rendering," a universal realignment of Goddess energies that would rebalance humanity and bring new peace and prosperity to the planet, she said. Erzsébet implored her followers not to turn to violence in return for the male-inspired violence, but to invoke the nature gods and goddesses for protection instead.

"I must remind our supporters – all people really – that at one time, humanity looked to the universal Goddess as their higher power. When women held power equal to men, the world was a much better place. But some men were jealous and not satisfied with egalitarian relationships, and so this hierarchy subverted the feminine principle and their alliance with nature so that they could hold dominion over the world, a situation lasting for over five thousand years."

The women gathered and the summer rains of central Europe began.

The weeklong deluge following the Harmonic Rendering retreat dampened the Exorcists' plans to avenge the men that shot one another accidentally. Everyone was amazed to see that only the gentlest of rains fell on the Castle Čachtice grounds and around the manor house where the tent communities now covered nearly every available inch of land.

I had to admit these Pagans were clever. Many Exorcists became disillusioned when God didn't help them vanquish their enemies. Some even suspected that they saw God's hand in the marshaling of natural forces for the Pagans' defense. Who else but God could allow these things to happen, some asked. Others became furious with the blaspheming Pagans and their assistance from birds, insects, and now, the weather.

"These demonic Pagans must be driven from the Earth," O'Malley declared in an interview. This declaration became the rallying cry of the Exorcist militia crowded around him.

The camera panned from O'Malley to his followers. "God gave us these weapons," a feisty Baptist preacher yelled, waving his AK-47 in the air in one hand and his Bible in another to a cacophony of cheers and dozens of rounds fired into the air in agreement. When the reporters concluded the interview, hundreds of O'Malley supporters marched to a field nearby to practice target shooting.

That same day, Father O'Malley sent a bold warning in the form of an electronic message to Erzsébet. "Either you give me the bracelet, Demon, or I'll turn my followers loose on your precious Dianics."

Erzsébet called another conference with the leaders of the various Pagan factions. We informed the Pagan leaders of the ultimatum given by O'Malley. A hush filled the room when Erzsébet suggested an alternate option to deal with the Exorcist threat. "It may be in the best interest of all concerned – for women and for Pagans specifically, to avoid conflict at this time. I would not want to see my friends and associates hurt because of Father O'Malley's personal vendetta to exorcise Jim Jackson and thus disrupt my influence in twenty-first-century cultural affairs."

I looked around, surprised at what just emerged from my mouth. I can honestly say I probably looked as surprised as the women gathered around me.

Esmé asked for a chance to speak and Erzsébet gave her the floor.

"This is a historic moment and a historic movement," Esmé said, her amber eyes gleaming. "You mention a personal vendetta by Father O'Malley, but his assault on you, Erzsébet, is an assault on women everywhere. We're on the verge of showing the world the power and the just governance of the natural religions. If we give in now, we may never have another powerful chance like this to demonstrate the righteousness of our beliefs."

"I agree that this point in history is critical," Erzsébet said, "but these misogynists will kill you all if they're able. I feel responsible for your welfare."

Esmé bowed her head in deference and remained silent for a moment. When she raised her head, her eyes brimmed with tears. "I believe that I'm speaking for all our denominations when I say I'd rather die than miss this opportunity for women involved in the worship of goddess to regain equality in the pantheon of world religions."

"This may not be the right time for the opportunity we seek," Erzsébet replied. "The historic record is filled with examples of how vicious men become when threatened. I see the ground of centuries littered with dead women and I am afraid for all of you. If we stand our ground, we must pray fervently to the Akasha Spirit. If the goddesses maintain the threefold law, we will not be harmed."

While Esmé led a group discussion about the pros and cons of continuing to confront Father O'Malley's forces, Erzsébet answered my questions. "The Akasha Spirit is the fifth element, the omnipresent spiritual power that permeates the universe," she explained. "Akasha is neither male nor female, but all things. The threefold law simply mandates that whatever energy a person extends into the world, be it positive or negative, is returned to that person threefold. So, if the Exorcists attack us, they risk the return of our magick, three times as strong."

CRYONIC MAN

Erzsébet agreed to the Pagan leaders' petition to wait a day while they determined what remedy they could summon to repel or defeat the Exorcist militias.

As the meeting adjourned, the rains stopped and the sun shone across the newly washed land. The Carpathian foothills blazed in brilliant emerald dotted by summer flowers of various hues. As Erzsébet and I watched together from the front entryway of the manor house, the largest rainbow I'd ever seen arched overhead.

A chorus of oohs and aahs rose from the woman fortunate enough to be outside to view the spectacle with us.

But our joy at nature's beauty was short-lived. A taxi carrying a petite woman with a child-like body and a mournful expression zoomed up the lane and stopped in front of us. I leaned forward to hear what she was saying. Erzsébet interpreted the local Slovakian dialect.

"Some concerned citizens who support our dear Erzsébet have planted Slovakian men among the Exorcists. The angry militants have dried and cleaned their weapons in preparation for action. The priest O'Malley has mobilized these rag-tag forces and they are approaching Čachtice by every means of transportation possible. Some are even on foot," the woman said, shaking her head so that her dark, bowl-like hairdo shimmered in the sunlight. "The priest has been secretly encouraging his followers to kill for Jesus. 'It is acceptable to God,' he preaches. 'The more witches you kill, the higher a place you will earn in Heaven.' You must rally your women and be prepared for their onslaught."

I thanked the woman. She nodded dolefully and signaled the driver to take her away. Erzsébet made me scurry into the manor house, calling for an immediate emergency meeting of the Pagan leaders. Within an hour, word circulated among the Pagan camps and the villages nearby that all Pagans available for the gathering storm must congregate upon the great hill of Castle Čachtice.

Women began streaming toward the castle. As the gathering grew, Pagan sentries atop the remnants of Erzsébet's tower spotted the first males arriving in Čachtice via tour buses. Soon, they could see a group of autos pulling to the shoulder of the narrow motorway just outside the village. Suddenly a military helicopter soared overhead, swooping low over the castle, as if gathering information. I wondered if the Slovakian authorities would stop the Exorcists or simply evacuate residents from harm's way. Or did they have confidence that the Pagans could rout the men as they did before? If so, they had more confidence than we did. I felt an equal measure of determination and fear emanating from Erzsébet.

An ever-growing cavalry of men began to march toward the ruins of Castle Čachtice. Erzsébet made me stamp to and fro, shouting out directives and encouraging the women to perform as many types of protective incantations as possible. The hills virtually vibrated with their prayers as they chanted and danced in large and small groups.

I could only speculate what must be on the men's minds as they marched toward the foot of the mountain. The most radical and hateful among them must be eager to start the slaughter. Those who lost faith after their own prayers remained unanswered must worry about what would happen when the "witches cast their spells," as they put it.

As the mob of men approached the mountain, I could hear the shouts as they prepared to scale it. Erzsébet astounded me when she made me concentrate upon the distant voices and tune in to one. I was astonished to hear him clearly, as though he'd been wired for sound.

"Did you feel that? The ground moved," the man said.

"Don't worry about a little earthquake," another replied. "I'm from California, and the earth shakes there all the time. There's no buildings to fall on you here. Just watch out for an avalanche."

But the ground continued to shake. It moved back and forth, up and down, harder and faster. Stones and old mortar broke away from the castle walls, sending many women scurrying away from it. I watched through binoculars as the solid ground below the castle softened and turned to a pudding of mud. Mature trees a century or more old teetered and fell with huge sucking sounds that echoed into the hills. Frightened, many men threw themselves down to try to find handholds on the ground, but found themselves sinking into the swampy muck.

Erzsébet helped me focus upon the pair of men who'd spoken first.

"I thought you said we didn't have anything to worry about other than a building falling on us," the first speaker complained. I could hear the exasperation in his voice as he must have tried to pull his legs from the mud, because I could hear watery sucking sounds followed by curses.

"I've never seen anything like this in Cali. Shit, my hand, grab it, I'm sinking," the Californian whined.

Panic spread. I watched and listened as the militia tried to escape the mud, miring themselves more deeply in the muck. They frantically worked in pairs to extricate themselves, but the more they moved, the deeper they sank. Many dropped their weapons, mortally afraid of drowning in mud. Some prayed while others moaned and started to cry, until they discovered they'd only sunk chest deep. In the far distance, I spotted two men in a black Mercedes who scanned the scene with binoculars from the road leading to the castle. Fathers O'Malley and Flynn, I figured, high and dry.

"No surprise that Father O'Malley doesn't fraternize with his troops. But I wonder why he hasn't yet used his magick," Erzsébet said. "Perhaps he's waiting for these fools to do his dirty work for him. If so, he shouldn't hold his breath."

A flock of the bravest and most accomplished Pagans descended the mountain to surround the mired men. A strange sound began to echo around them, becoming louder and louder with each cry.

"Oh no! Cats!" one man yelled.

Hundreds of cats dashed from behind the Pagans. Most of the muddied Exorcists had viewed the security video of cats viciously attacking the invisible Father O'Malley at the manor house in the news or online. Now they panicked at the thought of cats tearing them to pieces. As a wind rose and swept down from the castle mount, the gale mixed with the wails of dismayed men, aroused cats, and chanting women in a gigantic swirl of raw emotion.

Chapter 28

"Ah, I spoke too soon," Erzsébet said, disappointment and displeasure charging her thoughts.

O'Malley must have decided to use the magick he'd honed as Zsombor, because suddenly, a multitude of field mice swarmed toward the cats. The cats detoured from rushing at the men and began chasing and pouncing upon panicked mice.

The cats drove the frantic mice amongst some of the women nearby. Startled, some began to shriek.

"What a cliché," Erzsébet murmured. "Unbelievable." She began to mutter one of her seemingly endless incantations.

When a huge pack of dogs came howling out of nowhere, dashing down cats and mice alike, peals of laughter broke out among both distressed men and women.

"This mud spell may be new to Zsombor, but when he saw the cats he knew exactly what to do," Erzsébet said. "On the spur of the moment, I could only summon up dogs. Pathetic, but better than nothing."

"I'm impressed," I said, trying to cheer her. "Perhaps a comedic battle is better than a tragic one."

By now, O'Malley and Flynn had driven as close as they could to their men and stood on a boulder nearby. "Have courage, men,"

O'Malley shouted. "They send us cats and we counter with mice. It's no wonder we men run the world! The Pagans' world has gone to the dogs!"

O'Malley's face broke into a wide grin as he watched the dogs chasing cats, cats chasing mice, and the surprised looks on the faces of both sides.

The women quickly retreated, chanting additional protective incantations. With some ingenuity and help from fresh troops just arriving at the rear of their command, the mired men extricated themselves from the mud and returned to solid ground.

A news helicopter hovered overhead to capture the final scene with dogs, cats, and mice scattered among the open-mouthed Pagans and Exorcists. A short time later when the report broke on international newscasts, the world laughed more at the stuck-in-the-mud Exorcists than at the Pagans.

"Can you explain what just happened?" a newscaster asked Father Flynn in a follow-up interview. "There seems to be some parallel with Biblical stories of pestilences and punishments with the appearance of earthquakes, mud, cats, mice, and dogs."

Father Flynn appeared confused for a moment, as though weighing what to say. "It would seem similar, but all appearances were perfectly natural phenomena," Flynn replied. "The rain softened the ground and the earthquake turned it into jelly-like mud. The cats sensed the presence of so many field mice disturbed from their nests by the quakes and came to hunt them. The dogs were attracted to the scene and simply multiplied the confusion. But that the mice scared some of the women away probably saved their lives," Father Flynn said with an undisguised smirk.

"O'Malley must be proud – that's exactly the sort of thing he'd want Flynn to say," Erzsébet said. "O'Malley's supervising Bishop doesn't like to acknowledge that Pagans have any supernatural powers, despite all O'Malley's nonsense about exorcisms. And O'Malley certainly doesn't want anyone to know about his identity as Zsombor or the powers he possesses. "

Her opinion, as always, was spot-on, but a survey of viewers showed that many enjoyed the mad chase of cats, mice, dogs, and women, and believed that the event was caused by magickal spells, all attributable to the Pagans. Most loved it that the Pagans appeared to be victorious over their Exorcist adversaries.

Debates began to rage around the world about which group was right. President Josef Vladimir beseeched the Slovak Republic National Police to draft plans to keep the two groups apart, resulting in the creation of a new elite unit, the International Special Intervention Brigade. I could hardly believe their name – "Nádasdy-Báthory Guards."

"I told you, they love my family here," Erzsébet bragged.

Fascinated by the parallels between modern, reactionary Christian behavior and Christian behavior in centuries past, Erzsébet followed news reports closely. Reminded not only of the old and new witch-burnings in Boston, but also of the long-ago Christian inquisitions and the Crusades, she also spoke more about her personal travails before her death in 1614, when Zsombor and György Thurzó manipulated public opinion to seize her wealth.

"I guess some things never change – or maybe history really does repeat itself," I told her.

Modern Christians – at least those Exorcists focused on my case – had adapted a unique method of manipulation with the public performance of exorcisms after my rejuvenation and Erzsébet's appearance. These gained many converts because the result allowed the shamed victim to be welcomed back into society as "born again" – and more easily manipulated than ever before.

The media broiled with new reports daily about possession. Husbands accused wives, wives accused husbands, children accused parents, and parents accused children of spirit possession for the silliest reasons, the latest excuse for people to enjoy a few moments of media fame. Societies for the exorcised were springing up everywhere, and most people who experienced the procedure wouldn't associate with anyone who hadn't.

In the midst of all this uproar, the United Nations Security Council held talks about human rights violations connected with the

Saturday Night Exorcists. Sending a peacekeeping force to Slovakia appeared on one agenda. Finally, a UN committee hammered out an agreement with the Republic of Slovakia, the Catholic Church, and the World Federation of Nature Religions to schedule talks between leaders of the Exorcists and the Pagans, to be broadcast on an international cable network.

Father O'Malley didn't have much choice but to go along after Bishop Cheney agreed to the discussion, on orders from Rome. Erzsébet and her Pagan leaders welcomed anything that might cast the nature religions in a good light. My reservations about appearing in public kicked in, but the talks might just turn out to be my ticket to freedom.

Three weeks to the day after the mud and mice extravaganza and on the day of the much-anticipated broadcast, the online Times of London lead op-ed was an article titled "Gendered Mass Murder." The article outlined the nearly instinctive but irrational association between women and witchcraft, describing how women are historically cast as witches with an ability to coerce male-dominated Christian society for their own ends, and why the perception of that fallacy must change.

The UN Security Council selected representatives for the two sides – Bishop Cheney for the Exorcists, because he had extensive on-camera experience during the molestation trials of priests from his diocese twenty-five years before, and for the Exorcists, Professor Belinda Angier, author of several books about the persecution of women by the Church and a practicing Pagan herself.

Respected for his neutrality worldwide, Rufus Geerts, the popular journalist and host of "The Truth Hurts" on the FLIC channel headquartered Brussels, was chosen to moderate the debate. Geerts spiced his programs with a bit of contention – "If you can't stand the pain, don't ask Rufus" was the opening pitch line of his late-night talk show.

The midnight headliner had no set time limit, and Rufus decided when it was time to quit. If the debate went hot and heavy, he would let it flow until the rhetoric cooled down. Sometimes the show ran for hours and aired in segments. FLIC billed the confrontation between the Exorcists and the Pagans as "a marathon show."

"This confrontation will have more viewers than your championship fight," Erzsébet mentioned proudly as we scrolled through the morning news on my PVA.

As primary figures in this debate, we received complimentary tickets and airfare to the show. I wondered if Father O'Malley also came to see the show, but even with Erzsébet chanting incantations, I couldn't see him anywhere.

I conceded that there were certainly more cameras and reporters in the FLIC Amphitheatre than at my world championship fight. Equipped with huge video screens and a revolving stage operated via solar power, the venue seated up to 20,000 people. As I found when the show began, the amphitheatre also had extraordinary state-of-the-art acoustics even with the roof open to a clear sky when the taping began in mid-afternoon.

The FLIC CEO, dressed in a dapper tuxedo, welcomed the audience, introduced Geerts, Cheney, and Angier, who sat together at an oval-shaped table reminiscent of ambassadorial talks, and then left the stage.

Rufus directed his first question to Bishop Cheney. "Sir, will you tell us about the manuscript called 'Malleus Maleficarum' published by the Catholic Church in 1486?"

A look of concentration crossed Bishop Cheney's face before he answered. "Certainly. 'The Hammer of Witches' was published by Catholic inquisition authorities in 1485-86."

Ms. Angier's face tightened and her voice became hard when she interrupted. "The Inquisition – isn't that exactly what the Church is trying to resurrect again, Bishop Cheney?"

Cheney smiled beatifically at her loss of control. "Of course not, Ms. Angier. I'm simply answering a question."

Rufus intervened. "Do you have a related question for Bishop Cheney?"

Ms. Angier nodded. "Yes, Bishop, how many women has the Church murdered for allegedly practicing witchcraft?"

CRYONIC MAN

"I'll answer that question after you answer this one. How many human sacrifices have been carried out by witches and Satanic cults over the years? In the past decade, as the popularity of the so-called nature religions has flourished, authorities are discovering more frequently the grim evidence of animal and human sacrifices perpetrated by covens and Satanic cults," Cheney replied.

Angier frowned. "Let's talk about real statistics on both sides. Better yet, let's get straight to the point we all want to hear. Why is the church persecuting Jim Jackson?"

The camera panned to Rufus and he waved his hands and nodded. "Proceed," he said. "This is making my job much easier."

"Okay," Cheney said. "The Church is not persecuting Jim Jackson. We are reasonably certain he's possessed by an evil spirit and we are committed to help him rid himself of it."

"So, the plan is to force Jackson to have an exorcism?" Angier asked.

"When a person is possessed they can't decide what's good for them." Cheney said.

"How many of the priests who molested kids in their charge have been through an exorcism"? Angier asked.

"Why, none of them were possessed," Cheney answered.

"What you're saying is that these pedophiles weren't possessed and that their criminal acts were performed of their own free will. Now, a law-abiding citizen who has committed no crimes is allegedly possessed by a spirit and you're going to force him to have an exorcism. Is that correct?" Angier asked, drumming her fingers on the table.

"Law abiding has nothing to do with it," Cheney said. "He's definitely inhabited by a spirit, one who committed many crimes against humanity and the Church before she died in the seventeenth century."

"Perhaps the Church's child molesters may have behaved better if they were inhabited by a spirit. . ." Without waiting for his reply, Angier fired another question at him. "Even if Jackson is possessed as you say, how do you know it's an evil spirit and not a spirit sent by God?"

"Nowhere in the Old or New Testament does it say that God sends spirits to inhabit anyone's body," Cheney said.

Ms. Angier crossed her arms and leaned back in her chair. "So, now you can read God's mind! Because you say it's not written anywhere, does that mean God can't do anything He – or She – wants?"

"Both the Old and New Testaments make repeated references to the practice of witchcraft and sorcery," Cheney said. "These practices are always condemned by God. The Bible also condemns astrology and the reading of human and animal entrails."

"What if I told you that your Father O'Malley, who the Church sent to perform an exorcism on James Jackson, is himself possessed by an evil spirit?" Angier said.

Bishop Cheney glowered. "That's a preposterous accusation; I'd say you were lying."

"If you have a test for possession," Angier said, "I strongly suggest you use it on him."

"Ms. Angier, are you saying O'Malley is a tool of the Devil?" Rufus asked.

"No, I'm saying a spirit possesses him," answered Ms. Angier.

Rufus sensed a spectacular opportunity. "Why don't we invite both parties here and test them? Bishop, did you or did you not say there was a test to determine if one is possessed?"

"First, in deference to those in our audience who may not understand possession, you must consider the basic structure of the spiritual world," Cheney explained. "There is a hierarchy with God at the top, of course, and evil beings at the bottom. Fallen angels, originally members of the Heavenly realm, were cast out for their disobedience and now inhabit the lowest spiritual realms. Some of these fallen angels are demons; these spirits hate the human soul and seek to create chaos in the world. If a soul is spiritually confused or weak but still inhabits a live body, then an evil spirit can enter into the body. By terror and cunning, these spirits can wrest the soul's will to succumb to their will. Simply put, the human will and personality can be taken over entirely."

I was glad that I wasn't on stage because what the Bishop said I knew to be true and that's what Erzsébet did to me.

The camera panned to Rufus. "While I thank you for the clarification, it doesn't answer the question about a positive test for possession," he said. "Please enlighten us."

"Well, sir, a psychiatrist at the National Institute of Mental Health developed a different test in the late twentieth century, but cognitive neuroscience research has advanced significantly over the past two decades. The Church has perfected a simple procedure to discover if an unwelcome spirit inhabits a person by means of a combination of Functional Magnetic Resonance Imaging (fMRI) and hyperdigital electroencephalogram or hEEG. Other psychologists have confirmed the results of this sophisticated test. In simple layman's terms, the procedure involves shining a light at varied microscopic intervals into the eyes of the patient, whose brains and brain waves are then monitored on the fMRI and hEEG to register this activity. Each human brain reacts uniquely to light. The results of the two tests are digitally combined, then interpreted by computer software developed for this purpose. We have run control experiments in which researchers scanned a group of actors pretending to be possessed. These actors' roles did not cause significant variance from their normal brainwaves. Another trial tested psychiatric patients who thought they were possessed but weren't. Their brain waves showed no abnormality."

Ms. Angier nodded and appeared to be reassured by the mention of scientific trials.

Bishop Cheney continued his explanation. "On the group of people who manifested true symptoms of possession, each patient also manifested their own unique brainwave pattern. The demon or spirit possessing the human also displayed a distinct brainwave pattern of its own. In other words, a scan of a possessed person revealed two distinct brainwave patterns in one reading. This proved the patients were not acting or role-playing."

"So you'd be willing —"

Bishop Cheney looked impatiently at Rufus.

"He's boiling mad," Erzsébet told me. "I don't think he really wants to subject O'Malley to these tests."

". . . So in answer to your question, yes, I believe this is an accurate test, and I'll volunteer Father O'Malley to appear on your show to be tested if Mr. Jackson agrees to appear at the same time."

"Clever," Erzsébet said. "Cheney doesn't mind killing two birds with one stone."

Ms. Angier motioned to speak. "Mr. Geerts and Bishop Cheney, I'll need to study the accuracy of this test before I'll agree to have Mr. Jackson appear here and submit to it."

"Good point, Ms. Angier," Rufus said. "Now the question arises about how to interpret this test. Bishop?"

Bishop Cheney pressed his palms and fingertips together and held them at chest level. "That's both simple and complicated. The Church does not dispute spirit possession, but as you clearly know from Jim Jackson's case, modern psychologists and psychiatrists refuse to accept the possibility and refute the test results the Church advances as technical flukes caused by digitally merging the two tests. I'm not willing to continue this debate as it would be never-ending. Better that Father O'Malley and Jim Jackson are tested straight away. Likely we'll find that Jackson is clearly possessed and that our good Father is not nor has ever been possessed by an evil spirit," Bishop Cheney concluded.

Belinda Angier opened her mouth to speak and snapped it shut again, appearing to think better of it.

"Okay," Rufus said. "We'll continue this conversation if and when Father O'Malley and Jim Jackson consent to appear for a demonstration of the Church's protocol for testing spirit possession. As a preliminary, FLIC will petition the Church to provide scientific data for Ms. Angier. Meanwhile, if you have an opinion and want it expressed on "The Truth Hurts," please e-mail it to rufusmeerts at FLIC.be. Have a pleasant tomorrow, and remember, if you can't stand the pain, don't ask Rufus! Goodbye for now."

Afterward, as we rested at our hotel before our red-eye flight back to Budapest, talking heads on every news program we surfed through repeated just about everything said on "The Truth Hurts" and analyzed and reanalyzed it all.

So far, Erzsébet mentioned little about me being tested for possession. How would she deal with this?

"This is a break for O'Malley," she said, simultaneously commenting on the commentators and answering my question. In our case, I allowed you to remain even though your soul's hold on your body was weak after fifty years. Now, if you submit to the test, I may be exposed to Zsombor's designs because of that kindness."

Chapter 29

Belinda Angier reviewed the technical parameters of the Church's testing for possession and the UN Security Council scheduled a test just three days after "The Truth Hurts" debate. If I consented to the test, the truth about my possession by Erzsébet would be exposed in the next live broadcast from Brussels in just two more weeks. All the diagnoses of brain damage, emotional stress, or mental instability by my physicians, neuropsychologists, and neuropsychiatrists would be revealed as nonsense.

I'd desperately wanted to oust Erzsébet for so long that I found it hard to feel anything but elated at the prospect of finally getting rid of her. But O'Malley would surely demand I undergo an exorcism the day of the test when Erzsébet's presence was revealed. Then what would happen to her?

My elation turned to confusion. One part of me desperately wanted to be rid of Erzsébet and the other part wanted to prove her right to choose me as her champion. My anger at Cwia Alexander's death had not abated, and O'Malley's identity as Zsombor, though unknown to the general public, would likely not be revealed if, as Erzsébet said, Zsombor had patiently reincarnated as O'Malley. That meant that O'Malley was not truly possessed by a spirit, but moved instead by a conscious but evil soul. Clearly, he remembered his lifetime as Zsombor or he wouldn't be pursuing the bracelet. Although I desperately wanted to be free of Erzsébet, how could I allow Zsombor to get the bracelet?

Erzsébet ignored my hatred of her and studied everything she could about the Church's use of hEEG and the fMRI tests used for detecting possession, trying to find any weakness that could be exploited. She racked my brain for an alternate plan. I had no choice but to suggest she experiment on the same type of equipment used for the test.

Surprisingly, she thought my suggestion worthwhile and gathered the necessary equipment. "Since the exact timing of changes in the brain as well as the blending and interpretation of the tests is computer controlled, the computer software should also be able to determine precisely the time it takes for the visual stimulus to reach the visual cortex. The hEEG and fMRI records the active brain areas and are able to pinpoint the portions used by a possessing spirit. If we can find a way to subvert this. . ."

Erzsébet and I grappled with the technicalities of the apparatus, and after numerous attempts at deception, we failed.

"I'll have to leave your body while you're being tested or you'll fail and be turned over to the Church for exorcism," Erzsébet said.

I'm not ashamed to say the thought that I'd be free at last crossed my mind. Erzsébet immediately said she knew what I was thinking, as always.

"Jim Jackson, I'm leaving you with the bracelet, so if anything happens to me, it'll be up to you to prevent Zsombor from acquiring your bracelet."

"*My* bracelet? Why are you leaving it with me? I don't want it. Just take it with you when you go. You're better at defending it than I am."

"Haven't you yet learned the depth of Zsombor's evil? This nonsense he's doing as Father O'Malley is small beans."

"Causing Cwia's death wasn't small beans."

"No, but he's capable of much worse. Believe me, he'll find unheard of ways to cause as much suffering as possible. If he gains unlimited knowledge and immortality, the world will become a living hell. I'm more vulnerable if I wear the bracelet in spirit form. I'm showing complete trust in you. After all, Jim Jackson, I've shared your thoughts for two years now. If I don't return, it's up to you to stop Zsombor. You owe it to the people of the twenty-first century. This is why you ended up here, not the boxing championship."

"Where are you going, Erzsébet?"

"I'll be right beside you, but we can't communicate as we do now. All I've learned in the past two years will help me do what I must as a free spirit."

"Maybe we shouldn't take this test, then. Maybe there's a way out. Why take a chance you won't be able to come back?"

Finally, just days away from getting rid of this possessing bitch, and here I am, worried about her leaving. How could I be so uncertain about such an important matter? Two years of total togetherness made us one and now the fear of her leaving cut me like a knife. Could she literally be my soul mate?

"Listen to me," Erzsébet insisted. "We can pull this off. When Zsombor is examined, I'll enter his body. What I learned from my struggles with you will come in handy. I should be able to dominate his mind and he won't even notice what I am doing until I have control and it's too late."

"But what if you can't dominate his mind like you do mine?"

"I am not sure, but I have to try. I can't allow Zsombor to gain possession of both bracelets."

Leaving me the bracelet made sense. If Zsombor should prove more powerful than Erzsébet, he'd have both bracelets. So willing or not, I was now humanity's protector, honored to have this responsibility thrust on me.

At the very least, Zsombor's hEEG and fMRI would show two spirits in O'Malley's body if Erzsébet was able to enter it. That would turn the Church against him.

When the day of the test arrived, Father O'Malley and I were transported to the FLIC Channel studio temporarily erected at a secret location in Brussels just for this broadcast. The UN Security

Technical Team oversaw the setup – two identical cubicles situated side-by-side with a center wall dividing them. The occupants of each cubicle could not observe one another, but the TV cameras, Rufus Geerts, the medical examiners, and other broadcasting technicians could view both cubicles at the same time. There would be no live audience to avoid compromising the tests.

More people watched this broadcast than any other in the history of television. Rufus opened the show with his usual patter, then introduced the supervising technicians and assistants. Finally, he announced the commencement of the tests. Father O'Malley stepped from the left wing of the studio and into his cubicle. Then I stepped forward from the right wing of the studio and into my cubicle.

Suddenly, I felt a cold spot form on top of my head. As quickly as I noticed it, the spot warmed again and Erzsébet was gone.

Fear crept into my heart and mind to dominate any relief I felt. Zsombor was right next to me in the form of Father O'Malley, waiting to take the bracelet from my wrist. Like it or not, I had to proceed with Erzsébet's plan.

After we entered our respective cubicles, we each lay in the fMRI scanner. While Rufus explained the procedure, pointing out the display screens where images and data appeared and describing the images that would display if either subject were possessed by a spirit, the medical technicians placed the hEEG electrodes on our heads.

"This is history being made, right before your eyes," Rufus said as he gave the signal to start the scans.

Everything proceeded calmly. The scanners began to hum over our heads and the screens to alight with images of our brains. Suddenly, the screens on O'Malley's side went erratic, the numbers doubling and flashing wildly. His screen clearly showed the energetic profile of two separate entities.

The closed-circuit TV revealed the priest squirming out of the apparatus, ripping the wires from his cranium. "No! No way! Get out of my head," he shouted, clutching the sides of his head as though in severe pain. Rufus and the television crew and medical technicians watched, transfixed, as he shoved aside my technician and forced his way into my cubicle.

I ripped off my electrodes and stood to meet Father O'Malley. The priest shouted the incantation and made the bracelet on my arm flare with light. His right wrist glowed with the same fiery light. He pulled a long, serrated hunting knife from his sleeve. Brandishing it, he turned to threaten Rufus and the cameraman who abandoned his closed-circuit monitor to rush into my cubicle to try to grab O'Malley from behind.

Stupefied by O'Malley's actions, I froze to watch as he shrugged Rufus off, grabbed him by the hair, and tried to stick the knife into his throat. Rufus reflexively pulled back, escaping with a short, shallow cut near his jugular vein.

O'Malley grabbed my wrist and braced it against the table. He slashed the knife toward it. Coming to my senses, I hit him with my free elbow and tried to twist free.

Suddenly, Zsombor struggled as though attacked by an unseen intruder. His hand turned and he pointed the knife directly at his heart. With one hand, he struggled to stab himself, and with the other, to stop the knife's plunge. But the force holding the knife was stronger and it buried the knife deep into his heart. O'Malley sank to the floor with an incredulous look on his face, blood spurting from his chest.

Erzsébet must be responsible.

That Father O'Malley tested positive for possession and Jim Jackson found spirit-free was a major setback for the Exorcists and a major victory for the Pagans. An attempted murder turned suicide boosted ratings beyond all expectations as the FLIC replayed "The Truth Hurts" program multiple times daily over the next several weeks. A public uproar ensued over the bracelets of fire visible on Father O'Malley and me, but after I denied knowledge of the phenomenon to the dozens of reporters who called me day and night, they went elsewhere to dig up information.

After an investigation in Brussels by local authorities and the UN committee who oversaw the debate and tests for possession, I returned to Slovakia to collect the remainder of my things from the manor house in Čachtice. All the Pagans staying in and around Čachtice were packing and leaving as well. Esmé and Madame LeFleur and many other lovely ladies bid me a sad goodbye in one final sunrise ceremony at Castle Čachtice to honor Erzsébet.

It didn't seem possible either to me or to her supporters that she'd left my body. We all felt hollow. With both Erzsébet and O'Malley gone, the war between the Exorcists and the Pagans was pretty much exhausted for the moment. There would be future battles for the Pagans elsewhere.

When all the women trailed off after the final ceremony, I sat alone atop the castle hill, watching clouds etch the sky. Where did Erzsébet go when O'Malley died? Would she come back? I recited the chant to Marduk and watched the bracelet glow on my right wrist. I still had it, but what did that mean? Zsombor died as O'Malley, but he'd passed away before and reincarnated again, as we all do. Could he come back for the bracelet as another person? I felt totally lost without Erzsébet's guidance. Even here, at her previous residence, I had no clue what to do next.

Before departing Slovakia, I shipped the trunk with all the charts and magick formulas along with the golden amulets by armored express. Zoloti handled all the arrangements for me and locked the stuff in my bank's vault.

I headed home to Boston, alone for the first time since my rejuvenation. When I boarded my flight in Budapest and seated myself in first class, I recognized the rear end moving beneath the flight attendant's skirt as Gloria's. Her face lit up when she saw me. Nice to see her again, but with Erzsébet gone, I was in no mood for pleasantries.

"I lost a friend," I told her. She absorbed the news stoically and offered her condolences with genuine empathy for my grief. I promised to call her sometime.

As the plane droned over the Atlantic, I fell asleep and dreamt about Erzsébet telling me not to waste any time finding Zsombor. I awoke with a start, expecting to have a mental conversation with her. I'd taken it for granted that I always had someone to talk to and to share my thoughts.

On the positive side, I could use my five senses fully again and when I arrived in Boston, I went around my rooms at the Nine Zero touching objects to remind myself how things felt. I could take a shower in less than five minutes without bothering with a dozen lotions and potions. My freedom should have felt wonderful, but it didn't.

Joe called a few times during the trouble in Slovakia, but I'd only talked to him briefly, always deterred by Erzsébet's activities. He began to call daily after he read that I'd left Slovakia, but I put him off, not ready to share with him. And to think that I'd once wanted so badly to tell him about Erzsébet. . .

For the second time in my short life, I felt the dark cloud of depression wrapping its tendrils around me. I opened a bottle of Scotch, poured a tumbler full, and downed it in one long swallow and then poured another.

As I lay brooding on a couch in the Nine Zero penthouse in front of the 3-D TV, I watched as Bishop Cheney and Father Flynn discussed the possession test debacle on a talk show. I raised my hand to snap my fingers at the "off" position, then thought better of it and paused to listen.

"How could O'Malley be possessed?" the host asked Flynn.

Father Flynn offered his opinion. "I know he wasn't possessed before we went to the studio, because I tested him on the same type of equipment that was used in the Brussels broadcast numerous times. He never once showed any degree of possession."

"So," Bishop Cheney said, "Jackson loses his demon and Father O'Malley gains one. That strikes me as an answer to your question."

"Why would the demon then force O'Malley to try to kill Jackson?" the host asked.

"Demons work in mysterious ways," Flynn said.

People would debate what only I understood for weeks on end until something equally as bizarre captured their attention. I shut the TV off and went for a walk to think everything over. I returned home with another bottle of booze and opened it as soon as I walked through the door. I didn't bother with a glass. I chug-a-lugged a quarter of it before I felt relaxed enough to sleep, rinse and repeat. My days became tormented by thoughts and my nights dulled by whiskey.

As the weeks passed, current events began to overshadow the old conflict between the Exorcists and Pagans, as I predicted. A massive earthquake in China killed a half-million residents. The CIA uncovered a terrorist plot to explode a dirty bomb in downtown Chicago. The terrorist group who allegedly planned the event accused the U.S. government of infiltrating their inner circle and pushing the plot to eliminate a growing Muslim population there.

The world had certainly changed in leaps and bounds since I'd exited life in the '70s, and not just in technological advancements. I might have been interested in learning more about current affairs under normal circumstances, but normal for me meant sharing my mind with Erzsébet. The old cliché "can't live with her and can't live without her" came to mind. I began to curse my depression and my inability to shake it off. Could my affection for Erzsébet be some sort of spell she cast over me?

I pushed forward by finding a new fencing teacher in Boston. I continued to spar and jog daily to boost my mood. Though I retained my ability as a fighter, I felt like part of me was missing without Erzsébet egging me on.

Though I felt a little better, I continued to obsess about when I first became aware of her. She seemed evil, but after spending two years with her, I found her to be a brilliant, cunning, tough woman. She was forced to do some unsavory, hard-hitting things to survive and she was definitely a survivor. I believed many of the legends about her were concocted for various reasons. Zsombor planted some stories because he wanted the immortality bracelet, and some were planted by the king and Palatine Thurzó because they wanted her inheritance. The gory aspects, like the bathing in the blood of virgins, added shock value to the tale years later.

There wasn't a day that went by when I didn't think of Erzsébet or something in my life that was either influenced by or improved by her. To add insult to injury, on one particularly lonely day, Joe called to tell me that Emily had suddenly passed away.

"I'm so sorry, Dad. I know you've been busy and I just didn't expect her to slip away like this. Outside the Alzheimer's, her health was fairly good."

"I'm sorry, Joey. I've let you both down again," was all I managed to say before I choked up entirely.

While immersed in Erzsébet's drama, Emily became a faded memory. Now I felt like a low-down scumbag for not taking Joe's calls earlier, and worst of all, for not being at Emily's deathbed. But deep down I knew that staying away was probably best for both of us. Or was I kidding myself with all these excuses? Maybe I just didn't want to admit that I'd fallen out of love with her, Shallow, I know, and I wanted to blame it on our bodies' age differences, on Erzsébet, or even on Emily for rejecting me under the influence of the Alzheimer's. Confronted by two stubborn females and my youthful horniness, I'd just given up and let nature take its course. Only the object of my affection was a woman I couldn't even see or touch. I had to be out of my mind or under her influence.

While I dressed for Emily's memorial service two days later, I beat myself up again over not maintaining contact with Joe. I hadn't created many good opportunities to bond as father and son. I recalled him fondly as a baby and then my next contact was with this fifty-something doctor, and at a difficult time when I shared body and mind with Erzsébet. I'd watched Joe growing up from the spirit world but that felt like watching a character on television for many seasons. My obsession with winning the world heavyweight boxing championship hadn't helped either, then or now. It was hard to admit that Joe was more of a father to me than I'd ever been for him.

Joe was the one person in the entire world who cared if I lived or died and I vowed to do something about it.

Joe met me in the hotel lobby and we went directly to the cemetery for a graveside service, where a crowd was already gathering. My head brimmed full of regrets. Relatives from both sides of the family stared at me grimly, and rightly so, for abandoning

Emily. I hung my head, shamed. I understood their anger, but they didn't understand how much I regretted not being there for her.

After the service, Joe and I passed on the gathering with Emily's family and headed back to the Nine Zero. For the first time since my rejuvenation, I talked to him directly, without Erzsébet's control. I shared everything I could recall from the moment I'd died to the moment when I became conscious after the rejuvenation.

Amazed, he asked if I'd been possessed since he'd awakened me.

"Yes," I answered. "In the beginning I despised Erzsébet, but as I became acquainted with her, I began to understand her and as my understanding grew, I grew fond of her. Erzsébet's spirit is basically good. She came here to prevent her nemesis Zsombor, an accomplished but evil sorcerer, from acquiring the second bracelet that would make him immortal and all-seeing."

I'd forgotten all about the bracelet in my grief and confusion. I recited the incantation, and sure enough, it began to glow with its peculiar fiery light on my right wrist.

Joe's eyes widened in disbelief as the cool flames encircled my wrist. "Holy cow," he exclaimed. He grabbed a cloth napkin from my dining table and attempted to snuff out the fire with it. Once he put his hand near the bracelet, he discovered that the flame wasn't hot nor did it burn the dinner napkin or me.

He was full of questions. "That's miraculous. A flame that doesn't burn. Why does it erupt in flames when you say those words? How do you make it disappear? Will it appear again once it disappears?"

I couldn't help but smile, seeing his schoolboyish enthusiasm. "Erzsébet told me that the god Marduk created the bracelets and the sacred incantation to make them appear so those who wore his bracelet could be certain it remained with them and so they could choose their future incarnations."

The flames receded after a few seconds as they always did once I stopped reciting the incantation. I chanted it again, and once more, the bracelet burst into flames and became visible.

"Unbelievable. You're telling me by wearing a bracelet you'll live another life? What about the rest of us?"

"There's a spirit world waiting for everyone, Joe, and I can tell you much more about my fifty years there. But where you'll go, I don't know. It depends upon individual karma and maybe even preference. With these bracelets, the wearer can choose the circumstances and time of their next incarnation – and as far as Erzsébet knew, there is only a pair left."

"I'd like to study the composition of the bracelet, Dad. Maybe I can duplicate it. What do you think?"

"I don't know. Look how much trouble only two bracelets have been causing. It may not be a good idea to manufacture any more, even if you could."

"Well, of course my model wouldn't be the same. But stop by the lab when you have time so I can look at it through an electron microscope. Just to see what the composition is. What are your plans for right now?"

I could see the intense curiosity coursing through my son. My story about possession and eternal life, spirit worlds, and everything else either made him wonder about my mental health or made him realize that there truly is life after death. Perhaps his interests in cryonic preservation and rejuvenation would lead to scientific studies of the afterlife.

Still unsure what I should do, I couldn't answer Joe's question. I was totally confused about what happened at the studio. I assumed Erzsébet possessed O'Malley, but did he fight her off as he died? His intention was to cut my hand off and take the bracelet in front of the world. I had to be alive in order for him to get it. Once he acquired both bracelets, it didn't matter what anybody thought or did. He would be untouchable, and that's why he risked everything in front of the cameras. If he had been successful, the world would be a different place today.

"What actually happened during that horrendous telecast?" Joe asked.

"I wish I knew. I'm assuming Erzsébet got the upper hand with O'Malley and caused him to stab himself in the heart. But whoever wore the bracelet at the time of his death would be the one to reincarnate consciously. Erzsébet was in O'Malley's body when he died and so I can only wonder if they merged and reincarnated as one spirit or two."

"Maybe we can figure this out scientifically. If you'll let me study the bracelet, maybe we can gain a better understanding of what happened to Erzsébet."

"Let me think about it, son."

I knew Joe couldn't resist examining the bracelet to determine if there was any basis to my story and to understand better what had happened to me. But my priority was to find Zsombor, and to find out quickly what happened to Erzsébet. Maybe it would be smart to examine the ancient text waiting for me in the bank vault. Tomorrow I would think. Tonight I only wanted to have a few drinks to ease my grief.

"We both need time to process losing Emily. Let me get in touch with you in a few days," Joe said. We took the glass elevator that had frightened Erzsébet to go downstairs, and while he went home to mourn his mother's passing with Audrey, I prowled one of the hotel's lounges and ordered a whiskey sour.

As I nursed the drink and mused over the bracelet, I looked up. Sitting down the bar from me was the guy Erzsébet brought to my room nearly two years before, the one whose nose I'd broken. One look at me and he was out the door. I felt guilty at my brutal, un-twenty-first-century behavior.

Seeing him again stirred old memories I'd almost forgotten. I ordered another whiskey sour and before getting caught up in a walk down memory lane, I reached into my pocket for the digital communicator Zoloti had given me so long ago.

"I need an empty vault in the bank building to work in," I told him when he picked up, "and I need armed security 24/7."

"No problem, Mr. Jackson," Zoloti said. "Whatever you need."

Chapter 30

I drank so much after seeing the gay guy I'd beaten up that I woke up with a pounding headache. And with a sleeping body beside me.

Had I gotten so drunk I'd tried to make it up to him? Good God. I cringed as I slowly peeled the sheet away from the sleeping figure, expecting the worst. Relief washed over me when I saw the pretty blonde sleeping peacefully and noticed her clothes piled neatly on an armchair nearby. I reached over and held up a skimpy black cocktail dress. I didn't see any underwear and couldn't help but picture her in that little number without any.

She opened her eyes as though she sensed me staring at her and turned to look at me. "Good morning, Jim."

I was conscious that my breath might stink from last night's whiskey and pulled away. "Hello. Where did we meet?"

"Downstairs, in the hotel lounge."

"I'm sorry, I don't remember."

"No? Dude, you paid me five hundred dollars to spend the night with you and once we got to this room, all you did was talk."

"Oh, what did I talk about?"

"You went on and on about how you missed some chick named, um, Erz-something – like Elizabeth, and then you ranted about how you needed to find her."

Damn. Even when drunk and with a beautiful woman, all I could do was think about Erzsébet. Thinking of her now reminded me that the bank vault awaited. Time was truly of the essence and I needed to get started with my research. I pulled my trousers from the floor and pulled my wallet from my pocket. I figured the young lady would be satisfied with my addition of another hundred-dollar bill to the five I promised. I offered the money and my thanks, and then left for the bank without asking her name.

I met Zoloti as scheduled at the vault. He introduced the three large men accompanying him as Manny, Steve, and Izutu. From now on, this security team would never leave me alone unless requested. I needed privacy for my work, so I told them to wait outside the vault.

Three long old-fashioned oak tables with several matching chairs furnished the inside of the private deposit room of the vault, which measured about twelve by fourteen feet with an eight-foot high ceiling. Already sitting on one table was the old chest I'd pulled from behind the wall of Erzsébet's castle tower and the broadsword I'd trained with in Čachtice.

Seeing the chest again brought a lump to my throat. I started unpacking the scrolls and papers. As I arranged the contents neatly on the table, I realized the trunk contained more items than I'd noticed before. Had Erzsébet blocked this stuff from my mind? How could I follow the additional astrological charts to determine where Zsombor might have ended up? I needed to find him before he found me.

As I studied the charts, I despaired that without Erzsébet's brainpower, I'd never find him. With her, my own intellect increased tremendously, but without her, though I retained some learning and an expanded vocabulary, I was still pretty low on the IQ scale, a brain made more for fighting than analysis.

Báró Zsombor's and Gróf Ferenc Nádasdy's collection of documents were written in multiple languages and dialects as well as ancient glyphs. Without Erzsébet's linguistic skills, I hit a dead end. Maybe I could hire professionals who understood hieroglyphics and old tongues. If I divided the contents of the trunk by language and subject matter, and gave these parts to different experts, perhaps they'd be able to decipher their portion yet not understand the bigger picture. I wasn't dumb enough to tell anyone about the bracelets except the one person I trusted without reservation, my son Joe.

Joe arrived at the vault with his 3D interface touchscreen tablet soon after I called and requested his help.

He waved his hands at the tabletop full of scrolls and documents. "We can't let anyone have the originals, Dad. We'll scan everything into a database, and then we can print as many copies as we need. Then we'll use software to pre-evaluate whatever data we can come up with ourselves."

I hoped Joe believed Erzsébet's stories, but if not, he was really going out of his way to humor me.

"Here's how the voice-and-eye scanner software works, Dad. The 3DIT practically reads your mind by scanning your eye movements. You can also tell the computer what you want it to do. If you want to scan anything, just lay it on the touchscreen. The system will transfer everything into the drive and file of your choice."

"Like this?" I asked and lay a scroll face down on the wafer-thin, flatscreen monitor.

"Exactly," Joe said. "If you want to print a copy, just say print. He unfolded a plastic square that looked like a puzzle and transformed it into a working printer. "And if you want to open a group of documents or photos to view them together, you can arrange the images on the screen with your fingertip, like this."

I watched as he pulled pictures all over the touchscreen with his fingertip.

"If you need to type anything, just tap this corner for your virtual keyboard. If you'd rather use a mobile unit, just detach this rechargeable pen projector. It contains all the same files and software as the 3DIT and you can project your virtual screen and keyboard on any flat surface – a table, a wall, a mirror, or a piece of paper and do everything the physical touchscreen does."

"Amazing," was all I could say. I would never have imagined using this technology in the 1970s.

246

Within two hours, we managed to divide all the information by categories and languages, and scanned it all. By using the new database, it was much less intimidating to figure out what information needed more evaluation. Joe recommended that we give the same information to at least two different experts in each field in order to evaluate the opinions rendered.

Joe called a technology geek friend to design some software to do astrological tracking similar to what Erzsébet did by hand. While I watched, he forwarded our entries on the database so far by pulling a file with his finger into an electronic mailbox.

"Bill's Hyper3DIT will automatically do thousands of calculations when the file is received. If there are no mistakes in the software design or in the information we entered, we'll soon have some answers," Joe said.

"How will we know if there are any errors?"

"We won't. That's why we'll only use these results if we can get comparable results from our experts and combine them for a comprehensive inquiry."

Next, we would contact our experts in Egyptology, ancient history, and archaic languages such as Sumerian and Old Magyar, as well as experts in many other ancient dialects and glyphs.

Joe personally knew Professor Chin, an Egyptologist he'd gone to university with. Joe queried him about what questions we should ask. The following day, Chin made a trip to the vault with us and explained that hieroglyphic script represented only the consonantal skeleton of the words. "Today we do not have precise knowledge of what the vowels were. Fortunately, it's not necessary to know exactly what the vowels were in order to translate a hieroglyphic text."

Professor Chin went on to warn that despite this comforting advice, missing vowels could still make us miss something important. "The ancients considered this style of writing to be of a magickal nature. The individual hieroglyphs could possess a force either benevolent or evil," he said. "The same connection between writing and magick could also result in deleting names of unpopular people, demons, and even gods."

Professor Chin volunteered to help with the scrolls written in Coptic. He said he was also familiar with a cursive form of hieroglyphic writing used in the original *Egyptian Book of the Dead*. He had studied Demotic writing that surfaced during the Twenty-Fifth dynasty, also known as the Nubian Dynasty. He gave us the names of several other experts in various disciplines, and helped me find two archeologists well-read in Egyptian antiquities.

I hired two astronomers to track the bracelets using the charts, as Erzsébet had demonstrated, and two anthropologists to search digital archives for previous information about the bracelets. The Egyptologists also understood ancient Greek and Latin, so I didn't have to find experts for these languages.

I almost collapsed with relief when my information was transferred into the hands of competent people who might find the answers long before I could. It wasn't long before the astronomers contacted me, saying there was no trail to follow on the charts. Disappointed, I decided I might have better luck with astrologers, and after an internet search, found recommendations on two of the best. Both were happy to attempt to track the trail in the way Erzsébet had explained.

I went to bed that night thinking about Erzsébet. I knew she'd saved my life or at least had simplified it greatly the night she left me to inhabit Zsombor's body but I couldn't help but obsess about what had happened to her. Two spirits, one bracelet. Did both reincarnate, or neither? And who decided – or could neither one decide?

I knew if Zsombor was able to possess an adult body, he might already be looking for me. If Erzsébet managed to possess another body, where was she and why hadn't she contacted me? I had to find her or go insane trying.

I called Joe daily with any progress reports from my experts and to vent about Erzsébet. Evidently, Joe thought I needed help because he insisted I call Evergreen. I caved in and called Dr. Abrams, who referred me to his new partner, Dr. Gupta. A lovely Indian woman who wore a sari under her white lab coat, she prescribed a new tranquilizing psychiatric medication, a combination of Phenobarbital and some experimental anti-anxiety drug designated by a number. I thought to turn around and leave the appointment when she started pushing pills, but figured maybe it wouldn't hurt to calm down a bit chemically, since I couldn't force myself to meditate or to start a lifestyle change.

The night I started my drug regime, I dreamed in vivid technicolor. In one dream, or should I say nightmare, Erzsébet appeared and spoke to me in Magyar circa the seventeenth century. A problem, because without her, I understood only fragments of other languages, whatever phrases I could recall.

Anyway, Erzsébet had regained her former beauty, and as she pointed to the Egyptian star charts on the wall before her, I could see why so many were jealous of her. Though I'd viewed her historic portraits online, I nearly swooned, as the old-fashioned expression went, gazing at such exquisite beauty. I loved her totally – body, mind, and spirit. I tried to tell her how I felt, but the louder I talked, the further away she moved. I didn't know if she could hear me or not. I ran to catch her and just as I reached out to hold her hand, the alarm woke me.

Later that morning, some reports from my experts dribbled in. One of the most interesting came from my archaeologist at Boston University, who forwarded an electronic video of a discovery by a Dutch mission at Saqqara. The Dutch team found a new room containing many scrolls and charts in a tomb dated to the Eighteenth Dynasty. The tomb's owners were Ptahemwia, a royal seal-bearer, and his wife. This caught my attention because I knew from reading Erzsébet's documents that a seal-bearer was the one who made charts for pharaohs while they were tracking the bracelets. When I read that the star charts found in this tomb were exceptionally well preserved, I sent both my Egyptologists to gather any relevant information they could from the Dutch academics who'd studied the site.

In the coming days, my two astrologers gave me identical reports and both insinuated I should be searching the past instead of the future. These reports helped pique my interest in the ancient site at Saqqara. The archaeologists sent me an urgent V-SIM hologram about some scrolls written in an old Magyar dialect found in this tomb. In my ignorance of linguistics and of the archeological record, I didn't think much of it, as scrolls have been found in ancient sites written in numerous languages, such as Hebrew, Greek, Latin, Sumerian, and various Egyptian dialects. When I showed the report to Joe, he looked surprised.

"Dad, don't you see the significance of this?"

"No, do you?"

"According to the carbon dating of these relics, they were written long after Ptahemwia died. The documents were placed in the tomb at a later date."

Then it dawned on me. Could Erzsébet have planted these for me to find? After all, she knew of this particular tomb's discovery because it was in the news before she disappeared. Thoughts like these proved it was a good thing I was seeing a psychiatrist. I fumbled for the bottle in my pocket and popped one of my Phenobarb combos to help me cope with this revelation.

"Dad, take it easy on those, will you?" Joe said. "I think I liked you better when you were hyper."

That night, Erzsébet appeared in another dream. She took me on a tour of Turkey and pointed out Zsombor and her husband, Ferenc. The landscape around us was silent, littered with bodies of men, horses, and large dogs wearing spiked collars, as though a battle had recently taken place. I wondered why there were so many dead dogs and Erzsébet told me in English how the Hungarians often used trained battle dogs in skirmishes as the Romans had centuries before.

In my dream, Zsombor appeared in his prime, powerfully built with a cruel gleam in his beady eyes and a red beard that descended to cover the armor plate on his chest. His mouth twisted into a sneer of pure pleasure as he held up a wooden stake about twelve feet in length and three inches in diameter. I recognized the man standing next to him as Ferenc Nádasdy, and Zsombor seemed to be explaining the many methods of extracting information from prisoners as he sharpened the stake with his knife. Two guards forced a prisoner to his knees at Zsombor's feet. When the stake was finished, Zsombor nonchalantly asked some questions of the prisoner. The prisoner showed his contempt by raising his head and spitting at Zsombor, who dipped the stake's point in some animal fat. The guards leaned the prisoner forward.

I later learned that Zsombor lubricated the stake so that when he inserted it into the prisoner's rectum, it wouldn't tear his insides so badly that death would be quick. It seemed he wanted to prolong the torture as long as possible.

Zsombor jammed the stake into the crouching man's anus. The prisoner screamed and begged, but he couldn't flee from the pain. Zsombor drove the pole deeper into the victim's rectum. He then gave the signal for the guards to stand the pole up with the prisoner impaled upon it. The guards braced the pole in a hole prepared for this purpose, a living example of what the other prisoners could expect if they didn't cooperate.

Erzsébet's voice seemed to float on the wind. "This will be their fate if they cooperate or not."

I caught a glimpse of what she meant when a new vision appeared. Hundreds of men impaled in this manner filled the devastated battlefield nearly as far as my eye could see. All of them screamed in pain and horror while Zsombor observed them with a defiant smile.

"This is the world's fate if Zsombor recovers your bracelet," Erzsébet chanted over and over until I jerked awake, drenched in a cold sweat.

I had no choice. There was no way I could ever allow Zsombor to get his hands on Erzsébet's bracelet. I repeated the revealing incantation, relieved to see that the bracelet still encircled my arm, burning brightly in the early morning sunlight.

Later that same day I received a 3DIT message with the translation of the Magyar scrolls. Included in the electronic presentation was the story of the bracelets' creation. I skimmed over what Erzsébet had already told me about Marduk, but I re-read the portion about how men shared bracelets with women. An obscure part of the translation discussed women bearing children. It stated if a woman was with child and died while wearing one of the bracelets, both spirits would return from whence they came.

What the hell? I re-read the final sentence to be sure I had it right. *A woman and her unborn baby will return from whence they came.* My heart began to race. Was this the clue I'd sought? If I understood this correctly, when two souls inhabited one body at the time of death, they would return to the place they came from. In one sense, that could mean the spirit world between births. But it could also mean that both Zsombor and Erzsébet had returned to seventeenth-century Hungary.

I vowed to go back in time somehow, maybe even by killing myself. Then my better instincts kicked in. I'd better assess the situation before I acted foolishly.

How would this work? Assuming a person really could go back in time, could Zsombor and Erzsébet possess their own bodies again? Or did they have to find bodies to possess? If they reincarnated at the same instant and in one body, could Zsombor somehow kill or capture Erzsébet with his knowledge of magick? How could I find out? How could I return to the past and find Erzsébet?

I called Joe. As I read the new translation to him, I could hardly believe what I was about to ask. As a man of science, Joe was supposed to disregard any belief in supernatural happenings. Yet he couldn't deny that my interpretation just might be correct after seeing the immortality bracelet with his own eyes.

"Well, technically a mother and child have two bodies, but the baby is inside the mother and dependent upon her, so I'm guessing that the rule should apply if in fact Zsombor and Erzsébet were both in the priest's body when he died," Joe mused.

I held my tongue and called my astrologers to question them about new developments. Both said they tracked the bracelet to central Europe, but couldn't give me an exact date or an exact location due to the relatively small distances and timeframes involved. Obviously, where else would Erzsébet be but Hungary in the seventeenth century?

I racked my brain trying to figure out my next move. I came up with a crazy idea and figured it was okay to have crazy ideas, since I was seeing a shrink. I grabbed my passport and an overnight bag and immediately headed to the airport to catch the next flight to Budapest. Manny, Steve and Izutu, the bodyguards, crammed into my Ford air-driven multipurpose vehicle with me, and there was no room to spare. I had to reserve seats in first class for them so they wouldn't be cramped.

I questioned my impulsive action during the flight. Here I was, traveling thousands of miles on a stupid hunch, but I didn't have any other ideas. If Erzsébet somehow placed the scrolls with Magyar text in the tomb as I suspected she had, it meant my calculation that she'd returned to her time was correct. It also meant that maybe she'd left a message for me somewhere in Čachtice, perhaps in the castle tower. She always gave me credit for being smarter than I think I am. Blind luck and maybe a sense of romance led me to these deductions, but maybe she knew that's how I'd figure her scheme out.

During the long flight over the Atlantic, I still questioned my sanity. The one thing I couldn't get out of my mind was that Erzsébet had died in order to come back to the future. I still mulled over what form she might take in her past and my obsessive thought led me into confusion. If the evidence in Čachtice proved me right, then I'd know I was okay. If I found nothing, I'd credit my over-active imagination for my delusions.

On the ground, I hired two cars so I could ride in one and my bodyguards in the other. Happy to see me again, Mayor Ilionescu wanted to talk about the broadcast and Erzsébet's departure. I put him off, telling him we could talk at dinner. He agreed and gave me the keys to the manor house.

No townspeople turned out to greet me this time because they all knew Erzsébet was gone. Here I was, the oldest heavyweight boxing champion in history, and I may as well have been a field mouse for all the recognition I received. My bodyguards attracted more attention than I did simply because of their size.

At dinner, Mayor Ilionescu looked on with amazement at the quantity of food Manny, Steve, and Ituzu ate. I interrupted his dumbfounded gaze and asked his permission to visit the castle. "Of course, any time you want," he said through a bite of roast chicken.

"I'd like to do some more photography, if you don't mind."

"Do you need me to keep visitors away, like last time?"

"Just for a few hours tomorrow."

"Okay, I'll accommodate you in any way I can, Mr. Jackson."

The next morning I strolled over to "Eerie Foto," the photography studio on the village square, to rent some equipment. "Why do you call the shop eerie?" I asked the shopkeeper.

He laughed. "Because I'm known for creating weird effects with an infrared filter in my landscape photos."

"What's a filter do to make the pictures eerie?"

"I use an infrared filter that lets infrared light pass into the camera but blocks all or most of the visible light spectrum. People like my strange-looking pictures of Castle Čachtice and the surrounding area. You know, the 'Blood Countess' and all that." He picked up a round object. "This filter only works with film, so you can't use a digital camera."

Just for the heck of it, I bought an antique film camera with an infrared filter. The shopkeeper manufactured his own film using a machine he invented to supply antique photo buffs. He sold me a special electronic flash that would highlight different light spectrums to make more eerie effects.

When I returned to the castle, my bodyguards carried the photo equipment to the tower. I told them to wait outside. I shot a round of photos with the digital camera and a few with the antique camera so they'd see the flash and assume I was only there to shoot pictures. Then I removed the necessary tools from my photo bag to open the hiding place in the wall. Once I lay the heavy stone block on the floor, I put a bright photo light into the hole in the wall, and stuck my head through it. All the insects were gone. I looked around, then down at the floor, and didn't see anything. Disappointed, I decided to take pictures of the space for later study. Looking through the viewfinder, I caught a glimpse of something higher up than the opening. I aimed the camera and snapped several photos. When I finished shooting the interior space, I reached up for the item I'd spotted. It turned out to be an old piece of animal skin, vellum that probably once had writing on it, now faded to almost nothing. I lay it on the floor and photographed it from many angles. I didn't know right then who to send the vellum to for analysis. I finished up and replaced the stone in the wall. As before, it clicked as it locked into place.

I wasn't sure what I expected to find. Even if Erzsébet had left a sign, it would be four hundred years old, enough time for any message to deteriorate or disappear. I traipsed around the castle grounds and checked the village and the manor house more than once, but felt no other connection with Erzsébet.

I put the film in a lead-lined film bag so the X-rays at the airport wouldn't ruin it and booked the next flight home. As soon as I reached my apartment, I sent the film to a lab the next day and purchased three comfortable chairs to place outside the vault for the bodyguards. I would return to the vault to search for new clues when the chairs and the photos were delivered.

I wondered if somehow Zsombor could possess one of the bodyguards. If he did, what chance would I have? My gruesome thoughts inspired me to work harder to find Erzsébet.

Chapter 31

I was just settling into an early morning session in the vault viewing room with the package of my newly delivered photos from the Castle Čachtice tower when Michaela Davies, one of my archaeology experts at Boston University, pinged me online. She sent me a link to an early twenty-first-century article by a professor at Oxford University about an old find, a Gospel fragment among a collection of ancient Egyptian papyri. Part of a hoard of ancient texts uncovered in the late twentieth century, the fragment languished in the Oxford collection for over two decades, illegible until last month.

Researchers at Oxford had used an innovative photographic technique using infrared technology developed for satellite imaging to illuminate text on ancient and badly faded papyri. Many papyri dramatically revealed traces of writing not visible to the naked eye under infrared light.

I called Joe and requested he use his connections to call Oxford and find out what I needed to duplicate this infrared technology. I hoped to find any hidden secrets on my scrolls and in the photos taken at the castle tower that weren't visible after using the filters and film I'd purchased from the camera shop in Čachtice.

Finally, almost shivering with anticipation, I pulled out the photos.

I hoped they'd prove to be as provocative as the hidden information on the scrolls.

The first photo showed a bit of old graffiti on the tower walls, visible because of film and infrared filter. I shuffled through the pile and stacked them one by one, scrutinizing each for some sign that Erzsébet might have returned to Čachtice from the twenty-first century. Nothing seemed to present itself until I viewed the first photo of the scroll fragment that I'd found stuck high above the opening in the wall.

My heart skipped a beat. A previously hidden message scrawled in English leapt out at me. "Jim, Zsombor is coming for me. I'll be hiding, you know where."

Erzsébet had talked about where she preferred to retreat from society in her lifetime and I knew she meant Čachtice – Cséjthe in old Hungary – her favorite castle.

"Please come as soon as you find this." She'd signed the message with a single initial, E.

The implication floored me. She figured I'd return to Slovakia if necessary to search for clues to her whereabouts. What else did she know? Could the future be preordained, and if so, could Erzsébet possibly know what moves I would make? How did free will play into all this?

Erzsébet's request to join her in the seventeenth century reinforced my belief that it could be done. I had to go back in time to help her head off Zsombor. But how?

My PVA rang. "I was lucky to get through to Professor Owain Jones at Oxford before he left for the day," Joe said. "Be sure to use film and not digital. He said that infrared filters are sufficient for your purposes, as long as the subjects are illuminated with lights that emit the wavelengths with which you wish to record the photograph."

"Check," I said. I immediately sent Manny and Steve to purchase photo lights with differing wavelengths that might help me see anything I may have missed with the special flash I used. I started laying out the faded scrolls. I still had the infrared filter I'd used at the castle tower. Once Manny and Steve returned, they helped me set up the lights, and then I asked them to wait outside the vault again. I attached my camera to a tripod and set it for a long exposure time, and photographed each scroll and document. I hadn't yet tried the art of developing photos and had no darkroom setup, so I sent the film out with Manny to a premium one-hour shop nearby while I continued to survey the scrolls.

When Manny returned, I viewed the photos and the additional markings with excitement. I immediately scanned copies into Joe's 3DIT and forwarded them to my researchers along with a voice message clip asking them to call me ASAP with any news.

While I worked, I wondered whatever happened to Father Flynn. He'd dropped out of sight after public interest in O'Malley's death died down.

I could hear the muffled laughter of Manny, Steve, and Ituzu playing their usual round of cards outside the viewing room door. Suddenly, the sound of a scuffle alarmed me. My sword still lay in the chest, and I instinctively picked it up as a big man burst through the door with Manny right behind. The hunting knife in the stranger's hand prompted me to take a swing at him with the sword. When it cut deep into his knife-wielding arm, he dropped the knife and Manny dropped him with a karate chop to the nose.

We both rushed to the door. Steve and Ituzu were attempting to hold off four more men armed with identical hunting knives.

"Hold it right there," Steve yelled, pulling a pistol from a shoulder holster. One slashed Steve's hand with a knife, causing him to drop the gun. Ituzu thrust a powerful kick to the attacker's head. Despite his wound, Steve charged into two of the men like a football linebacker, knocking them backwards. Manny and I followed right behind him. I wondered out loud why in the hell these thugs chose knives to go up against my XXX-sized bodyguards.

When I looked into my opponent's face, I couldn't believe my eyes. Father Flynn in civvies, showing up with gang punks. My fighting instincts kicked in and I swung a hard right, knocking him to the floor. I ground one foot into his chest and put the sword tip to his throat.

"Time out," I yelled. All stopped to look. "Every man out or I'll run him through."

The look on Flynn's face rattled the others, who stared at one another as if measuring whether to stay and fight or cut their losses. Manny took advantage of their confusion and pulled an old-fashioned blackjack from the back of his waistband. He grabbed one of the stooges and slammed the blackjack into his face, causing a tooth or two to fly. He dropped and Manny went after the second guy. Steve grabbed the third attacker and pistol-whipped him. Ituzu grabbed the fourth guy by his collar – the one who'd entered the viewing room and now had a swollen, crooked nose – and flung him on top of the one on the floor, banging their heads together.

I dragged Flynn into the vault viewing room and locked the door.

"You okay, boss?" Ituzu yelled through the door.

"Yeah, you guys?"

"We're good. The one who still could, ran. We'll hold the others here until you decide what you wanna do with 'em."

"Got it." I turned my attention to Flynn. "What the hell do you think you're doing, coming in here with an armed gang?"

"I made a vow to pursue this matter to the finish. Father O'Malley told me about the bracelets and I wanted to acquire them for safekeeping."

"Bullshit!"

"Believe me. I had no choice but to work with O'Malley on Bishop Cheney's orders. He told me a little about the bracelets, not much, just enough to know he was after yours. I could see he had a screw loose and thought the best way to obstruct him was to pretend to be on his side. I'm the one who sent you the V-SIM holo chips."

"Yeah, of course you wouldn't be lying. I'm going to have you arrested for attempted murder."

"I wouldn't do that if I were you, Jackson. O'Malley's as powerful as you are with that bracelet, maybe even more so. He studied many esoteric things and knew a great deal about spirits and demons. If he reaches you from beyond the grave, he'll have both bracelets. That's why I wanted it locked safely away."

Now Flynn sounded just like Erzsébet, only he didn't seem to know about Father O'Malley's past as Zsombor.

"That's a helluva way to show your concern. Give me another good reason why I shouldn't turn you in."

"I can help you."

"Yeah, right. How?"

"The Vatican has equipment that will reveal the presence of spirits and if a person is possessed."

"I already know that, Flynn. What do you take me for, some idiot?"

"You don't understand. This new setup aims an electromagnetic beam at a subject. When the waves return to the analyzer, it instantly alerts you to the presence of spirits or anyone who has a second spirit in their body. Maybe you can detect O'Malley if he comes looking for you. Or detect anyone in your vicinity who's possessed. Those bracelets seem to attract trouble."

"And what about someone who is powerful but doesn't have two spirits in their body? This is far more complicated than you think, Flynn."

"Don't patronize me, Jackson. I've always resisted evil. I want to help you stop Father O'Malley from doing whatever it is he's planning on the other side."

"Why, just because you like me so much? Why didn't you stop him when he was still alive?"

"He was too strong, too determined. He would have crushed me. I sent you the hologram chips because I suspected if he wanted to exorcise you that you might be on the right side. I know the terror he'll cause mankind if he attains the second bracelet."

"And what if you simply want the same power? That seems to be the case, since you just swung from trying to harm me to wanting to help me."

We stood eyeball to eyeball for several minutes, neither budging a muscle.

I didn't know if I could trust Flynn or not, but if I went along with him, at least I'd know what he was up to. I decided to make use of his talents and instructed him to set up his detecting equipment in Joe's lab, so I could test *him* to see if he was possessed. I doubted it, but fooling around with the equipment might be some aid in finding Erzsébet, or like Flynn said, keeping other trouble away.

Then I realized I could keep him busy for quite some time by creating a diversion. Why not have him legitimately study spirit possession? The problem would be to find subjects. Where do you find people possessed by demons or spirits? A quick internet search located an article in which a social scientist explained that prisoners make excellent subjects for research because "they can be monitored at all times and their living conditions and diets are identical."

I unlocked the vault door and stuck my head outside. Manny, Steve, and Ituzu were lining the three scuffed-up men against the wall with their hands tied behind their backs. I waved Father Flynn outside. "Believe it or not, guys, these are friends not foes," I said. "Let 'em go for now."

I cast Flynn a look. "No more rough stuff, Father. Hope these boys aren't priests, but if they are, I bet they're from Hano. . . Better stay in touch – I have some plans for your equipment that will help us both."

I dusted myself off, returned the scrolls and sword to the chest, and headed over to Evergreen to pay a visit to Dr. Gupta, my new psychiatrist. When she had a moment between patients, I asked her how frequently she diagnosed patients who suffered demonic possession.

"Oh, I've read your old case histories, Mr. Jackson. Fascinating. Perhaps Dr. Abrams and your other physicians explained that psychiatry and psychology don't call the condition 'possession' any longer."

Dr. Gupta led me to her library, pulled a thick medical manual from the shelf, and read from it. "'Demonic possession is not a valid psychiatric or medical diagnosis recognized by the Diagnostic and Statistical Manual of Mental Disorders. Those who profess an understanding of demonic possession have sometimes ascribed the symptoms associated with mental illnesses such as hysteria, mania, psychosis, or dissociative identity disorder. DID itself is a controversial diagnosis described as the existence in an individual of two or more distinct identities or personalities.'" She placed the book back on the shelf and peered over her glasses at me. "There is, however, a mental disease called demonomania or demonopathy. This is a monomania, a type of paranoia in which the patient believes that he or she is possessed by one or more demons. So in answer to your question, I'd say it's not common, but it's not unheard of, either." She smiled with innocent self-satisfaction that she could so easily answer a difficult question.

Thinking of Erzsébet, I thanked Dr. Gupta and turned to leave.

"Oh, by the way," she said. "I can schedule a meeting for you with a local psychiatrist who has some experience with people who claim to be possessed. In fact, let me give him a call right now and I'll ask him to give you a jingle."

I couldn't believe all my incredible luck that day, especially when Michaela pinged me on the Star system in the aircar on my way to my next appointment. My photo expert was able to decipher a scroll photographed with infrared film. It contained a record made by the ruler of Urba from the time he first heard of the bracelets, up until the fateful day his over-confidence that caused his death. The bracelet on my wrist tingled with this news.

I wanted to wait for the remaining pages to read the entire report at one sitting with Joe so I wouldn't misinterpret anything. I checked my watch. He wouldn't be available until 5:00 p.m. and it was nearly time for the 3:30 appointment that Dr. Gupta booked with the other psychiatrist.

I parked at the medical center closest to Brigham Young Hospital in Boston and found the physician's office tucked back in a shady alcove, identified by his name on the door: *Dr. JD Kilroy M.D., Diplomat of the American Board of Psychiatry and Neurology.*

I knocked and entered. A receptionist showed me the way to Dr. Kilroy's office, a large, airy room with a waterfall cascading over the outside wall.

"Just call me Jack," Dr. Kilroy said, standing up and reaching over his desk to shake my hand.

"Jim," I said. "Thanks for meeting with me on such short notice."

We exchanged a few more pleasantries, sizing each other up. I'd gathered all available information about him before our meeting, and I'm sure he'd done the same about me.

"So, what can I help you with, Jim?"

"I have a somewhat unusual request. I'm researching Spirit Possession Syndrome and I have several questions about it. I'm aware that a small percentage of convicted murderers claim that 'the devil made me do it.' What percentage of convicts you've interviewed made this claim or a similar claim of spirit possession? Second, would it be possible to test these prisoners with some new equipment?"

Jack leaned back in his leather chair and stretched his legs out under the desk. "Before I answer your questions, let me advise you that since deinstitutionalization in the 1960s, the replacement of long-term hospitalization by community mental health services, jails, and prisons have also substituted for public mental health care, unfortunately."

"Are you telling me that all these guys are insane?"

"No, not at all. But the percentage of murderers who make this claim are larger than you might think. About four out of ten prisoners tell me they did not commit murder through their own volition. These say they felt possessed by a strong force that compelled them to carry out the act. From a psychiatric viewpoint, this claim is sometimes evidence of the strong emotion necessary to commit murder and sometimes a symptom of mental illness."

"What about the other six?"

"Well, most usually proclaim their innocence at first. When I convince them that our doctor-patient relationship is confidential, many say they murdered out of anger, jealousy, or sometimes as a result of trying to cover up another crime, usually while inebriated on alcohol or drugs."

"What do you think about the ones who tell you they were possessed by a demon or a spirit?"

"Usually I think they're making excuses or in denial. I've seen very few cases in which it seemed possible that the prisoner was truthful about being compelled or coerced by some outside force."

"I see. Can you answer my question about testing my equipment on prisoners who make these claims?"

"Of course. That would have been a problem in the past. With the expense of incarceration steadily climbing, some states have passed laws allowing experimentation on prisoners, with their consent, and for a fee."

"Who pays to experiment on prisoners?"

"Major pharmaceutical companies are more than happy to have test subjects who eat the same food, basically sleep the same hours, and are in a controlled environment. Couldn't ask for better subjects."

"I'll have to interview prisoners who claim they're normal and have never been possessed as a control group also."

"Of course, that goes without saying. You'll also probably want a control group who is normal but says they're possessed as well. I can put you in touch with the Massachusetts Department of Corrections."

"I'd appreciate that. I'd also be interested in hiring you to lend your expertise to my study. You have a relationship with many prisoners already, so would be the perfect coordinator. My associate, a Catholic priest, would work with you."

"Interesting," he said, his eyebrows raised at my oblique mention of Father Flynn. "I take it this equipment has something to do with detecting the presence or absence of spiritual possession. . . you and the Catholic exorcists were in the news quite a bit after that tragic death in the Boston Commons."

"Yeah, the death of my cutwoman, Cwia, inspired my research. And my experience with my own test in Brussels. . . also, my recollection of life on the 'other side' during my cryonic preservation."

I coughed, not quite knowing what else to say to this eminent physician. If I were to tell him the story about Erzsébet, Zsombor, and the bracelets of fire, he'd probably peg me for crazy.

But we forged a preliminary agreement for the project. "I'll have my attorney, Vince Zoloti, contact you to iron out the legal details with the prison system."

Jack stood up and shook my hand again. "Excellent, then we'll get started as soon as possible. It'll be a pleasure to work with you."

I kept one thought to myself for now. What if the equipment worked flawlessly, as Father Flynn claimed it would? Could it really be possible that as many as four out of ten murderers were forced to commit their crime by a demon or other external force? Did that make them not guilty because of spirit possession? As I was leaving, I asked, "Off the record, Doc, how many people in this country really have SPS, do you think?"

He laughed. "Jim, I think that's an answer you might reveal."

Chapter 32

After Zoloti navigated through all the bureaucratic red tape, Dr. Kilroy and Father Flynn began testing subjects in Massachusetts State prisons. The electromagnetic pulse analyzer worked perfectly, zeroing in on each victim of spiritual hijacking even before Dr. Kilroy confirmed those prisoners claimed to be possessed. None of the control test subjects told to lie about possession or subjects convicted of crimes other than murder showed any signs of the phenomenon.

Dr. Kilroy began to write a paper on the test study, saying when it was completed, published, and underwent peer review, it just might revolutionize psychiatry and the criminal justice system. Joe got involved with a few test sessions and said he would definitely add electromagnetic analysis to his rejuvenation procedures. There would be no chance that any of his future patients would ever have an experience like mine with Erzsébet.

I had a portable unit, no bigger than a pocket PVA, made for myself. Hopefully, if Erzsébet or Zsombor showed up in spirit form, I could detect either one immediately.

When Joe and I met to discuss my findings, he read aloud from the English interpretation of the Osmanlı Türkçesi text – Ottoman Turkish – of the scroll from Urba. Fascinated, he couldn't put it down, and if he had, I would have insisted he keep reading.

The ruler of Urba had done intensive research. The scroll contained the incantations Erzsébet taught me to make the bracelets visible as well as the incantation to remove them. But the ruler of Urba thought Zsombor and Count Nádasdy could not remove the bracelets from his wrists because he believed that Marduk, the all-powerful god who created them, would protect him while wearing both. He learned how wrong his belief was when Zsombor and Count Nádasdy cut his hands off. I sometimes woke up in a cold sweat, thinking about how Father O'Malley had almost cut my hand off.

The scroll also detailed how to track the bracelets through time by calculating alignments of the planets and stars, as Erzsébet had demonstrated. And it contained a line that Erzsébet often quoted and even used in her prayers: "In the domain of spirits, there is no time; everything that ever was or ever will be exists now and can never be destroyed."

Understood literally, this maxim meant that once I entered the spirit world, I had only to decide where and to what era I wanted to go and could will myself there, as Erzsébet had often said. Both past and future were open to me.

Now that I wore a bracelet that guaranteed me a conscious reincarnation, could I also choose a reincarnation while my body underwent a cryonic preservation? I'd never thought of trying to travel in time during my first cryonic preservation, but the possibility enticed me. I wanted to find Erzsébet and stop Zsombor, but committing suicide seemed like a risky way to go about it. I'd mulled this problem over for a few weeks while the spirit possession study progressed, fervently hoping that Erzsébet would understand my caution and that Zsombor hadn't harmed her.

Joe couldn't believe it when I steered the subject to a second cryonic preservation.

"You want to do what? Dad, this has never been done before."

"I survived a brain tumor. You revived me and that was a first. Now you're reviving two or three people every month. If this works, you'll know how to do it when a second procedure is needed by others."

"The cryopreservation process is more advanced now, but no healthy person has ever undergone vitrification to test some theory." Joe's face scrunched up as though he'd either punch the wall or cry. "I'll miss you if you leave again, Dad. We barely had time to get to know one another," he said, his voice muted.

I took both his smooth hands into my big, rough mitts. "If this works, Joe, think of all the uses for it. Astronauts could be preserved for space travel. People willing to time travel could research different eras."

"I don't know. What if a second procedure is too hard on your brain and nervous system? What if something happens to your soul in the seventeenth century?"

"I have every confidence that you can bring me back. Just give me a year. On my one-year anniversary, have me ready for rejuvenation and I'll come back, I promise."

"What if I refuse?"

"Don't make me choose, son. I need to find Erzsébet. I'll be back."

My heart almost broke at seeing the concerned look on Joe's face. He choked back emotion, composing himself for a moment before he could speak. "You're truly convinced by this old legend that you can reincarnate in the seventeenth century while your body is cryonically preserved?"

"With this bracelet, absolutely!"

"I don't know, Dad. Setting my personal feelings aside, a second cryonic procedure is still extreme. The medical ethics are borderline. It's one thing to do a procedure in order to save someone's life. But to do so experimentally? I'm not sure I can go through with this."

"My mind is made up. If you don't help me, I'll simply swallow a handful of my Phenobarb pills."

Joe's jaw dropped. "I can't believe you're willing to kill yourself to go through with this."

I crossed my arms in front of me. "I'll do whatever it takes, Joe. I'm deadly serious about this."

Joe shook his head and sighed. "Mom always did say you were the

CRYONIC MAN

most stubborn and determined man on the planet. In that case, I'd rather help you than see you kill yourself. God knows what would happen if you did, seeing that the Church considers suicide a mortal sin. Before we do anything, I insist you talk to all your old doctors, and if they tell me you're making a rational decision, I'll start the procedure."

Over the next week, I visited not only Dr. Gupta, but Dr. Abrams, Dr. Remus, and Dr. Dohmed. They all expressed their skepticism and felt my plan was outlandish, but deemed me certifiably sane.

I even visited young Dr. Thaddeus Dean, the grandson of my old family physician. He nixed the idea.

"Look at it from my point of view," he said. "You can save lives with cryonic preservation, but doing it a second time for a questionable reason borders on suicide."

I shared my astrological charts with the names and dates of the former owner's deaths and reincarnations with Dr. Dean, and then the photos of the note Erzsébet left in the tower, and explained why it had to be left by her.

"How else could it have gotten in there if not by her hand?"

"Did you ever stop to think this might be a hoax? You're dabbling in paranormal activity and there's lots of room for a scam by someone or something determined to trick you."

"No, I don't believe so."

"You know I can have you committed for threatening suicide."

"Well, yes. My shrinks said the same thing, but they were more open to my plan because of their interest in life after death. But nothing is going to stop me from hunting down Zsombor. If I don't get him and he ends up with my bracelet, this won't be a world you'll want to live in."

"Can I see this bracelet you keep talking about?"

I repeated the incantation and the bracelet glowed on my wrist. Dr. Dean stared at it in disbelief. He reached over and touched it, felt its cool glow and comforting aura.

"Is this some sort of trick to influence my decision?"

"No, I swear I'd never try to trick you. Everything I've said is the gospel truth."

"Well, seeing the bracelet proves you're not delusional," Dr. Dean said, "but I really can't give you permission to kill yourself."

"You're not allowing me to kill myself. You're giving me permission to take part in a scientific experiment for humanity's greater good. If I'm cryopreserved and returned to life successfully a second time, the results may be groundbreaking."

"There are far more pressing concerns for a population of eight billion souls," Dr. Dean said. "Cryonic preservation may be affordable in the West, but in much of the world it's still a rich man's pipe dream."

I racked my brain for convincing arguments. "But think of it. Astronauts could be vitrified for long space expeditions, and revived once they reach their destinations. Perhaps the world's energy problems could be solved with resources from another planet. Scientists could time travel to search for solutions to our current problems."

"You're a stubborn man, Mr. Jackson. Space flight and time travel are rich men's hobbies in a world where basic survival is at a premium. I still think your plan is suicidal."

"But Doc, an executive law has been passed."

"I don't understand."

"Human cryonic preservation prior to declaration of death is now legal, remember? So my second preservation can't be considered a suicide even if your opinion differs, otherwise some idiot prosecutor could charge doctors with murder. So you're not breaking the law by helping me. Anyway, I've already died once and I'm not afraid to die again. I've got a bottle of PB X9, and I'll use it as soon as I walk out your door if you don't help me."

Dr. Dean sighed. "I wish you wouldn't manipulate me like this. . . I need some time to think this over. Give me twenty-four hours before you act. Please?"

"That's the spirit," I told him. "If I don't hear from you in twenty-four hours, I'll definitely be calling you."

Joe called me later that evening, just after Dr. Dean had called him. After a long discussion about my threat to commit suicide if they didn't agree to another cryonic process, both reluctantly agreed to accommodate me. Both believed Joe could restore my life once again. If they didn't respond to my request and I succeeded in killing myself, they would never know what happened to me. I'm sure deep down they were both curious to see not only if a second cryonic preservation would be successful, but also to see what tales I might return with.

As soon as Zoloti completed the legal paperwork and assumed control of my assets as his father had fifty years before, Joe initiated the preparations for my second cryonic preservation. He assured me that he would supervise the medical team at the Cryonics Foundation during the advanced preservation process and supervise the rejuvenation as well.

That I wasn't dying was the only other difference this time. Joe and his team medically induced a coma with sedatives to inactivate my brain and slow my heart. The technicians monitored my brain closely, perfusing it separately from my body with special cryoprotectants.

My brain and body may have gone to sleep, but my spirit stayed wide awake. It tried to burst out the top of my head while the technicians perfused my brain, which it couldn't do until my heart stopped completely.

Then the technicians attended to my body, gradually slowing my heart while exchanging the rest of my blood for cryoprotectants. Finally, when my heart lay still, they lowered my temperature in stages until they could place my vitrified carcass in a nitrogen tank with a few more bells and whistles than the one I'd spent fifty years in. This time my body would float in the cold and dark alone, but I had little fear of it.

Suddenly, I was outside my body! As before, I realized my mind was synonymous with my spirit. I gazed upon the universe, our world and all the other worlds, totally aware of my destination. Around me on high lay worlds for the gods and demigods, one for angels, devas, and dakinis, and the worlds for demons and hungry ghosts far below. I knew all these things because we exist within "all that is." I even intuitively understood that potential worlds existed which had not yet manifested through creative thought.

Kind and friendly spirits surrounded me, and some snuggled close. Somehow, beyond my cozy cocoon, I felt Erzsébet as a magnetic force, drawing me toward her.

"I'm on my way to find my love," I told the spirits, sorry I couldn't linger in their sweet energy. "She's guiding me to her time, so I can save my world from a horrible fate."

I trusted I would find Erzsébet, but still had little understanding of how a spirit acquired a body. I prayed that Erzsébet would show me what to do. I remembered what she'd said about locating a specific time and place – "just think of it and you'll be there." I concentrated upon late sixteenth-century Hungary, hoping to find Erzsébet after Ferenc died but before her troubles began, and suddenly found myself hovering over what was known then as the Castle Cséjthe, nestled on a mountaintop in the folds of the Little Carpathian mountains. What a difference from the forlorn ruin known as Castle Čachtice in twenty-first-century Slovakia! The turrets and towers of the pristine palace gleamed in the morning sun, a hive of activity with people and animals streaming to and fro on various errands.

I knew Erzsébet, if she'd reincarnated fully, must be hiding from Zsombor either inside or somewhere nearby. I thought it best if I located him first to be certain he wasn't an imminent threat.

So I focused my mind and imagined myself with Zsombor. There were no surviving images of him in the twenty-first century, so I had to be content with Erzsébet's descriptions, the images from my recent dream, plus my intuitive thought that Father O'Malley resembled him.

Form followed thought, and there Zsombor stood, engaged in hand-to-hand combat with three men united against him. But he looked bigger, stronger, and meaner than all three. Although the expression on his face told me he wasn't winning his battle, he moved with an athletic grace and power that suggested he was having great fun nonetheless. I watched as Zsombor's sword rose upward and fell upon the left side of one opponent's neck. The blade was so sharp and his stroke so powerful that the blow sliced clean through, coming out under the man's left arm, virtually quartering him.

Obviously, my task here would not be simple. My fencing lessons could only be of marginal help if I ever engaged in such vicious swordplay. At least it didn't look as if Zsombor would hunt for Erzsébet today.

I withdrew mentally from the scene and willed myself to be with her, my mind unreeling invisible tendrils of love and hope into infinite space.

❧Chapter 33

When I opened my eyes, I found myself in a large, whitewashed room draped with tapestries beside a woman I assumed to be Erzsébet. I'd expected to see the beauty I'd dreamed about since the afternoon she left me in twenty-first-century Brussels, so the sight of this frail, elderly woman with a mop of braids and dreadlocks and clouded, unseeing eyes shocked me. Is this how Erzsébet appeared in the final years of her life? Or could she have possessed the body of an older woman?

Whatever the situation, this grizzled crone appeared to have led a hard life. As she stepped from a narrow four-poster bed to stand near a tall window, I reminded myself that my mission to protect Erzsébet was for humanity's benefit, not my own. And how could I not love her no matter how time had ravaged her body?

My mind drifted back to when I first saw Emily after my rejuvenation and she'd looked so fragile, so helpless. My heart went out to Erzsébet as it had to Emily. I only hoped she wouldn't fear me and banish me from her sight as well.

I tried to communicate with Erzsébet, but a spirit has no physical voice. I tried communicating telepathically as we'd done so many times before, but she didn't respond to my attempt. I tried again. The old woman glanced in my direction, at least, but either couldn't receive or couldn't understand my thoughts. She certainly could not see me even if I was in physical form.

Suddenly, the door opened. I did a double take at the woman with lush chestnut hair, creamy white skin, and full, sensuous lips. Her striking gray eyes sparkled with intelligence and her lithe, curvaceous body moved with grace. I felt stunned, as though witnessing a princess in a fairy tale.

The younger woman started to speak. "Anna. . ." Then the old woman pointed in my direction, her blind eyes glowing white in the gloom of the chamber. The beauty startled and gazed in my direction. "Is that you, Jim Jackson?" she asked softly.

The crone was not Erzsébet! I could hardly contain my joy at finding the beauty I expected.

"Jim Jackson, it is you," she said, evidently still maintaining the capacity to sense and communicate with spirits.

I answered her telepathically, the way we'd always communicated. "You gorgeous witch."

"Oh, thank God you're here," she said aloud, reverting to her Christian roots.

Erzsébet must have known I was coming because she showed little surprise at my arrival in the sixteenth century. But how wondrous for me to travel through time to hear her speak in these luscious, ripe tones.

"Is it really you, Erzsébet?"

"Truly," she said, her mouth blooming from a rosebud into a bright smile.

"It's a miracle I found you. What do I do now?"

"You must find a powerful body to inhabit."

"How?"

"Do you remember what I told you? How you may claim a body within moments of a spirit's departure?

"I do remember, but I don't know how in the hell to begin."

"You already know. Just find the right body, as I did with you, and think about inhabiting it."

"Okay, then. Before I go, tell me how you arrived."

"The magick of the bracelet worked for both Zsombor and me. Unfortunately, he retained his bracelet once we returned."

"Did you and Zsombor appear here side-by-side?"

She shook her head. "No, we both returned to the last place we inhabited in this era. I was the first to pass away, so I returned first and found myself somehow in my old life at Sárvár, as though I'd never departed. Zsombor also returned to his home, not so far away from here. He never knew that I did not bring my bracelet with me. I decided to live here, at my beloved Castle Cséjthe. Even if Zsombor suspects where I am, he won't dare to try to capture me, because the king protects this castle."

Now I knew why Zsombor hadn't returned to the twenty-first century to possess me and take the bracelet. He didn't know I had it. Maybe I should have remained in the future, but he surely would consult his star charts and come after the bracelet eventually. At least I could be here with Erzsébet. I gazed at her again, wishing I could embrace her.

"Let us go over this again, Jim Jackson. You must choose a suitable body, and by suitable I mean as large as possible, and strong and agile, because you must stand up to Zsombor. Do not worry about the intellect of this person, because your mind will control his body."

"Any suggestions?"

"Yes, I do have one. There's an execution scheduled in a village nearby. Ernö, a farmer, killed one of the king's soldiers when four attempted to collect some goats as taxes in the name of the king. He's to be executed by being drawn on a hurdle to the gallows and then hung."

"Hurdle?" I asked.

"A hurdle is fencing made from thin branches."

"Hold on a minute! You want me to inhabit a body that will be dragged around and then hung. What if his neck is broken before I take over?"

"I'm only telling you this so you'll understand why the jailer told me how Ernö is begging for poison so he can avoid the pain and degradation of a public execution. Maybe we can spare him this painful experience by giving him a sedative or even a poison. Then you can enter Ernö's body as his spirit leaves."

"But won't the body be dead when I enter it?"

"No, Marduk designed the bracelets to rejuvenate any newly acquired bodies damaged upon possession."

"But Ernö will be scheduled for execution when I enter his body."

"Then I will ask for a pardon once you've inhabited it. The king is my uncle, after all. I can request clemency. I have gold to bribe the guards as well. I can assure you that escaping the execution won't be a problem."

"Why can't you just save his life first? Why can't I possess his body while he's alive, like you did mine?"

Erzsébet sighed at my endless questions and arguments. "As I explained before, your connection with your body was quite weak after your death and fifty years of cryonic preservation. And you don't have the knowledge and experience to control another mind. A body must be dying or the spirit ready to depart for whatever reason, otherwise the possession requires many magick formulas as well as great skill and timing. Not only that, the farmer is a vicious man who deserves to die for his crimes, so you don't want to share his consciousness. He is abusive to his wife and children, but few dare oppose a man who abuses his property in these times. When he killed the soldier, his neighbors were relieved to see him arrested."

"I suppose I'll have to trust your opinion. After all, this farmer challenged four professional soldiers and killed one, so he must be tough."

"Godspeed, then," Erzsébet said, casting a loving, protective energy around my spirit. "Imagine yourself inside the village jail."

I wished I could take her in my arms. The sooner I gained a body, the sooner I might do just that. "I could do this only for you, Erzsébet."

I thought of the village jail and instantly found myself in one of two cells, a rank, dark cubicle with a straw floor and a high slit where a sparrow flitted in and out and a sunbeam illuminated a spider web on the ceiling. A youthful man of impressive size and condition stood in the manacles attached to the floor and wall. It appeared that he'd destroyed anything he could get his hands on, for a simple bedframe and chair were battered to splinters and a straw ticking shredded. He tried to reach the bars in front of him, but couldn't quite touch them, thankfully, because he looked capable of tearing them from the walls.

He strained against his chains and it looked like he might succeed in tearing them from the wall when an archer stepped into the entryway outside the cell. He loaded an arrow into his bow and aimed it at Ernö's face. "Stop right now or this arrow finds a home between your eyes."

"I'll stick that arrow up your arse," Ernö said, heaving the chains bound to his wrist manacles from the wall in a mass of flying plaster.

He must have hoped for a quick death and that's what he got. The archer drew his bowstring taut and released it. True to his word, the arrow hit the farmer directly between the eyes. Ernö crumpled to the floor, a look of relief on his broad face. The archer bent over Ernö's massive body and pulled the arrow out with a sucking sound. Blood spurted from the wound. In a flash of blue light, Ernö's spirit shot from the top of his head.

Thank God I'd not delayed any longer. Seizing the opportunity, I imagined myself inside the corpse. The immortality bracelet's magick healed the fatal wound as my life force entered the same channel that Ernö's exited. As this life energy flowed back into all his physical and metaphysical channels, his heart began to pump.

When I opened my eyes, the archer and a jailer stood over me.

"By God," the jailer exclaimed, "he lives."

"Quick, put his arms in chains before he stands," the archer urged.

My comprehension of the old Magyar tongue pleasantly surprised me. The blood that flowed into my eyes began to congeal and to obstruct my vision. The wound throbbed with pain, but the sensation moved outward, as if the wound were slowly healing.

Although master of this body, I had little control over the instinctive and inherited mannerisms of its former owner. For instance, I fought to

CRYONIC MAN

keep myself from picking my nose or scratching my ass. Exhausted from tearing the cell apart and the trauma of mortal wounding and death, I closed my eyes again and fell asleep.

When I awoke, the narrow window was dark. Erzsébet stood outside the cell with a candle in hand, peering through the bars at me. Desire coursed through my new body.

Erzsébet directed the jailer to wash the dried blood from my face. She took the damp rag from the jailer as he roughly swiped my face, and gently dabbed my eyes to soften the scabs there. Her soft touch moved me to ecstatic fantasies.

I tried to touch her but my arms were chained together because Ernö had pulled the original shackles from the wall. Flexing my arms and chest, I tested my upper body strength. My new hard-muscled form seemed nearly as good as my old body, stretched out over six feet and I estimated a weight of about two hundred and fifty pounds. There should be no reason that I couldn't tear the leg shackles from the wall.

I wiggled each of my fingers individually, and then each toe. The urge to pick my nose was strong. I ran my tongue over my teeth and found three missing on the left side.

When I heard the sounds of coins jingling, I turned my head to look. Erzsébet handed the jailer a small pouch. He loosened the drawstring, poured the coins into his hand, and examined them. A smile flashed across his face as he recognized the silver and gold. He grabbed a key ring from the wall and unlocked the shackles around my ankles and the heavy locks upon the chains around my wrists.

The first thing I did with my freedom of movement was to stick my right index finger into my right nostril. Shocked by the tacky mannerism, I quickly withdrew the finger, vowing to gain control of Ernö's old habit.

Erzsébet led me outside where two horses waited, a dappled gray mare and a dark, brooding stallion. The jailer watched from his doorway, probably speculating about why Erzsébet saved the life of this violent oaf. She mounted her horse, adjusting her skirt in the sidesaddle. I didn't know how to climb aboard my mount, because I'd never ridden a horse before.

"Mount on the left side by sliding your left foot into the stirrup, and swing your right leg over the horse," Erzsébet said, grinning at my inexperience. "I would think your body would intuitively guide you. Ernö was an excellent horseman."

I did this and found myself comfortably perched in the saddle. My left hand reached into my pants, and scratched my ass. I wondered what other nervous habits this body might have.

"Now just relax," she said. "Let your instincts take over."

I took a deep breath and relaxed as best I could, still reeling with a sense of unreality from traveling back to sixteenth-century Hungary and finding Erzsébet, all the while operating a strange body perched on a thousand-pound beast. After she allowed me to get used to controlling the stallion at a walk, Erzsébet dug her heels into the mare's flanks and we soon trotted along at a comfortable pace. We rode through the forested land separating Castle Cséjthe from the village, a green and fragrant place rich with darting birds, chattering squirrels, and bright wildflowers. Erzsébet rode ahead and I admired her from behind, perched regally upon the spirited mare. What good fortune to be chosen by her!

When we returned to Castle Cséjthe, Erzsébet introduced me to the castle steward as the new commander of the castle guard. When she informed her commander that I'd be taking command, his face registered his displeasure, but after looking my muscular body over, he voiced no protest.

"I have so many questions that need to be answered," I told her.

But Erzsébet insisted we wait to talk until she could be sure that no one could overhear us. "Spies are everywhere," she said.

After a young maidservant showed me to my chambers, Erzsébet sent a tailor to measure me for some decent clothes, and a manservant arrived to fill my bath and scrub away the farmer's dirt with an awful-smelling solution that nearly burned my skin and made my hair reek.

I protested.

"This will kill any nits inhabiting your body," he said, as he threw my

CRYONIC MAN

farmer's rags into the blazing fire that heated my bath water.

No wonder I'd scratched my ass and privates so often. My spirits lifted to observe the dozens of dark specks floating on the water's surface along with a dirty scum lining the copper tub. The manservant guided me from the water and he prepared another tub of fresh water to rinse myself.

The tailor worked fast. He fashioned a dolman, a long tunic of linen for warmer weather, fitted at the top like a shirt but with long flared tails to go over comfortable trousers that narrowed down to the ankles, similar to the garments worn by Turkish men. He also made a light vest of wool felt, and said he would procure sheepskins, furs, and woolen fabric when the weather cooled to make the high fur hat, fur and sheepskin vests, and the shaggy woolen mantle worn by military men. For more formal occasions, he would also sew a short, tight dolman with rows of brass buttons, similar to the Western European doublet, worn with short breeches, hose, and pointy shoes of soft leather, or for winter, high military boots. Before I could dress, a barber rushed in to trim my hair and beard.

When called to the dining hall wearing my new tunic and trousers, I felt silly as hell, as though I'd dressed in costume for a stage play. There were twenty or so people in the room, standing in small groups conversing. All the men were dressed in clothing identical to mine, thank goodness. A sudden silence filled the room as I entered, everyone turned to stare at me. I gazed at a window across the room and reflected back was my face and my finger about rim out my nose. I stopped my hand in mid-air and gazed at the glass again. A face stared back that might be considered handsome by some, but the features were broad and coarse. The arms and torso, however, were magnificently bulging with muscle. Surely, I would be a match for Zsombor in this body.

Erzsébet hurried to my side, dressed in a wine-colored gown of spun silk, a color highlighting her creamy white skin and gray eyes to perfection. Hard-pressed to take my eyes off her, I also craved the sweet aroma of her perfume. She took me from group to group to introduce me as many wondering eyes sized me up, wondering why a noblewoman would have anything to do with a coarse farmer like Ernö.

Everyone sat for dinner and all pretended pleasure to share the table with their mistress, but I noted fear, animosity, and jealousy on many faces. Any one of them might have alerted Zsombor to her presence if they could.

While lost in my thoughts, my farmer's body seized up with an attack of flatulence. Those sitting nearby pretended not to notice, but the smell around me changed from an overpowering sweetness to the aroma of a pig farm.

After dinner, Erzsébet informed me she'd held the gathering so Zsombor would hear of our presence at Castle Cséjthe. "We will lure him and take his bracelet," she announced.

"But how? Do you have some sort of plan or am I supposed to just kill him for it?"

"I've befriended a sister who knows many ancient secrets. Zsombor, as I've explained many times, is a master sorcerer who understands many magick spells. His knowledge makes it difficult to use magick against him, but my sister has learned a way to cause lightning to appear on her command, and I learned in your time how metal attracts electricity. Zsombor is usually the tallest man on the battlefield, and he always wears a metal helmet with a red plume on it and carries a long iron spear, so his troops can see and follow him. We'll meet him in an open field for battle. When he advances to the center of the field, my sister will create bolts of lightning. When Zsombor is struck, you can shift from Ernö's body to his body with my assistance before his spirit leaves, and thus have both bracelets."

"You trust me with both bracelets, Erzsébet?"

"Of course I do, Jim Jackson. Do not forget, I thoroughly know you, body, mind, and spirit. I know you have no need to rule over others. But there is one thing I must make crystal clear."

"What's that?"

"You cannot be captured under any circumstances while you wear a bracelet and we can never allow Zsombor to have both bracelets."

I took her right hand in mine and began to repeat the chant that would exchange the bracelet from my wrist to hers.

She tried to pull away. "What are you doing?"

"Returning your bracelet so Zsombor can't possibly wrest it from me. I plan to take his bracelet so we can return to the twenty-first century together."

Moved by my gesture of trust, her taut features relaxed and tears formed in her eyes. She'd seen so little trust it in her lifetime. But could I trust Erzsébet? I'd wanted more than anything to be with her again, but if I were killed while not wearing an immortality bracelet, I might never see her or my son again.

I shook my negative thoughts off, hoping and praying that Erzsébet would spend the night with me, but she suddenly informed me that she had a surprise for me in the morning, then bid me goodnight. Disappointed, I reasoned she didn't invite me to her bed because I lived in the body of a peasant. Maybe she observed me trying not to pick my nose during dinner. Surely she understood this to be Ernö's mannerism and not mine. Or perhaps she simply must show social distance as a noblewoman, or because in this treacherous age, women were burned at the stake for any stupid reason.

In the morning, I walked through the castle gate where my servant indicated that Erzsébet waited for me with two horses.

"Is this my surprise?" I asked, taking the reins of the big warhorse into my huge, calloused hands.

"No, this is." She held a sword identical to the one I'd trained with at the manor house in the twenty-first century in her outstretched hands. I wondered if it were the same sword, if perhaps she foresaw this moment in time and somehow had the ability to transport it back in time. Maybe it was the reason she insisted on my taking fencing lessons. If she foresaw this moment it would mean that she foresaw all that was happening now, including me returning the bracelet to her.

I shook my head as if I could shake the thought away. Once I began to speculate on what she did and didn't know about the future, I would drive myself crazy.

Erzsébet also carried a lance for me to practice with while riding the warhorse. Amazed at her vast reservoir of knowledge, I asked her where she learned the finer points of riding and fighting.

"I accompanied Ferenc on some campaigns and I learned by watching his training and his tactics."

She gave me a tour through the countryside and showed me various areas where it might be advantageous to lure and confront Zsombor and his army. Then she took me deep into the woods to meet the woman who could produce lightning.

I used to scoff at such things, but I believed anything Erzsébet told me now. Everything that happened to me since my rejuvenation had shown me that fiction couldn't get any stranger than my reality.

Soon we approached a tidy cottage set in the middle of a large clearing edged by blooming rose bushes and rows of grain and vegetables lining plowed fields.

"Eva, here I am," Erzsébet called loudly. She told me she warned Eva to give her time to remove the protective spells surrounding her cottage. I thought of the wicked witches in fairy tales with big noses and bigger warts right on the tip. But Eva stepped through the doorway and made my poor farmer's body frisky. Younger and prettier beyond my expectations, the sound of Eva's voice made me tremble with desire when she said hello. I tightly gripped that probing finger so she wouldn't see my disgusting habit.

"This is your witch?" I asked, grinning like a fool.

"Don't be misled by her looks," Erzsébet warned me. "She could make herself look just like you if she wanted to."

Erzsébet introduced us and Eva asked, "Are you comfortable in your new body?"

"Yes, I am."

"Good, then I can prepare you for Zsombor."

"Prepare me? How?"

"You know Zsombor will use magick to fool you."

"That's all I think about. How will I ever defeat a sorcerer like him?"

"The first thing he'll attempt is to cause you and your army to hallucinate each person's greatest fear. This is quite effective, especially if you're unprepared for it. Many armies have turned and fled because of this spell." Eva showed me how to make the protective symbol that each soldier and I needed to paint on our chests. The symbols would return the spell to the owner, and Zsombor's troops would hopefully panic instead.

"Do you know if you're wounded during the battle that your spirit can leave the body you're now in and possess another one that is dying or has recently died?"

"How can I do that, if I no longer wear the bracelet?

Erzsébet answered for Eva. "The same way I entered O'Malley's body while he was still alive. I used a spell and you can do the same."

"Surely Zsombor can do that too."

"Yes, he can. That is why we hope to strike him with lightning, giving you a chance to remove his bracelet before his spirit leaves his body."

"Eva, can you give him a demonstration of your talent?" Erzsébet asked.

"Of course," Eva said. She closed her eyes, rocking gently back on her heels as a look of deep concentration hardened her face. The sky over the croplands darkened, and almost instantaneously, a dozen lightning bolts forcibly erupted in a clearing before the field, causing small explosions and fires.

"Amazing," I said, dumbfounded. "What's the alternate plan if this doesn't work?"

Eva smiled. "You will also wear a faux bracelet that looks identical to the real one, the same trick Zsombor used on Erzsébet's husband. You will pretend to bargain with him in an effort to save Erzsébet by giving up the faux bracelet. If he falls for it and takes it from you and puts it on, the friction will cause small barbs to extend and release a deadly dose of poison."

"And if that doesn't work? What then?"

"Then you'll have to defeat him in combat."

"From what I have witnessed, that's easier said than done." I learned Zsombor had killed all the men I'd seen him in combat with, despite what appeared to be a losing battle.

"Your battle with Zsombor will be complex, because I have discovered that he communicates with the primeval gods," Eva said.

"You mean this guy talks to the gods and they answer?" I asked, half joking.

"This is grave," Erzsébet said. "You see, Jim Jackson, in olden times, the gods had tremendous influence in the affairs of mankind. As time went on, the gods became indifferent and only took an occasional interest."

"That is right," Eva chimed in. "But Zsombor has piqued their interest by promising that if he gains possession of both bracelets, he'll produce spectacles never before seen, such as nations exterminating other nations. He has promised ongoing torture and chaos on Earth."

For the first time ever, I feared getting into a fight I couldn't win. "You're joking," I blurted, "why would any deity enjoy something like that?"

Erzsébet scowled. "Why do men enjoy dogfights, cockfights, boxing, or any other cruel sport?

"For the amusement it provides, I suppose." I didn't mention my offense at her inclusion of boxing with dog and chicken fights.

"You've answered your own question," Eva said. "The gods want to be entertained and place no more value on man than man places on a dog or a chicken."

My head spun with all the contradictions. I had to fight a murdering monster who was also a master sorcerer *and* had the gods on his side. I might as well give up.

"Don't despair," Eva said. "I also talk to the gods and I believe Athena may help us."

Erzsébet cast Eva a despairing look. "Why didn't you tell me this?"

"Because I just made contact last night."

I recalled the times that Erzsébet called on Athena during our confrontations with the Exorcists.

"Athena mixes aggression, belligerence, virtue and benevolence. She'll take on any force and is victorious against any who challenge her. She always has the power to restore order and justice," Eva said, finally running out of breath in praise of her goddess.

All this talk of magick, deities, and justice made my head spin. Why did this have to be so complicated?

"Isn't there some way I can fight Zsombor man-to-man rather than with trickery?"

"No," Eva answered. "Zsombor has been an occult practitioner for years, and there is no such thing as a fair fight with him."

"Why do you even need me then?"

Erzsébet looked at me sternly. "You're one of a few who don't desire to use the bracelets' power for yourself and one of a very few who have a chance to defeat Zsombor in battle."

I wondered again if perhaps Erzsébet and Eva planned to bewitch me. Erzsébet had possessed me; was she also setting me up to engage in battle with the dominant predator?

"Too bad there's no pay-per-view television," I said. "This just might turn out to be the fight of the century. My second fight of the century, as a matter of fact."

Eva looked at me, puzzled, but Erzsébet's throaty laugh rang across the landscape. "The veil between the worlds is thin here, and why Eva chose to live at this spot. That is the best place to confront Zsombor," she said, pointing to a rocky plain beyond the patchwork of fields we gazed upon. Behind us was the forest we rode through – I could conceal any number of men there. Erzsébet explained how she would try to draw Zsombor into it when he came for her.

Fear began to chip away at me again. When I fought in the ring, I was only responsible for my own ass. Without any military training, how could I repel an army led by a warrior like Zsombor? This would put the lives of my men at risk. If we lost, we wouldn't just lose a fight. We'd lose our lives, and painfully at that. I didn't want to see any of my men or myself skewered upon Zsombor's poles!

Chapter 34

As the days passed in a dizzying succession, Erzsébet and I continued to meet whenever an opportunity arose to plot how we might engage Zsombor in battle and acquire his bracelet. We were careful to not socialize openly because she was bound by custom to associate with members of the royal class, not commoners like Ernö. I often pouted because she refused to spend much time with me.

Despite her status, I began to see her as a woman struggling to survive rather than the self-assured countess who outranked me. I began to appreciate just how much she depended on me to accomplish her goals and why she'd taken my body in the first place. I prayed I could fulfill her wishes before something happened to me or my year in cryogenic preservation ended.

"We need to move forward before my time runs out," I said after months of inaction. "Joe and his medical team will remove my body from cryonic storage in six months. You know what happens then."

Erzsébet gave me one of her maddening, enigmatic looks. "When he rejuvenates your body, your spirit will be drawn back to it, of course."

"What's Zsombor waiting for? I thought he was in a hurry to get your bracelet."

Erzsébet shook her head. "Perhaps he is waiting for the same reasons we have dallied, to be fully prepared, to make certain he is victorious. He will only act when he thinks the time is right."

"If Zsombor isn't going to make the first move, then maybe we should summon him on the pretext that you want to make a compromise to guarantee your safety."

"He will never fall for that," she said flatly.

"Since he discovered that you didn't have the bracelet when he died, how about starting rumors that you've taken my bracelet and I want revenge? He'll think I'm just waiting for a chance to kill you."

Erzsébet's face brightened. "That may work because Zsombor knows if you kill me, he must follow me to get the second bracelet. Maybe he will want to forge an alliance with you to get it." Her face turned thoughtful again. "Knowing Zsombor, his only true motive to meet you will be to destroy you."

"No different than my motive, of course. If we delay longer I may be called back, and what will you do then?"

"I do not know, Jim Jackson. You know how much I am counting on you. And when you leave, I will miss you terribly."

"Why don't you return to America with me?"

Erzsébet sighed and her shoulders drooped in contrast to her usual regal poise and relentless determination. "I would love to, but there are so many complications. If we can't wrest the bracelet from Zsombor now, then I must confront Zsombor myself. And I can't be certain what consequences I have created by coming back in time like this, nor can you. These bracelets are truly a curse."

"Bring the bracelets to my time, Erzsébet, and we'll return them to the gods so no one else will ever possess them again."

"How would we do that?"

"Drop them into an active volcano. Isn't that how so many of them were disposed of in olden times?"

"Yes, but that means I would live and die in your time."

"Of course, but don't you remember how much you enjoyed it? Hot running water, soft towels, motor vehicles, airplanes..."

"Except for the airplanes, you are right. I did love twenty-first century conveniences. But what would I do there?"

"You'd be my wife, and without the bracelets we'd enjoy a nice, peaceful life."

"A nice peaceful life sounds compelling, something I have never had."

All this talk was just a fantasy, a fairy-tale wish. I knew it and I believed Erzsébet did too. Even with all the bizarre things I'd experienced, even with my keen desire to have her, I still didn't believe in romantic fairy-tale endings.

So I feverishly set back to work. I berated myself for having knowledge of airplanes, tanks, and automatic weapons but not being able to figure out how to reproduce any of them. I did have one idea that might give us an advantage. Balloons. They'd been around before the industrial age. I figured I could easily build a few, fly over Zsombor's troops and bombard them with rocks.

I spent my free time talking to shopkeepers and farmers in various villages, looking for the right materials. During my best attempt, I tried heavy canvas sailcloth coated with pitch to construct a balloon, but the fire necessary to inflate the balloon melted the pitch and caused the air to escape. I knew that hot air balloons were introduced in the late eighteenth century, so I'd probably solve the problem with enough time, but I couldn't afford to waste any more time experimenting. I would have sold my soul to get online with my PVA to find out what materials were used in early hot air balloons!

I continued to absorb conventional military strategy. I learned a few tricks from the castle guard detail by carefully cultivating friendships with my men. I taught them modern calisthenics, weight lifting, and boxing strategy, and they taught me the finer points of sixteenth-century military maneuvers. When I'd learned as much as I could, I showed my attack plan to Erzsébet, a map I'd sketched of the area where Eva lived, marked with the lines and arrows of my strategy for exterminating Zsombor's army, complete with troop placements and sketches of the weapons I was constructing.

Pleased with my tactics, Erzsébet reminded me that the media called me a "ring general" when I trained for the world heavyweight boxing championship.

"I was proud of that name because I dominated the ring every time I fought. I'm beginning to realize that my confrontation with Zsombor is simply a bigger ring with more punches to throw."

Once again, I thanked my lucky stars for sending Erzsébet into my life. I never dreamed it could be this exciting: me leading an army and preparing for the one thing I loved, a good battle.

Not able to construct any modern weapons, I turned to history for ideas. I wanted something more lethal and dramatic than catapults, rams, and the medieval and post-medieval cannons used to breach castle walls and blast battlefields. After some thought, I recalled a medieval movie or two in which fiery balls were lobbed from castle walls or toward them with a catapult. Then I recalled the long sought-after formula for "Greek fire" written on one of the ancient Egyptian scrolls. It was a very old-fashioned strategy, but maybe there was a way to spray Greek fire on Zsombor's troops.

"That may work better than dropping boulders from balloons," Erzsébet said.

I knew a primitive flamethrower might intimidate Zsombor, or at least cause death, destruction, and fear among his ranks. The thought of killing so many appalled me, but the future of humanity was at stake. I had to win this battle by using any means available.

I figured out a simple pumping mechanism for discharging a stream of Greek fire, a mixture of ingredients that Eva and Erzsébet read on the scroll – naphtha, quicklime, sulphur, and niter. I felt relieved to conceive of an effective weapon after the balloon debacle. Eva and Erzsébet said they could add a little magick into the mix to make the fire colorful and more intimidating.

While I worked on my pumps, I fantasized about driving off attacks on the skirmish lines using this frightful secret formula. It had saved the Byzantine Empire from two Arab sieges and I was positive Greek fire could repel any sixteenth-century army just as it had in years past. Most men fear fire because it's such a painful way to die. And pouring water on flames caused by Greek fire would not extinguish them. On the contrary, water served to spread Greek fire and it was used effectively in ocean battles.

My officers and I heated our ingredients in cauldrons and then pumped the fluid out through large two-handed pumps. It worked like a charm. I had the castle guard mount four barrel-like pumps in the tallest trees overlooking our battlefield. We also installed four on the walls and parapets at Castle Cséjthe in case we had to make a retreat. Over the coming weeks, we also fashioned dozens of hand grenades from earthenware vessels with chambers for fluids that mixed and ignited when the vessel broke on impact.

I taught my soldiers how to carry and effectively lob these hand grenades. When they charged, they would stop and throw the grenades instead of following through with their assault. Fire, I hoped, would cause Zsombor's defenses to give in quickly.

I showed Erzsébet how I planned to lure Zsombor to the center of the field by leading our troops in a faux retreat, turning to fight when they passed the field's center point.

First, while Zsombor pursued my army across the field, my riders would ignite the tall grass on three sides of his army. We cleared an area of flammable material in advance where our troops would be able to gather safely while everything else burned.

Zsombor's troops could only move forward, directly into the assault with grenades and flamethrowers as well as the cannons and one-shot muskets of the artillery. Hell, even my unit of archers would stand ready – flaming arrows could be as effective as Greek fire.

My greatest worry now was that Zsombor would die before I could capture his bracelet. If that happened, the cat and mouse game would begin again. Neither one of us wanted a chase through all eternity for the remaining bracelet.

During the final days of planning and training my troops, I still questioned the wisdom of attacking Zsombor's superior force, but my time in the sixteenth century grew shorter every day. If I didn't succeed, Erzsébet would be no worse off than before she met me, but if I didn't act now, I'd wonder forever if I'd done my best to save humanity from Zsombor.

Erzsébet, Eva, and I spent our last evening together at Eva's cottage, copying the idea to construct a look-alike bracelet filled with poison that Zsombor had used on Ferenc.

When they finished, Eva handed it to me. I repeated what Erzsébet had said before: "He'll never fall for that."

"It is worth a try," Eva said. "Zsombor is so eager to possess both bracelets that he may forget to use caution."

Erzsébet sighed. "If nothing else, it will give us the opportunity to annihilate him and his army when they meet you in the open," she said. "Anna Darvulia taught me a special enchantment to grace it with."

"Okay." I put the bracelet in a drawstring bag that hung from a loose belt around my hips. "I suppose it doesn't hurt to keep all my options open."

Finally, three days before Joe was due to remove my body from the nitrogen tank, I sent word to Zsombor that I wanted to negotiate. He agreed that the open field made a good meeting place, a situation that would prevent any surprises. Just before his arrival, I showed the officers under my command how to paint Eva's protective symbol against Zsombor's magick upon their chests. As they took this information to the troops, I prayed that not one man would be affected by his spells, the first weapon he would unleash.

On the following morning, Zsombor and his five thousand troops lined up across the field. I didn't think my story credible at all, but Zsombor appeared to be as weary of waiting as I was. His heavily armored cavalry stood alert, off to one side upon their mounts. His infantry, the men who carried muskets and swords, lined up behind the artillery with their cannons and mechanical catapults. Perhaps Zsombor had heard rumors about my tactics and had some fiery plans as well. He raised his spear high, a signal to send a delegation of four forward. I did likewise. They negotiated, deciding Zsombor and I would meet alone in the center of the open space, our respective troops at ready behind us.

I rode toward Zsombor, mounted upon the fully-armored warhorse that Erzsébet had provided months before, dapper and gleaming in my polished helmet and specially crafted chain mail.

Zsombor wore matching armor of dull black metal and as foretold, a spiked helmet with a red plume protruding from the crown. My battle horse was as well armored as Zsombor's and I felt confident that my strength matched his strength.

I greeted Zsombor from a distance, shouting across the space between us. "Your agreement to come here today terrified Erzsébet. She returned the bracelet to me and you'll have to kill me to get it." I began to chant the revealing incantation, slowly showing him my left wrist where I had placed the decoy bracelet over a band of copper so the barbs wouldn't penetrate my skin. I moved my arm so that the bracelet flashed in the sun, hopefully making it seem as though I'd made the incorporeal bracelet (that Erzsébet still wore) appear as real.

Zsombor threw his head back and laughed from the belly, a sound that echoed into the forest behind us like a lion's roar. He clearly considered killing me as insignificant as squashing an insect. He suddenly began to chant the incantation to make the bracelets glow in a deep growl, and his bracelet began to flame on his wrist. I felt the fake bracelet tingle on my wrist and I knew that Anna Darvulia's spell had worked.

Zsombor tried to draw me nearer. Ernö's body wasn't going to be as easy to kill as Zsombor seemed to think. My adrenaline flowed and my muscles tensed, ready for any attempt on his part to overpower me. He urged his horse forward and extended his hand in a false gesture of friendship.

I ignored Zsombor and kept my distance because once I extended my hand, he would attempt to cut it off. In that respect, it didn't matter one whit whether I wore a real bracelet or a fake one. I hoped Zsombor didn't remember the spell Erzsébet had used to make a real bracelet vibrate in the presence of another bracelet when he had reincarnated as O'Malley. If he had used this incantation, then he would already know that I wore a fake.

Zsombor withdrew his hand and leaned on his lead-lined iron lance, an imposing staff that touched the ground and extended at least twelve inches above his head. His men declared that only he could carry his lance because of its weight.

The clear sky began to darken by slow degrees. I knew what was coming and reined my horse in to back away.

"What ..." Zsombor said, as the first bolt of lightning struck his lance, arcing through it as if held by a god. Soldiers on both sides shouted their surprise. But I knew what the others didn't. The metal shaft of the lance had acted as a lightning rod.

Both armies expected Zsombor to either die or to direct what they thought was his power at any second. He sat as though glued to his horse as bolt after bolt of lightning erupted through his lance. Both he and his horse began to glow in a blue-white haze. My warhorse lifted his legs high, stepping farther from the lightning as the antiseptic smell of ozone wafted through the field.

When the bolts of lightning ceased, a loud cheer rose from the ranks of Zsombor's soldiers. They saw him struck many times – or had he commanded the lightning? Yet he lived, a sure sign of victory either way, it seemed. His army began to surge forward without an order to do so.

I took comfort that Marduk, who had promised to assist Zsombor, was nowhere to be seen. I wondered if Zsombor had forgotten to invoke his help or if gods only observed from a distance.

Zsombor lifted his lance skyward and chanted something, maybe the incantation to make my men hallucinate, but no one seemed fazed in the slightest. As Zsombor's cavalry advanced to the center of the field, I gave my signal. A score of my fittest horsemen dragged burning bushes behind them to set fire to the tall grass surrounding Zsombor and his troops. They laughed at this because the path to us was wide open, but they had to advance quickly to stay ahead of the flames. A haze of dust and smoke added confusion to the orderly battlefield.

My rear guard galloped forward with the nozzles from my improvised flamethrowers. When Zsombor's troops reached my lines, my men deployed the devices. A deafening whooshing noise erupted as Zsombor's troops faced a solid wall of flame. Soon burning brush and burning flesh created an odor like pigs roasting on a spit.

But Zsombor's troops marched bravely forward into the path of the flames like hell's demons. I gave my cavalry the signal to attack. Zsombor's troops flinched when my soldiers stopped their charge and began to toss our chemical-laden earthen grenades. Flames and acrid, irritating smoke assaulted the advancing line of soldiers.

I lost sight of Zsombor and frantically gazed around, trying to locate him before he died or disappeared. I issued orders to find him at all costs, a grievous mistake. Zsombor had sent his reserves around and behind us in the cover of the smoke while he distracted our attention with a frontal assault. From behind us came the sounds of running horses. I turned to see a rip-roaring cavalry charge that took my army by surprise. All our defenses were looking forward, none to the rear. This caused escalating fear and confusion in the ranks that slowly started to retreat. Some began to run for Castle Cjsethe despite my shouts to stand and fight, and soon my maneuver turned into a complete rout, as every man tried to save himself.

I had no choice but to turn and join my men. About half of my army made it safely to the castle with Zsombor's troops in pursuit. The drawbridge creaked and shivered as it began to rise and my warhorse barely made it across before it closed.

Zsombor was smart enough not to approach the castle walls, rising thirty feet at their highest points. He had seen what my flamethrowers were capable of during the battle and suspected we had more on the parapets. He did what was usual for a siege in the sixteenth century: he ordered his troops to surround the castle. They began preparations to camp along the road up the mountain to cut off our supply lines. What Zsombor did do in an unusual manner was to march the several hundred captives from our battle around the steep perimeter of Castle Cséjthe. He ordered them to sit on the ground while his representative read a proclamation that any soldier of the opposing forces, including captives, could join his army at full pay and receive the personal freedom and rights all his armies enjoyed or face the deadly consequences.

⫸Chapter 35

To demonstrate his intent, Zsombor randomly chose ten prisoners as a sacrifice to Marduk. As they had in my vision of Zsombor, his soldiers impaled my men and raised them on poles. Their screams of anguish could be heard even behind the heavy walls of Castle Cséjthe.

If nothing else, terror spurred the remaining soldiers inside to ready for an attack. They hoped to free the living and to avenge their impaled comrades. To my surprise, not one had joined Zsombor's forces against me, perhaps not trusting his promise of forgiveness.

I mounted my warhorse and ordered the castle guard to raise the massive gate. The remains of my army surged forward as the captives desperately waved them back. Zsombor had captured two flamethrowers from the field and met our remaining flamethrowers on the parapets with a fiery assault of their own. For every man and line we succeeded in destroying, Zsombor's ranks destroyed the equivalent on our side. As in the field, the air on the flanks of the mountain became black with the acrid smell of Greek fire and burning flesh while the screams and shouts of wounded men scoured the hills. A fire began to rage in the woods bordering the castle and I feared it would turn into a major conflagration, fanned by the stiff winds rising from the valleys below.

Despite or maybe even because of the showy fireworks that Eva and Erzsébet's magick produced with our Greek fire, the first three ranks of both charging armies were incinerated. Our survivors turned tail toward the castle, a retreat from a fiery hell of magickal explosions, but too late. Zsombor's cavalry had ridden to our rear soon after we left the gate, blocking our way back. A small band of soldiers and I, mostly on horseback, fought our way through burning underbrush to get back inside, nearly overwhelmed by Zsombor's superior numbers.

Zsombor now held nearly one thousand of the Báthory family mercenaries, and many of the rest were dead or dying. One hell of a general I turned out to be, losing an entire army in one battle. Why had such a sure thing gone so wrong?

At least the castle walls had not been breached. The flanks of the mountain were much too steep to drag heavy cannons or catapults there in a short span of time, though these were likely still on their way from the battlefield. As my remaining troops regrouped inside the castle walls to consider our options, Zsombor rode among his ranks outside. His red plume fluttered in the breeze that blew the stink of burning flesh into the castle grounds.

My guard, consisting of roughly two hundred men and another exhausted, battle-weary one hundred, was all that remained to defend Castle Cséjthe. Erzsébet's relatives and all the civilians living inside the castle walls prepared to leave via the tunnels in the bowels of the castle under the cover of night. While the grooms led our exhausted horses away, Erzsébet appeared in the midst of my soldiers, dressed now in the same fashion as my soldiers in a gray dolman, long trousers, and boots. I did not notice her until she strode up to me, her fair hand resting on the hilt of what I presumed was Ferenc's old sword. A spatter of blood marked one cheek, proof that she had accompanied us outside under Zsombor's nose.

"If you wish to join my servants in leaving, they would be happy to have your protection. My son Päl is fortuitously away with his tutor, being schooled at court, and my daughters are in their own households."

I couldn't run from a battle even though the odds were overwhelming.

"You know I cannot." I nearly held my tongue, but wondered about the protection from the gods that she and Eva promised. "What happened to Athena?"

"I do not question her," Erzsébet replied, lifting her chin stubbornly as she always did when challenged. "There is always a reason for Athena's action or inaction."

In the wee hours, the evacuation proceeded quietly like the rustle of scurrying rats. Erzsébet insisted upon staying by my side. I instructed the second-in-command of the castle guard to take Erzsébet, by force if necessary, through one of the concealed tunnels when the final battle for Castle Cséjthe began.

At dawn, the sound of chopping upon green wood penetrated the castle. I stood alone and forlorn, gazing from a parapet as Zsombor directed his commanders to force another two dozen prisoners to chop young evergreen saplings surrounding the castle. Each prisoner then dragged his sapling to a point designated by Zsombor's soldiers. They were forced at sword point to peel the bark and sharpen both ends of the stakes they had fashioned.

The soldiers circulated among the prisoners, collecting the axes to prevent their use as weapons. On Zsombor's signal, four to five soldiers grabbed hold of each prisoner and impaled each one on their stakes. The soldiers hastily dug holes and raised the stakes into standing position with the flailing and screaming prisoners stuck like marshmallows on a stick. As Erzsébet had said, Zsombor must want Marduk to see how he would amuse them once he had both bracelets.

Those who had perished the day before began to fill the air with a stench, attracting carrion birds and insects. My stomach turned and I slid to my heels and crouched against the wall, the images, deafening screams, and stench swirling around me in a living nightmare.

I and I alone was responsible for all these poor souls. I vowed to get my hands on Zsombor so I could ram a pole up his ass.

We had only one more day before my body's scheduled rejuvenation. If Ernö's body did not survive Zsombor's siege, it was of little importance because I would be drawn back to the future into my own body. Still, a feeling of impotence at not being able to protect

Erzsébet or stay with her burned through me.

When she found me again, still dressed in a soldier's garb, I tried to convince her of the hopelessness of our situation. If she stayed, Zsombor would surely capture her bracelet and his horrors would engulf the world.

"Perhaps you are right, Jim Jackson," she conceded after staring at me for a moment. I cannot be responsible for that, so I must leave."

"Where will you go?"

"I don't know. As a member of the royal family, I have many options. We protect our own from savages like Zsombor."

"You mean everything to me, Erzsébet." I looked down at my coarse farmer's body. "I love you and I'm sorry it ends like this."

"Oh, it's not over between us," she answered, her eyes gleaming with mischief.

"The battle begins," cried the lookout. I jumped up and gazed downward. Below us, Zsombor's forces rallied once more, his cavalry leading a charge toward the castle gate.

"Man your stations," I yelled from the parapet stairs. I grabbed Erzsébet and planted a hasty but passionate kiss on her lovely lips, and we rushed hand in hand to the battlement. The advancing troops carried wooden ladders to scale the wall above the castle gate, the one side not protected by the steep mountain flanks. I ordered the castle guard to let Zsombor's troops raise the ladders, then attack them again with the flamethrowers.

"But if we allow the ladders to be raised, the barbarians will scale the walls," my guard cautioned.

"We'll roast them like the pigs they are before they climb," I said. "Ready the remaining grenades."

The attacking army approached the castle's high walls with their shields held above their heads, edges touching to form an overhead barricade against arrows, spears, and the Greek fire. The men hefting the ladders crouched between the shield holders until they reached the wall. Then they dashed from under cover, setting and holding the ladders against the castle wall so our defenders couldn't push them down.

A deep voice bellowed from below the first ladder in place. "Follow me!" Zsombor's plume bobbed from behind his shield as he began to ascend the initial ladder.

His men followed his example. The shield carriers escorting them to the wall scrambled up the ladders to do battle with the castle guard, who showed extreme courage in the face of what would be a grotesque execution for them if defeated.

There were ten ladders in all, a macabre scene of flame-enshrouded men jumping from blazing ladders lit by my archers' flaming arrows and the Greek fire. Perhaps a dozen men survived the onslaught of the Greek fire and made it to the top of the wall. Next came their newly arrived catapults, battering rams, and cannons. Because Zsombor had placed less than a hundred men inside the wall, he would have to infiltrate it quickly by force. Our defenders fought hard, energized by the sight of their comrades' impaled bodies and the smoking corpses of the newly dead enemy.

Above the yells of the soldiers, I could hear the thuds of the rams and cannonballs pounding against the battlement and the slow splintering of the castle gate, and then finally, a tumbling roar as part of the wall began to collapse. Zsombor's men began to scramble up the wreckage and through the splintered gate. The Greek fire, a barrage of loose stones from the damaged wall, and some well-placed arrows and musket balls, repelled some enemy troops. Hand-to-hand combat raged inside the wall, with nearly every man facing an equally-matched swordsman.

I turned from cutting down a young man dressed like me but in cloth of another color, not wanting to see his lifeblood cascading from the sickening wound I'd gashed in his skull. I opened my eyes to see Zsombor just a few paces away, slaughtering any soldier who came within reach.

I would now meet my match.

Many of our men lay strewn around us in the broken postures of dead warriors. As I stepped before him and looked into his eyes, Zsombor vanished into thin air.

"Search for Zsombor," I yelled. I dashed toward the steep, winding stairs to the castle's top parapet so I could view his remaining troops and predict their next tactic.

As I slowed to a jog on a landing just below the top of the stairs, my farmer's body ducked instinctively at the sound of a blade swinging through the air. I came up fast with my sword ready. Trapped on the narrow stairway, I barely avoided having my head severed from my body.

There stood Zsombor with his monstrous sword and a heavy leather and iron shield. He spread his blood-spattered legs and grimaced savagely at me, his eyes burning with hate. "There's no getting away from me now, you uncouth lout," he said.

I swung my sword low on a wide swath, trying to hit his exposed leg, which showed through a gaping tear in one boot. The blade missed, but when Zsombor lowered his shield to protect his lower parts, I drove the dagger in my left hand into his right shoulder.

Zsombor roared like a wounded animal. I matched his bellow with a scream of aggression as I went on the attack, flailing my broadsword in great, heaving sweeps.

Suddenly Zsombor laughed despite his pain and I could see he truly loved squaring off with me. His enthusiasm got my fighting spirit and the adrenaline of Ernö's body flowing. He began to sing in deep bass tones that matched the rhythm of our parries as he easily blocked my strokes.

What kind of man sings when he battles for his life? I realized that Zsombor wasn't singing, but chanted instead in a strange language, probably a magickal incantation that meant more trouble for me. I nearly stopped meeting his sword's strokes as I glanced dumbfounded at the flames encircling my wrist.

Suddenly, something clenched in my gut and I nearly fainted. My hand began to reach out as though I offered it to Zsombor in in a sacrificial manner. I tried to pull my arm back with all my might, my body trembling with the effort. I could not.

Zsombor brought his sword down fast and hard above the bracelet.

I couldn't believe my eyes when both hands and my sword hit the stone paving, blood gushing in two wide streams at my feet. I backed away, trying to think what I could do to defend myself. Zsombor laughed as he bent over to pick up the bloody severed hand with the bracelet still attached to the ragged wrist.

Dangling my detached hand in the air, he turned to me. "Thank you, Ernö, for bringing me the bracelet."

Of all things to think of at a critical time like this, I could only stare at the bloody index finger that had so often found its way to my farmer's nose, knowing it would never find a safe haven ever again.

Zsombor ripped the bracelet from my severed wrist and jammed it on his bare left arm.

Blood pumped from my wounds. I faded and fell with a smile on my face, knowing Zsombor had fallen for the same trick he had played on Count Ferenc Nádasdy.

Chapter 36

Ernö's body shuddered as it struggled to breathe before expiring. My spirit floated from an invisible opening in the crown of the farmer's head just as it had escaped from my body during my death years before.

The memory of how Erzsébet had entered Father O'Malley's body when he was distracted with our televised testing in the twenty-first century spooled in front of me like a movie. I watched again as she caused O'Malley to kill himself.

My thoughts drifted to Eva. Immediately, she stood before me saying, "If wounded in battle, you can enter another body." I recited the spell Erzsébet had taught me to enter a body without wearing a bracelet.

My mind continued to drift and I fought to focus it. I began to gaze through a fog that that swirled all around me in random shapes and forms. A new thought formed. If Zsombor had died from the snake venom (and surely he had, just minutes after me) then he would be born again and Erzsébet would never be safe. At this cue, a form began to materialize from the fog. Zsombor lay below me, contorted in the throes of a seizure. His skin had become a putrid yellow and he gasped for air like a beached fish. I made a quick decision to enter his body, to accompany him wherever he went. He still wore his authentic immortality bracelet that guaranteed him a conscious reincarnation. Erzsébet still had the other, so I didn't know where I'd end up.

Once I closed my eyes and repeated the spell, I found myself inside his body. Zsombor tried momentarily to expel me and then gave up, too weak for the effort. As he died, our intertwined spirits floated from his body. As our spirits entered the spirit world together, I felt my consciousness magnetically drawn toward something. What, I didn't know, but I could definitely feel the pull. Zsombor's spirit accompanied me, as full of hate as the living man, and if he could have harmed me in any way, he would have done so.

Suddenly thousands of gleaming spirits like orbs of light drifted around us, their revulsion of Zsombor clear without thought or speech. Somehow, I absorbed their thoughts and intentions to take him to the hellish world of demons far below. I wasn't allowed to go there, so they determined they must separate him from me. These spirits were Zsombor's victims in his past life and payback was due. They tried to form an energy field to surround Zsombor's spirit, but this maneuver didn't succeed. Knowing that I would not be taken to a hell realm, Zsombor had mixed the energy of our spirits together with his magick, knowing that by making us one that he was safe.

I recalled that Joe would have started my rejuvenation by now and set his nanobots to work repairing any damage caused by the cryonic process. Could I hope that he might apply electrical current to activate my brain at any moment? The spirits seemed to understand this and hummed around me with soft glimmers of sound and color that created a soothing sensation.

Although linear time and space do not exist in the spirit world, I had a sense of traveling somewhere, still intertwined with Zsombor's spirit. His spirit dimmed in fear at the presence of the vengeful spirits. As soon as this thought had manifest, thousands of colored lights swarmed furiously around us like a horde of feeding insects.

Zsombor's spirit darkened to an almost lifeless state as he cried out to Marduk, his protector god. A blood-red light flashed around us. All the victim-spirits retreated from it. Zsombor brightened a bit and thanked Marduk for coming to his aid. Suddenly, an even brighter green light flashed near Marduk. Athena made her presence known and simply indicated through her strong will that Marduk should stay out of her business. The murky red light began to wane, followed by the clear green light.

This answered my final question to Erzsébet. Athena was on our side after all.

When the bigger lights vanished, the victim-spirits reappeared with an angry, energetic glow, trying to rip Zsombor from me. I wished them all the success in this world, because I didn't want to face this rejuvenation with our spirits intertwined. I had no doubt that Zsombor would dominate me and use my body for his reprehensible desires. Having to participate silently in his torturous acts would be a living hell, something I wouldn't wish on my worst enemy.

We arrived in the barest fringe of the physical world, a sort of purgatory or holding area in which spirits prepared for rebirth. After being there for what seemed like just a few moments, I felt drawn to another form below and as I neared it, I recognized my old body. My spirit formed into a sphere and slowly drifted through the crown of my head and into my heart, still intertwined with Zsombor.

With the strange, hard-edged jolt that marks the beginning of physical life, a flurry of activity began to take place around me. Joe applied the electrical paddles to start my heart and some part of me floating above watched my body jump and gasp for its first breath. The medical team cheered, as it had before, and technicians gazed at the monitors lining the walls of the rejuvenation chamber. Everything looked familiar except for Father Flynn's device, connected to the fMRI machine to detect the presence of spirit possession in patients revived from cryonic preservation.

Flynn's detector beeped, of course, and the monitor showed two distinctive, individual electrical patterns in my brain. Joe barked an order at a technician to inject me with one of the drug cocktails. Soon my body drifted into a comatose state again, but my spirit remained aware.

Zsombor and I drifted like a rudderless ship in a formless, desolate world. The battle began as he tried to slip directly into my mind via my newly rejuvenated brain. I blocked him with all the mental energy I could summon. In turn, I attempted to enter his mind. He put up a furious resistance, perceivable to me as flashing sparks of light, but I continued to press into his consciousness until I succeeded in mingling my consciousness with his. After all, he had made us one by commingling our energies, so perhaps this made my task easier. In the same way that Erzsébet viewed my thoughts and memories, I saw Zsombor's, an endless parade of ugly, sickening scenes, the torture and mutilation of thousands of victims in his lifetime. If I had eyes, I would have squeezed them shut. I wondered how long I'd be isolated with Zsombor, and how long before I went insane?

I expected him to overwhelm me somehow, as Erzsébet always did, but he shut me out, attempting to block my awareness of all his dirty secrets. As he withdrew his energy from mine, I became aware of a vague separation, as though I were an egg yolk spooned away from the white. Gradually, Zsombor and I became two distinct spirits again.

Once the medical team verified and recorded on my chart that I'd returned from the cryonic state with more than one spirit, Joe called Father Flynn to perform an immediate exorcism. If the second spirit was an agent for good, an exorcism would do it no harm, but any evil spirit would be repelled. I hoped that Flynn would send Zsombor to the subterranean world where tarnished souls are cleansed by fire. In all the stress and confusion, I couldn't recall all the Egyptian rules about the bracelets, but I seemed to remember from one of my dual spirits discussions with Erzsébet that if the one holding the bracelet did not reincarnate, then the one who did would keep the bracelet.

Father Flynn arrived quietly with his assistants – two young seminary students with serious expressions incongruous with their baby faces – to perform the exorcism. Joe met them at the sterile lock at the room's entrance that looked rather like the opening of an airline jetbridge.

"Does my father need to be conscious for you to complete this?" Joe questioned Father Flynn as the three men took turns scrubbing and donning sterile hospital gowns and booties before entering the sterile field.

"No, his soul is aware and will hear my prayers."

"Of course, medical science recognizes that people maintain awareness even when in a comatose state," Joe said, texting into his digital medical records analyst, "but I wondered if this is applicable to this situation. I'm really uncertain how my father manages to return to his body with another soul in tow. . ."

"For my purposes, the reason is not important. What matters is my ability to expel the intruding soul or spirit," Father Flynn explained. "You've seen my work with state prisoners – in a sense, the detection of possession is based on science, but matters of exorcism are based more upon faith."

Joe looked on as Father Flynn and his assistant prepared to perform the ritual by setting twelve altar candles around my inert body. Next, he mixed a solution of salt and holy water along with an ointment used for anointing the head and body: three tablespoons of frankincense oil, three tablespoons of myrrh oil, six drops of clove oil and one half teaspoon of powdered garlic mixed in one-quarter cup of melted animal fat. He measured the temperature with a digital cooking thermometer to ensure the proper temperature.

"Does anything ever go wrong during an exorcism?" Joe asked.

"There have been problems – exorcism has caused a number of real-world tragedies over the years."

Visibly shaken, Joe said, "Maybe we better hold off, then."

"Don't worry. I should have mentioned those were all attempts by amateurs. I've exorcised over three thousand souls and never had an injury, let alone a death."

As Father Flynn continued his preparations, Joe's face relaxed as he observed the priest's efficient, expert movements.

Flynn directed his assistants to light all the candles. "Be vigilant. The candles must be kept burning throughout the exorcism. If they go out, they must be relit immediately," he said. "Now, light this incense made from Solomon's Seal and St. John's Wort. It must also burn continuously."

Finally, Father Flynn took leather straps from his bag and directed his assistants to strap my arms and legs to my hospital bed. He began to pray in a deep sonorous voice while he scattered salt across and along my body in the mystical sign of the cross. "With this Holy salt I baptize thee. . ."

Zsombor squirmed at these words. Then Flynn sprinkled holy water in two swaths along and across my body and Zsombor recoiled again.

"With this Holy water, I sanctify thee," he said, and anointed my feet, abdomen, the palms of my hands, and my temples with the ointment, repeating his prayer.

Flynn raised his voice a notch and held his hands over me. "Hear me, demonic spirit who possesses this mortal body. I command thee to depart at once, and return into this person nevermore! By the Holy, Almighty, and Everlasting power of the Supreme Being, I cast thee OUT! Depart from this mortal body at God's command!"

I prayed that that God was far more powerful than Zsombor's gods and that Zsombor would leave my body without taking his bracelet. Then I continuously repeated the incantation to transfer the bracelet from Zsombor to myself.

Vengeful spirits surrounded my body in spirals of clashing colors and a humming frenzy, waiting for Flynn to cast Zsombor's spirit out. The furious spurts of sound and color so terrorized Zsombor that he didn't seem to notice my incantation.

My body began to tremble and soon my arms and legs shook like a vibrating bed in a cheap motel. Zsombor fought to stay, but he shook too, anticipating with a sweaty, palpable fear what the vengeful spirits would do to him. I tried to push him away mentally. Like a sudden ray of light shining through a keyhole, a small separation between our spirits began.

I concentrated harder, visualizing myself physically pushing him away. Then I concentrated on two actions at once, trying to push him out to the spirit world where he would get what's coming to him, and at the same time, trying to attract the bracelet to my wrist.

Father Flynn repeated his simple prayers with new emphasis and a stronger conviction. A gust of cool wind swept through the room and blew all the candles out. Zsombor regained his strength until Flynn's assistants relit them. His strength receded when the last candle began to burn.

My body shook violently as the spirits formed a solid ball of light energy around Zsombor and tried to rip him from my body. They struggled at an impasse for a full twenty minutes until I thought I'd pass out or my bones would break from the shaking. The assistants stood on either side of me, holding my hands in theirs.

I didn't know if I imagined the horrifying scream or if Zsombor's soul had actually screamed when his spirit ripped apart from mine. Or perhaps I was the one doing the screaming.

Relieved and exhausted, I regained consciousness, looked into Father Flynn's eyes, and passed out.

Chapter 37

My body relaxed back into a drug-induced coma, but my spirit struggled to remain aware. I could hardly wait to discover if I had the bracelet or if Zsombor had taken it with him to the depths of the underworld where the spirits had dragged him. I didn't care what happened to him as long as he couldn't harm anyone else. Only the bracelet's fate mattered now.

As Father Flynn prepared to leave the rejuvenation room, Joe praised how well his detector had performed. In his excitement and his typical, clumsy effort to socialize, he questioned Father Flynn. "Do you know anything more about why my father picks up hitchhikers? What's the difference between ghosts and demons?"

Father Flynn looked up from the valise he was packing with his exorcism paraphernalia. "I still can't explain why Mr. Jackson is possessed during his rejuvenations. But I can answer your second question. A ghost is an "astral shell," an imprint, if you will, of an entity's soul that does not pass over to the spirit realm. Ghosts are usually attached to particular locations, because of either a sudden, traumatic death or a reluctance to move on. The obsession with a living entity by a ghost can cause sad and sometimes tragic experiences. Some ghosts compel people to commit suicide or murder. Ghosts can influence habitual behavior and lead people into drug or alcohol dependence or cause them to perform other negative acts. Demons are not from this world and possess the human soul from within, and this is the major difference. But possession is possession, whether by a demon or a ghost, and either must be cast out."

Joe nodded and thanked Father Flynn, still distracted with all my charts and data. The two shook hands as Flynn's seminary students exited the room through the sterile lock.

Equally exhausted by the effort of the long, painstaking rejuvenation, Joe waited until the following morning to try to bring me out of my medically induced coma. While he directed the injection of the stimulating drug cocktail into my IV, the medical technicians kept an eye on Father Flynn's possession detection device in the event another spirit might somehow appear.

Though I felt connected with my body, I had little sense of time passing, like a drowsy sleeper too tired to wake up but still aware of his surroundings. In a mental sense, I rolled over and went back to sleep as my body became more alive. A week passed before my eyes opened again. As I took my first glance into the worried face of my son, he asked, "Did you accomplish your objectives?"

How about, *Hello, Dad. How are you?* I couldn't reply because my throat was too dry, for one thing, and I didn't know what I'd accomplished, for another.

I tried to raise my right wrist to see if I retained the bracelet, but I couldn't move my arm because of the IV and all the gadgets attached to me.

I silently repeated the invocation, hoping to watch the bracelet glow. But I was lying flat and with medical bracelets and IVs on both arms and couldn't properly see my wrist. And Joe was too distracted or maybe didn't think of my need to see my wrist. I could only lie there in frustration and imagine what devious things Zsombor might do if he retained the bracelet. If he had, I'd be hunting for Erzsébet again.

A nurse entered my room with Joe and seemed to sense my predicament or perhaps only wanted to make me more comfortable.

"Well, well, Mr. Jackson, there you are," she said, raising the head of my bed. "Can we get you anything else? I bet you're ready for some real food!"

I tried to raise my right hand and found that I still couldn't move my arm. But at least I could see my wrist.

Joe noticed me staring at my wrist and thought I was worried about my atrophied muscles. "Hey, glad to see you're finally awake, Dad. I was beginning to wonder. Don't worry, after a week of massages and hydrobaths, you'll feel like a new man."

Joe couldn't stop smiling, obviously buoyed by a sense of accomplishment at having revived me a second time. I hoped he spoke the truth.

NTRS, Joe's research company, had greatly improved the subatomic nanobots since my first cryonic preservation. I found I experienced less disorientation and muscle stiffness from being inert for the past year than after the fifty-year preservation.

Another week of worry and remorse went by, but I became physically and mentally stronger. Finally, one quiet night when left alone for a bit, I raised my right wrist and in my raspy, newfound voice, I prayed to the gods, any gods who might listen, but particularly to Athena, Erzsébet's ally. I repeated the incantation and as soon as I'd finished, the characteristic glow of flames ringing my wrist appeared. I almost cried with relief. At least Erzsébet would be safe from Zsombor's relentless pursuit. This also meant that Zsombor likely went to a hell realm in the depths of the spirit world for his spiritual rejuvenation.

As before, Joe performed many neurological and psychological tests to determine if I had any physical or mental abnormalities, but he found nothing outside my obsessive interest in Erzsébet.

A few days after I viewed the bracelet, I began to walk and exercise, moving from bed exercise to the therapy room and then into jogging gradually but intensively because my efforts kept me from thinking about Erzsébet.

But depression finally cast its web around me and it wasn't long before Joe recognized the symptoms.

"What's bothering you, Dad?"

"Uncertainty. Have you ever loved a woman so much you trembled when you thought of her?"

"I'm pretty fond of Audrey, but no, Dad, I haven't."

"Well, that's how I felt about your mother when I married her and how I feel about Erzsébet now. I could return to her time with another cryonic procedure, but what if she's on her way here? I'm so confused; I don't know what to do."

Joe sighed and looked at his feet, something I remember him doing as a toddler when I observed him growing up with Emily. He'd aged a bit in the past year, and his receding hairline now reminded me of his babyhood.

"I want you to stay right here, Dad. Audrey and I would like to spend some time with you. If Erzsébet needs to wait for the opportune time as you say, why not wait and see what happens?"

"I guess you're right," I agreed reluctantly, my heart pulled in two.

As I recuperated at the Cryonics Foundation, I spent a great deal of time on the internet and asked Joe to acquire any books he could find about the history of Hungary in the post-medieval period. My reading list kept me busy. At last, I opened an obscure book written in 1650 by an Englishman named Leigh. He claimed to have been a young man in Vienna when the King of Poland sent Báró Zsombor, described as a patriot and a great warrior, along with the Palatine Thurzó to apprehend Erzsébet Báthory. Rather than arrest her, he ended up her murder victim, so this history went. I thought the Englishman deluded. Zsombor was definitely was no patriot and Erzsébet had definitely not murdered him.

History coined many unkind names for Erzsébet. She was always the "Infamous Lady," the "Blood Countess," "Lady Dracula," or even "the most evil woman in history." Anyone reading these exaggerated, inflammatory tales about her would take them at face value and write her off as a demented serial killer.

I personally found Erzsébet to be a tough but caring person who tried to help as many people as she could. Disgusted by all that I'd read on one particularly depressing day, I picked all the offending books up, bound them up in a bed sheet and threw the bundle into the trash. I decided then that I'd somehow rewrite history by thoroughly by researching Erzsébet's life to find the necessary evidence to portray her as the multi-faceted person I'd experienced.

The next day, Joe released me from the clinic and I went home with him to stay until I felt better oriented. This time, with full control of my body and senses, I was able to experience things on my own without Erzsébet's influence. Audrey's cooking tasted and smelled as delightful as everyone claimed and Joe and Audrey's home seemed even more beautiful than I remembered it.

I reminisced with Joe and Audrey about my first visit, recalling how frightened I felt that Erzsébet might pose a danger to them. I even shared with them how strange it seemed that I'd initially feared and resented her so much and yet became so emotionally involved with her. We shared a lot of laughs about my strange experiences, but neither Joe nor Audrey could truly understand them. Every time I mentioned Erzsébet's name, my stomach did flip-flops.

But two little negative thoughts nagged at me and I couldn't ignore them. Could my attraction be nothing more than one of Erzsébet's spells? Isn't romantic love really just a type of bewitchment? I asked myself these questions repeatedly during the coming weeks, mostly to settle upon some good rationalization that would make my non-relationship relationship with Erzsébet okay. After all, she'd hardly paid me any attention except to use me for her mission.

I wished I could will myself to despise Erzsébet again, but I couldn't. With little else to do, my heart and my mind spun around in circles, trying to justify my desire for her.

Chapter 38

Once I felt well enough to declare myself independent again, I decided to return to Slovakia and continue my search for Erzsébet and her true history. My hunch might prove right – I'd found a message from her at Castle Čachtice before; maybe I'd find another. A smart woman like her could surely find a way to leave another message, one I would recognize as dated after I'd departed with Zsombor. I couldn't imagine how she'd know I would try to find it, but I needed to search for clues to her whereabouts no matter how remote the possibility of finding one.

First, I rehired Professor Chin, my Egyptologist and history expert and requested that he and another historian at Boston University locate any old documents that might vindicate Erzsébet Báthory as history's most evil woman.

Then I tried to sort out the complexities of time travel. My head reeled with the paradox of multidimensional or circular time. Linear time simply meant that anything placed in a particular spot in the past could be located from the future if it hadn't deteriorated. Every time I tried to map out logically how Erzsébet could leave the present, re-enter her previous body in the past, then leave me a message that I would find that induced me to leave my body and travel to the past, and then return to the future, it blew my mind.

How could I make any sense of this? I nearly had a stroke trying to figure it out and simply gave up on the space-time conundrum. I would just have to trust that time in the spirit realm was fluid and non-linear.

On the flight to Budapest, Gloria Stefanowski swayed gracefully down the aisle, filling drink orders in first class. My mind remained fixated on Erzsébet though I felt pleased to see Gloria and surprised that her light touch on my shoulder excited me.

I slept for much of the flight, oblivious to everyone around me. Gloria slipped me her phone number as I exited the plane. "Call *anytime*, Mr. Jackson," she purred as I passed her near the cockpit entrance.

"Nice flight," I said, giving her a wink and a thumbs-up as I slipped her card into my pocket. I liked Gloria and if it weren't for my obsession with Erzsébet, I would have followed her anywhere.

When I arrived in Čachtice, Mayor Ilionescu implied I wasn't exactly welcome now that Erzsébet was no longer with me. Barely sociable, he peered at me over his glasses and growled, but allowed me four hours of exclusive time at the castle tower.

This time, I set up ultraviolet lighting to capture different wavelengths and snapped dozens of pictures, hoping something previously undiscovered would turn up. Grasping at straws, but what else could I do?

After I packed the equipment, downloaded the digital pictures to the 3DIT mobile unit and placed the 35mm film in its protective bag, I toured the castle ruins. I could hardly believe that this dead and desolate site and the thriving sixteenth and seventeenth-century community were the same. I scoured the countryside trying to find any information, any anecdotes or documents about Erzsébet. Most people weren't at all helpful. Like the mayor, they no longer had any use for me without her. I pored through every old bookstore, library, and secondhand shop I could find in surrounding villages, hoping I'd discover a clue to her whereabouts or some evidence of her former kindness.

I knew I should visit museum and university archives in Budapest and Vienna to research official documents after conceding that my small-time search in Slovakia was for nothing, but I hit a wall. Dispirited, I returned to the United States after two weeks, still undecided if Erzsébet cared about saving the world or if she was an evil witch who'd used me. Whenever I became angry or depressed about the situation, I felt comforted by the presence of remaining immortality bracelets. Wouldn't Erzsébet return for Zsombor's at all costs? Had she wanted the bracelets all for herself, surely she would have kept hers and gone after Zsombor herself.

My gut told me to duplicate the bracelet. The poison-filled fake ruse had worked twice, and if someone showed up and tried to take it, I wanted to be prepared. I went to a skilled watchmaker who made an excellent replica from a picture I drew for him. I would fill it with poison if and when the need arose.

More days passed without Erzsébet, then weeks. I began to understand what people meant about wealth not equaling happiness. I would have given everything up for a few moments with Erzsébet. I found myself considering suicide until I remembered that obliterating myself would be impossible as long as I wore the bracelet. Just the opposite – it would allow me a choice of birth time and place and probably more reasons than ever to obsess about Erzsébet.

Other than Erzsébet's pre-industrial world, I couldn't imagine living in any other era or place than America or Europe in the twenty-first centuries. It did cross my mind once or twice to try entering my old twentieth-century life with Emily, but if I couldn't change the past, I might get ill again and relive the same old events. Always, I circled around to the same problem – if I returned to Erzsébet's time, what would happen then? What if she was on her way here as I tried to enter her world?

When I returned to Boston, I took up residence in the Nine Zero penthouse to review all the photos I'd shot in the dungeon. I didn't see anything out of the ordinary or find any new information. Perturbed, I called Professor Chin to ask if he'd found anything.

His reply almost destroyed me.

"Mr. Jackson, I tracked the exploits of Grófnő Erzsébet Báthory de Ecsed from the date you gave me, and found a record that claims she lived approximately eleven years longer than other historical accounts portray. Many historians have recorded her death at the age of fifty-four in 1614 after four years of confinement in her castle tower, but a newly discovered death certificate records her death in Vienna at age sixty-five. Confusing, and there are official documents to substantiate both dates. I can't determine which one is correct. Neither record appears to be a forgery. I'm looking for more documents to substantiate the longer life span."

"Thank you." Devastated, I hung up without any other reply. Erzsébet's death at fifty-four had been recorded before she came to my time. Though we never talked about it, I always assumed that she'd spent years in the spirit world or in other lives and then possessed me, or rather, entered my body in 2026. Then, after she'd possessed O'Malley's body and he'd killed himself on network TV, she'd returned to the past and somehow resumed and redirected her life after Ferenc's death. I'd arrived in her life when she was forty-three and what Professor Chin discovered was accurate – Erzsébet lived another eleven years past her original date of death in her altered lifetime.

If she was trying to come back to the future, how could I help? I needed to answer this question somehow.

I stopped berating myself for my foolishness by burying myself in new research of medieval and post-medieval Hungarian history, trying to find anything to repudiate Erzsébet's reputation. I obtained a second copy of every book ever written about her, both in and out of print, and started reading all over again. Professor Chin provided me copies of sixteenth and seventeenth-century documents that I should have looked through myself on my last trip to Europe. Over the next two months, as my rooms became cluttered with dog-eared books and coffee-stained notes, I obsessively read and analyzed my data or paced my penthouse apartment. As I withdrew from normal life, I let my beard grow and my room-service trays pile up beside my door.

My mind circled and recircled on one track, not helped that history is written by the victorious, or that in the seventeenth century, history was written by men. I found little in any but the most recent books or the most recently discovered documents to change Erzsébet's history. Some modern historians and female historians in particular agreed that Erzsébet was framed or at least her crimes were exaggerated by Thurzó and Zsombor in order to gain her fortune. But there were still many questions about her alleged "discipline" of servant girls at her homes, especially in her final years at Čachtice. Many local families claimed to have lost their daughters during their employment with Erzsébet. Her notoriety and the lack of existing death records among the peasant class made it almost impossible to determine the truth. The court records and confessions seemed damning, although Erzsébet's most trusted servants were clearly coerced before they implicated her in the torture and murder of her servant girls. In their rush to justice, the male hierarchy never allowed Erzsébet to testify on her behalf, another weakness in their case.

I spent hours standing at the balcony railing that had so frightened Erzsébet, staring pensively at the activity in downtown Boston. Whether by light of day or by the glitter of neon at night, the endless parade of people pursuing business or pleasure below me had lives and I did not. When Joe and Audrey finally coerced me one rainy afternoon to get help, Dr. Thaddeus Dean diagnosed me with garden-variety depression and anxiety caused by losing a relationship. He prescribed different drugs in a trial-and-error effort to see what worked – first my modern combination with the numerical name that I'd taken before the second cryonic procedure, followed by some old standbys, the latest generation of Paxil and Eskalith, but nothing dispelled my longing for Erzsébet. If anything, the meds made me zombified and even less inclined to turn my life around. I finally confided to Dr. Dean that Erzsébet might have placed a spell on me. He pulled out his prescription pad and prescribed the most recent incarnation of Abilify.

"Take it at night. I think you'll see a difference in a week," he said.

I thanked him quietly and left via the back door of his office with the prescription in hand, glad at least that Dr. Dean had replaced his father's floral decorating scheme with a minimalist space-age design.

I guess the latest drug combination finally worked, because sure enough, I began to recognize my circular thinking and emotional addiction to Erzsébet by the end of the week.

To break the cycle, I dialed Gloria's number with the intention of asking her out. As her phone rang, I recalled how thrilled Erzsébet was with telephones. I hung up. I liked Gloria, but it wouldn't be fair to date her while I struggled with Erzsébet's memory.

But I had a Plan B. Ridding myself of the bracelet might be the key to my recovery. At any rate, its continuing existence was a danger to humanity. Psychopaths like Zsombor would always seek to possess both bracelets. If there was only one left in the world, so much the better.

A quick search on my TVA internet connection showed that about twenty volcanic eruptions occur on Earth daily. Mt. Etna in Sicily had the longest period of documented eruptions of all the world's volcanoes, the greatest variety of eruption styles, and erupts from both the summit and flanks from numerous vents. Not only that, Mt. Etna seemed to be the volcano nearest Erzsébet's beloved home in Slovakia.

Thoughts popped around my head like kettle corn while I planned my trip. Would I have to wear protective clothing if an eruption was expected? Would the bracelet melt in the volcano? If I jumped in wearing the bracelet, could I choose another incarnation before the bracelet was destroyed?

There were numerous eruptions and an earthquake over the past year, so a visit to Mt Etna might prove to be spectacular. I located a guide who consented to lead me around the volcano to the sites of accessible vents and I scheduled a tour for early spring, in case Erzsébet returned soon.

Three months before the tour, I returned to the vault to study the contents of Count Nádasdy's trunk. After all my experiences with astrological tracking using the scrolls to determine Zsombor's whereabouts, why shouldn't I be able to track Erzsébet's? After all, she presumably still wore her bracelet when she'd died twenty-one years after Zsombor. Why had I let this slip my mind?

I needed help. Within hours, one of my astrologers e-mailed a computer-generated astrological birth chart for Erzsébet, with transits from her birth in 1650 to the present day, and cross-comparisons using the calculations contained in the scrolls for tracking the existing bracelets. Erzsébet, or whomever she reincarnated as, seemed to be in the Carpathian region of Slovakia or Hungary in the present, give or take three years.

It wasn't logical to run off to Europe every time I had a hunch, but logic didn't enter the equation. This revelation was good enough for me. I booked airfare to Slovakia on the next available flight. The ticket agents and hostesses knew me by name because of my frequent trips back and forth.

While I inched forward in the security line at Logan International Airport for the red-eye flight to Budapest due to leave at midnight, a woman tapped my shoulder from behind.

"We've met before, Mr. Jackson."

"Esmé Deschamps," I said. "What a coincidence."

The Pagan leader's curly rainbow-tinted locks were straightened and now shone like polished platinum, but I recognized her as soon as she spoke.

"There are synchronicities but no coincidences," she said. "Don't take this flight."

"But my luggage is already checked."

"Believe me, Mr. Jackson, you don't want to take this flight." Esmé handed me an old journal, labeled on the front with faded but still legible ink. "Read it." She patted me on the arm with a wan smile and moved forward in the line of sleepy travelers approaching the security scanners.

I opened the journal's yellowed pages and trembled at the familiar tight loops and scrolls of Erzsébet's handwriting.

Chapter 39

I turned around and sat down at the electronic charging tree near the security station, opening the journal as the last-minute boarding directions for my flight sounded over the terminal intercom system.

Dearest Jim,

Please accept my apologies for your long wait. Circumstances have prevented me from ending my life here prematurely. I think of you daily and hope you will understand why I could not abandon my responsibilities at this time.

Thinking of the ancient scrolls now in your possession, I am reminded that because of your great generosity and foresight that I still have possession of one immortality bracelet, and thus I am able to choose the era and the body I wish to live in when this life is over. When I finally die and come to you, a relatively brief time will have passed in your era. I believe this extension of my life is for the best because you will have the freedom to adjust to your life again.

I worry that the body I acquire when I arrive may not be desirable to you. What would you do if I came to your world as an eighty-year-old woman? Don't answer, because we both know!

These are but a few of my many concerns — I hope you can understand why I did not immediately enter your world.

Sincerely Yours,
E.

Erzsébet had filled the remaining journal pages with spells and descriptions of events in the last twenty-one years of her life, after I died in battle with Zsombor at Čachtice.

On my way out of the international terminal, I informed AirEuro that I had urgent business and to notify me when my luggage arrived back in Boston. For the first time in months, I decided I'd like a beer, maybe a couple. I made a night of it, club-hopping in downtown Boston. Of course, I paid for the night with a stomping headache and muddled brain the next morning, a small price for all the joy I felt.

That feeling left in a hurry when I turned on the news.

"The sudden crash of AirEuro Flight 232 over the Atlantic approximately two hundred miles outside Boston. . ."

The flight I'd booked to Hungary via Paris had mysteriously gone down over the Atlantic. I thought of Gloria. She preferred to work on the late night flights from Boston and New York.

". . . just five survivors among the 256 aboard, three passengers and two crew members. . ."

Did Gloria survive? Then it struck me. Esmé had warned me not to take that particular flight. But I didn't think of a crash because I'd witnessed many strange events since Erzsébet had entered my life. When Esmé gave me the journal, it distracted me from everything else. Erzsébet and Esmé had saved my life by sending the journal at the appropriate time. But what happened to Esmé? She continued to board the flight despite her knowledge. Was she part of a plan?

The first thing I did was trash all my medications. My spirits lifted, knowing Erzsébet cared enough to contact me. Somehow, she would find her way to Boston.

Time slowed to a crawl. Every day I expected to hear from Erzsébet. Every night, I went to bed disappointed, falling asleep as I read her journal obsessively, looking for any clues to her whereabouts.

I fought to keep the waiting from getting me down. To get any maudlin thoughts out of my head, I started working out at my old gym daily. It was starting to look like a boxing gym should. Walls were scuffed and covered with graffiti, and rooms with drywall had holes punched or kicked into it every few feet, put there by frustrated boxers. The punching bags and the frayed ropes on the ring sagged with use. I felt more at home than when the gym was fit for royalty. The odor of old sweat filled the air, and unbelievably, it smelled sweet, reminding me the years I'd worked my butt off to become someone. Those memories were good ones now that I knew Erzsébet hadn't used me for nefarious ends.

Still, those old dreams had become meaningless. All I desired from life now was to spend the rest of it with Erzsébet. Some say this yearning for love is a sickness, but I could do little about my feelings and simply accepted them at face value.

One night over one of Audrey's outstanding dinners, Joe told me about a case he'd recently consulted on because of his experience in reviving patients. He went on to describe the AirEuro crash near Boston.

"I'm familiar with that crash," I said. "I was booked on it and a woman warned me not to take it."

"What!" Joe exclaimed. "Did you report the person who warned you to the authorities?"

"It's not like she was a terrorist or had anything to do with crashing it, Joe."

"Then how did she know it was going to crash?"

"However, fortune-tellers see the future, I suppose. . . I bumped into Esmé, a Pagan friend of Erzsébet's that I met in Slovakia, and she warned me in the security line."

He thought about this for a moment. "I wouldn't take that for an answer not too long ago. But after what we've been through the last two years, I'd believe almost anything. . . by the way, there was no sabotage or terrorism involved, according to FAA inspectors. But getting back to what I wanted to say – one of the survivors has been in a coma ever since the crash, a flight attendant. . ." He stopped speaking when he saw the look on my face.

"Gloria Stefanowski?"

Joe smiled. "You know *her* too, Dad?"

I nodded. "Being so absorbed with Erzsébet, I forgot about seeing if she was on that flight too."

Feelings of selfishness washed over me. How could I forget?

"Gloria was on every other flight I made to Europe."

Joe raised his eyebrows. "It's been three months. Her family is talking about discontinuing life support. Her doctors believe her only chance at recovery is with nanobot therapy."

"I thought that was routine in hospitals by now."

"Not quite. The patents are in place and the therapy is allowed after cryonic procedures because the patients are technically dead before the rejuvenation procedure. We're still waiting for full approval from the FDA to use nanobot therapy on living patients. I'm certain we can wake Gloria from her coma by repairing her brain damage with nanobots. I received permission to begin a trial on living comatose patients, and she'll be the very first."

"How soon will you start?"

"It may be several days. First, Gloria's physicians and I needed the family's permission. They were afraid she'd end up in a vegetative state for life. They said, 'She would rather die than endure that' –"

"I can't fault that sentiment."

Joe continued. "But we described the cryonic rejuvenation procedure, showed them the successful case histories involving terminal diseases like yours, and convinced them to take a chance.

"Although Gloria's doctors have done MRIs and other tests with some guarded prognoses, we'll have to do some fresh tests to determine what healing has taken place, if any. We've not worked with a case based solely upon traumatic brain injury, so we're still in the process of creating specialized robotic particles with extra immune system anti-rejection properties to repair damaged brain tissue. It will take two to four weeks minimum before the nanobots' work is complete. Then I'll use the same procedures to awaken Gloria that we use to revive cryopreserved patients."

"It sounds easy enough – all of your patients have cryopreserved brains, and once they're warmed up and restored by the nanobots, any damage is repaired."

Joe's eyes misted over. "If this works, it'll be revolutionary – to think that comatose patients with brain injuries can be healed and awakened! Just think of the medical advances inspired by your decision to be preserved rather than accepting an early death, Dad."

That my son thought my life and my ambitions worthwhile warmed my heart. I wrapped my arms around him and held him close until we both felt embarrassed by the long embrace.

"Can I visit Gloria? I'm sure she's had many visits from loving relatives and friends, but maybe. . ."

"Sure. It would be a real morale booster for her family. Why don't you come with me for my first examination? I'll only be there an hour or so. You can introduce yourself to her parents while I check her labs."

I prayed to Athena all night long that Gloria would recover. I really liked her and if it wasn't for Erzsébet, we might have clicked.

A call from Joe late the next afternoon verified approval of Gloria's transfer from Mount Sinai Hospital in New York to the Cryonics Foundation's rejuvenation center. The following morning I rushed to CF. Joe led me to Gloria's room and he told me to sit as he scrubbed and donned a sterile mask, gown, and gloves before examining her.

She looked peaceful, if only a shadow of her former self. Her once shiny hair stood out in dry wisps and I could have almost doubled my fingers around her thin wrists. I thought about how shallow I'd been, the way I'd gotten excited when I watched her walk down an airplane aisle. I sighed. Shallow or not, weren't men built that way?

It hit me then what Erzsébet meant when she worried about inhabiting a body I found attractive. She knew me as well as I knew myself. Was I a flawed human because I felt revolted by having sex with an older woman? I couldn't answer that, but I vowed to be a better person. When my son finished examining Gloria, I told him I'd be responsible for any expense that her treatment incurred.

"If she needs anything – a kidney, bone marrow – I'm more than willing to help. In fact, before we leave, I'd like to stop at the blood bank and make a donation. It's the least I can do."

Joe looked up from Gloria's bedside, surprised to see me so interested in someone else for a change. "Beautiful thought, Dad, but we're making organs from the recipients' own DNA now. And Gloria hasn't needed any transfusions so far."

Weeks went by, and I still hadn't heard from Erzsébet. I told myself not to worry, but all I did was worry. I worried if she'd know where to look, worried what she'd look like, and worried if she really did want my companionship. Then I worried about what to do if her real motive was to gain both bracelets. After all, the old legends suggested she wasn't any different than Zsombor and the lure of immortality and unlimited power seemed to be the motivating factor with previous owners of the bracelets.

Joe called me from the Cryonics Foundation three weeks after his first visit with Gloria. "Dad, you better get over here."

"Why, what's up?"

"Just get here as quick as you can."

When I arrived, there was a commotion in the lobby. TV crews and reporters jammed the reception area and the front entryway, and Joe had called the police to keep order.

A reporter surged past the police line toward me, shouting "Mr. Jackson, Mr. Jackson."

"What's going on?" I sputtered, annoyed at the commotion.

"She's back."

"Who's back?"

"Erzsébet Báthory."

My jaw dropped. "What are you talking about?"

"Your son brought the flight attendant out of her coma today and when he asked if she knew her name, she answered, 'Yes, I'm Erzsébet Báthory.' How do you feel about that, Mr. Jackson?"

The young man held his microphone in front of me, but I broke into a run trying to get to Gloria's room. The police held me back on the threshold until Joe came through the security door to get me.

"Dad, I can't believe this is happening. Reviving another person with the same spirit from the seventeenth century is unbelievable. Did you use the scanning equipment?"

"Yes, of course I did. We use it on everyone now. Gloria's brain showed just a single energetic pattern. She threw us for a loop an hour ago when she announced that she is you-know-who."

"Can I talk to her?"

"Sure, Dad, but don't stay long. She's in a delicate state at this point." He escorted me past security and into Gloria's room, then turned away, leaving us alone.

I stared at Gloria but saw Erzsébet when she felt my presence and opened her eyes. Erzsébet's dimpled smile greeted me and I swear I could see Erzsébet's gray eyes underlying Gloria's bright baby blues. Even her mannerisms belonged to Erzsébet. How could a change in consciousness alter a person this much? How did I look when Erzsébet animated me?

"Hello, Jim Jackson."

Gloria's high voice and Boston accent were altered by Erzsébet's commanding, throaty tone and her Hungarian inflection. My knees became weak at the sound of her voice.

"I know you like my appearance – at least you liked it when this body was inhabited by Gloria."

I felt conflicted, overjoyed that Erzsébet was finally here, but at what cost? Had she killed Gloria to possess a body she knew I'd like? Maybe I should walk right now while I still could.

As usual, and despite the fact we no longer shared a body, Erzsébet read my thoughts.

"The future is never fixed and I can't interfere with destiny, as you know. But the chance that aircraft would crash was great. Gloria died in the crash and I watched her spirit as it left her body. I was in no way responsible for her death and I chose her body because I knew you found it attractive."

As Erzsébet's words flowed from Gloria's sweet lips, I felt that old mind-numbing euphoria flooding my head. I couldn't argue with Erzsébet's logic. I lowered the bed rail, sat on the edge of the bed, put my arms around Erzsébet and told her how I'd discovered my love for her when she left me and how much I'd missed her.

"I know," she said. "I have missed *you* dreadfully, Jim Jackson, and I want to be certain we stay together for the rest of our lives. Please call that tour guide and make the trip to Mt. Etna for two. Our first act together will be to rid the world of these accursed bracelets."

She must have read my mind because I hadn't mentioned Mt. Etna, but I was overjoyed to hear these words. Her feelings for me felt genuine and not a pretext to fill any of her needs or desires.

Joe rapped lightly on the door and entered the room. He took a long look at the two of us entwined in each other's arms. "You'll have to leave, Dad, so Gloria, I mean, Erzsébet, can rest. I'm sorry about the hubbub outside. One of the staff must have leaked the news again."

I looked at my son, wondering if he hadn't leaked the information himself both times. He did love controversy and media attention. But no matter. I'd been through worse.

As I entered the lobby, reporters swarmed around me, their digital cameras held high over each other's heads, flashing in a bouquet of light. A flurry of shouted questions about the return of Countess Báthory echoed through the lobby – "Erzsébet, Erzsébet, Erzsébet."

"Is this the same Erzsébet who helped you beat the Arab for the championship fight? Is this some kind of gimmick? Is she actually in the flight attendant's body? Will there be another exorcism?" The questions went on and on as I pushed through the growing crowd, waving them away.

At the front entrance of the Cryonics Foundation, I turned dramatically to face the media and flashed the biggest grin of my life. "I've only one statement for the press. We're honeymooning in Sicily this spring to watch Mt. Etna erupt."

CRYONIC MAN

Spring rolled around with a vengeance, swathing Boston in rain and spring flowers. I carried armfuls to Erzsébet, who delighted in having the nurses scramble to find vases for all the daffodils, iris, tulips, lilies of the valley, and lilacs. Finally, on a day bright with blue skies and hope, Joe finally released Erzsébet from CF and we held a sweet, private wedding filled with ancient incantations and Pagan prayers to the goddesses in the garden at Joe and Audrey's home.

The only other thing to sully our spring romance was my big mouth. Manny, Dave, and Ituzu were glad to have us back on their client list and kept us insulated from the paparazzi and publicity hounds who nosed around us day and night. I experienced Erzsébet's mind and spirit in Gloria's knockout body as a dream made in heaven. I almost forgot that poor Gloria was gone, but now and then, that fact nagged at the corner of my mind.

Our honeymoon started the day we flew to Naples and took the ferry to Palermo, Sicily. We – along with Manny, Dave, and Ituzu – spent our first passionate weekend as man and wife at the Grand Hotel et des Palmes, a luxurious historic hotel that delighted Erzsébet. Angelu, our guide, met us there and escorted us to another historic resort spa at the village of Linguaglossa, where we shook off the remainder of our jet lag by the pool and in bed, making love, before embarking on our tour of the north slope of Etna. Manny, Dave, and Ituzu devised a diversion for the paparazzi with some models hired to impersonate Erzsébet and me so we could explore Mt. Etna and dispense with the bracelets privately.

Angelu returned on Tuesday morning, ready to lead us over the sharp, rocky flanks of the stratovolcano, which rumbled, groaned, and steamed at the verge of an imminent eruption.

"It would take too long to hike up and down the mountain to satisfy the local authorities, who may need to evacuate the south face of the mountain before it erupts," he informed us. "But don't worry; I have a permit to use a hover-car to glide all over Etna. We'll stop at all the best sightseeing points on the north and south slopes and the four major craters. We'll cover *everything* in all the hiking tours and will still have time to return before she blows. I hope you brought cameras – you'll love the spectacular views of the lava flows."

Erzsébet seemed to forget all about her fear of speed and heights – or perhaps Gloria's body and brain, accustomed to international flight, neutralized it. She chattered with excitement as we scooted over the eerie, smoky slopes and high, forested ridges. We even viewed a few picturesque farms who owed the fertility of their newly sprouting crops to the volcanic ash.

Though I enjoyed all the spectacular sights as much as Erzsébet, I felt more subdued, relieved that we would finally destroy the bracelets that dogged us both and caused so much mayhem throughout history. I'd even worn my duplicate along with the original, planning to destroy both.

Angelu found a wonderful spot near east flank of Etna's Southeast Crater cone, landed the hover-car, set up a shade canopy and started a fire to cook our lunch. We relaxed with flutes of champagne and watched from a safe distance the broiling, bubbling explosions and steam rising from the crater. After we were full of Angelu's delicious eggplant annelletti – prepared by him before the trip and baked in the hot ashes of the fire – and tipsy on the fine white dinner wine, we donned the protective gear needed to destroy the bracelets in the caldera, giggling and teasing one another about looking like astronauts.

We agreed it would be wonderful to watch the bracelets descend into the fiery pit under the golden glow of the late afternoon sun, a good omen, I thought.

As Angelu chauffeured us toward the crater in the hover-car, Erzsébet startled me by raising her arms and chanting in a loud voice in some unknown language. Angelu appeared not to notice, his hearing muffled by the earbuds of his personal music PVA that also piped the strains of some wild-sounding Sicilian folk music into the passenger pod.

So why was I surprised? Erzsébet had never made her occult practices a secret. I only hoped she would forget all the magickal stuff once we destroyed the bracelets and would choose to live a straightforward, normal life.

Before long, there seemed to be some chanting and howling coming from somewhere outside the hover-car, but I could see nothing but acres and acres of rocky ground appearing and disappearing beneath the smoke, and a small crowd of onlookers at another small vent in the far distance. Whether Erzsébet had aroused some nature spirits or some creatures that lived upon Etna, I couldn't say. Her ritual took only a minute or two and then she turned to me and gave me passionate kiss that almost made me forget about it. But when she leaned against me afterward, gazing at the landscape as Angelu maneuvered the hover-car for a landing, a chill crawled over my body. She somehow seemed more animal than human. What was the ritual meant to do? I opened my mouth to ask her and then snapped it shut again, scolding myself for mistrusting my beloved Erzsébet. I snuggled against her and we both looked forward as the hover-car settled gently into a dry lava field shelf below the crater.

Angelu covered his head with his protective helmet and escorted us from the hover-car. We set off down the rise in a jubilant mood, Erzsébet singing an old Hungarian folksong about a maiden stoking the home fire and keeping the stew warm for her lover returning from battle. Though I could just barely hear the melody through her helmet, I recognized a few snatches of the song as I listened to my breathing become louder and louder. The ascent became so steep on the final few hundred yards that I had to support Erzsébet and nearly drag her up the trail. It was far too hot to take the hover-car near Mt. Etna's blazing heart.

As Angelu led us to the most stable viewing point on the rim of the caldera, I motioned to him to stand aside as we agreed previously. Erzsébet and I approached the boiling cauldron holding hands. She stopped suddenly and leaned her helmet against mine as though plastering me with another passionate kiss. The thought of our sweet lovemaking made my blood hotter than the lava that bubbled in the crust below us. I wanted to lay her down then and there in the crunchy tuff under our feet and have my way with her.

We gazed into each other's eyes through the mica visors for a moment. I gave her a thumbs up, hoping her excitement was as keen as mine to rid the world of these bracelets forever. We joined hands and looked down. She leaned against me and yelled through the helmet, trying to be heard over the rumbling volcanic noise.

"What?" I yelled.

Erzsébet yelled again, mouthing her words dramatically. "Let me throw both bracelets in at the same time!"

My heart swelled with love. I repeated the incantation to make my bracelet appear and then the incantation to remove it. I handed it to her, thrilled to accommodate her wish. She placed it on her left wrist and motioned to the other side of the volcano. I gazed across the fiery maw but saw nothing unusual. She pointed vigorously with a forefinger again. I took a step closer for a better view. Suddenly I felt her hand on my back. I lost my footing and tried to scramble back. She pushed harder now. As I fell into the fiery abyss, I heard her yell through the helmet and over the bubbling, hissing noises of Etna. She gazed at me and mouthed the syllables. Her lips clearly formed just two words, another of her favorite lines from a vintage movie: "Thanks, Sucker!"

My past flashed before me in slow motion as I continued to fall, just as it had when the tumor ended my life so long ago. As I drifted in slow motion toward the broiling lava, a stray thought welled up into my awareness like a bubble rising in a deep pool. I'd inadvertently

CRYONIC MAN

given Erzsébet the duplicate bracelet to throw into Mt. Etna. I conceded that she had used me all along. I'd been an easy mark, taken in by her charisma and prone to rationalizing that she was a sweet, misunderstood victim.

My thoughts came to a sudden halt when I landed on a protruding ledge with a jolting thump. The searing heat nearly made me pass out and I knew this was the reason Erzsébet wasn't on her hands and knees looking over the edge to make certain I was gone.

I clung to the side of the rim, clawing my way up, cursing myself for thinking Erzsébet would ever agree to destroy the only two remaining immortality bracelets for mortal love. My desire for her turned to rage. I would punish her for every minute she'd caused me to suffer, from the moment I'd awakened from the cryonic preservation to the months I'd spent pining away for her. The whoring witch was responsible for poor Gloria's death. She'd even put poor Esmé at risk to help her possess Gloria's body during the plane crash, though Esmé had also been one of the survivors. All the evil stories about Erzsébet, though exaggerated, must be true.

As with Zsombor, I would do the world a favor by sending Erzsébet to the molten center of Mt. Etna.

As I inched up the last few feet of the rim, drenched inside the suit with what felt like gallons of sweat, I brushed away any thought that I might also be the kind of person who thrives on hurting anyone that crosses me. But who was I fooling? Hell, I was a boxer. My job was to hurt people, to hurt them as bad as I could and I'd always loved doing it!

Erzsébet ran no more than fifty feet from the rim before I overtook her. When I jumped in front of her, the hateful look on her face reinforced my thoughts about her evil nature.

"Erzsébet, we came to destroy the bracelets," I said, pretty much to myself since she couldn't hear me. I picked her up and carried her back to the caldera. She tried to fight me, a wasted effort. There was no way the petite witch could overpower a two hundred twenty-pound boxer. I twisted her arms behind her back until she cringed with pain, then let go and grabbed her by the shoulders, resisting the urge to shake her until her head rattled.

Erzsébet pulled her helmet off, gasping in the hot, sulphurous air. "Wait. . . an accident. . . I didn't mean to push you. . ." she tried to say, and I could barely resist putting my fist into her mouth to stuff that outrageous lie down her throat.

I recited the incantation and watched both bracelets glowing on our wrists with an eerie, fiery light. Holding Erzsébet around the waist, I leapt away from the protruding ledge toward the volcano's heart.

Erzsébet's ungodly wail nearly erased my last thought from my brain. Would I reincarnate again when we were dead and the bracelets melted?

Then it hit me. Why hadn't I tossed my bracelet into the lava first? Now Erzsébet might reincarnate in another era, and knowing her evil ways, she'd hunt for me no matter where I went.

I vowed to find her first. . .

Two smoking cinders, we spun and fell inexorably toward the liquid fire, dissolving into faint double tendrils of smoke just above the sputtering caldera. . .

Poised for a moment like two glowing silvery quarter-moons in the last fire of sunset, the two immortality bracelets splashed into the volcano's eternally seething heart.

CRYONIC MAN

&Bibliography

Codrescu, Andrei. *The Blood Countess: A Novel.* Simon & Schuster, 1995.

Craft, Kimberly L. *Infamous Lady: The True Story of Countess Erzsébet Báthory* – Second Edition. CreateSpace, 2014.

------. *Elizabeth Bathory: A Memoire: As Told by Her Court Master, Benedict Deseo.* CreateSpace, 2011.

------. *The Private Letters of Countess Erzsébet Báthory.* CreateSpace, 2011.

Johns, Rebecca. *The Countess: A Novel.* Crown, 2010.

CRYONIC MAN

Like the hero of Cryonic Man, author Joe DiBuduo grew up in Hano, one of the toughest neighborhoods in Boston. He became a writer and an artist, not a prizefighter, but in his rough-and-tumble youth, he never turned away from a street fight.

DiBuduo is the author of another mixed-genre paranormal novel, *The Mountain Will Cover You* (JD Books), the popular nonfiction title, *A Penis Manologue: One Man's Response to The Vagina Monologues* (JD Books), a historically relevant memoir, *Crime a Day: Death by Electric Chair & Other Boyhood Pursuits* (Jaded Ibis Press), collections of connected short fiction, flash fiction, his signature "poetic flash fiction," and a children's storybook. He also has short fiction and poetry for children and adults featured in online journals and in print anthologies.

See more about Joe DiBuduo and his work at joedibuduo.com.

CRYONIC MAN

TooTiE-Do pRESS

publishes quirky speculative fiction with a romantic twist.

YOU HEARD NOTHING HAPPENED ON DECEMBER 21, 2012, RIGHT?
NOT EXACTLY. HERE'S WHERE THE COSMIC SHIFT BEGAN!

If you loved The X-Files, you'll enjoy Heart of Desire: 11.11.11 Redux!

HEART OF DESIRE: 11.11.11 REDUX
KATE ROBINSON

ISBN 978-1500402280

"The cast of characters is a deft masterpiece in character development
that rivals Diana Gabaldon, George R.R. Martin, and Michael Crichton."

–Penelope Anne Bartotto, In'DTales

The Contest and Other Stories
Connected short fiction by Joe DiBuduo and Kate Robinson
Halloween 2017

BW interior ISBN: 978-0692973684
Full color interior ISBN: 978-0692962213

"Love the atmosphere and story narration. . . vivid and gripping. . .
The frame narrative is more compelling than expected. . . has hints of
beat literature, and the story arc about an art magazine is interesting."

–PekoeBlaze

1

⁂

A Lonely Death

As my cab arrived at Fairhaven Cemetery, I spied a lone Catholic priest standing by my Uncle John's coffin, a study in black and white. Heavy snowflakes fell in swirling eddies like confetti from heaven over the monuments scored with epitaphs for mothers and daughters, fathers and sons, husbands and wives, all long dead and in some cases, long forgotten. Soon the snow would blanket one and all for the long winter's slumber.

I exited the cab reluctantly and pulled my collar up to stop the snow determined to swirl down my neck. As surprised by my presence as I was by his, the priest locked eyes with me for nearly a minute as though fishing for my soul, then bowed his head to read a blessing for my recently departed uncle from a battered prayer book. When he finished praying, he nodded at me and turned to walk toward the street into the blowing snow, a raven-like figure bobbing through the storm. Two workmen, gravediggers, emerged from the flurries on a pathway beyond the open grave and when they arrived, they lowered the casket into the ground. I threw a clod of dirt onto Uncle's coffin, startled by the finality of the hollow thump as it met the polished wood. But the clod soon whitened and disappeared under the falling snow as the workmen began to shovel in syncopated rhythms from a low pile of icy, moist earth beside the grave.

I walked away and waved the cab on so I could stroll alone through the storm toward my office at First Fiduciary Savings. When I arrived, I lay my damp overcoat across a meeting table near my desk and grabbed a cup of steaming coffee from the employee's lounge. I tried to concentrate on the never-ending stack of paperwork filling my inbox, still shivering twenty minutes later. The phone jangled suddenly, startling me even though my secretary picked it up at her desk outside my door. "Line two, Mr. Rizzo," Ruth said over the intercom.

"Peter John Rizzo," a clipped voice demanded when I answered.

"Speaking."

"Are you nephew to John Rizzo of Brooklyn, New York?"

"Who wants to know?"

"Harold O'Neill, attorney at law, calling the nephew of John Rizzo, called Peter John Rizzo. Am I speaking to the aforementioned nephew or not?"

What kind of person would actually talk like this? "Yes, John Rizzo is my uncle, and my name is Peter John Rizzo."

"I'm very sorry for your loss," O'Neill said tersely. "The reading of John Rizzo's last will and testament is at half-past three at my office tomorrow. 211 Broad St."

Without warning, Mr. O'Neill hung up and left me to sift through my thoughts.

I had trouble attending to my work because I still couldn't believe Uncle John was gone. Granted, I'd not seen him for years, but I never thought about losing him permanently. My eyes brimmed with tears, but I held back the storm by taking deep breaths. Shuffling blindly through the papers on my desk, I could only think about him. Because he and Aunt Millie had no children of their own to grieve for them, I'd made the trip to the cemetery. I had little knowledge of Uncle's social life and concluded he must have been a loner after Aunt Millie's death. I'd expected to see my father present, supposing that in the face of death he would drop his bitterness about his only brother. That I carried his brother's middle name probably didn't help the situation any—I had no clue why Mother insisted upon naming me after both Father and Uncle John. I remember well how he snorted every time he heard my middle name when I was a kid. Father hadn't cared to remember his estranged brother at all.

❦

I was the only person present again the next afternoon in the tastefully appointed conference room at the law office of Harrison, Shearer and O'Neill.

"To my nephew, Peter John Rizzo, I leave my entire estate," Harold O'Neill solemnly read from the legal-sized sheaf of papers he pulled from a dark leather binder embossed with gold lettering.

Uncle John's entire estate consisted of "Classic Art Exposé," a bi-weekly magazine with art, and sometimes literature, as the main content, located in an old warehouse in New York City, plus seven hundred dollars in cash. I felt touched he'd thought of me, but I didn't have any interest in running his magazine because of my position at the bank and my need to placate my father.

O'Neill looked over his narrow reading glasses at me. "Peter John Rizzo, it's my duty to make certain you're aware that this bequest is conditional."

"Oh? What kind of conditions could Uncle John possibly place on a barely functioning publishing business and seven hundred dollars? I earn enough working for my father to buy and sell magazines like his anytime I want." After I spoke, I bit my lip, not liking the smarmy rich-boy declaration.

"I know you probably expected more, but your uncle went into debt to pay your university expenses."

"Wait a minute—I had a scholarship that paid for everything."

"Surely you did. But who do you think the donor was?"

My jaw nearly hit the floor. "Why did he do that if he couldn't afford it?"

"I'm not certain. Perhaps he wanted to annoy your father. . ." Mr. O'Neill said, speculating with feigned interest. "Here's the note for the loan he took out to pay for your scholarship." He handed me an itemized statement of loan payments and corresponding interest typewritten on a bank's letterhead.

Why would Uncle John go into debt just to annoy my father? I remember how proud he was that I showed the same inclination toward the arts that he had. I believed he wanted me to follow my heart. He knew how my father always manipulated people to do exactly what he wanted. My uncle wanted me to be free of that trait, and I suspect he may have been a bit envious of my father's wealth as well. To Father, my university tuition and living expenses were small change.

"Uncle John owned the magazine for years. Maybe he really could afford it," I stubbornly insisted.

"He chose to publish exactly what he wanted, not always what was best for the magazine. The business is breaking even right now, but Mr. Rizzo's notes are due in eighteen months. Unfortunately, he took out a second mortgage to pay for the scholarship as well as a loan to keep the magazine afloat. One of his conditions is that you increase the circulation from ten thousand to forty thousand. By accomplishing that, you'll have enough cash flow to meet his expenses."

Who, What, When, Where, Why and *How* streamed through my mind and I barely heard the financial details. Uncle John had paid for my education—my feelings were in turmoil. Why didn't he tell me? Did my mother know? I knew I'd never figure out the answers. Now that Uncle was dead, I couldn't even thank him.

"Your uncle felt you could easily meet this stipulation. He always said how clever you are, and he was proud of that."

I still couldn't say anything. It had been almost thirteen years since my uncle and I had communicated. Though we both loved the arts, I wondered where he got the idea I am clever.

"The condition attached to this stipulation is that if you can't increase the circulation prior to the due date of his notes, then you're to forfeit all assets to his creditors, and you must donate seven hundred dollars to the Artists' Benevolent Society. But if you do meet his stipulations, you can do whatever you desire with the business. Likely he wanted you to gain experience in his field and still be able to sell the magazine if you choose."

TooTie-Do PRESS

LoS ANGELES
REDWooD HiGHWaY 101
SAN DiEGo

www.ingramcontent.com/pod-product-compliance
Lightning Source LLC
Chambersburg PA
CBHW030553180626
46816CB00005B/1525